King

R.J. LARSON

BETHANYHOUSE

a division of Baker Publishing Group
Minneapolis, Minnesota

© 2013 by R. J. Larson

Published by Bethany House Publishers
11400 Hampshire Avenue South
Bloomington, Minnesota 55438
www.bethanyhouse.com

Bethany House Publishers is a division of
Baker Publishing Group, Grand Rapids, Michigan

Printed in the United States of America

Library of Congress Cataloging-in-Publication Data

Larson, R. J.
    King / R.J. Larson.
        pages cm. — (Books of the infinite ; 3)
    Summary: "As dark forces threaten the king, three friends must trust the Infinite's guidance when questions of love and faith become entangled with dangerous intrigue"—Provided by publisher.
    ISBN 978-0-7642-0973-4 (pbk.)
    1. Friends—Fiction. 2. Religion—Fiction. I. Title.
PS3602.A8343K56 2013
813'.6—dc23   2013007613

Cover design by Wes Youssi/M.80 Design
Cover photography by Steve Gardner, PixelWorks Studio, Inc.

Author is represented by Hartline Literary Agency

12 13 14 15 16 17 18   7 6 5 4 3 2 1

To Larson, Robert, and Katharin

Love always,
Mom

P.S. Thanks for cleaning the kitchen!

CHARACTER LIST

Akabe Garric \Ah-**cabe Gair**-rick\ Former Siphran rebel. The Infinite's chosen king of Siphra.

Barth of Siymont \Barth **See**-mont\ Royal page and son of Lord Ruis of Siymont.

Ela Roeh **El**-ah **Roe**-eh\ Prophet of the vanquished city-state of Parne.

Lord Faine **Fane**\ Akabe's chief advisor.

Ruis of Siymont **Roo**-es **See**-mont\ A lord of Siphra. Father of Barth.

Matron Prill **Prill**\ Ela's chaperone.

Cyan Thaenfall **Sigh**-an **Thane**-fall\ Siphran lord and suspected Atean. Caitria's father.

Kien Lantec **Kee**-en **Lan**-tek\ Military judge-advocate for the Tracelands.

Ishvah Nesac **Ish**-vaw **Ness**-ak\ The Infinite's chief priest of the vanquished city-state of Parne.

Dan Roeh \Dan **Roe**-eh\ Ela's father.

Kalme Roeh **Call**-may **Roe**-eh\ Ela's mother.

7

Rade Lantec \Raid **Lan**-tek\ Kien's father. The Tracelands' preeminent statesman.

Ara Lantec **Are**-ah **Lan**-tek\ Rade Lantec's wife. Kien's mother.

Beka Thel **Bek**-ah Thell\ Jon Thel's wife. Kien's sister.

Jon Thel \Jon Thell\ A Tracelands military commander. Beka's husband.

General Rol \Rawl\ The Tracelands' General of the Army.

Bryce \Brice\ Steward or Chief Servant of Aeyrievale.

Riddig Tyne**Rid**-ig Tine\ Akabe's field surgeon.

Ruestock **Roo**-stock\ Exiled former Siphran ambassador to the Tracelands.

Caitria Thaenfall \Kay-**tree**-ah **Thane**-fall\ Daughter of Cyan Thaenfall.

Bel-Tygeon \Bell-**Ty**-jee-on\ King of Belaal.

Rtial Vioc **Reh**-tee-al Vee-**oak**\ A commander of Belaal.

Dasarai \Da-**Sar**-ay\ Princess of Belaal. Sovereign of Women's Palace.

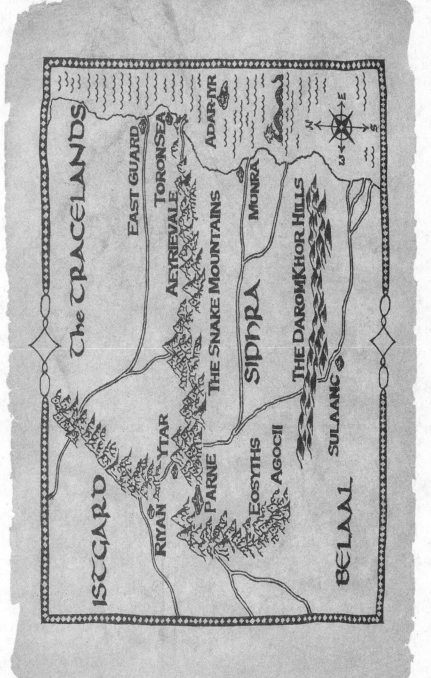

✦ I ✦

A salt-tinged ocean breeze lifted Akabe of Siphra's gold-embellished mantle as he stood on the uppermost white marble step before his country's razed, ruined Temple of the Infinite. Bracing himself, he called to the crowds below, "Today we have gathered to reclaim a treasure vital to Siphra, and vital to our journey through this life—the Infinite's Holy House!"

Earsplitting whistles and shouts of approval echoed all around Akabe, easing his fears. Affirmations of his decision to rebuild this place of worship, which had been toppled by his brutal predecessors.

As he waited for the enthusiastic uproar to fade, Akabe studied the multitudes in the white-paved public square below the steps. Arrayed in bright robes and mantles, the citizens of Munra, Siphra's capital, met his gaze, respectful, yet pleased. They quieted now, listening. To *him*. An almost-nobody rebel and hunter . . . turned king.

Who could ever dream of such a swift, unexpected rise to power? Not Akabe. Truly, his people were insane. Why had they accepted him as their king?

Yet he must honor their decision. Now he would earn his place—and their continued esteem.

Clearing his throat, Akabe proclaimed, "Therefore, as we celebrate the first day of work in restoring this Holy House, I ask you all to rededicate yourselves and this place to the Infinite! Let Munra and Siphra be worthy of such a glorious and sacred crown!

"In generations past, the Infinite's Holy House was Siphra's glory—a gathering place for our people as we worshiped our Creator. Now, as your king, I decree that this Holy House shall be built again, on this same historic, consecrated ground, acclaimed by the priests of old as the Infinite's own land. This place must ever be His alone in Siphra! This sacred site that our oppressors defiled, as they devastated . . . and killed . . . our defenseless people. . . ."

Akabe paused, remembering all the precious lives lost before the recent revolution. He eyed the crowd in a bid for composure.

No help there. Many of the women were now weeping into their scarves and veils, while here and there men sniffed and blinked, or rubbed their noses into their long sleeves. Not a family had been left untouched by the terrors of the previous reign.

Fighting back his own tears, Akabe forged ahead. "Today we remember our loved ones—torn from our lives by hatred! We recall their courage and their sacrifices as we feast with our workers at the very foundations of our previous temple. Let those who sought to destroy all worship of the Infinite in Siphra see that by the Infinite's mercy, we have survived! And I, your king—with all my might!—will guard your freedoms to worship our Creator! This Holy House will again become Munra's blessed crown!"

Munra's citizens yelled their agreement, the men stomping and cheering, the women waving colorful scarves in celebration. Akabe exhaled, acknowledging his subjects with a grin and a wave. Success! He might yet amount to something as king.

Akabe the First. Scruffy revolutionary. Rebuilder of Siphra's glorious temple.

Laughable thought. Sobering, actually . . .

Standing almost beside him as usual, Lord Faine—Akabe's chief advisor—leaned into view now, his elaborately sculpted and waxed gray beard twitching with enthusiasm. "Majesty, they're overwhelmingly for you!"

"Yes, and I don't understand why." Followed by his gossiping, overdressed entourage, Akabe walked with Faine across the ruined temple's vast stone terrace, their booted feet sending bits of pale rock clattering with every step. "Until now, I've done nothing to merit my people's approval."

Faine harrumphed disagreement. "You believe that protecting others during the revolution and then defeating Belaal—our most hostile neighboring country—in battle was nothing?"

"I did not defeat Belaal, Lord Faine. The Infinite did. Give tribute to the One who deserves glory."

"Ah, very true. Then, sir, it must be that your people are pleased because you've not asked for new taxes to rebuild this temple."

Akabe laughed. "Aha! At last, the terrible truth! They love me because I haven't spent their money." As he spoke, Akabe glimpsed a small flurry of movement to his left. Barth, his youngest page and heir to Lord Siymont, skittered across the broad stone pavings, his short official crimson cloak askew as he chased an undoubtedly terrified miniature lizard.

Biting down a grin, Akabe shot a look at the boy's stately tutor, Master Croleut, who obviously feared to break formation from Akabe's attendants—much less to physically restrain a powerful nobleman's heir.

When Master Croleut hesitated, Akabe sighed. "Barth!"

Instantly, the little boy straightened himself, but not his cloak. Flushed from the failed chase, he offered Akabe a gap-toothed smile and lisped, "Sir? I mean . . . Majesty?"

Akabe tipped his chin. "Time for lessons, Barth."

Barth scrunched his nose as if smelling something vile. He threw an accusing glance at Croleut, who hissed at the boy, "Sst! Young sir, manners! Bow to the king!"

Barth trotted to Akabe, bowed, then protested, "But, Majesty, I finished today's lessons."

A valiant plea, but worthless. For the sake of training, Akabe pretended sternness. "With Master Croleut, yes. With the prophet, no. And you'll behave for the Prophet Ela while I inspect the temple site, Barth. No arguing with her or with the other students. I command you."

"Yes, sir." The little boy's gloom deepened. But then he raised his dark eyebrows at Akabe in a teasing manner he'd obviously inherited from his father, Ruis, Lord Siymont. "Is she pretty?"

Beautiful, Akabe wanted to say. But caution restrained him. An unmarried king must avoid praising any lady overmuch, even to a child. Why provoke gossip? "You will like her. She's defeated monsters and survived battles."

And Ela had anointed him as king at the Infinite's command. One deed Akabe wished she'd left undone.

He'd never wanted to be king. Worse, the Infinite had given Akabe this appalling responsibility with no true explanation or direction. Not even from His prophets. Therefore, he must make his own decisions and work for the Infinite's glory and for Siphra's people.

Leading his retinue, Akabe crossed the gravel-strewn terrace, his conviction becoming more assured with each brisk step. Surely he couldn't have chosen a more magnificent, unifying task than to restore the Infinite's Holy House to Siphra. For the Infinite.

Surely the Infinite was pleased.

✦ ✦ ✦

Unwittingly testing Akabe's patience, Lord Faine talked nonstop as they marched across the temple site. Faine's broad, ring-garnished hands accented his intonations. " . . . and we are blessed, Majesty, that the foundations remain from the first temple. This will speed along the new temple and reduce costs." Lowering his voice, glancing around, Faine added, "As a result, Parne's treasury alone ought to easily fund the work."

His lord-counselor's caution was understandable. The distant and ancient city-state of Parne no longer existed. Yet Parnian refugees abounded here, brought to Munra last year by Akabe's own army after Parne's devastating besiegement by their mutual enemy, Belaal.

Mentioning the gold removed from Parne's own demolished temple—no matter how well-intentioned—could only wound the Parnians. Particularly their remarkable young prophet, Ela Roeh, who now waited to greet Akabe.

Her prophet's staff in one hand, Ela stood with her two formidable chaperones just beyond the fringe of her makeshift canopied study area. Akabe eyed the prophet's staff. The branch, Ela called it. An ordinary-seeming piece of vinewood. But he'd seen that branch glow like fiery-white metal, illuminating Ela's dark hair and eyes with the Infinite's power.

Healing her of fatal wounds.

Now the image of a model Siphran, Ela bowed. When she looked up at Akabe, her big brown eyes shone, serene. She appeared, for all of Munra, to be nothing more—or less—than a lovely young lady in a flowing tunic and embroidered mantle. Yet Akabe knew better than to be lulled by her delicate appearance. Strengthened by the Infinite's Spirit, this girl felled kingdoms.

Never, for as long as he lived, did he wish to become a target of this prophet's warnings.

Aware of his watching courtiers, Akabe acknowledged Ela with a nod and a polite smile. "Prophet. I have a new student for you." Master Croleut nudged little Barth of Siymont forward. Scuffing his boots over the pavings, the boy halted before Akabe with an unenthusiastic sigh.

Akabe struggled to sound serious. "Barth, remember what I said."

"Yes, Majesty." Barth looked up at Ela. His eyes widened and, ever Siymont's courtly son, he fluttered his lashes. "I have a loose tooth!"

"Do you?" Ela seemed thrilled. "Well, if it falls out during lessons, we must be careful to save it. Now, Barth, these are my chaperones, Tamri Het and Matron Prill. And they're very strict with me, so I must behave. You'll help me, won't you? Do you have a writing tablet? No? You may borrow mine."

Watching her, Akabe wished he could join the class.

Other youngsters approached, bowing shyly to Akabe before taking refuge behind Ela. Akabe greeted them with a smile, then departed to inspect the future temple's foundations.

Envying Barth.

✦ ✦ ✦

Kneeling between the silver-haired Tamri Het and the veiled young widow Matron Prill, Ela clenched the branch, fighting the longing to fidget. Really, she felt so restless that she ought to sit among her little students as they worked. Not good, these fidgets. They were no mere springtime restlessness. And the branch gleamed at her subtly, showing glints of light.

Infinite? What is about to happen?

Whatever it was, Ela prayed the trouble would wait until after class, when her students were safe with their parents.

Little Barth paused over his borrowed wax tablet, giving his loose front tooth a cautious nudge. Eager child. Very self-aware. Ela smiled. "Barth, did you finish your verse?"

He ceased his tooth-wiggling and flourished the wax writing tablet. "Yes—see? And I drew a scaln!"

Scaln! Ela shuddered and banished her memories of the venom-drooling, viciously clawed red beasts.

Goaded by Barth's exuberance, other students waved their work. Before they could accidently hit each other with their tablets, Ela said, "Very good, everyone! Let's recite our verse, shall we?"

Joining the children, Ela recited from the Book of Beginnings, "'Then the Infinite said, "Let Us form mortals in Our image that they may rule over the creatures in the ocean and the birds in the sky, over livestock and all the animals that move along the land. . . ."'"

Even—ugh!—the stinking scalns.

She worked with the giggling children until a distant horn from the work site signaled the noon meal. A feast—the first meal to be shared on the temple's groundbreaking day. Ela smiled, as excited as the children. Bless Akabe of Siphra for deciding to rebuild this place and to shelter Parne's sacred books! After Parne's temple fell, she'd lost hope of ever seeing another Holy House. But now she might live long enough to realize that dream. Infinite, thank You!

Ela clapped her hands. "Class is finished! Wait with me until your parents arrive to take you to the celebration."

As the last few children departed with their parents, Barth tugged at Ela's sleeve. "My lord-father is too busy and couldn't come to the feast. May I eat with you?"

"Of course." Ela took his hand. On either side of them, armed with scarves, mats, and baskets, Ela's chaperones, Matron Prill and Tamri Het, feigned suspicion. The thin, imposing Prill made pretend sour faces at Barth—though her joy in today's celebration peeked through.

And Tamri, an eightyish great-grandmother, flicked her festive crimson scarf at Barth while scolding Ela. "Celebration or not, I expect you to behave, prophet-girl!"

Ela pretended meekness. "I will."

Hand-in-hand with Barth and followed by her chaperones, Ela crossed the vast, stone-paved site to its eastern edge. There, massive platters of food waited—a hastily planned feast, honoring the king's unexpected proclamation of his intention to rebuild Siphra's Holy House. Roasts, steaming spiced grains, marinated vegetables, nuts, and fruits filled the air with their savory-sweet aromas. Nearby, hired men cheerfully bellowed at each other while they chipped at huge blocks of ice, spilling frozen slivers into metal and clay pitchers of juice.

Watching them and listening to their joyful banter, Ela's unease returned. Why?

As they settled down on their mats to eat, Prill arranged her food and then nodded at Ela and Tamri. "There! Now I'll fetch a pitcher of juice."

Before she could stand, a man called, "Prophet! Captivated as you are by your new student, you cannot keep him."

17

Ela turned, startled. The king approached and nudged Barth with a gold-embellished royal boot. "Move, young sir. I'll sit with you for an instant. Have you anything to drink? No?"

Though his courtiers hovered behind him, Akabe sent a servant for goblets and a pitcher of juice. While they waited, he addressed Ela. "Prophet, I spoke with your father. He's pleased by the progress his men have made thus far, and so am I."

"Thank you, Majesty. He's honored to serve the Infinite's House." As of this week, following Akabe's signing of the land contract, Father was in charge of the team refurbishing the temple's foundations and rebuilding the walls. And grateful for the work, Ela knew.

"Likewise," Akabe said, "I'm pleased you're teaching from the Sacred Books."

"It's my duty, sir." Ela adjusted a cloth she'd placed over Barth's obviously new crimson tunic to avoid food spots. "Most of Siphra's copies of the Books of the Infinite were destroyed during the previous reign. Sharing knowledge of the Infinite may prevent future losses."

A servant brought cups, then filled them with juice from a metal pitcher beaded with moisture. They all waited until the king lifted his cup. Following his lead, they drank.

Ela couldn't help draining her juice, despite its tartness. Let Tamri and Prill frown at her appalling manners—she was thirsty. Finished, she looked for the servant, but he'd vanished.

Beside her, Barth grumbled, "Mine tastes sour."

Akabe grimaced at the pitcher left in their midst. "True. The aftertaste is bitter."

Aware of an unpleasant icy burning around her lips and down her throat, Ela flung aside her cup. "Majesty!"

She wrenched Barth's half-empty cup from his small hands. He already looked sick.

Matron Prill threw down her own cup and said the word Ela feared to voice.

"Poison!"

2

Poison? Yes, it must be. Blisters bubbled in Ela's mouth. Searing pain scorched its way down her throat. Frantic courtiers and guards closed about them now, some calling for physicians, others kneeling beside the king, whose usually healthy complexion had turned waxen. Barth cried out and writhed against her. Prill and Tamri supported each other, gasping as if burning alive, and no wonder. Her own stomach seemed on fire.

Ela snatched the branch from the mat, pleading, "Infinite, what must we do?"

An image flashed within her thoughts, sped by a ferocious mental nudge from her Creator. *Hurry!*

Battling faintness, Ela grabbed a round of flatbread from Tamri's dish. The instant she lifted the bread, Ela saw the branch flare, its blue-white fire spreading through her and into the loaf. Frantic, Ela tore the still-glowing bread in two and thrust one half at Akabe. "Eat! Quickly!"

The king obeyed.

Ela dropped the branch and ripped off pieces of bread for Barth, Tamri, Prill, and herself.

In obvious pain, her chaperones snatched the bits of bread and crammed them into their mouths.

While Ela lifted Barth, she swallowed her own bite of bread. It went down her raw throat, quenching the poison's fire. Ela shoved a piece of bread into Barth's mouth. He squirmed and fought. "Chew!" Ela ordered. "Barth, swallow the bread—please!"

The little boy wailed. Ela covered his mouth to prevent the bread from falling out. Holding him, she begged, "Barth! Swallow the bread, and the Infinite will save you!"

She felt his jaw clench. The little boy gulped audibly, opened his eyes, and chirped, "I feel better!"

As the onlooking courtiers exclaimed their relief and praised the Infinite for His miracle, Ela hugged Barth and kissed his soft cheek. "Infinite, thank You!" But she trembled inwardly. Someone had tried to kill the king. With four of his subjects—one a child.

Infinite? Who would do such a thing?

No answer.

Ela turned to the king. Blessedly, Akabe's complexion was no longer ghastly. He shook off his fussing attendants. "I'm well. I give you my word. Step back, all of you." To Ela he said, "Prophet, thank you."

She rocked Barth. "Thanks to the Infinite, sir, for providing the bread that saved us. I'm grateful you're alive—that we all survived."

Barth snuggled into Ela's arms, seeming content. Soon the king commanded him, "On your feet, young sir. We must return to the palace. Your lord-father ought to see you're well before rumors reach him that you were . . . ill."

"He won't mind," Barth argued, but he stood. A grim-faced official in sweeping crimson robes nudged the child toward the steps, toward the royal cavalcade of horses in the street below. Akabe departed as well, surrounded by his anxious men.

As the crowd around them thinned, Ela grabbed Tamri's and Prill's hands. "You're not too shaken?"

"Oh no." Prill's mouth pursed testily. "Just another day tending our little prophet!"

"Sorry," Ela muttered.

Tamri's grandmotherly face crinkled as she smiled. "Well, we're alive for now, my girl. Do you suppose it's safe to finish our food?"

"Yes. I'm certain only that single pitcher was poisoned."

"The king's men took it with them," Prill observed. "No doubt they mean to test it."

"Yes, no doubt." Ela reached for her dish. Someone had kicked it, spilling half her food on the mat. She picked up scattered bits of bread and vegetables until a gruff voice stopped her.

"Prophet?"

Ela looked up. Two badged officials stared down at her, their expressions unmoving as masks. The gruff-voiced one said, "Will you answer a few questions?"

She nodded and set down her dish. So much for eating.

✦ ✦ ✦

"Huh." Akabe studied the dead flies floating in the gold bowl on his council table. "It's the most effective fly poison *I've* ever seen."

Unamused, his counselors stared at him, then at the bowl again. Lord Faine tapped his blunt fingers on the table. "Majesty, how did your enemies know so quickly that you'd visit the site today?"

"How indeed?" Akabe sat back in his chair. The celebration and his appearance were planned only this week, after he'd signed the land contract. "Is there a spy in my household?"

Faine sighed. "We must redouble our surveillance and your guards. Majesty . . . this was the second attempt on your life within the past seven months."

"I'm well aware of that fact, my lord. My knife wound from last year *and* this morning's blisters have made the dangers of kingship abundantly clear. What are you failing to say?"

Faine hesitated. "You need an heir. We've agreed you must marry."

"But have I agreed?" Akabe studied his council members' faces. To a man, they nodded, deathly serious.

"Yes, sir, you must." Faine harrumphed, adding with an awkward cough, "Duty."

"Ah." Duty. Perfect reason to marry. Nothing could be less inspiring to a prospective wife, Akabe was sure. "Do you believe there's a young lady somewhere in Siphra who is brave enough to live in this marble inconvenience of a palace—with a man who is clearly marked for assassination?" While they blinked at his acidity, Akabe continued. "Should we also warn her that she'd be sentenced to a life of cold food, perpetual gossip, and endless ceremonies? Surrounded—forgive me, my lords—by packs of staring royal courtiers who'd follow her to the privy to discuss business?"

His council members shifted guilty glances here and there. Faine attempted a joke. "Majesty, you make life in the royal court sound so *uncomfortable*."

"It is."

Lord Trillcliff broke their awkward silence. Stout and earnest, his eyebrows lifted in thick silver fringes over his ocher eyes. "Being the king, Majesty, you will have no lack of young ladies willing to share your . . . interesting circumstances."

Squelching further complaints, Akabe sat back in his gilded chair and stared at the dead flies. Poor creatures. A pity they'd suffered what he'd escaped. With as much grace as he could muster, Akabe conceded defeat. "As you say, then. Have you a list of courageous candidates, my lords?"

Faine sighed as if relieved. "Not yet, sir."

Akabe straightened. "Am I permitted to suggest a possibility?"

Clearly encouraged, Trillcliff gabbled brightly, "Any young lady of some social standing and impeccable reputation may be considered. However, sir, a foreign princess might bring—"

Princess? Akabe stopped Trillcliff with an upraised hand. Here, he must declare his personal battle lines. "No foreign princesses. And no Siphran ones either—if any exist."

His tone approving, Faine agreed, "Indeed, sir. Foreign brides bring foreign gods, and we've enough to deal with, trying to protect ourselves from the Atea lovers. One of those goddess-smitten fools is likely your failed poisoner from this morning."

Diverted by Faine's mention of the fertility goddess Atea—and her violently devout followers—Akabe asked, "Has the man who served us the poison been found?"

Faine snapped a look at Lord Piton, the youngest council member with the fewest silver hairs. Caught off guard, Piton stammered, "Er . . . um, n-not yet, sir. Your men are questioning everyone at the temple site, including the priests and the prophet."

"They're questioning Ela?" Akabe kept his outrage in check. "Do they suspect her?"

Piton moistened his lips. "Um, no, sir. But perhaps she saw details about the intended assassin that others have missed. And she could petition the Infinite for the man's identity."

Ela. He must speak of her before the opportunity was lost. Akabe pressed his fingertips together. "What I am about to say will not leave this room—does everyone understand?"

"Of course, sir." Faine and the others nodded agreement. "We hope you trust us."

Watching their faces carefully, Akabe said, "Ela Roeh is now Siphran. She's highly regarded by our people and is used to dealing with extraordinary circumstances. Not least, she's more dedicated to the Infinite than any person I've ever met. I'd prefer to marry her."

His council showed surprise, but no opposition. Trillcliff, ever aware of rank, lifted his silver-spiked brows. "The prophet's place is unique in Siphra. Difficult to dispute, should anyone mention her status. Though she's not highborn, she's quite presentable."

"And," Piton quipped, "considering her swift actions this morning, sir, no doubt you'd be marrying your antidote to future poisonings."

Even Faine laughed. But as Akabe enjoyed the joke, it upset him. Ela deserved better than to be considered a living antidote to future poisonings. Would she agree to wed a king?

Tomorrow he would seek information from someone well-acquainted with Ela.

Then he would visit with his favorite prophet and persuade her to marry him.

Faine harrumphed for Akabe's attention, his waxed beard twitching. "Now, to an equally important matter." He lifted a sealed leather pouch. "Thaenfall, Lord of the Plidian Estates, and previous holder of the temple land, has returned the signed formal agreement, giving Siphra full rights to the holy site." Pleased, he nodded to Akabe. "Majesty, you have signed, as has Thaenfall. Now, we—your council members—will add our seals to yours."

Opening the pouch, he withdrew folds of parchment . . . spilling ashes on the polished council table. His mouth sagging open, Faine displayed the agreement's charred remains with its singed gilded royal crest.

Akabe stood. "Thaenfall burned the agreement? Why? Does he want more money?"

"Majesty . . ." Faine rummaged through the ashes and scraps, smudging his fingers. "There's no explanation. But what can you expect? The man is Atean, and *they* would like nothing better than to see you fail, humiliated—with the Infinite's temple remaining as ruins."

By withholding *the* consecrated land, sacred to the Infinite from Siphra's beginning.

Seeing his dream of Siphra's restored temple dissolve amid the ashes, Akabe snapped, "Summon Thaenfall to Munra! We'll renegotiate in person. We *must* legally acquire that land—it's sacred—the only place we can build the temple!"

Trillcliff muttered, "No doubt Thaenfall is counting a fortune on the fact!"

"No doubt." Obviously, their celebration today had been premature. Fuming, Akabe departed the council chamber—and nearly stumbled over Barth. The boy was heedlessly sprawled on his belly at the base of a marble pillar, his small booted feet waving to and fro, his chin resting on his hands while he hummed.

Ha. *Someone* was happy. Pretending to scold, Akabe swooped

down, grabbed the back of Barth's tunic, and lifted him in the air like a sack of wool. "Idling on the job, are you?"

He shook Barth and swung him back and forth while the boy laughed himself breathless.

Cheered, Akabe grinned. It would be good to have a son to play with.

Yes, he would definitely speak to Ela of marriage.

✦ ✦ ✦

Ela wished Father would finish his conversation with that very talkative young man who'd stopped him as he was preparing to leave the temple site. She and Tamri and Prill were all but dozing off after this tiresome day. Pitying her chaperones, Ela said, "Father's right there. Why don't you two leave ahead of me? Stay home and rest tomorrow."

"Are you certain?" Tamri asked as Prill retrieved their baskets. "You won't need us?"

"No. I promised to help Mother tomorrow." And she intended to play with her baby brother, Jess. "It'll be wonderful to have a quiet day." Ela hugged her chaperones, praying blessings for them. "Thank you. I'm sorry you suffered the poison with me."

Prill sniffed, not too convincingly. "You'd best be sorry! Though I suppose it was an honor to survive with you and the king."

Tamri linked arms with the matron. "That's how we'll look at it, Prill, my girl! Not 'almost died,' but *survived*. Mercy, what will the child drag us into next? I need to retire."

"I didn't drag anyone into this," Ela argued.

"Bah!" Prill said. "You attract every sort of commotion, Ela— admit it. Our lives will be so much easier when you marry. Come, Tam. While we're both young enough to walk."

Pretending offense, Tamri scolded, "Hush, Prill, you are almost a child yourself. You may be chaperoning Ela, but *I'm* chaperoning you both!"

They walked away, arguing about who was chaperoning whom.

When you marry. Ela smiled and shook her head. She'd never marry.

Father finished his conversation and Ela picked up her basket and the branch. He scowled, however, as he watched the young man stalk off in the ruddy evening light. Curious, Ela asked, "Who was that?"

"One of the foremen. Asking for a responsibility I doubt he can manage." Dan Roeh glanced at Ela's basket and the branch, then sighed. "It's been a long day. We didn't need the king's men here questioning us half the afternoon—they set us behind schedule. But at least you didn't cause another revolution."

"I didn't cause Siphra's revolution!" Well, not entirely. She gave Father a fierce look.

He grinned. "If you say so, Prophet." As they descended the steps, Dan asked, "Have you reconsidered? About marriage?"

"No." Marriage. Again! Ela kept her tone mild, despite her growing frustration. "Father, why does everyone insist I must marry? It would be disastrous!"

"I'm not convinced it would be disastrous," Dan countered. "But your husband needs enough strength and status of his own to endure everything you'll bring to the marriage."

Ela's stomach clenched. "You talk as if you're considering marrying me off! Father . . . !"

"I could," Dan said, unnervingly quiet. "And I believe I should. You're nineteen and—"

"Please don't!" Ela begged. She halted at the top of the broad steps and clasped her father's arm, babbling in rising panic. "You know what Parne's elders always said. I'm a prophet. I'm supposed to die young. 'A silver-haired prophet has failed!' I *can't* marry. It wouldn't be fair to my husband. As for children, I don't know how I'd endure leaving them!"

Father patted her hand. "Ela. Calm yourself. Thus far, none of the men who have offered themselves could survive marrying you."

What? Ela blinked. "What do you mean, 'none of the men'?"

"Why do you think I was delayed tonight?"

"That man was asking you for *me*?"

"Yes, and do not yell," Dan warned. "It's unbecoming to a prophet. Unless the Infinite commands you to yell, of course."

"Sorry." Ela sucked in a calming breath. "Father, promise me you won't marry me off."

"Don't worry. I'll be sure it's the Infinite's will for you."

Infinite? What if he . . . Ela shut away the thought, sickened. No. She refused to think of it. Father wouldn't act hastily. He cared for her feelings. And if he was determined to marry her off, then only one man could be her husband. Though she hadn't heard from *him* in weeks.

Kien. Why hadn't he written to her? What was wrong?

✦ ✦ ✦

Inhaling the cool night air, Kien Lantec, Judge-Advocate for General Rol, leaned against the open window of his tower room in the Tracelands. Was this his last week of freedom? Soon he would endure the first day of his open trial before the Tracelands' Grand Assembly.

After four months of legal delays—at Father's insistence—Kien would confront his fate.

Freedom, he must admit, was not likely if he should be condemned and censured as he feared. Then he'd suffer fines and be cast out of the military and into prison. But for how long? Months? Years? All because he'd obeyed the Infinite.

And because he'd been richly and irrevocably rewarded for protecting his friend Akabe of Siphra from an assassin's blade. Yet not even Akabe's written plea, signed and sealed here on Kien's desk, would pacify Kien's most outspoken accusers.

Tracelanders, himself included, did not bow to kings.

Kien dared not use Akabe's plea. Yet he couldn't ignore it either. Siphra would be insulted if the Tracelands scorned their king's appeal, while the Tracelands would be equally offended if Kien offered the plea in his defense, causing a quarrel between the two countries.

Kien grimaced. He'd welcome wise counsel now. If only Ela were here.

Dear prophet! Kien returned to his desk and snatched a fresh piece of parchment. When had he last written to Ela? He couldn't remember. He'd been too busy. Too tired.

Perhaps she would come visit him in prison.

"Infinite," Kien murmured as he opened the ink, "please be with me, Your servant."

· 3 ·

Akabe stood as Ishvah Nesac, Parne's former chief priest, entered the royal study. "Nesac! Welcome!"

His thin arms laden with the scrolls and boxes needed for their weekly lesson, the young priest grinned and bowed. "Good morning, Majesty. It's a joy to see you're well."

"It's a joy to be well, thanks to the Infinite and our favorite prophet." Akabe motioned to a pair of chairs set before his massive, ornately carved worktable. "Sit, please. No ceremony." His own mention of ceremony caused Akabe to look at the study's entrance. Sure enough, two guards and a handful of courtiers lingered there, watching and listening. Akabe smiled at them. "Close the door as you depart!"

His guards slid suspicious frowns at Ishvah Nesac. No doubt they'd loiter outside, twitching, ready to break in and apprehend the scholarly priest at the slightest provocation. Doing their jobs, Akabe reminded himself. He stared until they obeyed and shut the door.

Nesac approached the table but silently refused to sit. Giving in to the man's wish to observe protocol, Akabe dropped into one of the gilded chairs. The chief priest reverently placed his collection of scrolls and a box on the wood's polished surface.

The box, itself an ancient relic, creaked open beneath Ishvah's thin, scholarly hands, revealing an ivory tablet yellowed with age.

One of Parne's Sacred Books—*Praises*. Akabe grinned. "Again? Do you believe I need to memorize *Praises*?"

"A spirit of gratitude pleases the Infinite, sir," the priest murmured, not entirely solemn.

"And you think I'm ungrateful?"

Ishvah sat in his designated chair, composed. "I'd never dare say such a thing, Majesty."

"Yet you think it."

"Only regarding your dislike of being Siphra's king."

True.

Ishvah cleared his throat. "Sir, if you're tired of *The Book of Praises*, I'll bring another next week."

"No. *Praises* will be fine." Akabe opened his writing box, eager to complete the lesson, then talk with Nesac. The priest was discreet, and he and his wife were Ela's friends. "I look forward to learning from all the Infinite's Sacred Books."

"Your priests and Siphra's faithful are glad." Nesac smiled. "Familiarity with the Infinite's Word will allow you to recognize false teachings if anyone should present them in the palace. Self-seekers invariably take verses out of context and build them up to fit their own purposes for the sake of gaining power."

"Well, if I must be a king, then I'll try to be a discerning one." Particularly while divine direction seemed so scarce. Akabe snatched a parchment and wrote the verse, translated by Nesac from Parne's ancient priestly script. *In all circumstances, praise your Creator. Those who love His name will take joy in Him. . . .*

Guilty. Akabe scowled. Yet he hated his circumstances—being king. Wasn't it honorable to confess reality? However, making everyone around him unhappy with his constant complaints wouldn't help this irreversible situation. Indeed, it would create bad attitudes among his courtiers and worsen matters. Better to be pleasant, win over his subjects, and find an understanding wife who would sympathize with his plight. Such as Ela. Sped onward by thoughts of Ela, Akabe charged into the verses. At the end of their discussion, he slapped his writing reed into its box. "Done! Now we talk."

Nesac's black eyebrows lifted. "Haven't we been talking, sir?"

"Yes. But now we must speak of confidential matters," Akabe persisted. "What do you know of the prophet's thoughts on marriage?"

Nesac's face went blank as he gathered his supplies. "Which prophet, sir? Siphra has many."

"Why, the only prophet I could marry, of course. Ela Roeh."

The young priest dropped a reed. Akabe laughed at his stunned expression. "You heard me. I'm serious. I want to marry Ela. Therefore, I need to know . . . does she speak of marriage?"

"No, Majesty." Nesac's tawny face reddened. "She refuses to marry because all of Parne's prophets have died young."

"She's a Siphran prophet now," Akabe pointed out, shamelessly delighted. "What else?"

The priest knelt to retrieve the pen, as if needing time to think. Settling, he coughed. "Well . . . before she was called as a prophet, Ela was pledged to marry a young man. But their agreement was broken, and he died at the start of Parne's siege. He was unworthy of her."

"Am I unworthy of her?"

"No." The priest studied Akabe as if trying to weigh his soul. "You are worthy. But would it be right? Would it be the Infinite's will?"

"She could ask Him."

"Er, indeed. But—"

Akabe leaned forward, determined to cut through the man's hesitation. "Has she spoken of anyone else? Or revealed fondness for another man since coming to Munra?"

"Not to me or to my wife, sir. She has close friends in the Tracelands—the Thels and Kien Lantec—but I've never heard her speak of marriage, except to refuse it. On her behalf, sir, may I say that she's not fond of public attention despite being a prophet. She might be uncomfortable as a queen."

"Well, I feel the same about being king. Ela and I could complain to each other whenever we escape the courtiers."

Nesac chuckled, relaxing visibly. "And I'd lecture you two on gratitude."

A victory. Akabe jabbed the priest's shoulder. "You'll say nothing, of course, until I speak to Ela this afternoon."

"You have my word, sir. I pray the Infinite pours His blessings upon you both."

✦ ✦ ✦

Accompanied by his father, Rade Lantec, Kien climbed the marble steps toward the Grand Assembly's meeting place, his gold-clasped black tunic, leggings, and military mantle drawing stares. His attire marked him as a dark raven among the Tracelands' dove-gray-robed officials—Father included.

Yet the military uniform gave Kien an excuse to carry his Azurnite sword. The prized, nearly indestructible blue blade consoled him, because the Grand Assembly members' gray robes undoubtedly covered a spiritual and political ambush. Kien would almost rather face scalns—stinking, venomous, hissing, soft-footed predators—with those bloodshot yellow eyes and reptilian red skin. . . .

At least scalns were straightforward about wanting to eat their victims alive.

Few greeted Father as they approached the huge bronze doors, but every gaze seemed fixed on Kien. Some unpleasant, others offering silent understanding, most noncommittal. Kien noticed one not-quite-concealed smirk from another black-garbed Tracelands soldier—the stuffily proper Subordinate Commander Selwin, his chief accuser.

Kien had hoped to not see the man on his trial's first day.

Father scowled. "Selwin's here already?"

"Of course." Kien's stomach knotted. "I'd call him to testify on the first day if I were prosecuting me." He deliberately grinned at Selwin, changing the subordinate commander's smugness to bafflement. "His testimony will make me a living joke to half the Grand Assembly."

"We need to find a way to counter your religious beliefs," Rade observed as they entered the huge marble-columned chamber. "Our foes are eager to condemn us for them."

Us. Kien grimaced at the word's truth. This trial named him as its defendant, but Rade Lantec, the Tracelands' preeminent assemblyman, might as well sit beside him in the chamber's arena-like center, equally accused for all his past policies. Political maneuverings were the reason Kien faced censure in the Tracelands' most public forum, instead of an ordinary court. He was being tried as Rade Lantec's son.

And as the Infinite's servant.

While Rade climbed the upper chamber's steps to his high seat—its placement revealing his status—Kien descended to his chair on the marble floor below, at the table of the accused. Selwin immediately strode to the witness chair.

Beyond Selwin, Kien recognized a particular smooth-faced, smiling, polished official. Assemblyman Cherne. Leader of the anti-Lantec faction. The man who'd insisted Kien be tried publicly, implying to all that the Lantecs might bribe a lesser court for Kien's acquittal.

After opening ceremonies, the lead prosecutor lifted his voice until it echoed off every marble column and curved wall, introducing Selwin, then bellowing his first question. "Commander Selwin, were you present at the fall of Parne, after the battle against Belaal?"

"I was."

"What orders did Akabe, king of Siphra, give concerning the allied forces' entry into the city-state of Parne?"

Deathly serious, Selwin lifted his chin. "He ordered the Parnians removed from their city. Anyone who resisted was to be executed."

A wave of outraged murmurs flowed through the crowd of onlookers in the marble chamber. Seething inwardly, Kien leaned toward his defending counselor, Alan, and whispered, "Anyone who raised *weapons* was to be killed—not those who merely resisted leaving the city."

Alan nodded and pressed his reed pen into a wax tablet, making notes.

The lead prosecutor raised his voice further. "What reason did the king of Siphra give for issuing this death order?"

The corners of Selwin's mouth curled, hinting at scorn. "He believed his orders were issued by his Creator, the Infinite, and that the Infinite decreed Parne must be destroyed."

"Commander Selwin, did you enter Parne under these orders?"

"No, sir. I disagreed with the king's orders and declined to enter the city."

"Do you know of any Tracelanders who did enter the city?"

Selwin nodded toward Kien. "Judge-Advocate Lantec rode into Parne against my advice."

Determined, Kien met and held Selwin's gaze until the man looked away. Interesting. The subordinate commander was consistently omitting any details that might validate Kien's actions. Well, well. The worthy Selwin would regret his choice of tactics.

Clamping his lips tight to suppress a grin, Kien snatched a reed pen, opened a new wax tablet, and pressed in rapid jottings of notes. His list lengthened as Selwin's testimony progressed.

Kien silently cheered the man onward.

✦ ✦ ✦

"Jess, hold still." Ela combed her baby brother's clean black curls, delighted by his shiny, perfect ringlets. Less pleased, the tiny boy stiffened, slid out of her lap, then crawled across the mat to Mother, who sat nearby munching on a crisp round of herbed bread.

Kalme Roeh wrinkled her delicate nose as Jess put a hand on her knee and offered her a three-toothed grin. Ela laughed while Mother cooed, "What do you want, young man? This bread is mine—the first thing I've eaten since dawn!"

Obviously certain of his welcome, Jess scooted into Mother's lap and stretched out one pudgy arm, reaching for the bread.

While her little brother was occupied, Ela gathered Jess's linens and cleansing oil. Before she could go rinse the linens, the front door opened. Father stomped inside, scowling.

Mother gasped. "Dan! Why are you home so early? Is everything all right?"

"I'm not sure." Dan frowned at Ela. "Have you had a vision? Anything I should know?"

"No, Father." Ela almost stammered beneath his ferocious stare. "Um, truly. Nothing's happened. We've had a good morning. Look . . ." She motioned to the branch, which rested in the corner as plain, unremarkable vinewood. "It's quiet, and I'm well. No headache, no revolutions, no poisonings—" Unlike yesterday.

"Then why have you and I been summoned to speak with the king?"

Ela blinked. "We have?"

"Yes!" Dan snapped. "Go put on your best clothes, and *hurry*. I must return to work."

"The king?" Kalme gave the bread to Jess. "Ela, what have you done?"

Why did her parents always presume *she'd* caused disasters? "I've done nothing!"

Kalme and Dan stared at her, their eyebrows lifted in unison. Only Jess was perfectly content, gnawing his pilfered bread.

"All right." Ela snatched up the branch and rushed to her sleeping chamber, praying as she opened her new clothing chest. "Infinite? Why should the king summon me, with Father—as if I'm a child, needing Father to vouch for me and approve my words?"

She waited.

But He didn't answer. And the vinewood remained bland, revealing nothing.

◆ 4 ◆

Ela lifted her chin and kept her eyes fixed on the corridor ahead as she and Father followed a royal servant to the king's audience chamber. Yet she couldn't help being aware of the courtiers on either side of her, clad in glittering, exquisite tunics and robes. Everyone eyed her. Some smiling, others not. All obviously curious.

Well, they weren't the only ones who were curious about her presence here—and particularly Father's. Infinite, won't You give me a hint?

The branch in her right hand remained cool and infuriatingly ordinary. It seemed she must be patient. She exhaled audibly. Dan gave her a searching look—as if he suspected she'd heard from the Infinite. Ela shook her head.

The servant led them into a quiet room with ornate walls, a large polished table, gilded chairs, and marble benches. A small crimson-clad figure dashed up to meet them. Ela recognized the little page. "Barth! How are you, sir?"

"Lady, I'm well." The boy bowed, then gave her a mischievous gap-toothed grin. "But I'll never forget drinking that juice and having those blisters—they *hurt*! And my stomach burned till I thought I was dying! Oh, and thank you for the bread. Lord Faine and Master Croleut said you saved my life and I must thank you." Before Ela could point out that the Infinite had saved him, the little boy raised a hand as if remembering instructions. "Wait, please. I'll tell the king you're here!" He ran out, his garments awry.

Ela sat beside Father on a cushioned marble bench. Dan grunted. "Talkative scamp."

"Very," Ela agreed. "He's a clever student and his drawings are quite imaginative." She shuddered, remembering his version of a scaln with overlong claws and fangs dripping venom.

The door opened. Ela stood in unison with her father as Akabe swept into the room, regal in his gold-pinned mantle and flowing robes. An energetic, handsome king, Ela decided. Unlike his apathetic, scrawny predecessor, Segere of Siphra. She practiced a ladylike bow. "Majesty."

Akabe grinned, dimples accentuating his engaging smile. "Master Roeh. Prophet. Welcome and thank you for coming. I apologize for the short notice; however, I wanted to speak with you before I'm locked away for a few days in serious negotiations."

Ela returned his smile. "I pray the negotiations proceed favorably, sir."

"They must." Akabe's smile changed to a rueful grimace. "The sale of the temple lands is now in question. We're trying to resolve the issue quickly." Before she could question him— and wonder again why she'd heard nothing from the Infinite— Akabe motioned to their bench. "Please sit." As they complied, he grabbed a gilded chair, placed it before them, and sat down. He studied Ela so intently that she blushed. "Prophet, thank you again for your quick action at the temple. I'm grateful. I hope most of Siphra is grateful as well."

Unable to resist his appeal, Ela smiled. "Majesty, Siphra is blessed to have you as its king."

Akabe gave a self-deprecating shrug. "Did Barth remember to thank you?"

"Yes, sir, he did." Recalling the little boy's sweet face and bright eyes, Ela melted inwardly. "He's an exceptional child. He remembers everything he's seen and heard."

"You sound pleased with him. I'm glad." Akabe matched his fingertips together before speaking again. "I'm not one to waste my subjects' time, so I'll simply say . . . or ask . . ." He looked directly at Ela, his golden-brown eyes as serious as they'd been the instant she pronounced him king of Siphra. "There's no young lady I admire more in Siphra. You are respected, beautiful, and . . ." Akabe paused, seeming to gather courage. "I'm told I must be dutiful and marry. Ela—" He'd said her name as if he considered it among the loveliest of spoken words. "You surpass every lady in this palace and beyond. . . ."

No. Ela felt the blood draining from her face as Akabe voiced the question she feared. "Will you honor me by agreeing to become my wife?"

Father shifted, turning to stare at her. Ela met his gaze and saw his emotions: shock, giving way to elation. She could almost hear his thoughts. The king. A worthy suitor, able to handle—as Dan had phrased it—everything *she* would bring to the marriage.

Ela gripped the branch, wishing a transporting current from the Infinite would sweep her from this room and this decision. How could she refuse without offending Akabe and infuriating Father? "Sir, thank you, but I've no wish to marry. I—"

"Ela," Dan warned softly.

Ela swallowed. Father wanted her to marry. He obviously wished to hand her over to the king this instant. And, legally, he could. Her heart hammered and her breath caught. How might she escape? Desperate, she looked Akabe in the eyes and whispered, "I love someone else! Kien Lantec. He's asked me twice. . . ."

Father gripped her wrist and made her look at him. "*What?* When?"

She hesitated, remembering. "Before Siphra's revolution. And after the fall of Parne." The heat of a blush worked over her face. The last time she'd seen Kien, he'd kissed her and promised he would never give up asking her to marry him.

Father's color also heightened, but with obvious frustration. "And you *refused* him?"

"I felt I should." Taking courage, she said, "I'd be a difficult wife—a burden."

His voice low, Akabe said, "I disagree. It would be an honor to marry you, Ela. And if you had said the name of any other man, I'd argue with you. However, disappointed though I am, I could never speak a word against Kien Lantec." He offered her a sad smile and clasped her free hand. "He counts himself as blessed, I'm sure."

To Father, Akabe said, "Please do not be angry with her, sir, and do not believe that I am angry with either of you—I am not. I'll greet you both at the temple site."

He left them quietly, through an amazingly concealed side door—its contours vanishing within the ornate wall carvings as he shut the door behind him.

Father glowered at Ela. "Because of your stubbornness, you've embarrassed that good man! I'm grateful he's kind. Any other king would have punished us, I'm sure!"

"I'm sorry."

Dan hadn't mentioned his own mortification, but Ela saw it in his eyes. In the way he rubbed a hand over his face. Oh, she'd humiliated Father. Badly.

Ela longed to crawl away and hide. Finally, Dan straightened, seeming to brace himself. "Let's go. Chin up, Ela. We need to walk past all those courtiers again."

She could not allow herself to cry. Would not. Akabe's look of hurt . . . Oh my.

Infinite, I wish I might have been warned. Kien . . . Ela ached to think of him.

✦ ✦ ✦

Finished telling of his rejection, Akabe sat back in his chair and waited for his council members' reactions. Their shock manifested in widened eyes and gaping mouths. Lord Faine shook his head. "How could she refuse you?"

Trying to cover his disappointment with humor, Akabe said,

"I'm in excellent company. She refused Kien Lantec—Lord Aey-rievale."

Lord Piton huffed, "Aeyrievale! We've seen no hint that she's communicated with him!"

"Really?" Akabe frowned at Piton. "My lord, how long have you been spying on the prophet?"

To his credit, Piton blushed. "Er, about three weeks, sir. A mere precaution. Nothing to discredit the young lady. We've decided to keep watch over all of Siphra's prophets—the Parnian and her lesser acolytes—scattered as they are while proclaiming the Infinite's will throughout Siphra. You know from experience what chaos one prophet can provoke."

"Yes." The most profound spiritual and political chaos. Not to mention personal misery.

He'd been refused. For the best of reasons, but still refused. Akabe planted his booted feet against the tiles. He would not resort to kicking something, but would deal with the humilia-tion and proceed. Straightening, he slapped his hands on the gleaming table. "What next, my lords? Have you created a list of potential prospects?"

Faine sighed. "No, sir. We were convinced the girl would accept you—and are shocked that she did not. I suppose that will be our next task." He paused, clearly choosing his words with care. "Majesty . . . Siphra's highest-ranked families will hesitate to enter a contract with you due to bloodlines. We know nothing of your past, sir. Despite your position as king, matters would be helped tremendously if you would give details of your family's history."

Lord Trillcliff added hurriedly, "Majesty, this is not to say we consider you unworthy. We do not. It is obvious you're educated and that you've the manners and deportment any nobleman would expect, but . . ."

"But what?" Akabe stared at each of his counselors in turn, making them shift and cough. "What's being said of me?"

"Well," Piton affected a shrug. "It's being wagered that you're illegitimate."

Illegitimate? Despite his shock, Akabe laughed. "My parents would be surprised, my lord. As would the priest who blessed their marriage."

"Then, Majesty," Faine pleaded, "who are you?"

Did he wish to reopen agonizing wounds? To provoke accusations that might shake his court and set Siphra's highest families against each other? Akabe shook his head. "I am the king. And I'm not illegitimate, though my parents are dead. Let it be enough. Have we received word from Thaenfall regarding the temple's lands?"

Piton cleared his throat. "Yes, sir. Thaenfall is now traveling to Munra for our meetings."

"Good. I want the land sale finalized. The workers are on site—I'd hate to send them away." Ela's father among them. Akabe stood and sighed. Enough. He'd had enough for one day. "My lords, prepare your list of potential brides, and I'll consider it."

Akabe marched from the room before his council could protest.

Until now he hadn't realized how much he'd depended upon Ela's acceptance of him as a husband. She'd appealed to him completely, and Akabe had allowed himself to contemplate sharing every aspect of his life with her. If only he'd known she loved Kien Lantec. Truly, Akabe couldn't fault her choice. Kien . . . Lord Aeyrievale . . . was descended from kings and had proven himself a true friend. Akabe only wished he could do more to defend him now in the Tracelands.

Had Siphra's formal plea been effective? When would Kien know the outcome of his trial? Akabe had heard nothing from him in weeks. Troubling, now that he considered the matter. Tonight, he must send a cipher to the Tracelands' General Rol through one of his household clerks, by way of courier bird. Surely a reply would arrive soon. "Be well, friend," Akabe muttered. For Kien's sake, Akabe must abandon thoughts of Ela.

He would not risk their friendship over a misunderstanding, no matter how deep the hurt.

Doubtless the Infinite expected such goodwill of him in all similar matters.

To no one, he muttered, "A bit of divine guidance now and then would be helpful!"

✦ ✦ ✦

His third day of trial. Kien glanced around the huge circular chamber, found Selwin, and smiled. Selwin frowned. Poor man.

Kien settled into his designated chair, then glanced over his shoulder at his family. Father sat with Mother today. Ara Lantec, elegant as always in graceful robes, perfectly coifed dark hair, and lovely gray eyes, beamed at Kien. Beside her, Kien's sister, Beka, settled herself. As elegant as Mother, but obviously pregnant, Beka threw Kien a sparkling smile. Kien grinned.

Until Father lifted a commanding eyebrow, silently reminding Kien to be dignified and serious. Father ought to be glad he could smile. Kien exhaled, seeking calm. "Infinite? Help me, please."

The trial judge entered the chamber, imposing in his black robes, his lined face austere. Kien wondered if he himself would ever preside over a criminal court. Not likely after this trial.

At least this chair was cushioned. No doubt he would remain in this seat for most of the day. Attempting to look pleasant, Kien watched the lead prosecutor approach. The man cleared his throat and raised his rich voice until it seemed to rebound from the very crest of the magnificent dome above. "Kien Lantec, remember you are sworn to speak the truth."

"Yes." But don't volunteer anything, Father's advisors had cautioned—as if Kien knew nothing of the law.

The first few questions were mundane and expected.

"Kien Lantec, what office do you hold?"

"I am serving as a military judge-advocate under the command of General Rol."

"What other duties have you undertaken for the Tracelands?"

"I served as ambassador to the country of Istgard and was

imprisoned there following the massacre at Ytar. I also fought as a volunteer in the battle of Ytar the next spring."

Murmurs of surprise and agreement lifted from among the audience. As if the Tracelands had forgotten he'd been imprisoned and nearly died for his country. The lead prosecutor looked irritated. "Were you present at the fall of Parne?"

"Yes."

"Did you indeed go into Parne under questionable circumstances as Commander Selwin testified?"

"Subordinate Commander Selwin forgot to mention that I entered Parne off duty, as a private citizen, to rescue Ela of Parne, whom I love." There. Let his love for Ela be recorded forever in the Tracelands' archives.

The prosecutor grimaced, then recovered. "You entered Parne knowing there was an order to execute any Parnians who resisted being removed from their city?"

"No." As the prosecutor gaped in obvious protest, Kien raised his own voice. "Subordinate Commander Selwin misunderstood the order, though he personally heard the king speak it, as I did. The king's orders were to kill anyone who lifted *weapons* against allied soldiers. I, too, was uncomfortable with the order, given Parne's circumstances."

Beyond the prosecutor, Kien noticed Selwin's pale fingers tapping restlessly against his black leggings. Nearby, the black-cloaked General Rol, Kien's imposing silver-haired superior and mentor, was scowling at the man. Within those two answers, Selwin was revealed as, at best, untrustworthily forgetful. At worst a deliberate liar specializing in omissions. And in each question that followed, whenever Selwin's testimony was mentioned, Kien solemnly repeated, "I regret that Subordinate Commander Selwin misunderstood."

At last, the lead prosecutor dropped all mention of Selwin. "Did you, Kien Lantec, obey the king's order, which was supposedly inspired by the Infinite?"

"I obeyed my own conscience and instincts, sir. While retrieving

Ela of Parne from a life-threatening situation, I defended myself against one man when he attacked me with a sword."

"Did you kill him?"

"Yes, sir. I have the right to defend myself."

"Are you a follower of the Infinite?"

"Yes." The circular chamber buzzed with comments. Some of the onlookers sneered.

The prosecutor smiled, remarkably bland. "And do you believe the Infinite's commands supersede any commands given by your own government?"

"A man must follow his conscience. If the Infinite's commands override others, then I obey Him."

"Interesting." His manner was so overly pleasant that Kien longed to shake him. Then the prosecutor changed the subject. "Did you serve in any official capacity in Siphra?"

"Yes. Because of my experience as an ambassador to Istgard, I also represented the Tracelands as a special envoy in Siphra's royal court last year."

"Did you save King Akabe of Siphra's life last year?"

"I did." Kien tensed inwardly, almost hearing the next question before it was asked.

"Did the king reward you as thanks for saving his life?"

"Against my will, yes. He granted me property and a title while his wound was being stitched." Indignant at the memory, Kien protested, "No government should work so quickly!"

Around him, the Tracelands' government officials laughed and repeated his statement to each other. When the hilarity faded, the lead prosecutor raised his voice again. "What title did the king of Siphra bestow upon you?"

Allowing everyone to see his aggravation, Kien said, "Lord Aeyrievale."

"And is this title permanent?"

"Though I've refused to act upon it, yes. Regrettably, the king's bequest cannot be rescinded in Siphra, on pain of death. I planned to destroy the document and run for my life, but the king's men locked away the record before I could snatch it."

"Indeed?" The lead prosecutor's voice lifted above the crowd's chuckles and murmurs. "Are you now considered a citizen of Siphra?"

"Akabe of Siphra termed it a joint citizenship—against my wishes. Yes."

Mildly, the prosecutor asked, "As a citizen and a lord of Siphra, are you in a position to establish laws and wield power in that country?"

Bad question. Kien exhaled. "I have not exercised *any* authority in Siphra. And I've no intention of doing so."

"But *might* you establish laws and wield power in Siphra, sir? Yes or no?"

Kien quieted inside. Why had the man phrased it that way? "Might you," instead of "do you"? Answer. He must answer before being reprimanded. "It would be possible, yes."

Though the questioning continued, Kien heard and responded in a daze. He knew what the prosecutor was planning. And what the now-frowning judge would be forced to decide. This would be no ordinary censure. Why couldn't they simply cast him from the military, fine him, and send him to prison? He slid a glance toward his parents and sister. Mother smiled at him, all her love in that look. Kien almost winced.

His sentence would crush her.

5

In the seclusion of his royal study, Akabe inclined his head toward the austere Cyan Thaenfall, Lord of the Plidian Estates. Then he nodded to Lord Faine, who opened the leather pouch and displayed the contested ashes.

Controlling himself at the sight of those ashes and his own seared gold crest, Akabe kept his voice serene. Neutral. "My lord, owing to this rather dramatic display, I presume you wish to renegotiate. Why?"

Cyan Thaenfall's smile did not brighten his cool brown eyes and stern voice. "I had forgotten a legal entanglement. Years ago, my youngest daughter's dowry was attached to this land to provide for her future."

"Then," Akabe murmured, "we will pay her dowry upon the sale of the land to Siphra."

Thaenfall didn't look pleased as Akabe had hoped. "Sir. The land, not its proceeds, is the dowry."

"Meaning?"

"My daughter will marry the purchaser of this land."

An uncomfortable chill prickled Akabe's arms beneath his fine tunic and cloak. Marry?

Lord Faine protested, "Thaenfall, your daughter cannot marry Siphra—which will purchase this land. Therefore you must name a sum."

"Must?" The proud lord's eyebrows lifted, almost regal. "Recite one law that prevents me from selling this land to whomever I choose, on my own terms."

Before the two could argue further, and before his own misgivings interfered, Akabe snapped, "Thaenfall, state your terms— I'm sure you've decided them!"

The lord of the Plidian Estates stared at Akabe. "It seems I've heard the truth. You are a . . . plain-speaking man. Very well, sir. Marry my youngest daughter and I will sign a document giving you control of the lands—in addition to the payment we'd originally negotiated. Those are my terms."

Marry his daughter. Akabe almost turned his back on the man. This known Atean. What were his ambitions? Merely to assure his daughter's future? To ultimately seat a relative on Siphra's throne? Or to further some Atean plot to disrupt the rebuilding of the temple?

Exhaling, Akabe said, "I will consult with my advisors and consider the matter. Until then, you and your family are welcome to stay in apartments within the palace as my guests."

Inwardly, Akabe groaned. Infinite? If only You would advise me through Your prophets!

But Siphra's lesser prophets had offered him no counsel from their Creator. As for Siphra's preeminent prophet . . . no. Nothing would induce Akabe to ask Ela's advice on marriage. His feelings were still too raw.

Well-enough. He was Siphra's king.

He must make his own choice.

❖ ❖ ❖

Enduring the fourth day of his trial, Kien clenched his hands into fists. Beside him, Alan mimicked his motion, then sat statue-still, staring at the judge, who sighed gustily, then read from the scroll, his tone sonorous and reluctant. "To the charges of corruption and subversion, this court must add an additional charge. An official question of the accused's loyalty to the Tracelands."

Alan threw a writing reed to the marble floor in mute protest. Whispers of confusion and indignation lifted among the onlookers. Kien heard his brother-in-law, Jon, growl. "Outrageous!"

Beyond the prosecutor, Cherne smiled. Gloating. *Laughing!* And why not?

What else could his or Father's opponents do to him beyond what they now intended?

Short of the death penalty, nothing. What a mercy his mother hadn't attended today. But Rade Lantec, his supporters, Kien's brother-in-law, Jon, and General Rol offered Kien looks of encouragement. They hadn't a clue. None!

While the judge pursed his lips and wrote notes, Kien muttered to Alan, "I'm doomed."

"Perhaps the magistrate will be more lenient if we offer Akabe of Siphra's formal plea."

"He won't be lenient. He can't. And the representatives will ridicule the king's plea. You know they will."

"Kien, we must offer the plea. To ignore it would insult Siphra."

"To offer it would provoke far worse insults to Siphra."

"I disagree. Siphra is our ally."

"Don't present the letter!" Kien grabbed Alan's heap of legal parchments to extricate the written plea. Where was it? "Nothing can be changed—it's all formalities now, and the letter will only cause a rift between the Tracelands and Siphra."

"Your opinion. Not mine."

Kien flicked through page after crisp page of parchment. "You know, Alan, for being my legal advisor, you're entirely too optimistic."

"Someone has to be." Reaching inside his formal black robe, Alan, the traitor, removed the document garnished with Akabe's official red wax seal, marched to the magistrate's table, and presented Akabe's formal plea that Kien not be held liable for his title.

Crushing the urge to yell and throw things at Alan, Kien shoved aside the heap of documents. As Alan sat down again, Kien said,

"You've just disturbed relations between two countries. It would have been better to tell Siphra the letter couldn't be presented!"

The judge skewed his mouth to one side of his face as he read the parchment. Finished, he hammered his mallet on the sound box. "I have here a formal plea for clemency on behalf of Kien Lantec . . . from Siphra and its king."

The prosecutor stood. "Irrelevant, sir! Kings may bellow, but *laws* rule the Tracelands!"

Behind him, Cherne intoned, "Tracelanders do not bow to kings! The Lantecs have become Siphra's puppets in the Tracelands—voices for a reckless king and his depraved country that feeds on the weak!"

"What?" Kien thumped his fist on the table before him. Even for an insult, that was foul. *And* being noted by the Tracelands' scribes, hunched at their own table near the magistrate's. "Sir, with respect, your deluded comments—when known—will cause an international uproar!"

Before Kien could continue, Rade Lantec leaped from his seat, motioning to his opponent. "This from you, Cherne, who accepts bribes from constituents! The Lantecs are never bought!"

A disharmony of hoots resounded from the anti-Lantec faction opposite Kien. They sounded like a barn full of owls. Kien started to stand. Alan shoved him down and stood instead. "With respect, sirs, we remind all in attendance that Siphra is our ally and—"

Cherne cut in, yelling, "Because of the Lantecs! *They* are why our country is bound to a despot king's policies—held by the whims of his capricious Creator!"

Wonderful. Kien seethed. Wild-man Cherne was now howling down the Infinite. If Ela could hear the man, Cherne would become an oil spot on the marble. If only . . .

The judge rapped the mallet ferociously on its sounding box. "Enough! *Sit,* everyone." Cherne, Rade, and Alan sat, all three glaring. The magistrate gathered his documents. "I've heard everything that's needful." He looked at Kien now. "Young man, with your legal training, you know what I am forced to rule. By our laws, my hands are tied."

Kien nodded.

Say it.

Obliterate Kien Lantec of the Tracelands.

The magistrate hesitated.

Clenching his hands on the table for support, Kien stood. "Sir, I await your verdict."

At last, the magistrate's voice boomed throughout the circular chamber. "Kien Lantec, all charges, save one, are dismissed. Regrettably, by your own admission, the question of loyalty is substantiated. No Tracelander can hold a position of power in another country, with the potential to create laws in that country and yet remain a Tracelander. Before I pronounce your sentence, which will become effective immediately, do you have anything to say?"

This was really happening. Throat tightening, Kien nodded and leaned on the table. Infinite! He needed to be composed now. No grieving and weeping like a child.

The silence lengthened as he summoned enough self-possession to speak.

Cherne finally yelled, "Lantec, if you've nothing to say—!"

Gouged by the taunt from his father's foe—from the man who'd undoubtedly forced this entire legal proceeding into the Tracelands' Grand Assembly to avenge some small political slight—Kien scowled at Cherne and his supporters. "Whatever you might think, sirs, this entire proceeding upholds my father's reputation, because you had to attack *me* to wound him! The Lantecs are not bought! Ever!"

Sneering, Cherne started to his feet. Kien pounded the table, leaning forward, yelling, "Sit down, sir! You've had your say, and you've achieved your goal! Be a magnanimous victor—*if* you can! I am speaking now!"

Cherne's face reddened. He sat. Perfect silence reigned in the Grand Assembly.

Willing his frantic heart rate to ease, Kien drew in a pained breath and continued. "Unlike most speeches given in this chamber, I'll make mine brief. Because you could find no charge to bring against my father, you've attacked me. And you succeeded in bringing me down for my so-called crimes." Would his heartbeat slow itself? He hoped so. He was trembling.

"To summarize . . . as a private citizen, I rescued the woman I love from a well in Parne. Yes, *after* the siege. Also, I saved a friend—who happens to be a king—from an assassin, and I was too well-honored by that friend despite my repeated attempts to reject his tribute. Most vital of all, I listened to my conscience and forced myself to be honest in evaluating my Creator's existence." Kien paused, deliberate. "The Infinite *lives*! I've witnessed His power. I've seen the words of His prophet fulfilled in the overthrows of kings, kingdoms, and His own beloved Parne. I will praise Him to my death! Those who sneer have not sincerely evaluated themselves or Him. Therefore, they mock in ignorance."

Remarkably, Cherne and his cohorts remained quiet. Staring. "As for your contempt toward the king of Siphra, sirs . . . " Kien straightened. "You are not in his place! You will never understand what Akabe of Siphra must endure. He is an honorable man, yet you scorn him, not knowing what he's facing for the sake of his people."

Cherne twitched, and one of the men beside him smirked. "So you say, my *lord*."

The magistrate hammered on the sound box. "Silence, or I'll have you thrown out!"

Kien eyed the man who'd smirked. "You called me 'my lord' as an insult. But you and your cronies are the ones who've made that word my reality! I did not ask for a Siphran title or wealth and lands for saving my friend's life. I rejected the title—as I rejected Istgard's crown last year! My father and mother raised me to love my country and to serve the Tracelands, and so I have. To serve has been my life! I've *never* sought power for myself."

R. J. LARSON

He wouldn't mention Father. Rade Lantec's ambition was too well known.

"But you, sirs, by trying to wreak havoc on my father to repay him for your political quarrels, have forced me to become a Siphran lord!" The thought choked him. Fighting the invisible cord burning and tightening around his throat, he rasped, "In conclusion . . . I have loved the Tracelands. I've been imprisoned and risked my life for the Tracelands. Now the Tracelands is about to repay me, thanks to you!"

Tears slid down his face now and dripped onto the table. Oh, perfect. Fine. He wouldn't wipe them away. He turned to the magistrate and stood at attention. "Sir, I am finished."

The man rubbed his face and coughed. Finally, he said, "Kien Lantec. For your guilt in the question of loyalty, you are stripped of all rights and status as a Tracelander. You will resign all offices and leave our country within five days. Dismissed." He hammered the sound box one last time, then stood and departed from the circular chamber.

Our country. Kien pondered the words from an emotional distance. Our country, no longer Kien Lantec's country. Numbed, he looked around. Father was slouched deep in his chair, hands over his face, his shoulders shaking. As everyone watched, Kien crossed the marble floor, climbed the steps, and leaned down, hugging Rade tight. Knowing that hope was probably wasted, he said, "We'll find some way to overcome this sentence!"

Rade gripped Kien, trembling. After gasping for air, he choked out, "Yes! Cherne will have a fight such as he's never seen!"

"Choose your battles carefully," Kien warned. "You must restore our good names first." *That* battle would take years. Beginning now.

Determined to fulfill his sentence publicly, Kien released Father and went to stand in front of General Rol. The general stood slowly, his thin face working in a clear battle against his emotions. "My boy . . ." he began.

"Sir," Kien interrupted quietly, "forgive me." He unbuckled

his sword-belt, lifted the military baldric from his shoulder, then folded the black leather against his cherished, nearly invulnerable Azurnite sword—the hilt gleaming in its scabbard, the glistening blue blade hidden like a treasured gem.

He'd loved carrying this sword. Best to never think of it again.

At attention now, he held the sword across both palms and offered it to General Rol. And waited. Rol finally accepted the sword, moisture edging his eyelids. After giving his military mentor an encouraging nod, Kien removed his own mantle with its Tracelandic military insignias and folded it with all the ceremony he could muster. Finished, he placed the gold-embellished fabric over the sword in Rol's hands, then stepped back.

As he suspected, everyone in the marble chamber was watching, their expressions and postures frozen in something resembling shock. Even Cherne looked startled, as if he hadn't reckoned on the sentence becoming an immediate reality he'd have to witness.

In the style of a nobleman, Kien bowed to them all and stalked from the Tracelands' Grand Assembly.

A Siphran.

✦ ✦ ✦

A night of prayer and a morning of meetings hadn't settled Akabe's thoughts concerning the marriage. Now he walked through the sunlit palace garden with his chief advisor, Faine, who sighed before confessing, "Majesty, last night we sent Thaenfall another offer—to add half again as much gold if he will release you from the marriage but sell Siphra the temple property."

Relieved, Akabe halted, his riding boots grinding on the paving stones as he turned to his advisor. "And?"

Faine tugged a parchment from his money purse. No, not a parchment, but scraps. "Thaenfall tore it up. Have our prophets imparted any wisdom?"

"No." And the Infinite remained silent. "It seems I'm to decide this for myself."

"Majesty," Faine murmured, sounding almost desperate, "do

not marry this girl—this Atean! This whole marriage scheme must be a conspiracy, and not the Infinite's will for you! Surely we can find another way to reclaim those lands!"

"Rest your fears, my lord. I have considered the risks. Even now, I am considering them. Legally, we've no other choice. The lawyers have . . ." A flash of movement crossed the tree-edged path ahead, drawing Akabe's gaze. A slender, elegant gray dog with a silver collar frisked toward a distant stone balustrade fronting the ocean beyond. A young noblewoman with long light brown hair trailed after the dog, seeming absentminded, hugging a dark mantle about herself as she moved. Her halfhearted responses to the lively dog suggested melancholy, prompting Akabe's curiosity, even as her flowing walk drew his admiration.

Beside him, Faine sniffed. "There's the lady—Caitria Thaenfall."

Admiration vanished, doused by the Thaenfall name. Yet his curiosity lingered. Akabe made up his mind. "I'll speak with her."

"Sir!"

Akabe waved off Faine's protest and marched through the garden in pursuit of Thaenfall's daughter.

✦ 6 ✦

As Akabe deduced, the insistent hiss and rush of the ocean's waves covered his approach to the ornate balustrade. Caitria Thaenfall didn't notice him until he stepped up beside her at the railing. She jumped, and her brown eyes widened with alarm, but she didn't shriek or run. Praiseworthy composure. Extraordinary eyes. Tall for a woman and gracefully beautiful, she'd clearly dressed for a brisk walk in plain robes and short, scuffed boots. Yet her elegant face conveyed refinement—truly a highborn young lady.

Trying to not frighten her further, Akabe smiled. "Forgive me, lady, but I wished to introduce myself as the cause of your current misery. I am Akabe Garric."

She blinked, then offered a polished obeisance. Her voice light and pleasing, she said, "Majesty. I . . . am sorry. I'll leave."

"You haven't interrupted me, if that's your fear. Rather, I've interrupted you."

"Not at all, sir." She nodded toward the dog that sniffed about. "Issa needed a walk, and Naynee is napping."

"Naynee?"

"My attendant. She's recovering from our journey."

"Kind of you to allow her a nap." The compliment escaped him, but he didn't regret it. Some of the young woman's melancholy faded, and she shrugged. If she weren't an Atean, and if their circumstances weren't so awkward, he'd find her very attractive. Ha. Enough self-deception; he found her appealing despite their circumstances. Not good for clear-eyed bargaining. Best to keep their conversation short. "Tell me, lady, what's your opinion of this agreement your lord-father has . . . offered?"

Caitria seemed surprised he would ask her opinion. Evidently taking courage, she looked around and then said, "You should not marry me."

Gently, Akabe asked, "Do I have a choice?" As she stared, Akabe explained, "My council has recommended that I marry for the sake of Siphra. Furthermore, rebuilding the Infinite's Holy House for Siphra is one of my primary goals as king, but legally, your lord-father holds the temple's sacred land. Our marriage would resolve both matters—yet I need to weigh the risks. I hoped you could help me to decide."

"I've given you my opinion, sir. Trust me. My . . . family . . . is wrong. They're overestimating their power and not seeing the situation clearly. This plan would bring disaster upon us all. *Please*, build on other land!"

"There is no other land for the Infinite's temple. The property was consecrated at Siphra's beginning." The fact that she'd asked him to build on other land proved beyond doubt that she didn't comprehend the Infinite's faithful ones in the least. Yet was she Atean? She seemed so vulnerable, wary as startled prey. "Perhaps, as you say, your family is wrong. But my true question ought to be, are you the wrong lady?"

"I am. Wrong for you . . . and Siphra, I mean." But she blushed, and the effect was so entrancing that Akabe caught his breath. "Sir," she persisted, "believe me! You mustn't—"

A young man's sharp voice called out, "Caitria!"

She turned, the glorious color fading from her cheeks. "Cyril?"

Tall and slim, with the same brown hair and eyes as Caitria, Cyril stalked toward them. Unmistakably one of her older brothers. But without her fascination.

Caitria stepped away from Akabe. "Cyril, you needn't worry. I—"

He cut off her explanation with a chopping wave of his hand. "Need I not?" The young man scoffed. His brown eyes cold, he grabbed his sister's arm and yanked her to his side. Caitria glared as if she'd like to stomp her brother's toes. But she remained quiet. He spoke to Akabe. "By your leave, sir, she went missing from her chamber without permission. My lord-father is worried."

Caitria's eyebrows lifted as if surprised. Then she puckered her lips in the most mesmerizing grimace Akabe had ever seen. "I couldn't allow Issa to wet the floor, now, could I?"

Cyril made a rude noise. "You should have shaken Naynee awake and sent her! Now, *move.* You've been away too long."

Keeping his voice low to soothe the young man, Akabe said, "My fault entirely. I greeted your sister and delayed her." He inclined his head to Cyril in farewell. "Sir."

"Sir." The young man insolently copied Akabe's formal nod, then all but dragged his sister away through the garden, with the elegant dog, Issa, following quietly. Cyril Thaenfall's sharp voice echoed back to Akabe in harsh, chopped syllables—obviously rebuking his sister.

Listening, Akabe tensed, reining in his defensive instincts. The young woman was clearly as trapped by this situation as he was. Yet she'd revealed spirit.

He could see her as a queen. But his queen?

How could he trust an Atean? *Was* she Atean?

Faine approached, seeming irked. "Shall I offer double the gold to halt the marriage?"

"Do we have double the gold to spare?"

"Not without Siphra taking on a sizable debt, sir."

"I doubt Thaenfall would accept it anyway." What was the man's motive? Power? Regardless, Akabe must outwit Thaenfall on his own battlefield. "My lord, I'm forced to accept this contract as is. Siphra *must* have that land."

Faine looked as if Akabe had punched him in the stomach. Recovering, he gasped, "Majesty, you *cannot* marry a Thaenfall—they're Ateans!"

"Then suggest another option for acquiring that land. Anything, my lord, and I'll consider it!"

Faine hesitated, silent.

"That's what I thought." Akabe exhaled. Wasn't this somehow the Infinite's will? It must be so—otherwise another option would surely present itself. Anyway, by all that was holy and dedicated to the Infinite, it was a disgrace that Ateans controlled what belonged to the Infinite. The situation must be settled.

By Siphra's king.

✦ ✦ ✦

Caitria stumbled and winced as Cyril wrenched her toward the marble steps. "Tria, what did you say to him?"

"The truth—that I don't want this marriage." Her brother's fingers dug hard into her arm, making her gasp. "Cyril, let go! You're hurting me!"

"*You* are hurting us! Furies burn your tongue! What were you thinking? You know what this agreement means to our lord-father—to our entire family!"

Family! Caitria stifled her disgust. What family? When, since Mother's death, had they ever concerned themselves with her? Naynee was now her parent, playmate, nurse, and friend. Of all her relatives, Cyril was one of the few who ever spoke to her. Cyril and her horrible "cousin," Lord Ruestock. Ugh! "The agreement was finished and *perfect* until dear Ruestock came creeping in, suggesting new terms to our lord-father!"

"You need to appreciate those terms—they've supplied you with a dowry and a future!"

"Oh!" She twisted her arm from Cyril's grasp as they entered the marble corridor leading from the garden. Behind her, Issa's toenails clicked and scrambled over the slick floor in skittish confusion as Caitria halted and glared at her brother. "Let's discuss how much I appreciate being ignored and sold to rebuild that temple despite my fears for the Thaenfalls, and for me! Let's discuss *everything* that could go wrong for us all!"

"There's nothing to discuss!" Cyril snagged her arm and rushed her through the corridor, muttering, "Lower your voice. In fact, just keep your mouth shut!"

She wanted to kick him and throw rocks at him—in her thoughts at least. Couldn't he ever speak to her nicely? She was his sister, not a mere interference to his drinking and gambling and rioting about Siphra.

Truly, the king had spoken to her with more kindness in a few sentences than had her whole family for years. The king . . . !

Oh, but why did that big, attractive man with those lovely warm eyes and perfect dimples have to be the *king*? Why couldn't he be some highborn nobleman whom her lord-father praised instead of cursed? If so, she would have approached this marriage joyously.

Instead, she'd become a pawn in some secretive power-game connived by that wretched Ruestock and her lord-father, who . . . who was waiting at the very entry of her chamber.

Seeing her father's jaw tense and his fingers curl into fists, Caitria faltered and reached blindly for Issa, who nudged at her, signaling fear. The poor darling's instincts were undoubtedly correct. They'd earned thrashings for their little jaunt this morning.

But it might be worth some pain if the king heeded her plea. In silence, she begged Akabe of Siphra, *Please*, build on other land! Don't drag me into your schemes—your religion!

Don't bring this disaster upon us! Please . . .

Caitria gasped as her lord-father shoved her inside the chamber and then swore softly and dug his fingers hard into the back of her neck. "Wretched, rebellious creature! If you have ruined my plans, I *will* throttle you!"

Pain-dazed, unable to speak, Caitria stared up at her father, her senses fading beneath his agonizing grip.

7

Akabe stared at Parne's chief priest, unable to believe what he'd just heard. "You refuse my request?"

Though Ishvah Nesac paled, he shook his head. "Majesty, she's an Atean! You, as one of the Infinite's faithful, cannot—must not!—marry an Atean!"

"Do you not wish to see the Infinite's Holy House rebuilt?"

"It is my dream, Majesty. Yet if this dream cannot be, I will mourn its loss, as I mourn Parne—until I draw my last breath in this fallen world." Nesac lifted his thin, scholarly hands, an imploring gesture. "Majesty, consider—I beg you!—an Atean wife could very well lead your heart away from the Infinite."

"Or I might lead her heart to the Infinite," Akabe argued. Did everyone consider him to be so weak?

The chief priest pressed a hand to his forehead, as if thinking were suddenly difficult. "Have you consulted Siphra's prophets? Have you sought the Infinite's will?"

"Yes. He has been silent. However," Akabe changed tactics, "if my decisions dishonor my Creator, won't He then tell His prophets to rebuke me? Yet how can rebuilding the temple displease the Infinite? Help me fulfill this work for Him, Nesac. *I beg you!* Otherwise . . ." Akabe leaned forward, meaning every word, "I will search Siphra for a priest who sees, as I see—that Siphra needs its temple, its strength, and its faith restored!"

Nesac closed his eyes, undoubtedly praying. After a long instant, he sighed and looked at Akabe. "I will continue to pray, Majesty. For you and your wife. And for me, that I will never regret blessing this marriage."

His words fell on Akabe's spirit so heavily that Akabe couldn't rejoice. Not that he wanted to rejoice. Thaenfall had set a snare, and Akabe had stepped into it, eyes open.

There was no other way. None!

He *must* complete this task he'd begun—this pledge he'd given his people for their temple. He would deal with his priests' opinions and his counselors' arguments as they cropped up. As for Caitria and her family . . . may the Infinite protect him!

He managed to smile at the unhappy priest. "Thank you."

✦ ✦ ✦

Formally attired and standing in the palace's ceremonial hall before his council and invited witnesses, Akabe sighed inwardly, feeling condemned.

He was about to marry an Atean.

Akabe hoped his people would understand. Their king certainly didn't.

Even so . . . Infinite . . . be with us. Akabe fastened a gold armband about Caitria Thaenfall's slender bicep, then clasped her cold hand. She stared straight ahead as Ishvah Nesac pronounced hesitant blessings upon the royal marriage. The blessings sounded more like a death sentence.

For consecrated land, chosen by the Infinite at Siphra's beginning.

As Ishvah's blessing ended, Akabe glanced down at his wife again. Caitria hesitantly looked up, wincing under Akabe's scrutiny. At least it was clear she didn't aspire to be a queen. Standing beside Caitria, Cyril obviously noticed her expression. He gave his sister a ferocious scowl that warned her to behave. Caitria glared at him.

Adjacent to the siblings, Cyan Thaenfall, Lord of the Plidian Estates, studied Akabe as if seeing an oddity that should not exist. And perhaps he was correct. As Siphra's king, Akabe certainly felt like a pretender just now. Particularly with most of his council members and courtiers showing hostile frowns, or—at best—bleak acceptance for this marriage.

Akabe nodded to Thaenfall, then led Cyan, Caitria, and Cyril into a meeting chamber. There a clerk waited, his worktable organized with vials, cords, parchments, pens, and a wavering lamp flame positioned beneath a warming stand, which held a small pan of melted crimson wax.

Seeing Akabe, the clerk produced two copies of the marriage agreement—so sniffily that Akabe nearly growled. He spoke to Thaenfall instead. "Here's the new contract, my lord. It's obvious I've fulfilled my obligation. Therefore, let's read and sign."

Akabe stood beside the haughty lord, reading his own copy of the agreement. Every clause seemed proper and concise. Akabe of Siphra agreed to marry Caitria Thaenfall, with the permission of Cyan Thaenfall, Lord of the Plidian Estates. Furthermore, having paid the negotiated sum, Akabe would bestow upon Caitria all the rights, lands, revenues, and marks of rank due to the queen of Siphra—never to be revoked without justifiable cause, noted in clauses, as long as they both lived.

Evidently finished reading, Thaenfall snatched a gilded stylus, jabbed it into an ink vial, and scrawled his name at the bottom of each parchment. Out of turn, yet Akabe wasn't about to rebuke the man.

Akabe signed both documents less hastily. The fussy clerk applied the royal seals, and Thaenfall grabbed his copy of the document. Flat-voiced, he told Caitria, "In nine months, I expect to hear that you've borne an heir for Siphra."

Thaenfall bowed to Akabe and departed, snapping his fingers at Cyril as if the young man were a dog commanded to follow at his heels.

Neither man looked back. Stunned, Akabe listened as their footsteps faded and the door closed with a muffled thud. Was Thaenfall always so rude and unfeeling toward his children?

Akabe looked down at Caitria, who still stared at the doorway as if unable to believe what had just happened. Sympathetic despite his own frustrations, Akabe wrapped his hands around Caitria's. She stared up at him now, dazed as a wounded creature.

Beyond them, gathering his pens, wax, and cords, the clerk said, "The queen should have signed the document, Majesty. Yet I suppose it's no matter. The marriage contract will stand."

Caitria's chin quivered.

Still furious with Thaenfall, Akabe held Caitria as she cried. Over her head, he gave the clerk a meaningful glance and sternly nodded everyone toward the hall. When all the witnesses had departed and closed the door, Akabe smoothed Caitria's hair, marveling at its sheen and delicious scent. "This whole matter was handled badly—you deserved better. I'm sorry."

She stiffened in his arms and pulled back, gazing at him in evident confusion. And hurt. "Sir, why should you care more about my feelings than my own family has?"

Akabe lifted a strand of Caitria's hair plastered to her cheek by tears. "Lady, I am now your family."

Caitria sobbed, covering her face with her hands.

Apparently not the answer she'd wanted.

✦ ✦ ✦

Akabe opened his eyes the merest fraction, aware first of Caitria asleep beside him, then of the door creaking open. A servant lit the hearth, then departed, softly closing the door. The first sounds of Akabe's day, as usual, made him hate being a king. Servants appearing and disappearing like shadows always raised Akabe's instincts to hide or to defend himself.

Which explained the dagger he hid beneath his pillow each night.

Any of these servants could be an assassin, the way they slipped through the palace. He must remind his guards to be vigilant. They'd failed him before. If they failed him again, Caitria's life would be equally endangered—a risk Akabe could not allow.

She was now, by all of Siphra's legal requirements, his wife. She merited his protection.

Hearing her stir, Akabe touched Caitria's tender face, then kissed her cheek. If only necessity hadn't forced him to marry a stranger—he hated being so unsure of his queen . . . his *wife*. But perhaps he could lessen their mutual emotional distance. He snagged his overtunic from the foot of the bed, flung it on, then stood. "Good morning, lady. I'm expected at various meetings today. Before then, however, let's share the morning meal."

She nodded and sat up, still seeming half asleep as she reached for her chamber robe and slippers. Akabe waited for her to speak, to say something . . . anything. But she moved about in that same speechless daze of last evening. How long would it take for her to recover from her father's harsh abandonment?

It might help if he corrected his own unhappy acceptance of their marriage.

As Caitria donned her robe and swept her hair off her neck, Akabe glimpsed a darkened mark on her pale skin. A bruise on her throat, just behind her ear.

Akabe strode around the bed, startling her. She froze, her brown eyes huge. Did she fear he would strike her? He halted within arm's reach and opened his hands gently, matching his cautious movements with hushed words. "Stand still, lady, only for an instant." He slid his hands beneath her hair, lifting the soft, sweetly scented brown waves off her neck. Not one bruise, but two. Someone had held Caitria by the back of her neck. Viciously and recently. "Who gave you these bruises? Your brother?"

"No, my lord."

"Your father then."

She waited, not arguing with his conclusion.

Akabe released her hair and stepped back, watching her. "Why was he angry with you?"

"Because I . . . behaved thoughtlessly, and . . . spoke contrary to his wishes."

"Concerning what?"

Caitria looked away, her elegant face setting in stubborn lines. Clearly, she would refuse to elaborate further. "It's unimportant now, Majesty."

Unimportant? Not by the look of those bruises. Akabe suppressed a frown. He could only guess that they'd quarreled about this marriage. She'd argued against it, failed, and suffered. For which he must bear the blame. Well enough. He touched her face, running his fingers along that stubborn, lovely jawline. When she glanced at him warily, he said, "This will not happen again. Granted, we've been compelled to accept this marriage, but for as long as I live, I will not allow you to experience further abuse such as this!"

Tears brimmed in her eyes, and she swallowed, so pitiable that Akabe felt compelled to hug and console her. In his thoughts, chief priest Nesac warned again, *Majesty, consider—I beg you!— an Atean wife could very well lead your heart away from the Infinite. . . .*

Was this how such a divergence of faith might begin?

A vulnerable instant.

The longing to protect . . .

The progression was more subtle and more treacherous than he'd believed. Would he be able to withstand such temptation?

Infinite? Guard my heart, I beg You!

❖ ❖ ❖

Caitria slid another glance toward her husband as he led her out into the echoing corridor to face her first day as his queen. Was he always so . . . protective? Truly, she'd experienced more tenderness and consideration from this "despicable fool," as her lord-father called him, in one day than from her entire family for ages.

Oh, it would be so easy to love this man if he weren't such a danger to her family. To her! Though she was descended from Siphra's most ancient noble lines, her family might be destroyed if she breathed a word of her fears and suspicions to Akabe—to the king.

She must guard her every word. Did he suspect—?

A bark startled Caitria from her thoughts. She turned and laughed, seeing her beloved nursemaid and her capering hound, both delighted to see her. "Issa! Naynee! You've stayed?"

She wasn't completely abandoned in this cold palace—such a relief!

Naynee beamed, her dear ruddy face alight with joy. "Your lord-father guessed he'd no reason to feed your dog or your servant any longer, lady. He left us here, if you'll have us."

"Oh, you know I will!" Unless the king refused. Caitria cast a fearful look at Akabe, silently imploring his agreement. He had absolute control over every aspect of her life now.

The king remained silent, studying Naynee as if trying to judge the influence she might wield. If only he knew how loving Naynee was! How disinterested in political maneuverings! Please . . .

Just as she was about to kneel before him and *beg,* despite the gathering courtiers, Akabe nodded. "I agree. Naynee and Issa will be the first official members of your household."

"Thank you, sir!" She stifled an undignified whoop.

The king seized her hand—a subtle smile lurking about his handsome mouth. "Now," he murmured, "one favor for another. . . . Come with me today, lady. *Majesty.* Not to the council meetings—I won't bore us both with those—but come visit the property we've granted Siphra. Nothing formal or announced. A surprise inspection."

The property they'd granted Siphra? That wretched temple land! She was grateful for his indulgence, but he could leave her out of his religion! Didn't he understand how vengeful the Ateans would be if she gave the slightest appearance of following the Infinite?

And yet, what else could she do? Would the Ateans understand the extent of her isolation? Her virtual imprisonment here—abandoned by her family and surrounded by hostile courtiers?

Forcing herself to think of less frightful things, Caitria nodded. "Of course, sir. I've never been. Can you imagine? My life's controlled by land I've never seen."

"You haven't traveled?"

"Not since Mother died ten years past. I've been isolated on our estates. My lord-father . . . has been busy." Too busy to do more than snap at her or lash out when she offended him. If only Mother had lived! Safer to not remember Mother now—risking a display of weakness before all these haughty courtiers.

As they walked along the huge marble-columned corridor, Caitria shivered despite the stunning surroundings. The palace was too opulent for her tastes. She loved coziness. Here highly wrought carvings of birds, flowers, and trees fretted the white marble columns, arcades, and walls like stonework embroidery— all coldly forbidding her to touch them. Semiprecious gems and gilding sparkled overhead on the soaring ceilings in massive sunbursts of gold and crimson that dazzled her and made her feel like an intruder.

But the king's chambers were worse. She couldn't move in those dim rooms without fear of breaking something priceless and irreplaceable.

Didn't he possess a refuge in the palace? A sunlit chamber where one could flop onto a couch or into a cushioned window seat with a favorite collection of stories, then read until a nap took hold? Did kings and queens even indulge in naps?

This whole situation promised a dismal life.

Silent, she accompanied her new husband as he ordered his servants and guards to prepare for the impromptu temple inspection. It seemed almost natural to ride beside him in a plain open chariot through Munra's streets. And, despite her predetermined loathing, the vast temple site amazed her with its white steps and immense smooth-slabbed paving stones, not to mention the multitudes of workmen.

Yet the king scanned the site, visibly tensing. Speaking so softly that Caitria almost didn't hear, he said, "Those men don't belong here. Too well-dressed to be workers. Not reverent enough to be worshipers . . ."

Caitria followed the king's gaze, eyeing the suspected

noblemen—for noblemen they were. They swaggered about, armed with swords and daggers, and . . . oh . . . was she imagining she'd seen them before?

While she sifted through her memories, trying to recall faces and names, Akabe signaled to four of his guards. "Sirs, follow me."

Tucking her mantle close, Caitria started after her husband. But a guard stepped in front of her. "Majesty, please wait."

"Very well." Curious, she leaned around her concerned guard and watched as the king hurried toward one particular supervisor, who'd been beckoned by the noblemen.

Busy overseeing his workers, the supervisor shook his head, refusing to leave his task, which irritated the aristocrats. Caitria frowned. *Where* had she seen these men?

Akabe called out, "Good sirs, allow him to do his job!"

The troublemakers turned and gawked, obviously recognizing their king. One recovered and lunged for Akabe, dagger drawn.

Assassins!

Caitria struggled as the guards pulled her away.

✦ 8 ✦

Akabe drew his dagger but had no chance to defend himself. Two royal guards tackled his foolhardy assailant, while the remainder chased down the man's cohorts.

Dan Roeh, who'd resisted speaking to these men and thereby escaped their trap, abandoned his work now and hurried toward the scuffle. "Majesty!"

Akabe halted Dan, noting smears of blood on the ground from the skirmish. Had the attacker suffered a wound? It seemed so. Infinite, let there be no more bloodshed! He snapped a look at Dan. "Is the prophet here today?"

"No, sir. Lessons are tomorrow. She's with her mother this morning."

"Good." Akabe sighed his relief, refusing to think of Ela beyond her importance to this temple. "We'll hire guards to protect you and your men. Until then, wear weapons as you work. That blood could very well have been yours, Roeh—bless the Infinite for His protection!"

"Bless Him, indeed," Dan mumbled, staring as the guards lifted their bleeding prisoner. "I'll tell my men about the weapons."

"Thank you." Akabe turned, glimpsing Caitria's approach.

She faltered, paling at the blood and the now-unconscious prisoner. "Majesty . . . sir . . ."

Aware of Dan Roeh's watchful gaze, Akabe gripped Caitria's hand. Was she turning faint? "It's not safe for you here, lady. Another time, perhaps. Where are your guards?"

"I—I ran from them, sir."

Akabe looped an arm around his wife and swung her away. "We're leaving. For now."

✦ ✦ ✦

"Sir," Faine mourned amid the hastily assembled royal council, "bad news. It seems the Thaenfall family was involved. They *are* Atean. They worship the goddess and wear her coils."

"Not the entire family," Akabe argued. "My wife hasn't mentioned the goddess Atea to me. And she has no marks of Atean worship." Only bruises from her lord-father.

"Nevertheless . . ." Faine reddened, betraying his annoyance. "Forgive me, Majesty, but we *cannot* trust the queen." Faine removed a money pouch from his belt and overturned it on the council table, deliberate and dramatic. Two rings spilled out amid the jangling of silver coins. "Majesty, these are signets taken from the suicides this morning."

Akabe winced inwardly. Of three attackers, only one escaped. The other two knifed themselves. "Who were they?"

Faine offered the larger signet to Akabe. "This was worn by Ison of Deerfeld. A Thaenfall cousin. His comrade was one Ezry Morside, a landholder of Deerfeld's properties. Both have remained away from court as our opponents."

Chilled, Akabe accepted the signet. How could Caitria not recognize her own cousin?

Before he could respond, Lord Faine warned, "As Ison's death reveals, the Thaenfalls are known for their loyalty to the goddess Atea. It may be that they're incapable of honoring you as their king. Remember, sir, the Sacred Books note, 'Those who hate the Infinite are corrupt. Their actions are evil and they know no good.' Be sure of those you trust, sir."

"I loathe living my life suspicious of everyone!"

"Majesty," Trillcliff argued quietly, "certain people must be suspected. Your wife might be blameless. But if she ever plots against your life—if you live—you will be unable to save her."

Akabe clenched the traitor's signet in his fist. Might his wife become part of a Thaenfall conspiracy? He must talk to Caitria.

✦ ✦ ✦

Firelight glimmered off the traitor's signet in Akabe's palm.

Sitting in the chair beside him in his silent bedchamber, Caitria shook her head. "No, thank you, sir. I've no need to inspect the ring. I've seen that seal in family records—though I didn't recognize my cousin."

Was that the truth? Akabe studied his wife. "How could you not recognize your own cousin?"

"As I told you this morning, my lord-father kept me mostly secluded from my family after my mother died. And I'm the youngest in my family. With the exception of Cyril, I hardly know my own siblings, much less some second cousin. Ison wasn't one of my father's hunting comrades." She eyed the signet in Akabe's hand again. "He tried to kill you."

"Yes." Akabe hesitated, hating his next question. "Also, I must ask . . . do you and your family worship Atea?"

Caitria's expression tightened. "The Thaenfalls have followed her for generations. Some more, some less."

"And you?"

She shrugged, but Akabe saw her defiance. "I suppose. Yes. Though I never attended the rites. As I've said, I was isolated."

"What if you were asked to cease worshiping her?"

She stared into the fire, her now-distant gaze reflecting flames. "I've not considered it. Nor will I discuss this further. It's part of my heritage."

"Heritage need not dictate your future."

She remained silent. Stubborn. Akabe leaned forward in his chair. "Lady, if there's the least chance we might make ours a true marriage, you must talk to me."

Something flickered across her face. Akabe couldn't quite name the expression. Hurt? Regret? Caitria stared at him. "I doubt we can ever have a true marriage."

He straightened. "Why?"

Caitria stared into the fire, shaking her head. "Because! I warned you not to marry—"

"You need not repeat yourself." Was she his enemy, then? Well enough. He'd suffered his fill of attacks plotted by Atean queens. Queen Raenna, Caitria's predecessor, had sent soldiers after him often enough. He would not endure verbal cuts from her successor. Akabe stood and crossed the room to his chest of hunting gear. He flung on his heaviest cloak, then grabbed a sleeping roll and slammed the chest shut.

Caitria startled within her chair and turned, her profile a graceful silhouette against the firelight. Akabe resisted the impulse to lash out against her and forced his voice to remain calm. "I wish you a blessed night, lady. Sleep well."

He strode to an elaborate wall panel and slid a carved, golden-winged, sharp-taloned aeryon to the left. A door shifted open, swift and soundless as a blink. Akabe stepped into the hidden stairwell and closed the panel. In absolute darkness, he climbed the familiar spiraling stone steps and let himself onto the wall-enclosed rooftop. His private fighting arena, crowned by a clear, star-jeweled night sky. No rain.

Infinite, thank You.

Akabe unfurled the sleeping roll and settled himself upon it to stare up at the stars. To consider his Creator. And his marriage. Infinite? Had he been too hasty in his desire to regain the temple's land?

How could he remedy this disaster?

He woke later to the sound of the door opening. To gentle footsteps. Caitria. She covered him with a quilt, then scooted beneath it to lie beside him. He felt her shivering. She nudged herself beneath his arm and sighed shakily. Had she been crying?

Not the behavior of a woman who hated her husband.

Confusing . . . but welcome. Akabe curved his arm around her slender body, drawing her closer, his thoughts speeding ahead. Here was the truth: Unless Caitria abandoned and betrayed him, he could not abandon her. He would learn beyond question if she truly followed Atean ways and if she was plotting against him with her family. If so, then he must fight to save them both.

We are caught within a battle, he told his wife in silence. If we are to survive, if we are to forge a true marriage from this debacle, we need a plan.

He stared up at the stars, no longer seeing them as he contemplated a defense.

✦ ✦ ✦

His travel cloak flowing about him, and accompanied by his mournful family, Kien crossed the Lantecs' main hall, ready to leave. Mother clutched his right arm and his sister, Beka, hugged his left as Father and Jon followed. Mother was crying, of course. Her pale gray eyes red and swollen, she pleaded, "Write! Tell us everything you're doing. Don't leave us to wonder. And don't forget us!"

"Do you think I could?" He kissed her wet face. "Mother, please, you'll dissolve me with those tears. Listen, we will restore my citizenship somehow, by the Infinite's grace. You'll see." He prayed his forced optimism might become reality. Until then, he must live within the present. For all legal purposes, whether they knew it or not, his parents had no son. He'd written as much to Ela, but couldn't bear to tell his parents.

As Mother dabbed at her tears, Beka picked at Kien's choice of travel clothes. "Why are you still wearing black?" Sounding resentful, Beka added, "You're out of the military, and you've no reason to honor *them*!"

Kien worked up a grin and gave his sister a hug. Her irritation was easier to cope with than Mother's tears. "I like black. It matches my mood right now."

Beka skewed her mouth in an aggrieved twist. "Well, I suppose it would. But we'll fight this decision, Kien! I'm circulating copies of your parting speech among my friends, and—"

"What parting speech?"

"You know . . ." Beka swiped the air with an impatient gesture. "The last segment of your trial. It's a perfect summary of your case. Jon brought me a copy of the transcript, and I cried when I read it. Kien, we must communicate your side of the trial and clear your name! And we will, even if I must haunt the Grand Assembly every day!"

"Furthermore," Ara sniffled, "all the ladies your sister and I have been writing to these past few months campaigning for your cause, have been sending us notes. They're pledging to join us, dear, to help change public opinion. And so has General Rol."

"Thank you." If Kien thought for one instant that inciting public fervor would change his status, he'd be the first to charge into that battle. But any hope of an actual reversal must have a legal foundation. And right now, he was unable to think of a fresh argument to use in his defense. Time and distance might clear his thoughts. Even so, perhaps copies of the transcript would sway attitudes in favor of the Lantecs. Moreover, fighting to restore their good name would probably help ease his family's grief. Already, Mother and Beka looked more cheerful just talking about their work on his behalf.

He hugged them, then reluctantly stepped back. "If I'm to reach the Siphran border by tomorrow night, then I must leave now."

Behind them, Rade Lantec cleared his throat. When Kien turned, Father gave him a sad smile and held out a long wooden case. "I bought this last year, intending it to be yours one day. Here it is, a few decades early."

A sword case? As Father held the case, Kien lifted its golden latch, raised the lid, and caught his breath. An Azurnite sword gleamed from within the case, its stunning, glistening blue water-patterned blade, silver hilt, and scabbard beautifully wrought with gold and discreetly etched with the name *Lantec*. Clearly every bit as serviceable as Kien's military sword, but more ornate. Worth a small fortune—and able to slice through ordinary swords as if they were twigs.

"Sir," Kien mumbled, his throat constricting, "there's no need . . ."

"You've more call for it now than I do," Rade argued. "The Tracelands demanded your sword. It'll comfort me knowing I've replaced a bit of what you've lost for my sake."

He couldn't argue with the tears in his father's eyes.

Infinite? Will I see them again?

Unable to speak, Kien hugged everyone again. Outside, his destroyer, Scythe—a gleaming black monster warhorse—waited. At least this irritable, never-dull mountain of a beast would carry him through any unexpected adventures with ease. Already Scythe tossed his big black head and stamped his colossal hooves as if urging Kien to hurry.

As he gathered Scythe's reins, Kien shuddered. Why did he suddenly feel like a wrongly condemned prisoner, going to his death?

Infinite? Why this chill? What am I facing?

Nauseated by the Infinite's telling silence, Kien goaded Scythe south, toward the windswept coastal road, and Siphra.

9

Shifting his gaze from Barth, who had crawled under a chair after a toy—which he wasn't supposed to carry while on duty—Akabe hid his concern as a servant readied a gold pin for the royal mantle. The pin's sharp point hovered too close to Akabe's neck for comfort. Imagine the irony if one bumbling servant accomplished what three Atean assassination attempts had not. A lingering, blood-poisoned death by gouging a vein in the king's neck.

Akabe braced himself, ready to strike away the pin if the man aimed it badly.

The servant jabbed the point into the crimson mantle, missing Akabe just as a rap sounded at the door. Lord Faine entered Akabe's attiring room and bowed, his waxed gray beard a-twitch.

Safely pinned, Akabe lifted his eyebrows at his lord-counselor. "My lord. What news?"

"Majesty. How did you know I have news?"

The twitching beard. Akabe grinned. Was it unregal and rude to toy with one's advisors? "I see it on your face. What news?"

"Good and bad, sir."

"Bad first."

"News from General Rol in the Tracelands. Lord Aeyrievale was condemned before their Grand Assembly. Our informants say your petition was mocked and scorned unread, though Aeyrievale defended your good name most spiritedly in his last statement. He—"

Akabe gasped. "Last statement? Did they sentence him to death?"

Faine blinked. "Death? Why, no, sir. The Tracelands stripped Aeyrievale of his citizenship and ordered him to leave *their* country."

Akabe grumbled while accepting a pair of riding gloves from his servant. "Faine, you near-killed me! I thought Lord Aeyrievale died because of my decisions. Anyway, his sentence is despicable enough." Kien loved the Tracelands—was a proud Tracelander. But no longer, thanks to the impulsive, idiotic Akabe of Siphra. "I'm sorry to hear of his exile."

"Which leads us to the good news, sir." Faine smiled. "He's returning to Siphra. We should expect him here within a week."

Perfect! Akabe swallowed his cheer. "Still, this is terrible news. Lord Aeyrievale deserved better than permanent exile."

"Indeed, sir. And Siphra deserved better than the insults pronounced against us in the Grand Assembly. We're drafting a formal protest against the Tracelands. If they'd an ambassador in our country, we would summon him today and tell him exactly what we think of such rudeness. Such uncouth—!"

"Yes, you are correct." Eager to cut off the brewing diatribe, Akabe asked, "Why don't we have an ambassador from the Tracelands?"

Caught mid-rant, Faine faltered. "Eh? Why, Majesty? Er, because we've been too politically volatile until these past few months. Siphra is regarded as dangerous and unstable."

Infinite, must every country in the civilized world be hostile toward Siphra? "I take it that, likewise, Siphra has no ambassador representing us in the Tracelands."

"The Tracelands ousted him last year, sir. You've met him. Lord Ruestock."

"Ah." The polished, conniving Ruestock. "Hmm. It seems he's been too quiet for the past five months. Find out what he's up to. And demand that the Tracelands allow us to replace him. Faine, let's create a righteously indignant defense in the Grand Assembly."

"Yes, Majesty. We'll deal with all that today." Faine's waxed beard twitched again. "We believe that today you also ought to formally set the record straight concerning your ancestry. Which of the Garric clans is yours? Northern or southern?"

"Southern, but why should it make any difference? My lord, I've made it clear that I don't welcome discussion of my family. You must trust me on this."

"Yes, sir." Faine straightened, turning overly formal. "However, it's not idle curiosity, sir, if questions are raised among your people concerning your lineage. You need to address the legitimacy concern."

Temper rising with the heat in his face, Akabe said, "I'll address this topic when I'm ready to deal with it, my lord. Not now, if you please. My legitimacy should have concerned my people last spring when they tossed me onto the throne. They must be bored if they've nothing better to discuss than my heritage. Meanwhile, my best friend is exiled, and the Tracelands have officially turned against us, robbing Siphra of an ally. I think that's enough for now, don't you?"

"Yes, sir." Still formal, Faine bowed, allowing Akabe time to banish his fury. As they walked outside, followed by Barth and saluted by Akabe's guards at the doorway, Faine coughed. "My wife and the other ladies will now attend the queen. Her apartments are prepared."

The queen. Where was Caitria? Akabe glanced along the corridor and saw Naynee walking Issa among the columns. Hadn't Caitria summoned them yet? Suspicious, Akabe tucked his gloves into his belt, beckoned Naynee, and whistled to the graceful dog. "Issa! Come here."

Issa trotted up and he scooped the obliging creature into his arms. Avoiding her licks, Akabe told Faine, "Go ahead of me to the council chamber. I'll be there promptly."

"Yes, Majesty." Faine marched off, motioning Barth to follow him. The little boy obeyed happily, still clutching his toy, a carved soldier.

"We must be quiet," Akabe murmured to Naynee and Issa. He crept through his attiring room and opened the panel into his bedchamber.

Just as he'd suspected. Caitria lay in the huge royal bed, sound asleep. Akabe marched over to the bed and plopped Issa onto the embroidered crimson covers. "Lady, if I must be awake now and wearing these wretched prettified clothes, then you must also play your part. Get up."

Issa evidently agreed, licking Caitria's face until she giggled and squealed. "No!"

"Yes!" While Issa capered over the pillows and barked, Akabe dragged off the covers. "Lady Faine and the rest of your entourage will arrive soon. You must be ready to greet them. You'll be moving into your rooms today."

Caitria sat up, eyes wide. "What?"

One would think the news upset her. Why? Caitria said no more than ten words per day to him. Had her family instructed her to spy on him and relay all his habits to them for some Atean plot? Akabe returned her stare, hoping his gaze was cool. Even sleep-rumpled, Caitria was entirely too pretty—devastating bait for a king. "Your rooms are prepared and the ladies will arrive soon. Time to take up your duties. *Majesty.*"

He kissed her cheek, then strode off to his council meeting. Entering the council chamber, Akabe heard, ". . . as I said, the southern Garrics have only three branches to the family. One suffered . . ." Seeing him, they stopped. Akabe eyed his council members. They looked away.

At the end of the table, a pair of small booted feet dangled over the gilded arm of a chair. Barth. Why should the boy hear a quarrel? Akabe cleared his throat and pulled the gloves from his belt. "Barth, hop down and take these to my attiring room. You can either wait for me there, or run errands for the queen and her ladies."

Barth whooped, scrambled off the chair, bowed, snatched Akabe's gloves, and ran from the royal council chamber. If only the royal counselors would as happily do the same.

✦ ✦ ✦

Standing in her chilly marble and gold apartments, Caitria nodded to her new attendants, Lady Faine, Lady Trillcliff, and Lady Piton. All older. And all Infinite-worshipers, she was sure. They eyed her, stern as three mothers. Caitria's lady-mother had never been so severe. If only Mother had survived her fever . . .

Caitria exhaled, forcing herself to ignore the tightening about her throat as she concentrated on her attendants. They seemed, for all the world, to expect her to chant some wicked incantations against them. It was almost a pity she knew none.

Lady Faine, all raised eyebrows, flowing embroidered robes, and meticulously coifed hair, looked as if she'd mistakenly eaten a grubby worm. "Majesty," she enunciated, as if certain that Caitria would fail to understand her, "we are to attend you and advise you in matters of palace etiquette. Be sure to ask us if anything is unclear, hmm?"

Smile. Never mind that the ladies Trillcliff and Piton were eyeing her as if she might taint them. Caitria could almost hear their thoughts.

Atean. Cousin to assassins. Enemy of the king and the Infinite. Not someone Siphra wanted as queen.

Hmph. Caitria must allow their words and attitudes to flow past like a stream to be skipped over. They would *not* bully her into their religion. Ever. Hadn't Siphra nearly torn itself to pieces for the sake of religion? Furthermore, these women didn't know her in the least.

Lady Trillcliff spoke, her voice as fluttery as her pale green veils and layered tunic. "Majesty, please follow us." She eyed Caitria's simple robes. "We've much work to do."

Caitria forced away a scowl. Why had Akabe sent these termagants—these scolds!—to plague her? And why was she being isolated in her own apartments? Did he actually hate her for their religious differences? This was not what she'd dreamed of after so many years of solitude. She'd dreamed of a husband who would at least speak to her kindly. Would she be cut off for her entire life?

Caitria closed her eyes for an instant, then lifted her gaze and chin. Courage. Face this with dignity. You are a Thaenfall.

Devise a plan!

✦ ✦ ✦

In his quiet, lamplit bedchamber, Akabe lifted a silver writing stylus from a nearby tray, tapped it in the crystal ink vial, then wrote, *Commanded and signed, Akabe of Siphra.*

Would this order provide enough guards to protect the temple site and its workers? Akabe winced, remembering how close Dan Roeh, his most knowledgeable stone mason—and father of Siphra's most renowned prophet—had come to being killed by Ison of Deerfeld.

Well-enough. He'd already relocated the Roehs to a walled residence, secured and protected by loyal guards. And his other workers would soon be as safely sheltered. . . .

A light tap and click at the door alarmed Akabe enough to reach for the dagger at his belt.

Caitria padded into his chamber, distractingly lovely, swathed in new embroidered robes, and armed with an attitude of cool defiance. As she dumped a small armload of gear onto his bed, Akabe frowned. "Lady? What's wrong? Does the queen's apartment have no bed?"

"It does." Not looking at him, she picked a square of fabric from her gear, settled into a chair before the hearth, and began to polish her fingernails. "But Naynee snores."

Oh? That was an excuse if he'd ever heard one. So she hated her new bedchamber and was planning to commandeer his? Or was she here to spy on him? Very well. He could, on occasion, speak to her of the Infinite—and perhaps deduce her motives.

"If you are determined to spend your evenings here, then you must at least begin to talk to me."

"As you command, Majesty." She studied her fingernails in the firelight, then resumed polishing. "With the exception of religion."

She meant with the exception of the Infinite. Could he be silent concerning the One who had sustained him through his agonizing, often bleak years as a renegade hunter in the Snake Mountains? Unlikely.

Smiling, plotting tactics, he selected a document and failed to concentrate on reading.

✦ ✦ ✦

A springtime breeze snatched at Kien's cloak in the evening light. Reining in Scythe, he adjusted the flapping garment, looked ahead, and grimaced. ToronSea—that barnacle of a border town—clung to either side of the coastal road, framed by the ocean to the east, and bright green meadows and distant stands of evergreens to the west. The last time he'd been here, Kien suffered a sling-stone strike that nearly got him trampled by his horse.

Not to mention being flung into the ocean by the Infinite as an abject and rebellious failure.

Kien shuddered at the memory and goaded Scythe forward. Things would be different this time. For starters, Scythe would defend him against attack—unlike last year's scatterbrained little horse. And this time, Kien would ride straight through ToronSea. Camping in the woods again this evening was preferable to this place.

But words rang in his thoughts. *You will stop here.*

His Creator. Speaking to him.

Kien swallowed. Fine. "Infinite? May I ask why?"

◆ 10 ◆

The hair on Kien's scalp seemed to crawl the instant he asked why.

The Infinite's voice, amused—amused!—slid into his mind. *Do you believe your work in ToronSea is finished?*

"No." Even as he spoke, Kien's mind was flooded with last year's instructions to him. Trying to contain the sudden rush of words, Kien dropped the reins and clutched his head. *You will warn My faithful in ToronSea of My displeasure because they are beguiled by certain Siphran worshipers of Atea. Tell the one who speaks for them that he must be faithful to Me and seek My will. You must also speak to certain deceived ones who love Atea. Tell them only that I see their failings and seek their hearts. The wise will hear Me.*

Kien's brain reeled with the effort of bringing his senses under control once more. No wonder huge visions sent Ela into a spin. At last, still dizzied, Kien regathered Scythe's reins. The beast had stopped, his big black ears flicked back, clearly listening and waiting for Kien to recover. Unnerving, this destroyer's perception. Kien forced out a queasy command. "Walk."

Scythe grunted, moving forward tentatively as if he'd gauged Kien's headache to its exact level of endurable pain. Kien took deep breaths as he rode, trying to quell his nausea. To distract himself, he looked around.

ToronSea hadn't changed much in a year. A muddied main road, edged by rough walls and small stone houses, many with miniature towers. And the inn, rustic yet welcoming. Until someone yelled an alarm from within the building. "Monster!"

"They're referring to you," Kien told Scythe.

The huge beast snorted and stomped, sending vibrations through all the nearby buildings.

Shrieks echoed up and down the street. Shutters slammed closed. But the inn's door opened and a man peeked out, brown-haired, thin, smooth-shaven, and understandably nervous. Kien recognized him. Giff, leader of the Infinite's faithful in ToronSea. Infinite, thank You!

Kien grinned. "Good afternoon, Giff."

Disgruntled, Giff sidled out of the doorway, clutching its frame. "You again—and riding a monster this time. You don't quit!"

"I'd like to." Kien raised his voice. "Now, Giff, you know what I'm going to say. Politely this time."

Giff backed up against the door, watching Scythe. "So say it."

"The Infinite is displeased because His followers in ToronSea are beguiled by worshipers of Atea. They, and particularly you, must be faithful to our Creator and seek His will."

Looking from Scythe to Kien, Giff's expression changed, not easing, but quieting. "I'll admit last year I was angry with you. But I've considered your warning every time I see . . ."

"Every time you see one of the Ateans?"

Giff nodded. "Yes. I feel the Infinite's Spirit, waiting and watching."

"Not comfortable, I'm sure, if you've been ignoring Him." Kien looked around. "Where are the Ateans?"

"Where *aren't* they?" Giff complained. "Look for their symbols and you'll find them."

Symbols? "Thank you." Kien nudged Scythe onward, scanning ToronSea's stone walls until he saw the serpentine goddess coils, all death-dark, worn by entrenched Ateans. Worn by Akabe's first would-be assassin. "Infinite? Have the Ateans deepened their grasp on ToronSea?"

Yes. But there is more here than you perceive. Do as I have commanded.

"Lead me," Kien prayed. "I am Your servant." He eased Scythe's reins, watching, sickened each time he glimpsed the goddess coils painted on ToronSea's buildings. When Scythe grazed before a fine stone residence with a particularly large goddess coil incised on its open gate, Kien asked, "Here?"

Yes. Speak only to the ones who answer the door.

Bracing himself to confront whoever lived in this residence, Kien dismounted. While Scythe watched, leaning his big, dark head over the wall, Kien entered the courtyard, crossed it, and rapped on the heavy wooden door. Whoever answered would surely slam the door; he looked disreputable in his rumpled, travel-begrimed clothes.

A pretty young woman opened the door. Clad in soft green, her hair hidden by a knotted scarf, she gaped at Kien, her blue eyes widening, particularly when she saw Scythe. "Oh!"

Behind her, a grizzled older man stared suspiciously. "Sir?"

A sensing of the Infinite's compassion and His love for these two struck Kien with an almost-physical impact. He smiled at them. "The Infinite has seen your failings and seeks your hearts."

Paling, the young woman clasped her work-smudged hands to her throat. "What do you mean?"

Kien lowered his voice, realizing he'd frightened the poor girl. "I'm only His servant. That's all I was commanded to say. I'm sure that if you speak to your Creator, He will answer."

Praying he hadn't said too much, Kien bowed. And started to leave.

An imposing, dark-cloaked man appeared from a side gate adjoining the residence, eyeing Kien as if considering him an enemy. "Who are you?"

Mindful of his orders, Kien departed in silence, aware of the three watching him ride away on Scythe. Had he looked foolish?

He certainly felt foolish right now. And why should he have ignored that arrogant man? Kien looked up at the graying sky. "Am I finished here?"

Yes.

"It seemed too simple."

I require simple things. You, My children of dust, always complicate matters.

"Guilty." And forgiven. Kien grinned. "What now?"

Munra.

Ela! Kien rubbed his knuckles into Scythe's massive shoulder. "Find Ela! Go!"

Scythe bolted, galloping through ToronSea, leaving tremors and screams in his wake.

❖ ❖ ❖

Freshly scrubbed and properly clothed, Kien stared at his apartment within the palace and shook his head. Who would believe he'd spent the last few nights sleeping on sodden grass near muddy roads, guarded by an irritable, ever-hungry destroyer?

He settled at his desk and wrote two notes. One to Aeyrievale's steward, Bryce, the other to Akabe, thanking him for offering shelter while Kien sorted out his legal and financial issues.

Finished, Kien sealed the notes and paid a servant to run them to their destinations.

Just as he was considering a brief nap, a thump sounded at Kien's chamber door. He shook out his still-damp hair and flung open the door. Three vaguely familiar, richly attired graybeards stared at him, and their eyebrows lifted in unison, as if by pre-arranged signal. One, boasting a spectacularly curled and waxed beard, inclined his head. "Lord Aeyrievale. I am Lord Faine, calling with regard to a matter of some importance. Lords Trillcliff and Piton wished to accompany me."

He motioned toward his comrades, who bowed to Kien as if the move was choreographed. Alarming. Kien bowed and retreated, holding open the door. "My lords, please step inside." What was Siphran courtly protocol for receiving unexpected nobility? When in doubt, practice good manners. "Are you thirsty? May I request drinks for each of you?"

Lord Trillcliff's thick upswept silver eyebrows rose all the more, looking oddly spiked. He shut the door. "No, Aeyrievale, thank you. We've come to welcome you and to warn you."

The third lord—Piton?—chimed in, "The king will send for you this evening, my lord, no doubt. However his circumstances have changed."

"Changed?" Kien looked from Piton to Faine, then at Trillcliff. "Is he stepping down?"

Faine sniffed and lowered his voice. "Hardly, sir. He's now married. To a girl from an Atean family."

"Atean!" Kien couldn't hide his shock. Akabe, of all people, married into an Atean family? Impossible! "Sirs, how did—"

"Shh!" Piton interposed. "Aeyrievale, lower your voice! Though we argued against the matter, the king married the young lady to legally acquire the temple site. Guard your words around her, my lord. She might prove to be a spy. We're trying to think of ways to . . . ahem . . . mitigate any power she might ultimately wield."

Wonderful. Kien rubbed a hand over his chin. In the palace less than half a day and already swept into court intrigue—surrounding Akabe, no less! "I'm sorry to hear of it."

"Another thing . . ." Faine sniffed. "You're partly to blame for one of the king's recent disappointments."

"I'm to blame?" Kien shook his head. "How? I wasn't here."

Trillcliff leaned toward him, widening his golden eyes, almost ferocious. "Sir, the king's previous disappointment involved the rejection of his marriage proposal to Ela of Parne—after he'd long cherished a most tender and hidden admiration for her. She refused to marry him—first, because she wishes to never marry, and second, because she loves *you*!"

Oh. Well, now Akabe's disappointment made sense.

Sounding offended, Trillcliff muttered, "If the prophet didn't love you, and if *he* had married *her*, we wouldn't be fretting about this Atean queen now."

Almost prim, Piton murmured, "Conversely, had he known you'd offered marriage to the prophet, my lord, and that she loves you, the king would never have suffered such sharp distress. He would have honored your friendship—as he did the instant he realized the situation."

Nodding, Faine added, "If you two hadn't kept the true nature of your relationship a secret, there'd be no potential awkwardness now. Just to warn you."

Kien almost winced, humiliated. But why? He'd done nothing to be ashamed of. "My lords, you make my understanding with the prophet sound scandalous. It is not!"

"Nevertheless," Trillcliff sighed, "be prepared for the king's possible displeasure. Talk to him of the temple to . . . distract him."

"I'm sorry. And I pray that the king's marital difficulties are soon resolved."

Leaning closer, Faine said, "Help us to resolve them! Legally, if you can think of a way."

Piton lifted a cautioning hand. "Do not mistake us, my lord. We are genuinely concerned for the king. He is a remarkable man. Potentially one of Siphra's greatest kings—the rebuilder of our temple and the restorer of our country's reputation! But this marriage could *ruin* his legacy."

The noblemen nodded together, and Kien nodded with them. Wait. He hesitated. Did he want to be in agreement with this ambush of lords?

However, these three noblemen truly respected the king and liked him. And, unless Kien could be somehow reinstated as a citizen of the Tracelands, these lords were now part of his life. Best to accept the situation. He smiled at the three, meaning it. "Thank you for warning me. Your regard for duty is invaluable to the king and to Siphra." As they straightened, subtly, yet visibly pleased, Kien continued. "Rest assured, my lords, I am equally concerned, and I will do everything possible to help protect the king from any Atean threats."

Lord Trillcliff beamed. "We'd hoped to depend upon you." His golden eyes lit with sudden inspiration. "Do you know anything of the king's lineage, my lord?"

"No, sir. I suspect he's of some highborn family. Why?"

Piton sighed as if defeated. "Because of your friendship, we hoped he'd mentioned some hint of his past to you. He's said almost nothing to us, and it's important that we know."

Lord Faine shrugged and turned to the door. "Until this evening, Aeyrievale."

"Thank you, sirs." Kien closed the door, pondered his situation, then grinned. Grabbing his cloak, he strode from his rooms, asking directions at every turn to navigate this maze of a palace. At last he reached the royal stables and his gluttonous destroyer, who was tended by a handful of nervous stable hands.

Clearly intimidated by Scythe's monstrous form and by the huge crescents he'd bitten into the rim of his water barrel, the stable hands backed away. Scythe grumbled threats at his hapless handlers while crushing a chunk of wood between those gleaming destroyer-teeth. The stable hands fled. Kien stifled a laugh. "Hush, you monster! And enough wood. You'll give yourself indigestion."

Scythe curled his equine lips slightly, but continued chewing as if Kien didn't exist.

Fine. How might a master best gain his irritable monster's attention? With one word. "Ela."

The black ears perked, and the chewing halted. Kien grinned. "Let's shine you up a bit, then we'll depart. You can track her down for me—at a quiet walk."

Poor unsuspecting prophet. A good thing she'd never been able to predict what Kien Lantec might do next, because he wanted to catch her completely off guard.

She must answer for the blame he'd just accepted.

✦ II ✦

Finished tidying her study area at the temple site, Ela kneeled in the evening light with Tamri Het and Matron Prill beneath the canopy to wait for Father. "It's been a long day. But at least there's been no trouble. And, look. . . ." She dug into her leather coin purse and pulled out her newest treasure. "Barth gave me his latest baby tooth!"

Tamri laughed. "That is an honor, Ela-girl. He's in love with you, I'm sure."

"He's a flirt, but a wonderful student." Ela smiled at the small white tooth and tucked it safe inside her purse again. Barth's class was her favorite by far.

Matron Prill's thin face puckered with worry. "Are you truly keeping his tooth?"

"Of course, Prill. I must. Knowing Barth, he's going to start every class for the next month by asking me if I still have his tooth."

"True," Prill admitted. "But you'd think his parents would want it."

"We'll offer it to him next time we meet, just to be sure. I—" A shadow passed through the sun's evening rays, dimming everything beneath the canopied study area. Ela glanced toward the light's obstruction, then looked again. A massive black beast was crossing the temple site, approaching her. A destroyer? Recognizing the animal, Ela's spirit leaped. *Her* destroyer. "Pet!"

And Kien! Oh, Kien . . . Even within the shadows, she saw his dazzling grin—gorgeous man. Safe. And here, finally! "Infinite, thank You!" She snatched up the branch and rushed to greet her favorite monster-horse and his master.

Behind her, Tamri called in a warning tone, "Ela-girl, don't you dare run away!"

"I won't!" But what a wonderful thought. If she were anyone else . . .

Pet—she *wouldn't* call him Scythe—greeted her with a tender nose-nudge and a gusty wood-scented sigh. Careful to avoid smacking Pet with the branch, she tiptoed and hugged as much of his neck as possible. "Dear monster! I've missed you!"

Jumping off the last rung of the destroyer's war collar, Kien protested. "What about me?"

Ela looked up at Kien and caught her breath. She must *not* hug him, and certainly no kissing. That would be bad prophet behavior. But how dare he look at her in such a way—admiring her openly, his gray eyes gleaming so avidly that she blushed. "Yes, I've missed you too. How long will you be visiting in Munra?"

The joy faded from his eyes. "You didn't receive my letter?"

"No. Only a tiny cipher yesterday, noting that you'd arrive soon. Were you acquitted?"

Seeming pained, he spoke so quietly that she barely heard, "I was exiled."

"From the Tracelands? For how long?"

"Life."

He'd been permanently exiled from his home? "Kien, *why*?"

"When my letter arrives, as it should have several days ago, you can read the whole miserable account." His voice flattened to bleakness. "Never mind. I'm here to visit you." Glancing around the site, Kien's beautiful, pale eyes brightened. "This is where the Infinite's temple will stand?"

"Yes, and I'm so grateful!" Ela's heart lifted, her soul soaring with the thought. "I've mourned over Parne's temple. I never knew how much I loved the Infinite's Holy House . . . how much all the survivors loved the temple until we watched our own fall—and rightfully so." Smiling, watching Kien survey the site, she added, "Parne's refugees have been rejoicing ever since the king issued his decree that the temple must be rebuilt. Though the Ateans are threatening the work. Father—"

"Ateans!" His elation fading, Kien turned, his cloak swirling with the movement. "Of course they'd try to destroy anything that the Infinite's faithful cherish." He sighed. "Let's discuss a slightly different matter."

"All right." She'd tell him of Father's near-death later. Determined to be patient, she clicked the end of the branch on the pavings beneath her sandaled feet. "What are we discussing?" Because if he offered marriage a third time she'd say no. She would. And hopefully she'd be convincing to Kien and herself.

Still somber, he lifted a dark eyebrow, looked around at others working on the site, then whispered, "Ela, before I'd even unpacked my gear this afternoon, three of the king's advisors called on me. Accusing me of hiding my relationship with you, thereby causing the king severe emotional distress. *And*—not to bring up such a hateful subject again—he's married an Atean."

"I've heard the queen's an Atean, and I hope to speak with her. But . . ." Ela felt herself blush, remembering the king's proposal. "Are his advisors blaming me because I refused to marry Akabe?"

"Me. They're blaming me, Ela." He grimaced, captivating her with that wry twist of his lips. "But I'm worried about your reputation."

"Wait." Ela lifted a hand. This conversation had just shifted to something worse than simple blame. "*My* reputation?"

"Yes." Kien leaned closer and murmured, "Once this story becomes known, if the queen's a rabid Atean like her predecessor, you might be condemned for rejecting the king. Do you think Siphra will ever forgive you?"

If Akabe's new wife was truly Atean like the former Queen Raenna . . . Ela shivered. In the end, after Siphra's revolution, Queen Raenna had succumbed to madness. Possessed by ghastly soul-shadowing deceivers—servants of the immortal

Adversary—she'd dashed herself to death on the rocks below the royal terrace. Within that same evening, King Segere hanged himself in his beloved Raenna's apartments. *Would* the Siphrans forgive her if Ela had inadvertently brought another queen like Raenna into power? "I suppose not."

Kien clasped Ela's hand, startling her with the warmth of his touch. "Once malicious gossip starts, it's nearly impossible to stop. Believe me. We must work together to mitigate this Atean situation. Meanwhile," Kien's tone softened, "the most sensible thing you can do to stave off gossip—and the fairest compensation for my sacrifice in accepting the blame—is to marry me."

Oh? She stared at him. Kien smiled. And his gray eyes lit with mischief. Was he enjoying her embarrassment? He was. Actor! Schemer! "You're hoaxing me!"

"Not at all." He grinned. "It's the truth. Though you're not helping matters by yelling—"

"I'll yell if I want to! You're bullying me!" She swung the branch at him.

Kien snatched it from her hand. "I'm not bullying you! I . . . Hey . . ."

Ela followed his gaze and stared at the branch. In *his* hand. He'd never managed to touch the miraculous vinewood before, much less take it from her. Infinite! She lunged for her treasured insignia. "Give that back!"

"Ha!" Kien whipped the branch out of her reach and wrapped his free arm around Ela's waist, restraining her. "I win!"

Pet trotted around them in a nervous circle now, obviously agitated by their squabble, his big hooves drumming the ground. Beyond him, Tamri, Prill, and a growing crowd all stared.

Really, despite Kien's fine words about fearing for her reputation, he certainly wasn't helping matters. "Kien!" Ela yanked at his long mantle, then his sleeve. "Give. Me. My. Branch!"

"No!" He whooped and swung her in a half-circle, definitely celebrating. "This means something, doesn't it? I have the Infinite's approval to marry you!"

"You don't know that!"

"And you do?" he taunted, setting her down, but still holding her tight. "*Do* you? Did you ask the Infinite about our marriage, Ela? *Ever?*"

Well, no, because she'd presumed . . . Horrified, Ela shut her eyes. Infinite? Is it true? Must I marry him?

Unperturbed silence answered her question. A waiting calm that told her nothing. Infinite—not helpful! However, couldn't this silence mean that the Infinite was impartial about the situation? Then the decision was actually hers. Reassured, and—if she must admit it—smug, Ela poked Kien's ribs. "Let me go. I don't have to marry you if I don't want to!"

Dan Roeh's deep, stern voice interrupted, "I disagree."

Father! Ela gasped and shoved at Kien. He removed his arm from her waist, but held her hand. To protect her? Or to protect himself?

Pet loomed behind them now, calmer despite Dan's threatening stance.

Dan glared. "I've had enough! Ela, I'm tired of chasing off your suitors. You'll marry this man, or I'll give you to the next one who asks—no matter who he is."

"Father!"

Ignoring her, Father nodded at Kien. "Lantec. Send word to your parents, then let me know when they'll arrive in Munra. We'll celebrate your wedding the following day."

"Yes, sir," Kien murmured, looking suitably meek.

"Meanwhile . . ." Father grabbed Ela's wrist and pulled her away from Kien. "No more public scenes. If you want to visit my daughter, you'll have to request my permission."

"Yes, sir."

"And"—Dan scowled at Pet—"you keep this destroyer off the temple grounds until the building is completed. Those vibrations he throws off are shaking the foundations!"

"Sorry, sir." However, Kien looked anything but sorry. He offered the branch to Ela with a courteous nod—so polite that he might have been returning a dropped scarf. But his eyes glittered, and he bit his lip.

Obviously laughing inside like a wild man.

"Huh!" Ela snatched the branch and turned away, huffy as Pet in a foul mood.

✦ ✦ ✦

Wearing his finest dark blue clothes, which were creased from the journey, Kien strode into Siphra's throne room. No surprise that he'd been ordered here. Before so much as speaking to the king, Kien must do the one thing he'd never in his Tracelander's life expected he'd do.

He marched up the length of the throne room, aware of Siphra's courtiers all staring, eager to see him accomplish this first ceremony as a Siphran. Fine. Let them stare. Throughout his childhood, he'd been thoroughly trained by every etiquette master that Rade and Ara Lantec could gather. And his training had been cruelly polished in the royal courts of Istgard facing the despotic King Tek An. He, Kien Lantec, could surely survive Siphra's royal court.

Kien halted before Akabe, who watched from his throne on the dais, somber as one about to pronounce a death sentence. And, in a way, this was a death.

Resolute, Kien unbuckled his Azurnite sword and placed it at the king's feet. Then he knelt and offered Akabe his bare hands. Looking the king straight in the eyes, he said, "Majesty, I pledge before all and the Infinite that I will faithfully serve you, Akabe of Siphra, as my king. I will never cause you or your heirs harm and will defend you completely, in good faith and without deceit before all living."

Akabe leaned forward and gripped Kien's hands. His voice formal and carrying throughout the throne room, the king said, "I accept your pledge and will honor your place as you ever deserve." Now Akabe grinned. "Stand, Lord Aeyrievale!" Beneath his breath, he muttered, "Welcome, my friend!"

Unable to speak, Kien nodded and stood.

His voice still low, Akabe said, "My lord, this is my wife and queen, the Lady Caitria."

A solemn young woman, who'd been sitting on a low cushioned bench near the throne, stood and held out an elegant hand to Kien. With long-lashed eyes, light brown hair, and a cautious welcoming smile, this lovely queen was surely too young, too vulnerable, to be an entrenched Atean. At most, Caitria was Ela's age. Nothing like the hard-eyed, conniving schemer Kien had feared.

Mindful of his manners, Kien kissed the young queen's hand and smiled. Inwardly, he frowned, puzzled by her demeanor. She stepped nearer to Akabe, watching Kien as if expecting him to bite her. Interesting. Though he hadn't said a word to the Lady Caitria, she didn't trust him. Should he trust her? Infinite?

✦ ✦ ✦

Finished with Kien's letter, Ela sat on her sleeping pallet in her parents' new fortress-like home and stared through glistening tears at his signature on the parchment. No wonder he'd been unable to speak of his trial. This, written in sprawling script, was the letter of a man in utter despair, grieving over the loss of his home and family.

Ela, legally, I have no parents. I am no one!

So the hurt she'd glimpsed this afternoon wasn't feigned. Kien still mourned.

If she'd read this letter earlier, before seeing him again, she would have hugged and comforted him the instant they met—never mind the gossiping onlookers. But perhaps it was best for all concerned that the letter arrived today.

Come to think of it, however, the result would have been the same: She must marry Kien.

A complication unsuited for her short-lived future as a prophet.

And yet, hadn't she longed to marry him for more than a year?

Ela folded Kien's letter, tucked it away like treasure inside her painted storage chest, then kneeled beside her bed and hid her face in her folded arms, praying fiercely. Infinite? I love You! Remember Your servant, and remind me always of You! Thank You. But won't I become too distracted by my marriage? Will I continue to serve You as I should?

Praying, she waited for a time, then curled up beneath the coverlets on her thick pallet and fell asleep.

Terror woke her. She was sitting up, and dawn's light sent luminous slivers through her shuttered windows. "Infinite?"

Are you My servant?

"Yes."

Listen!

Images slid into Ela's thoughts, sending shivers of fear over her skin. Tormented screams of dying men shrieked from within her mind. Ashes dimmed her sight. "Wait! Please!" She clutched her head and huddled on the tiled floor, rocked by agony. "Infinite!"

The vision opened, drawing her inside. Gasping, Ela looked around, her heart hammering with her soul's terror. Stone walls, a window, and a girl Ela identified as the queen—a thin, beautiful young lady, who screamed, her huge eyes pleading for safety that Ela couldn't provide.

And as Ela wept, soldiers died. Horribly.

Kien! Where was Kien? Her thoughts warned him away. Begged him to survive.

The image widened, becoming many. Biting down screams, Ela curled into a ball and fought the torment. Enemies whispered their hatred. Their plans. Decisions had been made in the Tracelands. Were being made in Siphra, and in the nearby country of a vengeful god-king.

All merged and flowed toward her. Toward Siphra's king. Toward the Infinite's Holy House, in a tidal wave of malice. Darkness threatened consciousness. "Infinite . . . help . . ."

Released from the stream of images and emotions, Ela muffled sobs, pressing her face against the cooling tiles as she fought to recover her senses. Clearly, this marriage to Kien—the love she'd resisted so fiercely—would be her only brief mortal sanctuary amid the coming chaos.

"Father?" Ela scrambled to her feet, praying as she ran.

For Father. For Kien. For Akabe and the temple.

And for the young queen she could not protect.

✦ 12 ✦

The instant the servant departed, Akabe set aside his half-eaten morning meal, opened a gilded silver box, and removed Caitria's official bridal armband—exquisitely cast in gold with two aeryons in flight supporting a crown. Akabe studied the piece for flaws. None. If the goldsmith held any resentment against his king or queen, or the Infinite's Holy House, he hadn't allowed them to show in his work. Satisfied, Akabe carried the armband into his bedchamber.

Stepping inside, he smiled, admiring Caitria, who'd—as usual—remained in bed, her slight form lit by a glowing cluster of gilt bronze lamps. How she loathed their early mornings. "Lady."

Caitria sat up, suddenly alert. "Majesty?"

Akabe lifted the armband. "Siphra's gift to its queen."

She allowed Akabe to fasten the gold around her arm without protest. But by her pitiable expression, the gold ought to have been an iron shackle on her left ankle instead, denoting imprisonment. Caitria fingered the band and sighed. "Thank you. It's heavy."

"Not unbearably so, I hope," Akabe murmured. "However, if it becomes intolerable, tell me. We don't agree on everything, but we've each been brought here as captives to our situations and, therefore, I'll understand. Unless . . ." He looked around at the dimly lit, windowless, trinket-cluttered royal chamber. Safe, yet suffocating. "Unless you actually like this place."

A smile lit her drowsy features. "No, sir. I hate this place! I hate feeling so trapped, so watched! I hate . . ."

Akabe could almost hear the words she'd just stifled.

I hate the circumstances that brought me here!

And he was the instigator of her misery, yet he couldn't free her. Guilt descended upon him like a sodden cloak. As he bent and kissed her hair, frantic tapping sounded at the antechamber door. Faine's muffled voice beckoned, "Majesty—a message from the prophet! She waits in the council chamber!"

The prophet! With a message? Heart thudding, Akabe spun on his booted heel and charged from his bedchamber, dread chasing his steps.

⁜ ⁜ ⁜

In his temporary rooms within the palace, Kien finished his morning meal and studied the documents just offered by his steward, who was already attending to legalities on the opposite side of the decorative table. "What are these, Bryce?"

Thin, brown, and businesslike, Bryce continued to prepare blue wax and cords for sealing the documents. "My lord, the first is your declaration of intent to reopen Aeyrievale's sapphire mines, which we closed during the rebellion, and this is your formal request for the release of Aeyrievale's funds."

"Hmm." He supposed he needed funds. As for sapphire mines—well, if Aeyrievale possessed them and wanted to use them, it meant jobs. Kien scanned the documents, found them in order, and accepted the reed pen and ink, politely offered by Bryce. Still disliking the look of his name, he signed twice. *Kien Lantec of Aeyrievale.*

Would he always cringe inside whenever he wrote *Aeyrievale*?

Bryce slid the parchments away from Kien and applied Aeyrievale's official seal within a puddle of bright blue wax. "That was the last of the legal concerns for this morning, my lord.

I'm told the king's revenue clerks will release the funds to your control today. You can decide how best to use the money later."

With a sigh, as if relieved of a long-carried burden, Bryce placed the sealed parchment inside a box, then offered a sketch on a small square of parchment. "For your signature of approval. The future Lady Aeyrievale's gold—her wedding band."

Ela's wedding band! Kien studied the sketch. It appeared to be a cuff, fashioned to resemble a stylish, curling plume-like feather. "Why a feather?"

"Aeryons, my lord. In Siphra, they live only in Aeyrievale, and they are our unofficial symbol. All the former ladies of Aeyrievale, in succession, wore an armband similar to this one. The original was confiscated by Queen Raenna—may she rot forever—after the last Lady Aeyrievale's murder, more than ten years ago."

Tracing the sketched outline, Kien asked, "Were there no heirs?"

"No, sir. Lady Aeyrievale's only child died of a fever at age five. But even if the girl had survived a few months more, she would have died with her parents at the queen's command."

May Raenna rot forever, Kien added silently. "I wish your previous lord and his family had survived." He signed approval to the sketch, then sat back. "What now?"

"We wait, sir. I've sent out a few invitations to various people who might be interested in joining your household. And you'll make additional wedding plans. Unless you'd rather follow Aeyrievale's ancient custom."

"Which is . . . ?"

"Steal the future Lady Aeyrievale from her family."

Kien laughed and shook his head. "No! You're a wild lot in Aeyrievale."

"We're trying to improve, my lord, but this custom continues. The former Lady Aeyrievale paid bribes to discourage weapons—your wife might consider resuming the practice. It was becoming rather popular."

"You'll have to speak with Ela about the bribes. She—" A

light tapping sounded at the door. Bryce hurried to answer it, admitting a young, crimson-clad page with rumpled hair, who looked as if he'd just been dragged from sleep.

The little boy bowed, gave Kien a bleary, gap-toothed smile and lisped, "My lord, the king requests your presence in the council chamber."

Careful not to laugh, Kien asked, "How did you lose your front teeth? In a fight?"

The page's eyes widened, and the gapped smile reappeared. "No, sir. But I wish so."

"Wild man! You must be from Aeyrievale." Kien stood, donned his sword and cloak, then checked his attire. All in order, he nodded to the little page, who'd perked up considerably. "Lead on, young sir." Over his shoulder Kien called, "Bryce, enjoy your day! I'm sure I'll return before this evening."

Just as they reached the end of the corridor, a sturdy ruffian with bashed features rounded the turn, wielding his sword. Instinctively, Kien whipped his glistening blue Azurnite blade from its scabbard and edged the little boy aside.

Recognizing his would-be assailant—Akabe's fightmaster—Kien tightened his grip on his sword. "Lorteus!"

The royal fightmaster gloated and tapped Kien's decorated Azurnite blade with his own plain sword. His voice low and gritty as ever, he laughed. "Good reaction! And what a pretty toy. Come, Lord Aeyrievale! You are summoned, and I intend to accompany you."

"Why?"

"Danger, m'lord. I'm like your destroyer, smelling trouble before it happens. The beast's waiting in the courtyard, you know, and your little prophet now stands in the council chamber. If there's to be a battle, I'm in!"

"Ela!" With Scythe waiting? What was wrong? Kien scooped up the astonished page boy, holding him in his left arm, still clenching the Azurnite sword in his right fist. Plagues, but this wing of the palace was a labyrinth! "Young sir, which way to the council chamber from here?"

Clearly speechless, the child pointed and Kien ran, with Lorteus at his heels.

✦ ✦ ✦

Not bothering to sit in his chair at the head of the table, Akabe faced Ela, who stood before him like a delicate guard. In her hands the slender prophet's branch glimmered, its mysterious light reflecting in her eyes—a silvery gleam, so alive that Akabe shivered inwardly. "Prophet, what was your vision?"

"The temple site will be—"

Clattering echoed at the chamber's tall carved door. A servant dashed inside as if chased, and Lord Aeyrievale entered the chamber, sword readied, with Barth under his arm. As the servant departed, hastily closing the door, Kien offered the barest of bows and set the little boy on his feet, then sheathed the Azurnite sword. "Majesty. Prophet, what's wrong?"

"The temple site is about to be attacked." Ela stepped toward Kien, but looked up at Akabe, tensed, her words abrupt. "Majesty, I've warned my father, but there isn't time to warn away all the workers and send them to safety as they arrive—you must bring more soldiers to the site at once. Your enemies plan to use arrows and bolt throwers to besiege the temple."

Akabe motioned to Trillcliff and Piton. "Call out my garrisons and order men stationed at every street corner. Send for my horses, and have my guards bring weaponry and battle gear, then command that the palace gates be locked and guarded the instant we leave—*and* I want my council alert against trouble!" Trillcliff and Piton hurried from the chamber, their mantles billowing with their haste. Akabe studied Ela's somber face. "What are your plans, Prophet?"

She hesitated and shook her head, clearly baffled. "The Infinite commands me to stay away. I'll wait with my mother. Majesty, this conflict is yours."

Kien stared at her. "I don't know whether to be relieved or appalled. Why did the Infinite command you to stay away?"

"I asked. He waits . . . silent. I'm praying for you, Majesty, and"—Ela touched Kien's arm in a clear, silent plea for his safety—"I'm praying for the men who accompany you."

Akabe paused. Why did her words and manner disturb his spirit so? But he had no time to fret over inert details now. As she'd said, this conflict was his. All his warrior instincts keen for a fight, he nodded to Kien. "Let's go."

Barth piped up now, his lisp young and eager. "Me too, Majesty?"

A pity to disappoint such an enthusiastic future soldier. Kien opened the door—revealing Fightmaster Lorteus pacing outside. Akabe nudged his page through. "No, Barth. You'll remain here. Go find Master Croleut for lessons."

His page frowned and kicked at the floor. "Aw!"

✦ ✦ ✦

Clad in armor, Akabe guided his warhorse along Munra's main thoroughfare as heralds rode ahead, trump-calls blaring around them. His guards bellowed, "All citizens to the safety of your homes! By official orders, clear the streets!"

As Akabe had commanded, archers now manned the rooftops of the main thoroughfare's public buildings, while soldiers from the royal garrison waited at each street corner. Silent and grim, the men's crimson military cloaks, polished plate armor, and gleaming weapons warned enemies that Siphra's Holy House would be protected.

Infinite, I beg you, let this be enough. Protect us this morning. . . .

They rode toward the temple, horses huffing, armor and swords clattering. Kien led the way on his giant black monster-horse, which was haphazardly buckled into a cobbling of chain mail created for smaller horses. Akabe grinned at the sight. If nothing else inspired his people to hide from the coming fray, the destroyer's resonant huffs and his giant hooves thundering against the pavings convinced them. All along the main street, doors and shutters were slamming shut, muffling panicked shrieks within the buildings.

"Now," Akabe called to his men as they crested the final approach to the temple, "with our people hidden—we smash this siege before it takes hold! Look around!"

Even as he spoke, something slashed past Akabe's cheek, embedding itself in a nearby wall. An iron bolt, undoubtedly barbed and meant for him. Kien's giant destroyer, Scythe, rumbled a low, merciless threat and turned, breaking file to charge a slender tower to Akabe's right—one of several overlooking the future temple. Obviously attuned to his monster-steed, Kien raised his shield to cover himself. Akabe bellowed, "Shields!"

Akabe lifted his gaze to the tower's crest. There, a graceful white cupola sheltered a bolt-thrower and three archers, all taking aim at Akabe and his men. "Break ranks—*move!*"

He turned his horse aside, and his men scattered just as arrows and another bolt flew past, gouging the paving stones. "Take that tower!"

Scythe reared and slammed his hooves against the tower's stone walls, then against the iron-bound door, which broke from its hinges. Akabe froze. Was Kien planning to invade that tower alone? "Aeyrievale—no! Check the other towers!" To his foot-soldiers, Akabe called, "Surround and capture everyone inside! Let no one escape!"

Distant screams from workmen now arose from the temple site and smoke billowed into the morning air, signaling an attack on the foundations. Followed by his guards and Fight-master Lorteus, Akabe urged his warhorse toward the screams. As they crossed the paved open court, an onslaught of flaming arrows sliced downward from another tower to his left, igniting oiled tarps and supplies—undoubtedly terrorizing the workmen trapped within the foundations below. Had some of the men been killed?

Akabe's own archers were now answering their enemies, and Akabe glimpsed an arrow-pierced body slumping onto an embrasure in the nearest tower. He called to Lorteus. "Secure that tower! Take some men with you!"

Akabe waved half his guard to follow Lorteus. The fightmaster departed, roaring his eagerness to raid the tower. "You firebrands are coming *down* after those arrows!"

Shielded by Lorteus's attack and his archers' reprisals upon the towers, Akabe motioned for his remaining guards to follow him. His pulse quickening with their pace, he urged his horse around the burning cedar logs, using the flames and waves of heat as his screen to approach the temple's foundations. Infinite, let the workmen be alive!

There, sheltered in the shadows of the sacred ancient stonework, Dan Roeh waited with his men, safe. All praying aloud as they watched for their enemies. Relieved, Akabe withdrew, circled the burning mounds of supplies, and rode to help Kien and Lorteus secure the towers.

✦ ✦ ✦

Within the confines of Akabe's antechamber, Faine mourned, "Majesty, *why* must these Ateans kill themselves whenever they fail? Without the chance to interrogate them, we have no way to counteract their plots. Moreover, their deaths only feed their comrades' fury."

"Provoking them to conspire anew," Akabe agreed. The deaths made him look like a bloodthirsty tyrant—the same as his predecessors. Was he? He couldn't help but question his actions as he recalled seeing those Ateans' bodies after they'd been removed from the tower. How might he neutralize their future schemes and prevent more deaths? "Faine, order *all* the workmen and the priests removed to protected residences."

"All? And . . . the priests, Majesty?"

"Yes. They'll be targeted, as in the previous regime. Best to protect them now."

Akabe's bedchamber door opened and a whispering of trailing fabrics alerted him to turn. Elegant and pale in gold-embroidered

red, Caitria hesitated, clearly wary of Faine. Undoubtedly sensing and reciprocating his queen's mistrust, Faine bowed. "Majesty, as soon as you've rested, we will attend you in the council chamber."

The instant he departed, Caitria approached, studying Akabe as if perplexed. "Forgive me, sir, but you left with no explanation." Her frown deepened as she stared. "How did you receive that grazing on your cheek?"

Grazing? Akabe touched his face. A sting reminded him. "Oh. A bolt flew too close."

"A bolt?" Confusion played over Caitria's fine features.

Had she led such a sheltered life that she'd never seen a bolt? To explain, he removed a dagger from his belt. "A bolt, lady. An iron projectile about as large as this blade, flung by an apparatus manned by my enemies. It missed."

"Almost *not*, by the mark on your face." She dropped into a gilded chair, pressing her hands to her own face. "You were in a battle this morning?"

"A skirmish. Some . . . rebels . . . attacked the temple site and threatened the workers. We defeated them and all's well—the Infinite protected us."

"No, all's not well!" Caitria shook her head. "Is this temple worth dying for—losing your kingdom for? Why should your Infinite demand such sacrifices? Such risk? I don't see that He's done much for either of us, sir, except to cause misery!"

Akabe controlled his tone, deliberately gentle. Calming, he hoped. "I'm alive, lady. My kingdom stands, and my people are safe."

"But you're not safe!"

"I am this instant." Unless his angry wife decided to attack. "And, by the way, yes. Some things are worth dying for, lady, because we love them. I love my Creator *and* His temple!" Though He seemed to not notice Akabe of Siphra now.

As Akabe processed the pain of that thought, Caitria stood,

inclined her head, then swept from the antechamber in a flaring tempest of crimson and gold.

He didn't follow. An armed skirmish seemed safer.

✦ ✦ ✦

Inside her husband's bedchamber, Caitria sagged against the wall, trembling, trying to recover enough strength to return to her apartments. The dim chamber seemed even darker now, and she'd turned giddy. Stars and sunsets, was she about to faint?

She sat heavily beside the door, dazed, holding her head. Akabe had faced another attack. Likely from more Ateans. Would the next attack succeed? Had her family been involved? Now, for the first time in ages, she appealed to the goddess in silent prayer.

Atea . . . save me . . . save us!

But since when had the goddess considered her worth anything—least of all worth loving? Akabe's voice rang again in her thoughts, impassioned, his face alight with fervor.

Some things are worth dying for, lady, because we love them. I love my Creator, and His temple!

He hadn't mentioned his wife.

Couldn't he care for her despite their differences?

For a long time, she sat huddled against the door, shivering. Trying not to weep.

✦ ✦ ✦

Nudged toward the stone-framed gate by the fretful Scythe, Kien nodded to the guards, crossed a fine stonework courtyard, and rapped on the Roehs' door. Ela answered instantly, studying his face. No doubt checking for wounds. Evidently satisfied, she flung her arms around him. "I prayed for you—for everyone! Is my father safe? And the king?"

"The Infinite honored your prayers, dear prophet. Not counting a few bruises, scrapes and sprains, plus a mark on the king's face from a passing bolt, everyone's well. And I spoke to your father." Kien nodded to Kalme Roeh, who approached, listening. "He's safe."

Kalme sighed, tension fading from her lovely face. "Thank you!"

"You're welcome." Kien kissed Ela's forehead, then stared into her big, dark, beautiful eyes. "Now, prophet of Parne, what are you not telling me?"

Sucking in a pained breath as if the vision still lingered, she whispered, "The Infinite's enemies want Him to fail! After our wedding . . . others will be waiting, conspiring to kill the king . . . and us."

Kien tightened his arms around her slender, shivering shoulders, praying even as he whispered, "Whatever happens, we know the Infinite will never fail!"

Infinite? Spare Ela, I beg You! Even if I must die, save her. . . .

✦ 13 ✦

Ela kissed her baby brother until he laughed and grabbed small fistfuls of her hair. "Don't you grow up too much while I'm gone. Oh, Jess," she crooned, "I'll miss you!"

From behind her, Kalme Roeh said, "Perhaps by this time next year, you'll have a baby of your own."

A baby. Ela's breath seemed to halt in her lungs. Kien's baby . . . Despite her longing, she argued, "Mother, how could I endure having a baby, knowing I might not live to—"

"Stop," Kalme ordered. "You're tormenting yourself, and it's useless." She gave Ela a stern nudge. "Rejoice in the blessings the Infinite gives you!"

"Mother, you should have been the prophet."

"I'm telling you what I've learned since *you* became His prophet." Kalme lifted Jess from Ela's arms, pausing just long enough to unwind Ela's curls from the baby's pudgy hand. "When you first left Parne, I nearly killed myself with worry. But, being pregnant with Jess, I had to stop fretting over things I couldn't control. Instead, I treasure my current circumstances."

"Well, at least one of us is learning something."

Laughter and a clatter at the door announced visitors. Tamri Het and Matron Prill let themselves in. Seeing Ela, Tamri scolded, "Prophet-girl, why are you not dressed? Your husband and guests will arrive soon!"

Determined to torment her dear chaperones to the end, Ela affected a mock frown. "He's not my husband yet."

Prill brushed past them both, murmuring to Tamri, "I'll set out her clothes. We'd best drag her inside to prepare. Kalme Roeh, how did you—the sweetest of souls—end up with such a dissident daughter?"

"It's Dan's fault." Mother shifted Jess in her arms, then pointed Ela toward her room. "Follow Prill."

Hiding a smile, Ela marched after the matron. Hmm. Prill's tunic was obviously new—a festive violet-red, embroidered with tiny flowers. Her boots, however, clunked against the Roehs' tiled floor. Heavy boots. As if Prill expected to hike or ride. "Matron, do you think I'll have you digging trenches or fleeing for your life on my wedding day?"

"I've found it's best to be prepared for anything if I'm around you." Prill stepped aside to let Ela into her room. "But, no, I don't expect to dig trenches. Bryce has enlisted me to help you in Aeyrievale."

"You're remaining with me? Wonderful! But . . ." Ela hesitated. *Bryce* had invited Prill? She turned and frowned at the matron. "You're calling Kien's steward by his first name? When did you two become friends?"

Prill met her gaze, seeming perfectly serene. "Over the past month. He's consulted me often while making arrangements for your wedding. He noticed us at the temple site, then remembered me from Parne as your chaperone, and didn't want to disturb you or your mother."

"Oh?" Ela donned a pretend look of disapproval. "Sounds more like a flirtation to me."

Prill blushed. Prettily. Bright as the embroidered flowers on her gown. Bryce and Prill? Oh my. Kien would love this. Ela dropped all pretenses as Tamri and Mother entered her room. "You just wait! When I'm married, I'm chaperoning *you*!"

"Really, Ela—"

"What's happened?" Tamri asked, chaperone-stern, alert as always to mischief.

"Nothing!" Prill snapped. She hurriedly dug into Ela's clothing chest, then coerced Ela into the delicate gold-embroidered layered white tunic. Proper and bossy as ever, the matron grabbed several tiny pearl-edged combs and nodded toward Ela's only chair. "Sit."

They'd just finished combing out Ela's hair when a musical, feminine voice called from the front door, "Ela dear?"

"Kien's mother!" Ela started from her seat.

Prill pushed Ela down again, and Tamri leaned out of the room, clearly delighted. "Ara! She's in here. We're trying to keep her settled long enough to hand her off to your son."

"Oh, well let me help you!" Ara swept into the room, so ladylike and flawless in a silvery tunic and gauzy shawls that Ela felt like a frump. The instant she saw Ela, Ara's bright gray eyes lit with joy. "Darling, you're not even put together yet and you look charming! And what perfect timing—Beka insisted I bring this to you." She opened a wooden box and offered Ela an elaborate, fragile half-circlet of silver and gold leaves, centered with a dangling dark blue gem. "Do you like it? Will you wear it?"

Speechless, Ela nodded at the dazzling headpiece. Mother snatched the pearl combs from Prill and said, "Yes, it's wonderful!"

"Oh, good," Ara sighed. "We must humor Beka during her last few months of waiting. Darling, she's a delightful tyrant, isn't she? Anyway, I wore this tiara on my wedding day, and Beka wore it when she married Jon, and *oh* is she furious because she can't travel!" Chattering, Ara extricated the comb from Prill's hand and began to arrange Ela's hair. "The gemstone centers over your forehead, with your hair half-up, half-down—Ela, I'm so glad you have such lovely curls! Where are those pearl combs? And pins! Heaps of pins!"

From that point on, Ara did all the talking and no one minded, Ela was sure. She could listen to Kien's mother all day. Ara described her enchanting visit with Kien, the king, and the queen—who was so shy she said not five words, poor dear—and her own exciting journey with General Rol and his sweet daughter, Nia.

Not to mention Rol's destroyer, who was in the same interesting condition as Beka, but even more irritable.

At last Ara sighed and shook her head. "Are you certain you'll be able to handle that destroyer when Rol returns her to you, Ela-dear? She's a true monster, make no mistake!"

"What?" Flame? Scythe's beloved? Ela turned her head, causing Ara to lift her hands. "General Rol is returning Flame to me? But he can't!"

"Darling, he must. He's leaving the military and offering himself for service in the Grand Assembly. He's sure to be elected, *if* he gets rid of that destroyer. Beka's at home arranging his campaign as we speak. I'm sorry . . ." Ara busied herself, pinning Ela's hair again. "You didn't know, did you?"

"No. The Tracelands has lost its finest general. And Flame is pregnant!" Appalling! What would she and Kien do with three destroyers? Dear though the monsters were, they'd overrun Aeyrievale!

Stunned, Ela sat mute until the ladies sent for Father.

Dan Roeh loomed in the doorway, looking prosperous and handsome in dark green robes. He held a hand out to Ela, but his smile weakened and he turned misty-eyed. "You don't look like my little girl."

"Well, I am." She snatched up the branch and rushed to hug him. "Father, stop! You're making me cry!" Not good.

Dan exhaled. "Let's brace ourselves. Everyone's waiting."

They wiped their eyes, then paraded outside to the courtyard, which was filled with celebrants and all the trimmings for a wedding feast. Yells, cheers, and whistles from their friends greeted Ela's appearance. Ela also recognized several noblemen from the royal court. And—She gasped inwardly, almost stopping.

A face from her vision.

Brawny and cold-eyed, the man ought to be clad in soldier's gear. But he wasn't. Instead, he wore a nondescript brown tunic, mantle, and boots. Clearly, this apparition come-to-life stood among the crowd not as a celebrant but as a spy, fixated on *her*.

His dark, calculating gaze lifted chills of fear along Ela's bare arms. "Infinite?"

Father guided Ela through the crowd. She followed his lead, grasping at composure. Why *was* that foreign soldier standing amid her family and friends on her wedding day? Surely it wasn't yet time for . . . Infinite, please!

She looked again, trembling. The soldier hurried away through the courtyard gate, walking quickly as if to put distance between them. Would he not stalk her again for a few months? Or was this the last time she would see her family and friends?

Before she'd gathered her fragmented thoughts, Father kissed Ela's forehead in farewell and placed her hand in Kien's. His gray eyes wide and serious, Kien bent toward Ela, whispering, "What's wrong?"

He mustn't know. Not yet, at least. She hugged her soon-to-be husband and murmured, "I love you!"

Immediately, his concern vanished, replaced by an apprecia- tive grin. "Not as much as I love you! Ela . . ." He breathed her name as if overcome. "You are amazing! Beautiful!"

She willed herself to smile. And to admire his magnificent gold-edged blue garments and his dazzling smile. "So are you. I mean—" Oh, she could stare at him forever.

Parne's chief priest, Ishvah Nesac, stepped forward, splendid in his blue-and-white priestly attire. "Now, you two, save your com- pliments for when you truly need them—after you're married!"

Everyone laughed, and Ela calmed herself as Nesac prayed, asked the Infinite's blessing, then witnessed their marriage vows. Kien slid a lavish gold armband up Ela's left arm and fastened it over the thin scar on her bicep. The instant the priest pronounced them married, Kien swept Ela into a hug and kissed her, his lips so warm and lingering that she gasped for breath when he finally released her. Around them, their guests cheered, ready to celebrate and feast.

Ela glanced around. No sign of the soldier-spy. A reprieve? Infinite, please, let it be so! Guests clustered about her and Kien, offering hugs, kisses, and blessings. Father. Mother. Ara Lantec and the tearfully happy Nia Rol. Prill. Tamri. Survivors from Parne . . .

At last, General Rol, resplendent in red-and-blue robes, greeted Kien with a hearty slap on the shoulder. But he kissed Ela, almost as teary-eyed as Father. "Ela, dear girl, you look beautiful. Have you heard my news? I'm retiring in favor of the Grand Assembly. I need you to take ownership of Flame."

Ela sighed. "Sir, is this truly what you wish? Flame will be heartbroken."

The general cleared his throat. "She and her foal will be too much for my few fields, and I doubt it's good for her to be separated from Scythe. Come along." He offered Ela a supportive arm, gallant as ever. Masking his sadness, Ela realized. She walked with him and Kien to the gate.

Flame waited outside, huge, shimmering-dark, and moodily chewing through a pile of hay. Rol beckoned her fondly, smoothing her glossy neck. "You've been a joy, you beautiful monster, but it's time you settled with a family. Look at Ela. Remember Ela?" Rol cleared his throat and commanded the destroyer sternly. "Obey her. Do you hear? Obey Ela."

The impressive monster-warhorse grumbled, an aggrieved noise that echoed through the entire wedding party, temporarily halting all conversation. When Rol tried to pat Flame again, she swung her big head away and moped, as if deeply betrayed. Ela smoothed the destroyer's gleaming coat. "I'm sorry. I know you've loved the general. But you'll see him again!"

Flame huffed. Ela sighed. "All right. Pout. I understand—he's a good master, so you're right to grieve. But wait here. Stay!"

As gloomy as the destroyer, Rol sighed. "Ah, well. Let's return to the feast, shall we? Ela, Kien, introduce me to all your friends."

While they returned to the celebration, Ela cast another look around for the spy. Still nowhere to be seen. Thank You! She merged with the crowd, determined to visit.

If this was the last time she would see her family and friends, she must hug *everyone*.

✦ ✦ ✦

Kien glanced up at the sun. Still full daylight, but definitely leaning toward evening. Well past the time they should have departed. He'd tried twice to draw Ela away from the feast, to no avail. However, she was lovely to behold, laughing and talking with the guests. . . .

Standing just behind Kien with Prill, Bryce murmured, "My lord, forgive me, but unless we leave now and travel quickly, you won't spend your wedding night in the lodgings I've rented for you. Instead you'll be camping, *most* uncomfortably, alongside the road." Blandly, he added, "There's something to be said for Aeyrievale's customs, sir."

"Fine." If he was truly Aeyrievale's lord—and Kien supposed he must be—it was time to act the part. Kien marched over to Ela and caught her by one arm, branch and all, and then bent swiftly, hauling her over his shoulder.

She gasped, "Kien!"

Balancing her trifling weight, he swept his Azurnite sword's glittering blue blade from its scabbard. Strictly for show, of course. Laughter and cheers erupted around them as he strode from the courtyard. Dan Roeh yelled, "Don't bring her back!"

Ela swatted Kien's shoulder, making him laugh. "Kien, this is *not* funny!"

"Oh, yes it is!" Outside the gate, Kien ordered Scythe, "Kneel." Grudgingly, the destroyer obeyed. Kien seated the offended Ela sideways on Scythe, slipped the Azurnite blade into its scabbard, settled himself behind his wife, then gathered the reins. "Scythe, stand."

Grumbling, Scythe stood. Flame glared at Kien. Ela sniffed, unbearably pretty. And annoyed. "Why did you haul me away like a sack of grain? All you had to do was tell me it was time to leave."

"I did. Twice. Didn't you hear me?"

"Yes, but—"

Kien interrupted her with a kiss. "We're late, and we must hurry. That's why." He nodded to Prill, who now waited in a cart, then to Bryce in a nearby chariot. "Ready!"

✦ ✦ ✦

Ela slipped the branch into its place on Pet's war harness and looked around, composing herself. How like Kien to create a scene. Stolen from her own wedding! So unprophet-like. Totally without dignity. However . . . She glanced up at Kien. He grinned at her, infuriatingly irresistible. Ela bit down a smile and looked away. "Hmph!"

Kien laughed and hugged her. "Oh, admit it! You're amused!"

"I won't." For now.

Pet's gait quickened, seeming jaunty. And Flame kept pace behind them, looking less disagreeable. Bryce, meanwhile, took the lead in his chariot, dignified despite his ordinary little horses. Prill, ensconced on the wicker passenger seat of a two-wheeled baggage cart, also rode ahead of Ela and Kien. Eyeing her former chaperone, Ela leaned into Kien, whispering, "Bryce has been flirting with Prill! Kien, we must keep watch over those two."

"We will. But for now, I'd rather watch you." He pulled her closer, sighed into her hair, then gave her an exultant one-armed hug. "We're married!"

"Yes, we are!" Enjoying his delight, Ela squeezed Kien's forearm. Um, daunting. He'd gained more muscle since the siege. Curious, she tested one of his biceps. "Have you been fighting much?"

"Nearly every day. With Jon, then the king, and Lorteus, and Bryce." Kien tipped her back slightly. "Why?"

"Just wondering." He was prepared to fight. All the better, considering her visions. She hugged him and suppressed a shiver. Infinite? Save him! Let him live. . . .

Kien disrupted her thoughts, kissing her hair as he breathed, "I love you!"

Tears threatened, and Ela hugged her husband tighter. "I love you too!" With no regrets, she snuggled against him, determined to cherish every precious instant of their lives together. Infinite? Thank You!

✦ ✦ ✦

Feigning sleep, Akabe opened his eyes the merest bit, watching the servant pause after lighting the morning fire. Why was the man simply standing there?

A sudden glint of firelight reflected off a blade, answering his question.

Infinite, be with me! Akabe slid his hand farther beneath his pillow and grasped his hidden dagger, hoping Caitria would stay put while he fought this would-be assassin.

◆ 14 ◆

Focusing on his attacker, Akabe whipped the scabbard from beneath his pillow and threw it at the man's face, then charged from the bed, dagger ready. A hollow thwack and his assailant's pained grunt proclaimed a direct hit.

Seizing his brief advantage, Akabe roared and lunged—a feint. The attacker lunged in turn, aiming for Akabe's heart. Deflecting the blow with his forearm, Akabe grabbed his assailant's arm and twisted it. Turning, he locked his right leg behind his foe's, threw him to the floor, and wielded his dagger to incapacitate the man but not kill him outright. The failed assassin yelled and recoiled.

Behind them, Caitria screamed as if Akabe had wounded her instead of the man at his knees. "Oh no! Guards!" He heard her scramble out of the bed and run from the chamber. "*Guards!*"

Now, even wounded and weaponless, the assailant fought, snarling curses, clawing at Akabe's throat for a chance to kill him. Akabe bashed the wretch with his dagger hilt, trying to subdue him. Alive—he needed this fool alive! Pinning him, Akabe bellowed, "Surrender!"

"Phaw!" The man spat toward Akabe, but the sticky globule landed on his own chin, provoking another spate of curses and maddened thrashing.

Gritting his teeth, Akabe held down his assailant. "Enough!"

He glared into the man's face . . . and stared. The eyes, the coldly proud features . . . undeniably variants of . . . "Thaenfall!"

The man sneered, intensifying his resemblance to Caitria's father.

A clatter of weapons sounded at the door. One of Akabe's guards cried, "Majesty!"

"Oh, welcome . . . now that I've got him down! Grab him! Bind his legs!"

They struggled anew until someone—his field surgeon, Riddig Tyne—dragged Akabe from the skirmish. "Majesty, are you wounded?"

"No." At least not that he knew. Akabe sucked in a breath, trying to calm himself. But he couldn't bring himself to release his bloodied dagger . . . not yet. Might there be more attackers? "Where's the queen?"

"My wife is tending her," Lord Faine announced from the doorway, barefoot, his hair and robes tousled—clearly a lord scared from his own bedchamber. "She's in hysterics."

For his sake or her own? Had Caitria conspired with this relative? Loathing his suspicion, Akabe snapped at the guards. "Have your comrades search the entire palace and post sentries at each doorway. Question everyone! Particularly this man. But don't take him away yet. Riddig, tend his wounds." To Faine, Akabe muttered, "Go find some boots and a comb for yourself, my lord. After I'm scrubbed and clothed, I'll summon the queen."

Before he departed, Faine quietly asked, "Do you believe she had something to do with this attack, Majesty?"

"No." Akabe prayed she hadn't. "But I want to see her face when she recognizes that man. And I want my guards replaced. Question them as well. Separately." Had they been asleep at his doorway or gambling behind the pillars? He could not excuse their failure. He'd warned them weeks ago of this possibility, yet they'd ignored him! Were they bribed?

Scowling, Akabe waited for water and clothes. Simply scrubbing the blood from beneath his fingernails took an infuriating amount of time. Particularly while the Thaenfall relative cursed guards, fought his ropes, and bellowed threats as Riddig Tyne opened his case of surgeon's tools. Riddig, however, seemed delighted to pour caustic cleansers over the man's flesh, then repeatedly stab him with a needle and a drainage tube while suturing his side.

Just as Akabe clasped a mantle over his clean tunic, Lords Trillcliff and Piton edged into the chamber. Their tense expressions eased when they saw Akabe. Trillcliff bowed. "Majesty, bless the Infinite!"

A small, dark-haired figure leaned between the two lords. Barth looked up at Akabe, worry fretting his small, pale face. He bowed and lisped, "Majesty, are you hurt?"

Breath catching in his throat, Akabe rushed across the chamber and swept up the boy, hauling him into the next room. Six years was too young to stomach the sight of a defeated assassin trussed on the bloodied floor like a near-slaughtered beast. "I'm well, little sir. But you wait with the ladies or Master Croleut this morning. I'll send for you later."

Barth whooped and kicked the air, reassuringly elated. "Yes, sir! The ladies are prettier and kinder than Master Croleut."

"Flirt with the ladies then." Akabe set the boy down. "Just don't marry anyone without my permission." Even as he spoke, Akabe realized the ladies and the queen waited in the room, listening. The instant he looked at them, they offered elegant bows.

Properly garbed in layers of embroidered pale green, Caitria straightened, silent and red-eyed, her indecipherable gaze searching his face.

Looking for . . . what? Almost seven weeks of marriage, and he still couldn't interpret her expressions. Akabe held out a hand. She hurried to him at once, her fingers cold as they touched his own. Akabe guided her into his bedchamber, threading a path between his lords and the guards. Riddig stood, smug, his bound patient neatly stitched and quiet at his feet. "Majesty. Your prisoner will live long enough to face trial."

Obviously weakened, the failed assassin found enough strength to snap, "Death take you before me!"

Ignoring him, Akabe eyed Caitria, almost daring her. "Do you recognize this man?"

"He—" She faltered and gripped Akabe's arm. "He resembles . . . my lord-father. Or my brothers."

Akabe's foe smiled thinly, all cold charm. "Do I? The last time I saw you, Cousin Caitria, you were singing and playing with your maidservant. Not much has changed, except that you're taller. And Siphra's queen." Sweeping an icy glance at Akabe, Caitria's relative added, "As for your newest servant—may he die swiftly!"

Eyes wide, Caitria shook her head. "I cannot believe this."

"Believe it, lady." Akabe motioned to one of his guards. "Have you checked his arms for the goddess coils?"

A guard bent and slashed his prisoner's sleeves, tearing them apart, revealing dark, intricate etchings over the man's biceps. A visible pledge of his life and soul to the goddess Atea. Akabe stared at the coils, then at this unknown Thaenfall, suspecting at least part of his motive. "Is this revenge for a relative's death—Ison of Deerfeld?"

"He failed!"

"And so have you." Akabe tightened his grip on Caitria, feeling her tremors of fear. Would she try to run? Much as he hated the thought of restraining her, Akabe needed his wife to face this situation. Evidently she'd known nothing of this attack, but Akabe wanted her to confess her devotion to the goddess. She remained maddeningly silent, staring at her cousin's black-etched arms. Akabe told the man, "Wearing those coils need not determine your soul's fate."

"And you think you might?" the man hissed. "Spewing inanities of the Infinite—rebuilding that symbol of His oppression! We'll be rid of you and that temple soon enough!"

The man's hatred of the Creator and His temple struck Akabe with an almost physical force. But why not? By all accounts, the Thaenfall clan considered the Infinite absurd. They'd embraced

Atean beliefs from birth. Willing Caitria to listen, Akabe asked the man, "Have you ever truly stepped back from your traditions and the lures of the flesh to question the object of your worship?"

Again the cold sneer. "Have you?"

Akabe met his look evenly. "I have. My life would have been far easier if I'd turned Atean. However, despite my unworthiness, the Infinite has proven Himself to me in more ways than I can count." He stared at this Thaenfall relative. "Has your goddess defended you? *Ever?*"

Now silent as Caitria, the defeated man turned his head, scorning to answer.

If only Ela or Kien could be here now. They might win him over. Akabe gritted his teeth. "Because of what I represent, and because I wish to restore the Infinite's Holy House to Siphra, you wish to kill me. But *I* want you to survive—or at least to be freed of the spiritual coils which ensnare you."

"Fool," the cousin muttered. He closed his eyes, refusing to answer another question.

Exasperated, Akabe nodded at the waiting guards, who hauled the wounded man to his feet and dragged him from the chamber.

Still trembling and staring at the bloodstained floor, Caitria spoke in a monotone. "Majesty, you should set me aside."

Was she serious? Aware of his lords watching and listening, Akabe said, "We will discuss this later."

"May I be excused to my rooms, sir?"

"Of course. Send Barth to me if you need anything."

She departed at a sleepwalker's pace, seeming oblivious to everything. *Set me aside,* she'd said.

No doubt half of Siphra would approve, despite the sacred land provided by her dowry. And yet . . . She'd been trembling as she said the words. Not looking at him to convince him of her sincerity.

Around him, Faine, Trillcliff, and Piton waited. Akabe motioned the three to remain quiet. He nodded to Riddig and the guards. "Thank you. That will be all for now. Close the doors as you leave."

The instant they were alone, Piton lifted his hands in a gesture of frustration. Apparently fearful of listeners at the door, he whispered, "How do we rid ourselves of these attacks?"

"Draw out the Ateans," Trillcliff suggested, equally quiet.

Faine nodded, his voice barely audible. "We need a plan, sworn to silence between us four."

"Six." Akabe sank into a chair, his thoughts speeding ahead. "Whatever the plan, it must include Lord and Lady Aeyrievale when they return to Munra."

Trillcliff's bristly silvery eyebrows lifted, and he nodded. "Most suitable, sir. We agree."

The three lords pulled footrests and stools near to Akabe and seated themselves. Arguably displaying the most courage, or the least wisdom, Faine cleared his throat. "Majesty, about the queen . . ."

"I will deal with the queen."

Gently, Piton said, "If evidence is found of her complicity, she must be brought to trial."

"I will deal with the queen!" Remembering Caitria's apparent shock and her request to be set aside, Akabe shook his head. Did his advisors not see a vulnerable young woman hiding behind that cold façade she showed to his court? A wife Akabe might cherish if he could reach her? He stared at his advisors until they shrugged, exhaled, or looked away. "Now, my lords, let me hear your ideas for finding these enemies who wish to kill me and keep our temple in ruins."

✦ ✦ ✦

Lulled by Scythe's ambling pace and nearly two days of travel, Ela dozed. Until Kien jostled her awake. "We'll be in Aeyrievale soon!"

Perking up, Ela straightened in Kien's arms and studied the meadows on either side of the road, which curved up into foothills, then rugged mountains beyond. "Are those the Snake Mountains?"

"I believe so. Bryce said our fief shelters in the Snake Mountains and escapes beneath its fangs, so to speak, where the river finally empties into the sea."

Ela frowned. "Then while traveling between the Tracelands and Siphra, we've crossed your lands, not knowing it."

"Our lands," Kien corrected. "And, yes, you're right."

Lindorms plagued those mountains. Ela squelched her fear of the vicious, lethal giant snakes. Surely Bryce would have alerted Kien and Prill to local lindorm infestations. But she shuddered, watching for the beasts as Bryce led their procession among the winding foothills.

Gradually the landscape changed, drawing her admiration. Towering, castle-like formations of gray rocks and steep cliffs walled a lush, stunningly green river valley. Here and there, rough stone walls protected rural stone dwellings. And herds of sheep grazed in bright meadows. Soon shepherds waved and yelled enthusiastic greetings to Bryce.

But, to a man, the shepherds' excitement shifted to frowns when they saw Ela and Kien.

Matters didn't improve as Bryce guided Ela and Kien through a rustic town. Fleece-clad men shook their heads, turning away in obvious disgust. Wool-clad women pursed their lips or clicked their tongues audibly before stomping into snug stone homes roofed with straw thatch.

Kien muttered to Ela, "We've displeased them without saying a word. What will happen if we dare speak?"

Before Ela could answer, Flame snagged a huge mouthful of thatch from a cottage roof and ripped it away, causing the roof to buckle.

Screams echoed from inside the cottage.

❖ 15 ❖

Flame! No more!" Ela reached over Kien's arm, beckoning her sullen still-chewing destroyer. "I know you're hungry, but thatch roofs are not food!"

Flame gulped the mouthful and tilted her dark head away from the beleaguered home, outwardly obedient. However, Ela caught a rebellious glint in those black monster-horse eyes. Wonderful. If she and Kien couldn't find a suitable food source for these ever-grazing beasts, they'd be barred from Aeyrievale. Meanwhile, they must apologize.

Kien whispered, "Let's dismount and be sure those people are unharmed!"

Dear man. If this situation weren't so distressing, she would kiss his beguiling lips.

They dismounted, and Kien rapped on the home's carved wooden door. A plump woman finally answered, her tawny eyes round, her mouth crimped tight as if suppressing a scream. Kien inclined his head. "I am Kien Lantec. This is my wife, Ela." As Ela offered the woman a sympathetic smile, Kien continued. "We're sorry. We'll pay for repairs to your roof and forbid our destroyers any foraging in the village."

"Huh!" the woman sniffed, recovering her evidently formidable spirit. "The beast may's well gnaw on our homes—an' why not? Just addin' to the aeryon's attacks!"

Kien unleashed a warm smile and murmured, "We'll be sure your homes are protected. Your name is . . . ?"

The woman blinked, then stammered, "M-Mallissa Nones. The husband's Naor." A rough-hewn man stepped up behind Mallissa now, giving Ela and Kien a scornful nod.

Ela sighed. Oh, Infinite, why—apart from the ravenous destroyers—did these people dislike her and Kien? "Again, we're sorry."

Mallissa looked Ela over, clearly disapproving her riding boots, soft-layered blue tunic, the gold armband, and Ela's long braid. "I'm sure."

A dismissal if Ela had ever heard one. Kien gave the irate villager another charming smile, then offered his arm to Ela with a courtier's grace. "Let's depart before Scythe's appetite threatens another roof."

Ela shot a warning look at Pet. "No eating houses!" He shifted and turned—obviously feigning disinterest in the nearest thatch roof. Kien helped Ela climb onto Flame, then he seated himself on Pet and nodded to Bryce, who waited, cool and composed in his chariot.

Without inflection, Bryce told Naor and Mallissa, "Come up to the manor tomorrow and state your damages to me. I'll pay and order the roof repaired."

Clearly respectful of Aeyrievale's steward, Naor nodded. "As you say, sir."

Following Bryce, they set a brisk pace along the slab-paved main road. At the village's edge, Bryce diverted from the main road onto a broad, walled stone track carved into a gray cliff.

Was this home? Ela almost gasped, looking upward along the stone track. A series of gated arches, terraces, and towers led her gaze toward a succession of magnificent buildings that crowned the cliff's sheer drop into the valley below. Vines and a misted waterfall tumbled over the highest cliff, dissipating as it neared the ground.

Suspicious, roughened, weapon-carrying men eyed Kien and Ela at each gated terrace, seeming reluctant to allow them through. As it was, because of Pet's height, Kien had to duck slightly to avoid striking his head on the stone archways.

The uppermost stone gate led into a paved courtyard. Ela slowly dismounted, still staring. How could this now be her home? Impossible. Entirely too grand. However . . . she noted that some of the tall shutters were splintered, while those vines—pretty as the flowers were—ought to be trimmed and trained to remain on their trellises, which looked badly weathered.

Bryce approached, followed by Prill, whose dark eyebrows couldn't be lifted any higher with her astonishment. Prill gasped, "Ela, how are we to manage all this?"

"A bit at a time?" Ela guessed.

Bryce's thin, tanned face glowed with enthusiasm as he addressed Kien. "My lord, now that revenues have been restored to the fief, we might plan repairs. The buildings themselves are solid, but the embellishments need refurbishing."

"Wasn't Aeyrievale in control of its own revenues?" Ela demanded.

Sobering, Bryce shook his head. "No, lady. All our profits were taken by the court and divided among several Atean lords. But their abuses will end now that your husband has taken control of his lands."

Ela winced. "That can't make the Atean lords happy."

"It hasn't," Bryce admitted. "Yet, if they quarrel, Lord Aeyrievale can afford to hire an army to fight them off."

Kien grinned. Ela winced. Enemy-lords and hostile locals. Not reassuring. Infinite, help Kien! Particularly if she didn't return from her forthcoming mission. Kien swooped an arm around Ela. "Let's see to the destroyers, then explore the place!"

Helpful, Bryce nodded toward a large lower building with a particularly wide enclosed terrace. "I've ordered a small mountain of hay to the stables. Your apartments are in the uppermost rooms in the building above us—all unlocked." He removed a broad ring of keys from his belt and offered them to Ela. "Enjoy your new residence, lady."

"Thank you." Ela accepted the keys. With a sidelong look at Prill, who was watching Bryce, Ela announced, "Matron Prill, you'll accompany us, please."

Kien swung Ela aside, hissing, "Surely we're not being chaperoned in our own home!"

"Not at all," she whispered, loving his nearness. "I simply want to be sure those two are kept properly away from each other."

"Not a problem." Kien looked around at the imposing buildings. "I must have a few barred cells or secured dungeons somewhere in these piles of stonework."

"Kien!"

"Fine! I was only half . . . well, mostly . . . serious."

✦ ✦ ✦

Moving softly to avoid waking Kien, Ela finished braiding her hair while admiring her sleeping husband's own dark, shining hair—and his whiskers. Her mortal love. Oh, he was so handsome and delightful! How could she be so blessed?

Truly, Kien looked as if he belonged here, sleeping in the huge carved bed situated within this lordly, tapestry-hung room, which glowed in the morning light. Who would have ever thought, when they both chose to follow the Infinite, He would lead them to such a place? Even if Aeyrievale's natives scoffed at them both.

Rueful, Ela tucked away her comb and stood, pulling her heavy woolen outer robe close as she looked around. Exceptional stone carvings graced the walls, and the tapestries were a bit faded, but she liked their wilderness patterns of trees, cliffs, and waterfalls. Probably scenes from various places around Aeyrievale. Lovely inspiration to explore today. Perhaps they'd spy aeryons and—

A brisk pounding on the bedchamber door startled Ela from her reverie and woke Kien from his sleep. As he sat up and blinked, Ela rushed to open the door.

A sturdy woman nodded, her freckled face pleasant, and pushed a linen-draped tray at Ela. "Here's the mornin' meal, lady, seein's how yer late." She turned away, adding, "Leave the tray where ya stand—I'll fetch it later when I've strength to climb all th' stairs again."

By now Kien stood beside her in his wrinkled robe, sleepy-eyed but pleased. "Food!"

Ela carried the tray to a nearby table and set it down while Kien arranged their chairs.

The instant Ela whisked aside the cloth, and the inverted basket that served as the tray's cover, a stench assailed her nostrils, making her lean away. "Ew!"

Kien grabbed a knife and poked at the scorched eggs and what looked like cubes of brown cheese. "I was afraid of this."

"What?" Ela stared at the meal, certain she could bounce these eggs off a wall, if she'd been the sort of person who wasted food.

Kien grimaced and stabbed a brown cube. "It's the local Bannulk cheese—a character test in a dish."

Wary, Ela nudged a brown cube with her knife while quizzing her doleful husband. "Is it too salty? Sour? Bitter? Sharp?"

"Solidified bile. And we're expected to like it. Therefore . . ." Kien picked up a cube, paused as if encouraging himself, then ate it. After swallowing, he said, "I dare you."

She popped a cube into her mouth and chewed. Mistake! Ela almost spat out the stuff. "Ugh!" Bile was almost right. Vomit was exact. And she was supposed to like this? No doubt they'd face it at every meal. Infinite, protect me, please! Eyes watering, she swallowed. "How did you eat that cheese?"

"I've eaten worse."

"Impossible!"

"Trust me, love, it's true." He grinned now, his handsome face alight with inspiration. "We could bury this in the garden."

"The trees would die. Anyway, we'll be forced to eat it often, I'm sure." If they survived. Ela nudged Kien and braced herself. "Courage! The sooner we finish, the sooner we explore the valley and look for aeryons."

Nose to nose with her, he said, "Ela, I love you."

"After I eat this, Lord Aeyrievale, you'd best love me forever."

"I do and I will." He nudged her. "Let's finish this bile and escape before the cook offers us second servings!"

They choked down their food, then donned warm outer tunics. While Ela tugged on her oldest short-boots, she asked, "Why do you suppose the locals dislike us? We've done nothing offensive that I can think of—apart from Flame's bad judgment in selecting food."

"I don't know. However, I'm more than willing to console you."

Ela laughed, backing away as he approached. "I'm sure you are, but save your kisses for later." She retrieved the branch and hurried to the stout iron-bound door leading to the terrace. Kien swept past her, unbarred the door, then escorted her outside, grinning mischievously.

✦ ✦ ✦

Kien caught his breath against the morning's chill as they walked out onto the broad, stone-paved terrace balcony. Ela hurried to the stone balustrade and rested her elbows and the branch on the ornate stonework as she stared at the view. Looking away from his beguiling wife, Kien paused and stared, his delight fading. The entire valley lay before them in a vast panorama, bathed in golden dawnlight, verdant and spectacular. An amazing landscape. And *his*. He'd be responsible for everything in this valley—and for some distance beyond—until his death. Stunned, Kien stared from east to west, trying to absorb the realization.

Infinite? How can I possibly manage all this? Help me!

Just as his silent plea and prayer faded, Ela distracted him by skittering across the garden-like balcony and down a stone stairway tucked against the wall. Kien grinned and followed his wife's delicate form. He was badly smitten. Besotted. Love-struck.

He caught up to Ela on a shadowed lower balcony, snaring her in his arms and kissing her before she could breathe a word of protest. Her lips, skin, and hair were so soft and deliciously sweet, and her lively spirit was simply refreshing. Beyond doubt, he was the most blessed man alive. If it weren't for Ela, this exile would have driven him half mad. He couldn't have endured. . . .

A man's voice, harsh and complaining, lifted from the courtyard below—adjoining Bryce's office chamber. "All well 'n good, Bryce, sure! So we've a new lord, but he's a boy!"

What?

Boy? Kien straightened and turned as a woman's voice chimed in, unmistakably bitter. "We've enough worries without rearin' a pair of kids till they're fit to protect Aeyrievale."

Was this the reason he and Ela were so poorly received? Their supposed youthfulness and lack of experience? Kien released Ela, determined to confront the misled whiners and set them aright. Ela clung to Kien, locking her arms around his waist while shaking her head. Fine. He supposed Ela was right. It wouldn't do to quarrel with the locals on their first full day in Aeyrievale. Besides, Bryce was hushing the infuriated pair, Naor and Mallissa Nones.

"Naor! Lissy, enough. Give them a chance—you don't know who you're speaking of."

Lissy protested, her voice as disgusted as yesterday when Flame had dismantled her cottage roof. "They're babies!"

"Hardly! Lord Aeyrievale has survived battlefields, taken down an assassin, endured a foreign prison, *and* he refused Istgard's crown last year. Moreover, Lady Aeyrievale is the Infinite's prophet!"

"She ain't." Naor hesitated. "That pretty little girl? Nah, I don't believe it!"

"Believe it. She deserves your respect and so does Lord Aeyrievale. Moreover, he's the same age as the king, and they're friends. Now, take your money and stop complaining."

As if needing further reason to argue, Naor said, "He seems nothin' like the king! In all his years hikin' these mountains, the king never behaved so grand—wearin' fine clothes and ridin' giant warhorses!"

Bryce snapped back, "Mind your tongue! He's Aeyrievale's

lord, and I'm grateful! As for the king, I daresay you'd be amazed at how well he's adapted to his royal place!"

Naor had met Akabe? Intrigued now, Kien listened as the man continued, "E'en so, these *kids* know nothin' of our ways—we'll have to teach 'em that much."

"They're more than capable of learning." With a trace of humor, Bryce said, "Actually, Lord Aeyrievale stole his wife away from her family on their wedding day."

"Huh! Did they fight for her—knives 'n all?"

"They were too shocked."

"Prob'ly glad to be rid of her," Lissy snipped. "I hear prophets are naught but trouble. An' who knows if she's true! All prattle, I'd say."

Kien bit his lip. Hard. Laughter would give away their presence. Ela's grip loosened from his waist, making him look down at her.

She glared toward the balcony and huffed beneath her breath. "Oh!"

Clearly choosing a decorous retreat rather than beating Lissy with the branch, Ela flitted up the stairs once more. Kien followed slowly, trying desperately to keep quiet. Being caught eavesdropping on the locals wouldn't enhance his boyish reputation.

By now Ela was leaning against the highest balcony's decorative rail, clutching the branch tight. Probably praying for patience with Lissy.

Just as Kien climbed the last steps, an enormous shadow swept over them, and a huge golden beast flew down at Ela like a hawk stooping toward prey, its big talons extended.

Ela turned, screeched, and lashed out with the branch as the creature struck, lifting and knocking her over the rail. "Infinite!"

Amid a burst of light and gilded feathers, Ela dropped as Kien screamed her name.

✦ 16 ✦

Helpless, unable to scream, Ela glimpsed a giant form gusting past her toward the courtyard below. Was her beast-assailant turning for another attack? Impossible—the ground seemed to speed toward her. Ela shut her eyes. Oh, Infinite . . . !

"Unh!" All breath vanished from her lungs as she landed against something reasonably soft. And warm. With huge golden wings and gleaming fur-like down. An aeryon!

Surrounded by plumage, Ela fought for air to scream. Infinite? Help me!

Her Creator's voice whispered, *Look*.

Daring frantic glances from side to side, Ela realized the aeryon was sprawled lifeless beneath her, half-hawk, half-feline, its upper talons and lower paws outstretched, incapable of clawing her again. If only she could breathe, she'd run! On the stairs above her, Kien screamed her name, but she couldn't catch air to call him. Her lungs and throat refused to work.

"Lady!" Bryce came running from his small office. "Remain still. I've sent Naor's wife for Prill!"

Remain still? Excepting her eyes, she couldn't move in the least. Tears streaked her face as she fought pain and the horrible breathlessness. Just as her eyesight began to darken and dim, she finally managed to suck in a whisper of air, clearing her sight and thoughts.

Infinite? Thank You!

She didn't regret the prayer, but the breath—ugh! This dead beast stank worse than the taste of Bannulk cheese, with overtones of scorched feathers.

Ela squirmed and willed her throat and lungs to pull in more air.

Kien reached her now, touching her face and staring her in the eyes. "Infinite, bless You! Ela, hold still! Bryce, how did the beast catch us unawares? Not a sound! No warning—where did it come from?"

If ever a man sounded penitent, Bryce did now, and his thin face looked so pained, so earnest, that Ela longed to console him as he apologized. "My lord, my lady, forgive me. I should have inspected the abandoned towers. It's likely a pair of aeryons are nesting above. They are viciously protective of their territories."

Kien scowled as he smoothed his hands over Ela's face and head, and along her neck. "Well, now that Aeyrievale has reclaimed its revenues, those towers will be manned from this day onward! If a nest is found, remove it—relocate it! I don't care what you do or spend, just protect our household and the village from further attacks."

"Yes, my lord."

Behind Kien, Naor said, "I'd say 'twas th' same beast scarin' my Lissy last week. Hates women! Dunno why."

Veils fluttering, Prill scurried toward them now, accompanied by the gawping Mallissa. Prill gasped, "Ela! What happened!"

Wasn't it obvious? Ela squirmed again, catching another breath, and glimpsing the huge stark-dead aeryon. The creature lay ingloriously on its back, spread-winged, its crested head oddly turned, the long beak open, and those cruel, curving talons out as if forever attempting to reach for prey.

"Ela," Kien scolded tenderly, "hold still and let me finish checking you for injuries."

She looked up at him and finally managed to speak. "I'll live."

He sighed and kissed her. "You must!"

By now, Prill, Mallissa, and Naor were staring down at her, all horrified, intensifying her longing to escape. And from far away, Ela heard shouts, whistles, and destroyer-calls. Pet and Flame were undoubtedly trying to reach her despite their chains, the gates, and mighty walls of stone. Kien, however, ignored everything but her. Cautiously, he pressed her hands and arms. "Tell me if this causes pain, love."

As Prill began to check Ela's feet and legs, Naor complained to Mallissa and Bryce, "I'm smellin' burnt feathers 'n flesh."

The three inspected the dead aeryon's talons, flanks, and feline rump and paws. Lissy gasped. Bryce coughed. "Lady Aeyrievale, you struck this beast with the prophet's branch, am I right?"

"Yes, I—" Ela managed to force some strength into her words. "I was trying to defend myself." The branch. Where was the branch?

By now, Naor was nudging Lissy, who giggled. Bryce actually chuckled. Ela feared to ask why. But Kien scowled while checking Ela's ribs. "What are you three snickering about?"

"Well, my lord . . ." Bryce coughed again. "Lady Aeyrievale roasted the aeryon's hindquarters mid-flight."

"I didn't!" Diverted from her concern over the missing branch, Ela grabbed Kien's arms and struggled to sit up.

Naor whooped, obviously unable to contain his laughter. "Ha-ha! Beware the lady's cookin'!"

As Ela turned to see the damage she'd inflicted on the aeryon, Kien stopped her. Prill shrieked and whipped off her veiling. "Oh my! Ela, hold still."

"Why? I don't feel anything—it can't be as awful as my scaln scratches." Even as she spoke, a trickle along her shoulder blade hinted at a bloodied injury. All right. Now she felt a stinging and the myriad pains of emerging bruises. She froze, allowing Kien and Prill to wad the veiling against her shoulder.

Obviously trying to be optimistic, Kien murmured, "You've got a gouge where the aeryon hit you. We'll clean it thoroughly, love—but I fear you'll have quite a scar."

"Another one?"

Naor sobered, his voice doubtful. "Did you say scaln scratches?"

As Kien supported Ela and pressed a fabric pad tight against the oozing wound, Prill pointed to the rippled scars along Ela's ankles and shins, briefly allowing the gawking couple to inspect the pink-purple striations before she smoothed Ela's robes, covering the marks.

Naor stuttered an incoherent protest. "How . . ." Clearly flabbergasted, he tried again. "How'd you survive? Scaln venom 'n all."

Did she hear a bit of respect in the man's voice? Mallissa was leaning forward, obviously straining to catch Ela's reply. "The Infinite healed me, though I didn't deserve it. Just as He protected me today."

"Yes," Kien smiled, some of the tension fading from his face. "Praise the Infinite, and pray my wife behaves while healing."

Ela widened her eyes at him, indignant. Kien grinned and kissed her. "If you intend to appear threatening, love, that look won't succeed." He drew back slightly, imitating fear. "I suppose I ought to be afraid of you—roasting aeryons alive!"

"Searing the aeryon wasn't my idea."

"Whatever you say, Prophet."

Infinite? Did the aeryon have to be roasted? She'd never—for as long or short as she lived—be able to suppress this story and the jokes about her cooking. But she'd had nothing to say in the matter. The branch had seared that—

"The branch!" Ela looked around. "Infinite? Where is it?" She closed her eyes and prayed.

Light flashed between her fingers and solidified into her precious insignia. Ela cradled the branch, exhaling her gratitude. "Thank You."

Kien recoiled a bit, startled. "Don't toast me!"

"I'll want to if you're forever teasing me about this!"

"I'm glad you have the strength to threaten me. Now I'm going to carry you inside." Gently, Kien scooped her into his arms and stood. "Tell me if I'm causing you more pain."

Aware of the silence surrounding them, Ela glanced at her companions. Having seen the branch materialize from nothingness before, Bryce and Prill were reasonably composed. But Naor and Lissy lifted their mutual gazes from the sacred emblem to her, visibly terrified.

Fearing they might run away in fear, Ela said, "Don't worry. You're not in the least danger."

Mallissa looked and sounded faint. "Indeed . . . lady?"

Naor braced his wife as he spoke to Kien and Ela. "M'lord. M'lady. We'll drag th' aeryon from here 'n save its feathers 'n down for you. Just tell us whatever else needs doin'. It'll be done."

Kien nodded, admirably solemn. "Thank you both." Ela managed a smile. A victory. Painfully won, but a victory nonetheless. Even so, she hurt everywhere now. And . . .

Infinite, she *didn't* want to be remembered as the Lady Aeyrievale who roasted aeryons!

Too miserable to complain, Ela drooped against Kien as he carried her inside the manor. While Bryce and Prill marched ahead of them, opening doors—with Bryce calling orders to the servants and Prill requesting bandages and ointments—Kien whispered to Ela, "If anything happens to you, love, I will not recover!" His every inflection conveying fear, he breathed, "You must live, or let me die before you! Do *not* leave me alone in Siphra!"

She stared up at him, unable to offer the reassurance he needed.

✦ ✦ ✦

Loathing his formal robes and the necessity of this process, Akabe released a silent breath of prayer as his guards led the Thaenfall cousin into Siphra's throne room. The man was clean, but gaunt, sallow, and so hostile he was snarling as the guards forced him to kneel before Akabe. Amazing energy for a man who'd half-starved himself during the three weeks he'd been questioned and investigated.

Nearby, Caitria—pale in her crimson-and-gold tunic—shifted slightly on her cushioned bench. Her movement, faint as it was, drew Akabe's attention.

And her cousin's attention.

The man's gaze narrowed, condemning Caitria. "Majesty. You're no Thaenfall if you do nothing while your people are being robbed of their freedoms!"

Akabe fought to keep himself from reacting. Was the man trying to goad Caitria into rebellion?

"What are you saying, sir?" Caitria lifted her chin, a furious blush tingeing her face. Akabe watched, captivated while she continued. "Have the Thaenfalls concerned themselves with me, ever? No! And now, though I've honored my family, I'm here, abandoned!"

The Thaenfall cousin smiled, distinctly unsympathetic. "Abandoned? Yes. And condemned. After all, you and your lord-father are both traitors . . . selling *him* that land. How long will you survive me, cousin, eh? You should have resisted—"

"Stop!" Akabe leaned forward, furious. "You will not threaten the queen. She was unable to prevent the sale and should not be condemned for it!"

"Tell that to your enemies—I'm finished!" the man snapped. He gazed past Akabe, his gaunt face now a hollowed mask. And he refused to say another word despite requests from his own legal advisor.

The public ordeal continued. The royal guards and the king's surgeon, Riddig Tyne, testified that this Thaenfall relative was the same man who'd attacked the king three weeks past. Sickened, Akabe declined to pass a sentence.

The royal council, seated below his throne to the right, condemned the Thaenfall assassin to death.

Convicted, the man shot a final accusing glare at the silent Caitria before the guards led him away to his execution. Though she didn't move, unshed tears glittered in Caitria's eyes.

As Akabe clasped his wife's cold hand and led her from Siphra's throne room, she whispered shakily, "By all I've read, sir, a hated queen is never forgiven, and you have enough troubles. You should set me aside."

Were her fears for him as much as for herself? Akabe prayed it was the truth. For all her stubbornness, Caitria wasn't the one to be blamed for her situation.

He was.

Could he protect her from vengeful Ateans if he set her aside?

Aware of his courtiers all staring at them, doubtless trying to read their faces and lips, Akabe murmured, "Lady, you've read the wrong books. And you've been queen for two months—too soon for anyone to pass judgments. I won't discuss setting you aside."

Even as he spoke, Akabe's thoughts sped through his plans. He'd been so zealous to acquire those temple lands that one thing hadn't occurred to him: The instant he'd married Caitria, she and her family had become traitors to the Ateans for bringing the sacred land into his control. He'd made her a target for death. Which brought up another thought. "Have you heard from your lord-father?"

For an instant, she hesitated, as if unable to speak. Then she said, "I wrote to him one month ago, asking for my books . . . my other belongings. My message was returned last week. The servants said that after our wedding, my lord-father and Cyril paid their debts, then left on an extended journey and refused to divulge their destination. But I believe they're hiding, because of the temple."

Hiding? Akabe hoped so. Otherwise, after such a long absence, Caitria's father and brother must be dead, executed by Ateans for enabling the temple to be rebuilt.

"You should have told me about your lord-father."

Toneless, she said, "Perhaps it's best he remain hidden."

As she should be hidden.

Infinite? Akabe eyed his wife as they walked. How could he save her?

Barth scampered toward Akabe from where he'd been standing with his mannerly father. Lord Siymont offered gracious obeisance as his small son trotted behind Akabe to follow him. "Majesties," Siymont murmured.

Caitria's somber face lit with a smile, beautiful to see.

Understandably she was fonder of Barth than anyone else in this marble prison of a palace. Akabe suspected she would be a doting mother . . . if they survived to become parents.

Yet a child would surely present another battleground, a realm of emotional conflict, pitting the royal council against the queen and her Atean family.

Sickening thought. Not the sort of life he'd ever imagined for his wife and children.

Infinite, let my plan work! Save us and let my enemies be confounded.

Let my wife turn to You. . . .

He *must* implement his plan and send for Kien and Ela. Now.

✦ ✦ ✦

As her smile faded, Caitria nearly stumbled, bringing herself to reality once more.

Today, one of her cousins would die a traitor.

Today, she'd faced a silent, unseen court of enemies while her father and brother had fled unseen, abandoning her like cowards. Had they joined Atean conspirators? Swallowing, she forced herself to accept the truth. Her own relatives might kill her.

And she could do nothing but continue to walk beside the man who'd unintentionally fomented this lethal tidal wave of hatred that would claim both their lives.

But *why* must Akabe die? He was very nearly perfect, except that he believed in that ancient, antiquated Infinite. *And* he persisted in building that horrid temple!

Caitria paused. Oh . . . Had she—like some naïve little fool from an epic poem—fallen in love with her husband despite their differences?

Even as Caitria faltered over the realization, Akabe squeezed her cold hand, warming it within his own. When she looked up at him, Akabe smiled, his golden brown eyes and those dimples encouraging her to pretend that they might survive the coming maelstrom of Atean conspiracies.

✦ 17 ✦

Heedless of her wild hair and her randomly snatched tunic and robes, Ela ran through the dawn-lit courtyard toward the huge arched stone gate. Wonderful, after four weeks, to finally rush around without pain! Unless, of course, she stepped on a jagged rock and gouged her foot.

Behind her, still descending the stairs, Kien yelled, "Slow down, Ela! You'll trip and hurt yourself again."

She turned and waited, folding her arms to express her impatience. "My lord, you sound like some old married man! And you're walking too slowly."

Though he was certainly worth waiting for.

Infinite? Wasn't a month of marriage supposed to cure her of infatuation?

Kien's reply was obliterated by a low, vibrant destroyer-call. Remembering her reason for standing barefoot and rumpled in the courtyard before breakfast, Ela tugged her husband's sleeve. "Pet's calling, and Flame is waiting!"

"Which is why you don't need to run. And his name is Scythe." Kien wrapped an arm around her shoulders and squeezed, provoking a jab of pain.

"Ow! The shoulder . . . careful of the shoulder."

He winced in sympathy, sliding his hand to her waist. "Sorry. You've seemed so perfectly healed that I forgot."

They hurried through the highest gate, nodding to the grinning guard before descending into the huge stable arena. Pet leaned over a stone barrier, whickering invitingly. Ela kissed the destroyer's big face and smoothed his neck. "Will she allow us to see your baby?"

But even as Ela asked, Flame beckoned her from the wide, stone-sheltered pen adjacent to Pet's. Ela crooned, "Ooo, there's the beautiful mama!"

Ela approached her destroyer cautiously, relieved when Flame nosed her in welcome. After scenting Ela's hair and brooding over the tender shoulder wound, Flame retreated toward the darkest area of her pen. A shadow moved just beyond the mother destroyer, black upon black; then a form appeared, all gangly legs, blocky body, long neck, and handsome little destroyer face. A second shadow moved behind the first, its inky mirrored-image. Ela slapped both hands over her mouth to stifle shrieks. Twins!

She danced around Kien and hugged him, whooping beneath her breath, "Twins! Twins!" Oh. Twin destroyers. "Oh no . . ."

Kien laughed and kissed her hair. "Well, that was a short celebration. What's wrong, Prophet? Are you envisioning destroyer-disasters? Don't worry. We can afford them."

"But will Aeyrievale survive toddler-destroyers?" She returned to Flame's pen and stared at the handsome babies. They eyed her as if she might be food. Oh, dear. Best to command this pair at once. She scowled and lowered her voice to absolute sternness. "No biting us! Not Ela, not Kien, and . . ." She hesitated, distracted as Bryce and Prill entered the stable yard. "Particularly no biting Bryce and Prill! See them? Obey!"

Small destroyer-grumblings answered, with stomps and huffs. Flame herded away the foals, who squealed in protest as if disgusted by the loss of potential food sources. Flame tossed her elegant head. Pet curveted. Which reminded Ela. "No kicking either!"

Bryce approached, a slight smile tracing his thin sun-browned face. "It seems Aeyrievale will now be known for aeryons, sapphires, and destroyers." Somber again, he bowed to Kien, offering him a heavily sealed parchment. "My lord, this arrived last night after you retired."

Obviously reluctant, Kien removed a dagger from his belt and slid it beneath the seal. He read the message, not appearing the least surprised. "A summons from the king."

Bryce shut his eyes hard, then opened them as if preparing himself for bad news. "My lord, the last time Aeyrievale received such a parchment, our previous lord and lady were killed. I don't intend to sound superstitious—I'm not—but is there any way to escape this summons?"

"No." Ela cringed inwardly, wishing she'd bitten her tongue instead of speaking.

Kien stared at her, one dark eyebrow lifted. "Prophet, what haven't you told us?"

"I can't tell you much," Ela replied gently. "But I notice you're not surprised either, sir."

Prill leaned into the conversation, her thin face as worried as Bryce's. "Ela, what's about to happen? Are you two in danger?"

The truth. "I don't know." She looked from her dear former chaperone to Bryce. "Ask everyone in Aeyrievale to pray for us while we're gone. And pray for the king and the queen. Our enemies are gathering."

For one chilled instant, looking inward again at her vision once more, Ela studied the young queen. Was she Atean? Could she be persuaded of her Creator's love?

Sickened, Ela retreated from her vision.

From ashes and death.

✦ ✦ ✦

With Kien and Prill looking on, Bryce placed a locked metal box on his worktable and handed Ela a key. As she accepted the key, Bryce explained, "We finally managed to retrieve this yesterday from our treasury—the tunnel leading up to the chamber was flooded. These are the few pieces that remained after our former Lady Aeyrievale's death."

Her murdered predecessor. Infinite? Did she love You?

Yes, His voice assured. *She is now beyond her enemies' reach.*

But Ela, prophet of Parne, was not.

Beside Ela, Kien slid an arm around her waist and kissed her cheek, somber. "It's all right. Open the box, love."

Ela pressed the key into the lock and slid its iron bar aside. Nestled among several leather pouches, an exquisite feather-patterned tiara of white and yellow gold glimmered with clear, intensely violet-blue sapphires, some dangling in elegant face-framing pendants.

Prill gasped. "Ela, it's beautiful!"

Stunned, Ela could only nod. Slowly, she opened a leather pouch and withdrew its contents—a matched pair of intricate sapphire bracelets designed to cover the backs of her hands like mitts. She, plain Ela of Parne, was supposed to wear these? "These are spectacular. But—"

"Necessary," Bryce interposed. "You represent Aeyrievale at court, lady. If we reopen our mines, you'll have more to choose from within a few years."

"Reopen the mines," Kien told Bryce. "Continue with our plans as we've agreed."

"Very well, sir. But if anything happens to you, we will close the mines immediately. Why pour Aeyrievale profits into Atean hands?"

Kien scowled—so ineffectively stern that Ela almost smiled. He said, "Bryce! Enough fretting. Reopen the mines! Let's clear out our documents today and finish up any business before I leave."

Back to business. Ela tucked the sapphires into their box and closed the lid. The jewelry reminded her of another yet-unfinished task. "We need to return your mother's tiara to her."

Gloom shadowed Kien's face, no doubt provoked by distress for his still-grieving family. "Box it up and I'll send it to the Tracelands with my next letter. We'll also see to pasturing the destroyers. Naor found a near-perfect place. A meadow walled off and unwanted by the villagers or the aeryons, for this season at least. What else?"

Bryce cleared his throat and raised an eyebrow at Prill. She blushed. "Ela, we'd prefer to be married before I leave with you for Munra."

Remembering her visions, Ela shook her head. Before the pledged couple could misunderstand, she said, "Prill, you're not accompanying us to Munra, so you'd best marry Bryce. While we're gone, we'll trust you to manage the destroyers and work on the improvements we've discussed—the chambers, the windows, and the gardens."

"Good," Kien said. "Now we can stop chaperoning those two."

"Oh!" Prill sniffed. "We've never been the trouble you were, my lord—admit it!"

"Me? Trouble? Never!" He nudged Bryce. "What are the civil requirements for marriage in Aeyrievale?"

"Your say-so, sir."

"I say so. Sir." Kien grinned at Prill. "And *lady*. We'll gather with all the villagers this evening, before sunset. Send word to Aeyrievale's priest and go find your wedding clothes, both of you!"

As the betrothed couple hurried off, Kien touched Ela's face. "You've been preoccupied this morning. What aren't you telling me?"

What could she tell him? Trying not to revisit her vision, she hugged her husband tight. "We're in danger. All four of us. You, me, the king, and the queen. Because of the temple, and our love for the Infinite. Truly, it won't matter where we are. Our enemies will find us."

Kien's gray eyes darkened, somber as approaching clouds. "Will we die?"

"I don't know." Fragments of emotions and images cut at her now, so sharp that she flinched. Desperation rising, she explained, "I see only the queen, and—much as I wish I could—I can't help her! I don't know where you are, but I want you to be safe, and I'm praying for you and the king!" She shut her eyes against the tears, saw the vision, and stopped. Better to be with her husband now than in the vision. Hugging Kien again, Ela hid her face against his chest, inhaling his scent. "Promise me, whatever happens, you'll stay alive and fight! If it's a choice between somehow saving me or saving the king, then you must save the king! Promise!"

"What?" Kien held her at arm's length, making her look at his now-ashen face. "Will I be forced to choose?"

"I don't know. As ever, I can't see your path. We must depend on the Infinite. But for Siphra's sake, and the temple's, the king is first—promise me!"

Kien shook his head. "Do not ask this of me! Don't expect this of me, Ela, please. I'll fail!" He pulled her close again, kissing her hair fiercely, his now-hushed words sounding like a tormented prayer. "Infinite, I will fail!"

In silence, Ela prayed. Oh, Infinite, sustain my husband! Let him live. . . .

✦ ✦ ✦

Twining his fingers around Ela's and breathing the ocean air, Kien paused and scanned the crowded, mazelike palace garden. Any reception, informal or not, was torment enough to make him flee. Except that with the courtiers scattered throughout the garden, he could speak to the king with less danger of being overheard. Akabe stood near an ornate fish pond, talking with Faine and Trillcliff while the queen lingered nearby, flanked by her noticeably *un*talkative ladies.

Leaning down to whisper to Ela, Kien admired her poise. She looked as if she'd been wearing golden hairbands and sapphires from birth. "Are the ladies shunning their queen?"

"It seems they dislike her. Poor lady." Ela's beautiful eyes reflected genuine compassion.

Amazing, that compassion. Particularly considering that this same young queen might soon draw Ela into a life-threatening situation. Must he choose between Ela and the king? No . . . He could not lose Ela. Not again.

Infinite? Please protect my wife! Kien lifted Ela's hand and kissed her fingers, avoiding Aeyrievale's sapphires in favor of her incredibly soft skin. "I love you!"

A nobleman's cultivated, too-familiar voice interrupted from behind them. "Most moving, my lord. Such an example of wedded bliss should be honored by the entire court."

"Ruestock!" Kien turned, his free hand instinctively moving to his sword as he glared at the oily, no doubt Atean lord—this conniver who'd once stolen Ela and whose scheming had contributed to Kien's exile.

He'd gladly pay for one good, defensible reason to strike this man!

Even as he finished the thought, Kien glimpsed a flash of light in Ela's hand—the branch, taking form. And Ela turned, her dark eyes mirroring its fiery white glow.

✦ 18 ✦

Ela clenched the prophet's branch, longing to beat the sleek-haired Ruestock. Infinite, please?

No. *Ask him, "How long will you test the Infinite?"* Then *warn him that he has chosen the wrong path.*

All right. Ela held the glowing branch before the startled nobleman. "Lord Ruestock. How long will you test the Infinite? He warns that you have chosen the wrong path."

He moistened his lips and stepped back, clearly unnerved. Yet, as ever, he sneered. And quibbled. "I . . . take it that this is a prophetic utterance, Lady Aeyrievale? A meaning quite apart from the garden path on which we now stand?"

"Yes." Spirals of light expanded from the branch like unfurling vines, flowing over her, reaching for Ruestock.

The nobleman's eyes widened. He bowed, then swiftly walked from the garden. What was the scoundrel planning? Infinite? I'm curious . . . how many times will You warn him?

As many as I please. He sent her a stern mental nudge, making her turn again.

Oh. Ela hid a wince. Everyone—servants, courtiers, king, and queen—stared at her and Kien, all unmoving, as if waiting for some unavoidable disaster.

Wonderful. Her formal introduction to court, and lovely sapphires or not, she was already an object of fear.

Kien adjusted his sword, then offered Ela his hand. "Prophet, shall we greet the king and his queen?" As they walked and smiled soothingly at the nervous courtiers, he asked, "What is Ruestock plotting?"

"Everything possible, I'm sure."

"Is he Atean?"

"Yes, but for himself more than his goddess. He's a meddler, schemer, and instigator." And lecherous. But she couldn't mention this to Kien. He'd fillet the man and end up in prison.

They approached the king and queen and bowed. The instant they straightened, Akabe's formality lapsed into a warm grin, almost as charming as Kien's. "Lord Aeyrievale. Lady Aeyrievale. Welcome."

As Ela smiled, Kien said, "Majesty, thank you."

Akabe nodded, some of his pleasure fading. "I'd say we've been bored without you, but, unfortunately, that wouldn't be true. Lady Aeyrievale, you haven't met the queen." He looked down at the slender silent young woman standing beside him. "Caitria, this is Lady Aeyrievale. Parne's prophet."

Her gaze fixated on the still-glowing branch, Queen Caitria nodded and uttered one word. "Welcome."

"Thank you, Majesty." Ela shifted the branch away and smiled, trying to look harmless. Infinite, please, let the queen not faint. She'd be blamed, and—considering what they were about to face—she needed to earn the queen's trust.

Infinite? A few hints? Please?

As the king and Kien turned away, talking with the other lords, the queen seemed to compose herself. "Lady Aeyrievale, these are my . . . companions, Lady Faine, Lady Trillcliff, and Lady Piton. Will you join us?"

"Gladly." Or rather as glad as she could be. "Thank you." A tremor of premonition slid over Ela's skin. The young queen's future terror presented itself now, making Ela's heart race so violently that she had to take deep, calming breaths. Forget the ashes and death! Closing her thoughts to the vision, Ela focused on the queen, who was talking, her lovely face as wary as her voice.

"We saw you speaking to Lord Ruestock. What did you say to each other?"

"Lord Ruestock offered his compliments and I offered him guidance from the Infinite." Noticing the haughty silver-haired Lady Faine's suddenly avid expression, Ela added, "Ruestock was advised to reconsider certain choices he's made."

Lady Trillcliff aimed a prompting glance at the queen. "Introspection is always useful for self-improvement. It's advice we might all accept."

The queen looked away, her slim jaw visibly tensed. Obviously this wasn't the first none-too-subtle hint she'd caught from Lady Trillcliff. Worse, Lady Faine and Lady Piton both nodded, approving their friend's indirect criticism of the queen. As if stuffy lectures would delight anyone!

Be calm, Ela warned herself. Swatting thoughtless noblewomen wouldn't help this situation, and no doubt the Infinite wouldn't approve. Didn't the queen have any attendants her own age?

When Lady Faine cleared her throat to speak, the queen turned to Ela in obvious desperation. "Lady Aeyrievale, will you walk with me to those steps? There's a marvelous view of the ocean."

"Yes, Majesty. Thank you. I love the ocean."

"So do I." Keeping herself warily away from the branch, the queen quickened her pace as they left the other ladies. When they were a safe distance apart from everyone, the queen burst out, "One more 'you need to improve' remark and I'll scream!"

"Understandable, lady."

"Furthermore, I hate Lord Ruestock! I wish the king would send him from court."

Ela shuddered, unable to hide her disgust. "I agree. He's . . . overly flirtatious!"

"With you too?" The queen stared as if contemplating a freak. "But you're a . . . a prophet."

Definite royal mistrust here. And did she sense . . . loneliness?

Hmm. Ela kept her tone pleasant. "Lord Ruestock seems unable to control his, er, compliments to women, no matter who they are—prophet or not."

Caitria reddened and looked away. "Lord Ruestock is one of my second cousins, and he hunts with my lord-father. Once, about five years ago—I was thirteen—Ruestock told me I was so pretty he ought to marry me and offer me to the goddess. And the look he gave me . . . I was terrified. But my lord-father overheard."

Ela halted, sickened. "Obviously your father protected you."

"If locking me away from everyone might be called protection." She began to walk again, leading Ela up to a curving stone balustrade. A breeze swept up from the ocean far below, loosening light brown tendrils from her softly pinned hair. "Yet it's not as if Father cared enough to speak to me beyond pronouncing punishments. Worse," she continued, bitterness edging her voice, "he still hunts with Ruestock."

"I'm sorry." Ela sighed, thinking of her own father. Dan Roeh was a stern parent, but he often joked with Ela. And he'd always cherished Ela and her little sister, Tzana. Remembering her fragile baby sister and Dan's grief at her death before Parne's siege, Ela fought a stab of sorrow. She mustn't burst into tears now. How sad that the queen never felt as loved by her own father.

Leaning on the balustrade, the queen hesitated. "Forgive me. I've said too much. But I'm half-wild after being lectured all morning. I trust you'll not breathe a word of our conversation."

"As I live, Majesty, I'll tell no one."

Caitria studied Ela now, seeming perplexed.

To gain royal insights, Ela dared her. "Say what you're thinking."

The queen paled. At last, evidently fearing Ela already knew, she said, "I think you're not . . . tall enough. Or frightful enough. For a prophet."

A laugh escaped before Ela could stifle it. Well, she'd asked. "I'm proof that the Infinite considers the heart rather than outward appearances. You expected someone more dignified. More—"

Hypocritical, pretentious, condemning, and small-minded.

Infinite! Bracing herself, Ela repeated, "Hypocritical, pretentious, condemning, and small-minded."

Caitria gasped. "I didn't say so!"

"No. But your Creator hears your thoughts concerning me and the other ladies." As the queen blinked, seeming stunned, Ela added, "I don't blame you. Thoughts can be impossible to control. And mortals *are* often hypocritical, pretentious, condemning, and small-minded, no matter what they believe."

"True." Queen Caitria tensed both hands on the balustrade now, as if she longed to leap over it and escape. "While we're being so honest, I've no choice but to speak with you. My lord-husband all but commanded it." She almost smiled at Ela. Almost. "At least for now I no longer think you hate me, or that you'll strike me dead. But . . . you're worrisome. Do you know all my thoughts?"

"Rest assured, Majesty, most of your thoughts remain known only to you and to the Infinite. I don't see or hear everything." Noting Caitria's relief, Ela continued. "Soon, however, you'll make your own choices concerning your life and your soul. Because other lives will be affected by your choices, you must be careful."

"Yes, Prophet." Caitria sounded dry-voiced now. Definitely one who'd heard too many lectures. "I can guess what those choices might be. You sound as if—" She stopped, interrupted by a sleek gray dog, which trotted up and daintily licked her hands. Instantly, the queen crooned, "Issa! Dear thing! Did Naynee feed you? Did she?"

As the queen smoothed her dog's shining coat, Ela looked around.

Kien, talking with Akabe, caught Ela's glance and grinned, luring her thoughts toward him. Gorgeous man! How dare he distract her?

✦ ✦ ✦

Akabe turned and saw what—or rather who—had distracted Kien mid-sentence. He should have known. And he understood. If Caitria had cast him such a loving smile, Akabe would have abandoned this impromptu conference altogether. But Caitria petted Issa, ignoring everyone else. Therefore . . .

Akabe backhanded Kien's shoulder. "Stop flirting with your wife and pay attention!"

Kien shot him a mock-threatening look. "I am your servant, sir."

A headstrong and unexpected servant, Akabe agreed silently. But most welcome.

Faine coughed, gaining Akabe's attention. "Are we agreed on our plan, sirs?"

Trillcliff and Piton nodded. Kien asked, "When?"

Relieved to have the decision made, Akabe said, "Day after tomorrow. Weapons, silver, plain clothes, and not much gear. We want to remain inconspicuous and travel swiftly. Is everything arranged for the decoy royal household?"

Piton twitched as if overcome by nerves. "It is, sir. We'll set out before dawn and see you safely away. And to verify . . ." A shamed expression crossed Piton's lined face. "Aythan Garric?"

Father. Just hearing his name reopened a gash in Akabe's soul. Was he ready to face this? Was Caitria? What if his plan failed? Would she die? Would the temple be lost to Siphra?

Infinite . . . be with us, please. Bless us with Your presence. Be with my friends. He nodded at Faine, Trillcliff, and Piton. "Yes. Aythan Garric. Only you three know where to locate me. Guard yourselves!"

If he died, no doubt his advisors would soon follow him in death.

Faine shifted from foot to foot, clearly uncomfortable. "Our goal, sir, is to ensure that you survive and your enemies are captured. During the previous reign, fear made cowards of too many of the Infinite's faithful. We will not allow ourselves to be overcome by terrors now."

A little boy's happy shout made Akabe turn. Barth ran past, calling again, "Prophet!" Apparently released from his afternoon lessons, he seemed oblivious to his duties, favoring his pretty prophet-teacher more than his king. The boy probably wanted to show her his new teeth.

As the little page hugged Ela, kissed her bejeweled hand, and chattered like a well-trained bird, Kien pretended offense. Particularly when Ela laughed and knelt, hugging and kissing the boy in return. "He's trying to steal my wife! Excuse me, sirs."

"Aeyrievale!" Akabe lifted a hand. "Bring Barth to me, please. I need him to fetch Lord Ruestock." Unless Siphra's lady-prophet had frightened the irksome nobleman beyond use.

What better use of a meddling Atean lord than to send him throughout the court hooked with bait? To snag the assassins who longed to spill Akabe and Caitria's blood and halt work on the temple.

Would Ruestock carry a casual comment to Akabe's enemies to assist Atean plots?

If so, then Ruestock would be brought to justice. However . . . what if Caitria's brothers or her father were involved? Or worse, Caitria herself?

No. Akabe gritted his teeth, rejecting the possibility of losing Caitria. Or of sending more Thaenfalls to their deaths.

His plan must not fail.

Bringing his thoughts to the present, Akabe smiled at his counselors, and at Barth's father, who approached, polished and so perfectly clothed that Akabe felt like an interloper. Siymont bowed. "Majesty, I—"

Siymont's greeting was drowned by a chorus of shrieks and laughter from the queen and her ladies, and howls from young Barth—to the courtly lord's obvious, grimacing dismay.

✦ ✦ ✦

"Kien!" Ela gasped, then laughed as her husband kissed her, snagged Barth, turned him upside down and—bellowing pretend threats—carried the screeching boy across the garden to Akabe and his lords.

"Hmph!" Lady Trillcliff sniffed. "What an uproar. Lord Aeyrievale's certainly returned to court." She smiled at Ela, but sent her an admonishing look. Was this a silent command for dignity? An unspoken request for Ela to control her husband? As if she could!

A cautioning mental nudge from her Creator made Ela smile. She linked arms with the startled noblewoman, guiding her away from the others. "Lady, perhaps one day you'll succeed in taming the Aeyrievales. Now, tell me—and I say this with complete respect—do you remember being eighteen?"

"I do, I assure you." She lifted her chin, decidedly a lady who remembered everything.

"Good! Tell me, Lady Trillcliff, do you recall your thoughts when elderly acquaintances or relatives did nothing but scold and lecture you continually, without befriending you?"

The elegant woman opened her mouth as if to vow she'd never needed scolding or lecturing as a young lady. But an uneasy look flicked over her proud face. "You're referring to someone in our company? Perhaps to the . . . ?" She tilted her head slightly toward the queen.

"You know I am." The branch shimmered in Ela's hand as she voiced a gentle warning. "Only the Infinite is her true judge. Meanwhile, endless unpleasant lectures will make her Atean background more appealing than becoming one of the Infinite's seemingly ever-sour faithful. Shouldn't we share His joy and His undeserved love for us with others, in addition to His wisdom for our lives?"

Lady Trillcliff's expression puckered in dismay. "We *have* been suspicious and untrusting."

"Caution is good, my lady. But kindness is better. Will you warn the other ladies?"

"I will." She looked down at Ela now, thoughtful. "How can you be just nineteen?"

"The truth is, I usually feel much younger. About toddler-tantrum age. However, the Infinite offers the wisdom and maturity I lack." She smiled, compelling her elder to reciprocate. "Lady, do you suppose we could persuade the queen to walk with us on the beach?" Before the lady could protest, Ela approached the queen and offered obeisance, begging, "Majesty, may we have your permission to leave our sandals here and walk down to the water?"

As Caitria hesitated, Ela persisted, "We could! The king and our lords are all busy. But if they care—well, they'll simply have to chase after us."

A lovely smile crossed the young queen's face. "You may. But only if I'm first." She rested one jewel-sandaled foot against the balustrade and untied it. Her ladies stared, then followed her lead with rusty, unsure movements. Ela swiftly copied the queen, then they all descended the stairs, barefooted, to the beach below.

Just as Ela was digging her toes into the sun-warmed sand, the men spied them from the terrace above and shouted, clearly indignant at not being informed of their wives' plans.

Even Lady Trillcliff laughed, and Lady Faine smirked at Lord Faine's gawping expression. "*Now* he pays attention! Ha! Just once, he can forget his politics!"

Ignoring them all, Queen Caitria swept up her fluttering robes and ran toward the sparkling waves with Issa frolicking and barking at her heels.

Ela followed her, laughing at Kien's indignant yells. Let him chase her.

✦ ✦ ✦

Caitria halted in the sand, drawing in deep breaths of the damp, salty air. If only she could cross this ocean and escape! A royal runaway. Perhaps stealing Akabe for company. They'd be nobodies, no longer fearing assassins, or—in her case—enduring snippy little lectures from prim-mouthed etiquette fiends. Not to mention mind-reading prophets who scared her to bits. Caitria slid a glance at Lady Aeyrievale, so delicate and pretty and harmless-looking as she splashed at waves.

Who had Akabe inflicted upon her now? Was he *this* frustrated that she wouldn't discuss her beliefs with him? In silent protest, she kicked a frothy wave.

I love you, but leave me out of your religion!

✦ ✦ ✦

In the predawn dimness of his lamp-lit bedchamber, Akabe coaxed his wife from bed and handed her leggings and a full tunic. Dressing sluggishly, she asked, "Where are we going?"

"We're running away." To save their marriage. To save her. And, he prayed, Siphra's temple. Dropping a thick gray cloak over Caitria's head, Akabe taunted softly, "Don't tell me you don't want to escape! Not after seeing you run to the beach yesterday and the day before. Lovely sight, that."

Instantly, Caitria stood and yanked the cloak around her shoulders. "Where are my boots?"

✦ 19 ✦

In the secluded royal courtyard, beneath the starry remains of the night sky, Akabe spied a shadowed form that could only be Lord Faine. Beyond Faine six horses waited, loaded with supplies, attended by three silent cloaked figures. Immediately, Akabe identified Ela's delicate hood-draped form and the branch in her grasp. Kien loomed beside her, one hand unmistakably readied to draw his sword, while his shifting stance betrayed eagerness to leave. Just behind them, Akabe's military surgeon, Riddig Tyne, glanced about, tense and equally ready to use his sword or bow and arrows against any threat.

Caitria lagged now, obviously unnerved by the presence of others. But if Akabe had warned her that they'd be accompanied on their journey, would she have followed him without resistance? Despite visiting with Ela again at the beach yesterday, Caitria still didn't trust the prophet. Akabe hadn't missed his wife's suspicious glances and the usual stubborn silences. She clasped his hand and whispered, "My lord, what about Naynee and Issa?"

Akabe kissed his wife's fingers and covered her hair with her cloak's hood. "Naynee and Issa will be cared for while we're gone. I've commanded Faine to take charge of their well-being. Don't be afraid. You'll see them soon." If his plan succeeded.

Faine bowed. "All's ready, my lord. We'll see you away. Surely within three days we ought to have some resolution with the Ateans after baiting Ruestock and the one other lord."

His council had withheld information? Akabe scowled. "Another lord? Who?"

"Forgive me, sir, but for your sake I'll tell you only if our suspicions are confirmed—you'll receive our message within a week, I'm sure. We must set off before sunrise. I'll await you with the others in the main courtyard."

Akabe suppressed his frustration. "Thank you, my lord. Above all, be certain the temple is manned by additional guards—protect the workers and priests!"

"Indeed, sir!"

As Faine hurried off, Akabe assisted Caitria onto her horse, then nodded to Riddig. The burly man answered with a wordless salute, then rode ahead, alert and mistrustful enough to please even Fightmaster Lorteus.

Glancing over his shoulder, Akabe watched Caitria draw her horse just behind his as they rode through the gate to the main courtyard. Kien and Ela followed her on their own designated horses, both watchful. Akabe almost smiled at their cloaked forms. Ela had slipped the branch within their gear, mostly concealing it. Was any king so unconventionally guarded?

No one spoke as Akabe and his party joined the courtiers and servants, who were arranged in a decoy royal procession of covered chariots and armed horsemen. They left through the palace's stone-arched woven metal gates. In perfect silence, the procession threaded through Munra's broad pale streets. Only the muffled thuds of horses' hooves, the creaks of leather tack, and occasional metallic clinks of weapons and gear disturbed the predawn calm.

The few citizens to be seen hastily stepped toward the buildings and watched the shadowed royal procession pass. Munra's night guards eyed them from their posts near the city's outer limits. Normally, Akabe would have greeted them. Now, however, he lowered his head, shielding his face beneath his cloak's hood.

At last, as the first rays of dawn fell over a crossroad in open countryside, Akabe leaned over and snatched the lead reins on Caitria's horse. Her eyes widened with alarm and indignation. But she allowed him to proceed in silence.

Good. Akabe nodded farewell to his courtiers, then led Caitria off to the south with the Aeyrievales, Riddig, several packhorses, and twenty plain-clothed guards. Despite his concerns, Akabe's spirit lifted as their horses trotted along the muddied road. He'd not experienced such freedom since becoming king. Grinning, he offered Caitria her horse's reins. "Forgive me, lady. I didn't want to lose you."

She answered with an anxious smile. "Sir, where are we going?"

"A distant hiding place. Regrettably, we'll be uncomfortable because we're traveling disguised and avoiding towns. I apologize in advance."

Caitria shrugged, focusing on her horse's dark mane. But a rueful grimace worked at her lovely mouth. Was she regretting coming with him? Perhaps upset by his lack of trust? Or wishing she'd found some way to warn her family? So be it.

Surely during their time away, he and Caitria could settle into their marriage. Indeed, they must. Caitria offered his only hope for a true family, *if* they learned to trust each other.

Contemplating trust, Akabe scowled. Evidently Faine and the royal council had hidden certain matters from him. Had another lord been pinpointed and baited as an Atean? Akabe considered several, disliking the potential of each man's betrayal. Ruestock certainly—

An approaching rumble from the nearby eastern woods, a quivering of the road, and his horse's sudden agitation caught Akabe's attention.

His guards closed in protectively. Riddig Tyne half-drew his sword and turned, his bristly white hair showing beneath the edge of his dark hood. "Sir!"

Akabe heard Caitria gasp, and he turned just as her nervous

mare shied, skittering to the right. But Caitria held her seat. To Caitria's left, Ela crooned and soothed both their horses.

Kien, however, began to yell.

✦ ✦ ✦

"Scythe!" Kien bellowed, infuriated, recognizing his destroyer's ground-shaking pace emanating from the woods to the east. "Walk! Do you hear me? *Walk!*"

Sure enough, the tremors jarring the road eased. Scythe walked from among the trees to the east, huffing, tossing his gleaming dark head. How had the beast escaped his handlers and the stone and iron-barred stable area? Kien ground his teeth together, aggravated. So much for incognito. He hoped Scythe's handlers were still alive.

As the horses settled, Ela called to Kien, her expression a pretty mix of frustration and wry humor. "We forgot to command Pet to 'stay.'"

Evidently. And Scythe's unbridled path-carving through the Siphran countryside had likely diminished the king's chances of hiding himself and the queen until their potential assassins were snared. By his grim expression, Akabe feared the same. How could they remedy the situation?

His huffing intensifying, Scythe thudded toward Ela and Kien, adding a resentful you-forgot-me glare that blamed them both. The smaller horses sidestepped, ears flattening. Kien snapped a look at his destroyer. "Stop!"

The monster horse grumbled, but halted at the edge of the muddied road. As if disdainful of his smaller equine companions, he curled his lips back from his huge teeth.

Akabe exhaled. "I suppose something had to go wrong. Well-enough. Scythe might be useful."

Relieved and mortified—an experience he didn't appreciate—Kien dismounted from his small, trembling horse. "Majesty, forgive me. I thought he was secured. We cannot cover his tracks to this point, but what about from here to our destination?"

"Good question." The king surveyed the surrounding land. "Beyond those trees at the next turn is the Inaren River." He turned and frowned at Scythe. "Is that beast afraid of water?"

Obviously irked by the king's doubtful tone, Scythe snorted and stomped one mighty hoof. The lesser horses went skittish. Kien lunged for his smaller beast's reins. "Halt!" To the king, he said, "No, sir, he's not afraid of water."

"Perfect. You can cover his tracks somewhat by walking him in the river awhile. And . . ." Akabe mused, "we should shelter early and travel by dark, beginning tonight. There's simply no hiding that beast."

Scythe grumbled once more, but Akabe laughed. "Destroyer! Calm yourself. We're friends, remember? I've fed you before. You know I'm right!"

Kien offered Ela his smaller horse's reins. She responded with a tender look, as if she wanted to kiss him. If only she could. Kien sighed. "I'll trade places with Riddig and ride ahead to calm the others." He approached the gleaming, barebacked destroyer. "No war collar? Fine. Kneel so I can climb you!" Kien mustered a cold-eyed stare. "And try to be less conspicuous!"

✦ ✦ ✦

As they approached the river, unease slid over Ela, warning her with a chill. On the broad road ahead, four bronzed horsemen were riding past Kien toward her. All four horsemen were muddied and travel-worn, but acutely attentive to the destroyer. And to her. Recognizing the fourth man, Ela muted a gasp. The soldier who'd spied on her the morning of her wedding!

She couldn't suppress this dread. Not with each of those men staring her in the eyes as if they found it difficult to ride past her without saying a word. When the horsemen had passed her, Ela prayed, summoning courage. Infinite? Have all four of those men seen me before?

Yes.

Memories broke apart in Ela's thoughts, reassembling

themselves like a puzzle shifted to reveal a fresh and horrifying viewpoint. Parne, seen by Bel-Tygeon, king of Belaal, and his defeated army. . . . Months ago, she'd stood on Parne's now-broken walls, seen by these same soldiers while warning them of their impending defeat.

Infinite? Do they seek revenge?

Yes.

What must I do?

Silence answered. Why? Perhaps she didn't want to know. And she didn't want to face those men. Good thing that she and the others would soon be hidden in the forest. Gathering her wits, Ela drew a calming breath and looked around.

The queen rode beside her now, which was odd, considering her mistrust of Ela. Yet, for all her caution, Caitria watched Ela as if concerned. "Lady, are you ill?"

"No." Fearing the queen's worry might halt their progress, Ela straightened and smiled. "But thank you, lady. We'll be camping early, so even if I'm ill, it wouldn't matter."

After a wary glance at her husband, Caitria leaned toward Ela and whispered, "Prophet, do you know where we're going?"

Not exactly. "South, lady. I know we're riding south. Beyond that, we ought to pester the king for details."

Her majesty appeared miffed. "Some prophet you are!"

🟆 🟆 🟆

Sheltered amid ferns and trees beside a rocky, rushing stream south of the Inaren River, Kien swiped his destroyer's glossy coat with a rag. "If I'd had the proper tools, this would have been easier. If you'd stayed *clean* instead of carving canyons through Siphra, this would have been easier. Above all, if you'd stayed in Munra, this would have been easier. But you didn't—*did* you?"

Crunching on nearby fronds, Scythe closed his eyes, ignoring Kien's rant. Finished with the grooming, Kien swatted the beast with the rag. "Because I didn't command you to stay, we've caused a multitude of difficulties for the king!"

Iّll stop.

"Kien." Ela stepped from one smooth gray rock to another, making her way toward him along the riverbank. "Evening meal is ready—such as it is."

"Late midday meal is more like it," Kien grumbled. He gave Scythe's shimmering neck another swipe, though fonder now. "It's your fault that we're eating so early! But do you care?"

Clearly unrepentant, Scythe leaned toward Ela and greeted her with a blissful sigh into her hair. She hugged the beast, so small beside the massive horse that Kien melted. He swept Ela into a hug, then lost himself in the softness of a kiss. Until Scythe whooshed a soggy breath down Kien's hair and neck. "Ugh!"

"Food," Ela reminded Kien. She rapped her knuckles against his boiled-leather vest, concealed for his protection. "Their majesties are waiting."

"They need not have waited." Trusting Scythe to follow them, Kien slid an arm around his wife's waist and hiked with her through the trees beyond the stream. What would his life be like without Ela? Kien frowned at the thought. Doubtless, he'd still be moping over his exile from the Tracelands and fretting over his family's despair at their lack of legal progress on his behalf.

Guiding Ela up a rocky, mossy incline, Kien composed the first line of his next letter to East Guard. *Dear Father and Mother, while no news would please me more than word from you that my sentence has been reversed, please do not fear for my comfort.* Unless discomfort included this evening as he slept in a forest . . .

On level ground now, with Scythe lumbering behind them, Ela linked her arm in Kien's. "You've become so serious, my lord."

"I'm thinking of my family. I miss them. Without you, I'd have gone half-mad these past two months, trying to devise a way to conquer the Tracelands' legal system."

Sobering, she hugged his arm. "Remember, whatever happens, the Infinite is good."

"Now you're the serious one."

"We've much to consider and pray over."

"True. Such as crossing half of Siphra unseen, despite a certain monster warhorse."

"I'd say we both failed by not telling him to stay in Munra."

They entered a sheltered clearing, passed the guards' small encampment, and headed for the king and queen. Riddig sat on a thick gray blanket eyeing the untouched food—dried meat, tiny red berries, and flat rounds of bread Ela had packed the night before. After they'd prayed, Kien said, "You didn't need to wait for us, Majesties."

Akabe grinned. "I prefer to divide everything fairly." He took a bit of leathery meat, then nudged Caitria. "Have you tried the berries, lady?"

Not looking at the king, Caitria shook her head. "Berries give me rashes, my lord."

Rashes? Kien studied the queen obliquely. Was she pouting? Could she be trusted?

Clearly reluctant, Akabe finally took Caitria at her word and divided the berries among himself, Kien, Ela, and Riddig. "When we finish, we ought to be sure the horses are tended and tethered, then seek rest. At dusk, we'll share the last of the bread, then be on our way."

Kien nodded, as did Ela and Riddig. But the queen's silence weighed over the remainder of the meal like a sodden cloak, and the shadowed woods around them seemed more oppressive than sheltering. Kien finished his berries, trying to deny his growing concerns over this little jaunt through Siphra.

✦ ✦ ✦

In the fading daylight, Ela tied her waterskin onto her little dun horse. The creature's muscles quivered beneath her hands. Poor thing probably recognized Pet's scent on her clothes. She soothed the dainty gray-brown horse and its tethered comrades. "You have no reason to fear Pet." Unless the dun and its comrades ate his food.

Best to keep the horses separated.

She glanced at the far side of the small clearing, watching Pet nose a shrub, clearly determined to prune the helpless plant to the ground before their departure. Adjacent to the massive black warhorse, Akabe was talking with Riddig and their guards. Meanwhile, Caitria waited near the king, much too wary for an eighteen-year-old, queen or not.

Where was Kien? She'd thought he was with Pet. Hmm. Focused on the last buckle, Ela heard the rustle of footsteps behind her, and she smiled. "*There* you are, sir. I'm almost ready."

A choking wave of aged sweat warned Ela that the footsteps weren't Kien's—just as a big, leather-mitted hand clamped tight over her mouth. Was she being stolen? No! Wait!

Ela kicked, clawed, and tried to scream as her abductor carried her into the dusk-darkened trees. Infinite!

✦ 20 ✦

Finished lashing his gear onto Scythe, Kien gave the monster-horse a nudge. "Kneel."

Still chomping on a mouthful of leaves, Scythe grunted and kneeled, huffing, as if urging Kien to hurry. Kien bit down a grin. "What right have you to complain? If you don't like kneeling, then you should have planned ahead and brought your war collar! Anyway, I don't *need* to ride you—I do have another horse." Though much smaller and nowhere near as interesting.

The destroyer's dark ears suddenly perked in the deepening twilight, and a quake ran through his massive body. Jolted, Kien grabbed the beast's reins and leaned forward, aligning himself with Scythe's huge neck and shoulders. "What?"

The destroyer lunged upright and took off at a full gallop toward the opposite side of the clearing where Ela was tending her little horse.

Where Ela was *not* tending her little horse.

Ela! If Scythe had turned wild and Ela was gone, then—!

Kien snarled. Whatever creature threatened Ela . . . *Dead!*

The lesser horses squealed and dashed aside just before Scythe bolted past them toward the woods. In the trees, amid the shadows and rustling leaves, the destroyer slowed just enough for Kien to draw his Azurnite sword, its metal shimmering an intense blue even in this dim light.

Ahead in the murky trees, ferocious thrashings and muttered threats drew Kien's attention—and Scythe's. The monster-warhorse charged toward the confusion and bit down on one of four shadows milling between the trees. A man's agonized scream cut through the twilight. Scythe flung the offender against a tree, then charged the others.

A second shadowed form separated itself from the others and rushed toward Kien. Seeing the muted metal gleam of a sword, Kien braced himself, swung the Azurnite blade in a wide downward arc, and felt it sink into yielding mortal flesh.

His target fell, silent, writhing on the carpet of leaves until Scythe stomped him while lunging for a third shadow. The third man roared in pain. Scythe crushed him into a tree, let him fall, then finished him with a tremendous backward kick.

Judging by distant huffs and the hoofbeats of horses, a fourth man was fleeing on horseback. Scythe turned to follow him. Kien loosened his reins. "Did he take Ela?"

The destroyer halted. Breathing hard, he shook his head and mane now, as if coming to his monster-senses. Kien repeated, "Did he take Ela?"

In answer, Scythe moved forward, bent, and nosed the ground to the right. Something thrashed and rustled amid a clump of ferns and last year's leaves. Kien slid his sword into its scabbard, then swung himself down, using the destroyer's neck and thick mane for support. On his feet now, he stepped into the shrubs and grabbed a squirming bundle of fabric.

Stifled screams and uncontrolled kicks greeted Kien's touch. Aha! One angry little prophet. Thank You, Infinite! He scooped her up. "Ela! Calm down. It's me."

She sagged in Kien's arms. He felt her sides heaving as she took in rapid breaths. Her head and arms were entangled in ropes and heavy, reeking cloth, but Kien hugged her. "Let's get you into the clearing, and I'll unwind you."

Ela kicked the air in obvious frustration. Kien grinned. "Stop, or I might drop you."

Whimpering, she stilled—flinching only when Scythe nuzzled her.

As Kien carried his wife toward the clearing, he shifted her several times. The movements didn't seem to cause her pain. Evidently her abductors hadn't hurt her.

Infinite, bless You!

Akabe waited in the clearing with Riddig and the guards, their swords readied—all surrounding the queen, who held her hands over her mouth as if fighting screams. Brushing aside his fretful guards, Akabe hurried toward Kien. "What happened?"

"Four fools believed they could steal my wife and survive." Kien knelt and placed Ela in the grass, warning, "Ela, hold still while I cut these ropes."

She obeyed, but he heard her inhale deeply as he lifted the malodorous fabric away from her face. A strip of cloth covered her mouth. The instant Kien cut it away, Ela gasped. "Kidnappers always stink! Ugh!"

Akabe laughed, then coughed. "Forgive me, lady. Aeyrievale, did they escape?"

Kien helped Ela to sit up. "One escaped."

Ela clutched his shoulder as if desperate, and a wounded noise lifted in her throat. "The others are dead!"

"Yes." Kien pulled her close. Ela hid her face against his neck, drooping, all her natural feistiness gone. As she wept, Kien murmured, "Ela, it's done. It cannot be changed. You're my wife—I couldn't allow them to steal you!"

Infinite? Was there another way? Could I have spared them?

No, the Infinite's voice whispered, interlaced with sorrow. *They chose their own paths.*

Exhaling miserably, Kien smoothed his wife's mussed hair.

Low-voiced, the queen asked, "Lady, are you hurt? Why are you crying?"

"They're in torment, and I c-can't help them!"

"Your abductors are in torment?" Caitria frowned. "What do you mean? They're dead."

Sniffling, Ela forced out sob-punctuated syllables. "Their souls . . . They are in . . . agony! I wish I could have stopped them!"

Kien compelled her to look him in the eyes. "Ela, it's nearly dark, and for the king's sake, we must leave now. Come ride with me on Scythe." Merely mentioning the destroyer's name drew a fretful equine nudge on Kien's neck. "You've made us both feel guilty."

He should have guessed that his little prophet would mourn for renegade souls.

✦ ✦ ✦

As they rode, using the narrowing stream as a path, Caitria shivered. Silvery moonlight glistened icily over the rushing current, adding to her chill. How unsettling . . . watching Ela crying over dead enemies' souls.

If the enemies had been her own and Akabe's, Caitria would have been relieved by their deaths. Unless, of course, the dead were from her own family. Did that make her coldhearted? Hopefully not.

And souls. Caitria grimaced. She'd never considered souls. Her childhood books and Naynee's stories—full of Atean poems and Siphran epics—all praised love and life as it was, promising only a vague "rest" beyond death, which she'd interpreted as . . . *nothing.*

But was there more? Might a part of her actually continue to exist beyond death?

Shivering again, Caitria watched her husband as he rode ahead. Though he'd expressed frustration at his Creator's silence, Akabe never questioned his Infinite's existence.

He protected us, Akabe had said after the attack on the temple.

Well, if she must be honest, Akabe certainly *seemed* protected, considering the fading scar on his cheek and all the previous failed assassination attempts.

Did the Infinite actually exist?

Caitria stifled the notion and snatched back a wisp of an impulse that reached for the awful, improbable Infinite.

Really, she was turning daft. Falling in love with Akabe, and now wondering if she might have a soul!

Yes, quite daft. Dangerous for a queen. Truly, because of her heritage and that dreadful temple land, she'd already brought enough chaos to Siphra. Akabe should set her aside.

She blinked at the thought, dashed aside tears, then forced herself to concentrate on the frothing, chilling stream to guide her.

✦ ✦ ✦

Her arms around Kien's solid, leather-protected waist, Ela listened as Scythe clomped and splashed in the rocky stream. Dear monster, he'd been so concerned for her. She sighed shakily, hoping her tears were finished.

Infinite . . . ? I hated feeling so helpless—for myself and for those men.

Am I not with you? As for those men, you could not make their choices for them.

Even as He scolded her, consolation slid over Ela like a second cloak, provoking remorse. She'd been in similar situations before, so why was she having such difficulty coping tonight? At least Kien, Pet, the king and queen, and their guards were safe. A blessing.

Infinite? Forgive me, please. I don't deserve Your loving-kindness.

Ela leaned against her husband once more, making a face at the unforgiving toughness of his boiled leather vest, wishing he didn't need to wear soldiers' gear. He patted her hands. Low-voiced, he asked, "Have you forgiven me for those men's deaths?"

"You've done nothing to require forgiving. I was upset, wishing I could have warned those men."

He smoothed her hand and turned slightly, his profile a dark, clean-cut outline in the moonlight. "Reasonable. But fair warning, my love: in similar situations, my reaction—and Scythe's—will be the same."

"I know. Thank you both for saving me."

Pet grunted and nipped at a low tree branch. They rode through the stream bed until it narrowed, providing less water and almost no protective screening. As they stopped to rest and fill their waterskins, the king said, "From here, we'll cut out to a paved road. We'll travel more quickly on less rocky ground."

Riddig spoke, bowing slightly to the king and Kien. "Sirs, with your permission, I'll lead again. The horses are now more settled in the destroyer's company." He hesitated, then addressed Kien. "My lord, I believe the four men who tried to abduct Lady Aeyrievale passed us on the road before we reached the river. The way they stared at her—I'm certain they'd seen her before."

Ela swallowed. Best to confess. "They recognized me. I knew they had. But I was sure we'd be well-hidden from them in the forest, so I didn't trouble anyone."

She heard Kien's exasperated sigh in the darkness, though she couldn't see his face. "Ela, I wish I'd known. One of them escaped! Why did they try to take you?"

"They were soldiers, defeated in Parne. They sought retribution."

Akabe spoke, uneasy now. "Defeated in Parne? Then those men weren't Siphran. Prophet, is this situation unique, or is Siphra overrun with foreign soldiers?"

"Unique, Majesty." How much information should she offer? She could not—must not—endanger the king's life for the sake of her own. To her relief, he asked no more questions.

But he sounded troubled as he guided Caitria toward the horses. "Let's be on our way. At dawn, we'll try to buy food at a market—without the destroyer. Then, I pray, we'll find a safe place to sleep."

✦ ✦ ✦

Disquiet sharpening all his senses in the moonlight, Akabe goaded his horse to follow Riddig's. Ela—Lady Aeyrievale—had been recognized and threatened despite their precautions. She might have died. And he wouldn't have forgiven himself. He should have brought more men. Though twenty should have been enough to discourage this attack. More than enough. Yet he'd been careless. Overconfident. Fool of a king! He must send a cipher by courier bird, requesting that Faine send more guards to their destination.

At dawn Akabe led his friends and his men across the bridge spanning the dark, sluggish River Darom. After hiding Scythe in the nearby woods—and silencing the chittering, singing birds with his presence—Akabe wrote his cipher. While he worked, Kien, Ela, and a handful of guards entered the nearby Rhimton market, bargained for food, then returned to the woods.

With the horses tended and the guards eating while they stood at watch, Ela unpacked her purchases from a rugged basket. She set out soft bread, fresh herbed cheese, grilled chicken, and pickled vegetables. With an apologetic glance at Caitria, she unsealed a plump little crock of spice-scented fruit preserves and placed it in the center of their picnic blanket. "Majesty, I was promised that no berries were used in this—it's all stone fruits. Peaches and the like. If you cannot eat this, I bought some honeycomb as well."

Busying himself with bread and cheese, Akabe sneaked a glance at his uncommunicative wife. If she turned her nose up at these offerings as she had at the berries Ela picked yesterday—

Caitria blushed and threw Ela a tired little smile. "Thank you, Lady Aeyrievale. I'm sorry to be such trouble."

Akabe almost dropped his bread. A bit of genuine warmth toward one of his friends—finally! Even Kien and Riddig seemed to relax at Caitria's meek apology. Perhaps his chary wife would finally begin to trust them. At least he might hope. Meanwhile, considering their perilous situation, he must establish a strict watch schedule and new rules.

When they'd finished off the food, Akabe swept all of his companions with a commanding look. "For the duration of this journey, no one will say the words *majesty* or *lord* or *lady*. Is that clear?"

Kien, Ela, and Akabe's men agreed. But Riddig tugged the shoulder strap of his leather baldric as if the command chafed. "Yes, M—sir. If we must."

"Furthermore, we'll establish three separate groups, with two watches per day while we're hiding—myself included. Thus, every third day, each of us can expect a bit more sleep."

As Ela nodded, Kien said, "We'll stand watch today."

Taking refuge within a tree-sheltered patch of ferns and leaves, Akabe unrolled Caitria's pallet and his own, then arranged his cloak and weapons. Caitria touched his arm, then hid her face within his cloak. Caught by surprise, Akabe held his wife. Was she in a panic?

Shivering in his embrace, Caitria whispered, "Are we running from more assassins?"

"Hiding." He could tell her that much, at least. Akabe paused, recognizing his own mistrust. Hypocrite! How could he expect her to talk with him honestly when he harbored his own secrets—among other things, his suspicion of her and the Thaenfalls? Awash in guilt, he kissed her tender cheek. "Cait . . . Cait! Don't be afraid! Whatever our differences, you've been tossed into this situation through no fault of your own—and you've persevered wonderfully, my brave queen—so endure me awhile longer. Believe me, I'll protect you with my life!"

Caitria huddled against him, clearly fighting sobs.

So much for talk. Akabe sighed, smoothing Caitria's soft hair and holding her tight. Sweet, courageous wife! Here was the truth—and his fear: Despite their secrecy, despite his guards, they'd already been followed and attacked, proving he'd placed his friends and his wife at risk. Had he and his counselors miscalculated? Fatally?

If so, he'd be killed before reinforcements arrived—leaving Cait vulnerable. And with his death, the Infinite's temple might never be restored to Siphra.

Sickened, Akabe bent, kissed Caitria's hair, and prayed with more ferocity than he had in months. Infinite? Protect us. Save Your temple. And Caitria. Let her turn to You!

Let her survive!

✦ ✦ ✦

Cait? He'd called her "Cait"?

Choking down fresh sniffles, resting her head against Akabe's shoulder, Caitria tested the name in her thoughts. Cait. Her family had only ever shortened her name to Tria. But she'd never liked Tria.

"Cait" sounded so normal. So *accepted* and cherished. Particularly when pronounced by her husband. Was Akabe beginning to love her? Did she dare hope?

She drew back slightly and peeked up at his handsome face to see . . . anguish. He masked the emotion instantly with an enchanting, heartening smile. But that brief glimpse was enough.

Caitria looked away. If her husband was beginning to love her, it was too late.

With one unguarded glance, he'd told her the worst—her own fears.

He believed they would die.

✦ ✦ ✦

Unable to quell his worries and aware of the others watching them, Akabe faced Ela in the forest's deepening evening shadows. "Prophet, surely you know what I'm about to ask."

"You seek the Infinite's will." She closed her eyes and averted her face, as if praying.

Ela recoiled in apparent shock, and a sickening drop in Akabe's gut told him the truth. His Creator was somehow displeased. Ela opened her eyes, and Akabe saw one of the sights he'd prayed to never see: a prophet aiming a warning at *him*. "Sir . . . you have hated His silence, yet this is the first time you've truly sought His will concerning your recent decisions regarding this journey, and—" she faltered—"Siphra's Temple."

Silence pressed in around them, building like a force. A wall.

The Infinite's Holy House? Akabe flinched, forcing himself to meet Ela of Parne's gaze. "How could it be wrong of me to rebuild His temple?"

A tear slid down her cheek. "Rebuilding the Temple was your will, for your name, not His. The time was your choosing, not His. I blame myself, too. For simply accepting—"

"For accepting my decision," Akabe finished. Infinite? What have I done?

Aware of the darkening sky above and their need to continue the journey, he asked, "Am I now His enemy? Has He no word for me?"

Ela covered her face with her hands, swaying. Akabe waited, afraid to breathe, aware of Kien and Caitria both drawing near, both alarmed. Ela lowered her hands, trembling visibly as she looked up at him now. "The Infinite loves you as ever, of course. You are His beloved child, but . . ." She looked around. "Here we are now, according to your plan, with our enemies approaching . . . plotting our failure. We must pray and walk this path together."

A path he had decided for them.

Too horrified to speak, Akabe allowed her to turn away first, as he begged in silence: Infinite, forgive me! Show us Your mercy. . . .

✦ ✦ ✦

Akabe watched five bedraggled travelers ride past them on the dirt road, their expressions disinterested in everything but the destroyer. Understandable. He'd deliberately extended this night's journey past dawn, into the trees and winding valleys of the DaromKhor Hills, guardians of Siphra's border with Belaal and stoic witnesses to his past—to this place, which was the start of his life's journey. And perhaps its finish. Each bend in the road revived a memory. Provoked fresh pain. And sharpened his guilt over leaving these hills eleven years ago. Infinite? Was I wrong to return? Will You not protect us?

R. J. LARSON

Scanning toward the left, he saw the road. Overgrown now, nearly hidden amid the trees, vines, and fallen evergreen limbs. Akabe called over his shoulder, "Everyone, remain close."

Caitria, Ela, Riddig, and Kien nodded, staring about as the horses picked their way through a litter of crackling twigs, leaves, and shrubs rooted in the road. Did his comrades realize their journey ended at the crest of this overgrown path? But what had he done? Akabe tensed. Infinite? I am not prepared to confront this place! All the more, knowing I've failed You. . . .

Beyond the final turn, he saw the hill's crest—bare-rocked as it had always been—encircled by a vine-covered wall. Crowned by the bleak, lifeless stone tower.

Verging on ruins, as was he, Siphra's vainglorious king.

❖ 21 ❖

This was their destination? Kien stared at the neglected walls. The stone tower's shutterless windows opened to the landscape, blank as dead, staring eyes. And the tower's uppermost crenellations looked half broken as if someone—most likely many someones—had tried to dismantle the structure and finally abandoned the task.

A desolate wreck of a fortress. Kien shuddered. He should have expected ruins. Akabe never spoke of his kindred. But why speak? This skeleton-fortress gave eloquent testimony of the devastation Akabe—and, most likely, his family—had suffered.

Summoning all the reverence required of one approaching a personally sacred site, Kien goaded Scythe after the king, following the last turns of the overgrown winding pathway. Even the destroyer seemed affected by the air of gloom permeating this place, eating only a few snatches of leaves along the narrowed road.

Without explanation, Akabe rode through the gateway, the left half of its huge metal-studded wood gate sagging open as if surrendered to despair. Inside the heavy, curtain-like stone wall and sweeping central yard reflected disaster. Heaps of rubble—stones evidently cast down from the crenellations—stood amid overgrown grass and briers. Piles of scattered grayed, weathered wood. A large broken clay water jug partially embedded in the soil. An entire fortress left to decay.

Following Akabe's lead, Kien dismounted, using the destroyer's thick mane for a handhold, swinging himself down along Scythe's massive black neck. The warhorse lowered his big head, allowing Kien's booted feet to hit the ground. Kien muttered, "You're obeying well, for a runaway monster. You deserve extra rations."

Scythe huffed, shook out his heavy mane, then swung around to watch Ela. She'd dismounted and was removing her vinewood branch from its leather casing alongside her little horse's saddle. Why? Kien fixated on the branch. No, not glowing. Even so, did Ela have a premonition that she might need the sacred insignia? He smoothed Scythe's glossy neck and spoke quietly. "Feel free to trim all this grass. We're safe." For now.

He crossed the huge, overgrown yard and offered Ela his arm as if they were at court. When Ela leaned against him and sighed, he whispered, "Prophet, what will happen here?"

"When I know more, I might tell you." She stared up at the tower, looking squeamish, as if the sight made her ill. "This was Akabe's home."

"Apparently. How else would he know of such a place—much less bring us here?"

Ela looked from the barren tower toward Akabe. "I wish it weren't so."

By now, Akabe—followed by Caitria and Riddig and several guards—had crossed to the far corner of the yard. Seeking some indication of Akabe's plans, Kien led Ela toward them.

"Sir," Caitria asked Akabe, "why are we here?"

"For me, this is where everything started." At the jointure of the fortress wall and the shaded stone foundation of a long-vanished building, Akabe kneeled, removing a dagger from his belt. He tore at the thick, moss-cushioned grass, casting handful after rustling handful aside. Finished, he studied the wall, then aligned the blade with a seam, slid it into the dark, bared soil, then pried it up as if digging for something. Clearly wondering aloud, Akabe asked, "Has it been stolen?" He eyed the adjoining stones, then slid his dagger through the bared furrow again, deeper this time. When the blade snagged, he dug into the soil.

A grimy, broken gold chain emerged, bearing a clod-encased pendant. Akabe rubbed the damp soil between his fingers, cleaning the chain and slowly revealing a delicate, crushed, gold flower pendant. He stared at the flower for a long time, a war of emotions turning his mouth, bringing a glint of tears to his eyes. Showing the pendant to Caitria, he said, "This was my little sister's. Deeaynna. I found it after we buried her, and I feared she'd miss it. My horsemaster refused to disturb her or my parents and older brothers. I'd guessed this line to be just above where she's placed."

Obviously stunned, Caitria stared at the fragile, smashed golden flower, then at the patch of overgrown grass. "Are you saying . . . your parents and siblings . . . are buried here?"

Sickened, Kien watched Akabe gently run his fingers through the grass, as if touching his long-dead family. "Yes. They were attacked as ordered by my predecessors. The night before, I'd coerced Beniyon, my horsemaster, to help me escape our unexpected company. Some long-winded government officials and their servants had arrived, all droning on and on about potential laws my lord-father was supposed to endorse. I couldn't bear the thought of listening to them when I might be hunting instead. No one saw me enter the hall or leave it. Beniyon and I snatched our gear, stole food when Cook was distracted, and we rode off.

"I hid in the DaromKhor Hills through the next day, supposing I'd be punished for abandoning my duties in waiting on my lord-father." Akabe continued. "I never dreamed my family welcomed their own murderers. Our servants . . . were herded into the keep's stables, then slaughtered and burned. Even a day later, the stench was nauseating. As for my parents . . . my family—and a serving boy evidently mistaken for me—I found their bodies arranged in order like fallen trophies. For some reason, the fire didn't touch them." Akabe fingered the gold chain, gazing at it. "I couldn't believe they'd killed Deeaynna. She'd just learned to write her name."

Cold fingers entwined with Kien's. Ela. He turned and saw her staring at Akabe, tears sliding down her face. She sniffled moistly, but said, "They would have killed you as well, sir."

"Often I wished they had. However—" Akabe managed a pained grimace of a smile. "Beniyon insisted I live. We buried my family by night, then he dragged me away."

Kien winced. If Ela or his family and friends had been massacred, yes, he would have shared Akabe's wish to die—he'd traveled that particular path of grief before. "From here, you fled to the Snake Mountains as Akabe of No Name?"

"Yes." Akabe slid the gold chain into his money pouch, caressed the grass once more, then stood. "It was easy to deny my name. If my family never existed, then neither had they died. Though I had nightmares for years. . . ."

He left abruptly, striding through the unkempt yard, whistling sharply at the horses. Most likely attempting to bury the remnants of his sorrow with work.

Caitria stood, drawing Kien's attention. Not looking at anyone, she returned to her horse, evidently focused on removing her gear, though she moved with a peculiar dazed blankness.

"Someone should speak to her," Kien murmured.

"Someone speaks to her now. Caitria must choose to listen." Ela caressed Kien's whisker-roughened cheek. "Let's go tend the horses. And Akabe."

✦ ✦ ✦

Hearing footsteps, Akabe turned. Not Caitria as he'd thought, but Ela and Kien, with Riddig trailing them. Accompanied by the guards, they worked alongside him in mute, sympathetic companionship, grooming the horses, then testing ropes and buckets to access the well. Good friends, indeed. But they weren't married to him. Drawing a sharp breath, Akabe slid a glance toward his wife. Caitria was rummaging through her gear as if she'd not heard him speak of the massacre. Had he mistakenly supposed she might care?

Never mind. He couldn't speak to anyone right now. Not Ela, not Kien, nor Riddig and the guards. Least of all, the perplexing young woman he'd married.

Infinite? Does she hate me after all? Should I set her aside as she insists?

No answer, of course. Despite this, he would persevere. He must. Giving up would hand the victory to his enemies.

Akabe finished tending the horses, then looked up at the tower. Time to face it now. This would be their shelter until they received word from Faine that it was safe to return to Munra in several weeks. He scooped up his gear and Caitria's bedroll, crossed the yard, climbed the stone steps, then strode through the doorless entry into the tower's main hall.

Musty silence, cobwebs, mice droppings, and a dust-filled central hearth greeted him. Bird nests festooned some of the carved brackets that supported stout ceiling beams, reminding Akabe of the floors above. Were the upper chambers intact? Surprisingly, for all the dust, droppings, and birds' nests, the beams appeared sound. He started for the stairs. Riddig followed, his boots thudding a rushed rhythm of haste. The military surgeon darted in front of Akabe, his silver hair seeming to bristle in alarm. "Sir, please, allow me, with the guards, to inspect the building first. If you or the queen drop through a rotten step or floorboard, the blame will be mine."

Akabe nodded. "Do your work, then." As Riddig and several guards stomped up the stairs, Akabe dropped his gear and the bedroll and glanced around, still hoping to see Caitria. Kien and Ela followed him instead. Ela's red eyes and damp lashes revealed she'd been crying.

If only the tears could be Caitria's. Not that Akabe longed for his wife to be miserable. But even the slightest show of sympathy might offer him hope that she cared. He paced the tiled floor, listening as Riddig scuffled and thumped through the chambers above. The timbers sounded sturdy; at least the guardsman hadn't fallen through. Folding his arms, Akabe halted, waiting.

Just as Riddig clattered downstairs into the hall, his expression satisfied, Akabe noticed a shadowfall at the entry. Caitria carried her few belongings into the main hall. Rumpled, obviously exhausted, she sat on her bedroll, refusing to meet Akabe's gaze. Her unspoken loyalties must be with the Ateans.

He'd suffered worse sorrows. But a pang cut through him. He'd failed her.

Trying to shield himself, Akabe focused on Riddig, who offered his report. "There's some splintering of the planks and timbers below the windows, sir. Beware. And it's clear that the furnishings and decorations were stolen long ago—everything's bare wood and stone, though habitable. And"—Riddig grinned—"several doors above are intact."

Akabe nodded. "Good news, indeed. We'll choose sleeping quarters, prepare some food, and take turns at the watch. Perhaps we should nap today and sleep tonight as normal people. I'm sure we'll be safe enough this first night—and we can hunt for food in the morning. No one knows we're here, yet."

Riddig shifted the quiverful of arrows, then his sword, checking his weapons as if unnerved. "If it's your . . . wish, sir."

"Yes." Akabe grabbed his gear and Caitria's belongings and headed for the stairs. Caitria followed him at a distance. No doubt reluctant to be near him, yet fearing to be alone.

He climbed the spiraling stairs, aware of her presence with every step. At the uppermost floor, he chose the old room he'd shared with his brothers. Riddig was right. The place had been looted, stripped to bare stone walls, wooden floors, and a shutterless window. Fresh stabbing grief halted Akabe in the center of the dusty chamber. Nothing was left of the thirteen-year-old he'd been. Nor of his brothers, Jorem and Matthan. Akabe swallowed.

A soft footstep told Akabe that Caitria had entered the chamber. Akabe dumped their gear, then turned and stared at Caitria. She averted her face. Akabe stifled a growl of frustration. "Have you nothing to say?"

She sat on the rolled pallet, still avoiding his gaze. Her tone almost lifeless, she said, "Sir, again, you should set me aside."

Emotionless as her words sounded, they sliced into his already wounded spirit. Akabe turned and left the chamber. She didn't follow.

✦ ✦ ✦

In the darkness of their chamber, Ela nestled beside her husband on their shared pallets, cherishing his warmth. Loving him. "Tell me your plans," she whispered. "I saw you talking with the king."

Drawing out his words as if reluctant to speak, Kien murmured, "We need meat, and Akabe wants to survey the surrounding hills. Some of the guards will remain here."

He turned and slid an arm around her. "Why do you ask? Are you worried?"

"Of course I'm worried. Yet we must trust the Infinite's plans." Ela wished she could see Kien's eyes in the darkness. Not to mention his handsome face. "I don't know much of what's to happen in the next few weeks, but I must warn you . . ." She propped herself on one elbow to emphasize her words. "Whatever happens, hunting or not, you must be sure the king never crosses the Siphran border into Belaal. If he disobeys, he will be captured. And so will you."

"By Bel-Tygeon?" Kien's voice turned frosty as he spoke the name of Belaal's king.

"By his men." A prompting image of what might be made Ela shiver and hug her husband close. "Belaal will kill Akabe and take Siphra. You mustn't fail."

Kien tensed in her embrace. "Do Bel-Tygeon's men know the king is here?"

"No." Ela soothed her husband with a kiss. "They don't know he's here." But they suspected her presence. Ela shook off the realization. Akabe and Kien were her chief concerns now. "However, my warning is serious. Promise me you'll not let the hunt or anything carry you from Siphra."

"I give you my word, Prophet, I'll heed the warning. Don't worry—it's only one day."

"Yes, but this will be the longest separation we've faced since our wedding."

Kien chuckled. "Poor love. Again, don't worry. I'll think of you every other instant." He sealed his pledge with kisses, coaxing Ela to set aside her fears and lose herself in his embrace.

✦ ✦ ✦

Moving around the dais, Ela gathered the morning meal's utensils and bowls in the dim light. Through the hall's open doorway, she heard the men talking quietly to one another and to their horses. Pet grunted and stomped a foot, sending a tremor through the tiled floor.

Cranky, bad-tempered monster-warhorse.

But why call Pet cranky and bad-tempered when she was just as unsettled and irritable this morning? Not to mention tired and sore . . . scared and . . .

She ran outside, down the steps and into the predawn light, her short boots and mantle sweeping through the grass. "Kien!" He turned. Ela charged into his arms and hugged him in farewell, breathing in the odors of smoke and furs he'd used to mask his scent for the hunt. Infinite? Was this the last time she'd see her husband? "Be safe. Remember the warning."

Kien's laugh hinted at indulgence, and his lips were warm as he kissed her. "I'll never forget a warning from my favorite prophet! Ela, don't worry. We'll return by sunset, but if we're going to reach the ideal place to harvest some venison, we must leave *now*."

Fighting tears, she watched him climb onto Pet's back. Ela smoothed the destroyer's face, then waved as Kien rode off with Akabe, Riddig, and fifteen of the guards. When they'd vanished from sight, she returned to the hall.

Trying to ignore her disquiet, she prayed, washed the dishes in a bucket, rested awhile, prayed again, then climbed the spiraling stairs. She needed more sleep. As she turned toward the chamber she shared with Kien, a muffled, tortured sound halted her. Sobs cut through the closed door from the chamber at her left. "Lady?"

Ela rapped on the chamber door and peeked inside. Caitria lay on a pallet, crying with all the despair of someone in deepest mourning. Surveying the barren room, Ela gasped.

This chamber . . . that window . . .

Fighting nausea, Ela stepped into her vision's beginning.

✦ 22 ✦

Ela kneeled beside Caitria, trying to focus on the young queen's grief instead of her own dread. Time. They still had time.

Infinite? I realize the queen doesn't acknowledge You. But for the sake of Your Name, my beloved Creator, please give me Your wisdom.

Calm dropped over Ela—an unseen spiritual mantle, temporarily separating her from fear. Heartened by His unspoken agreement, Ela touched Caitria's thin shoulder. The queen stiffened, audibly gulping down a sob. Ela lifted her hand. "Majesty—"

Caitria gave in to fresh sobs. "D-don't call me that! I don't deserve it! Ela, I'm nothing but evil to him." Her words becoming a mourner's cry, she added, "He m-must set me aside!"

Oh. Ela stared at the sobbing girl. "You do love your husband."

Caitria sat up and hugged her knees. Her delicate nose was bright pink, her eyes red and swollen. Had she been crying ever since she'd left their morning meal? A violent shudder wracked Caitria's body and words. "E-ever since . . . I first s-saw him, I think. Yes, I'm infatuated! Oh, Ela! I love him. I *do*! But I c-can't endure this—I'm all to pieces! If Akabe dies because of m-me, I . . . I'll . . ."

Seizing upon the queen's trailing words, Ela asked, "Why would he die because of you?"

Caitria wiped her eyes, sniffling moistly. "M-my family scorns

201

Akabe, though he doesn't deserve their contempt." Her expression hardened now, tears giving way to anger. "You should have heard my father and my brother Cyril when they learned Akabe's beliefs as king! They said he and the Infinite's followers were fools—spiritually oppressive. And Ruestock called Akabe a peasant nobody. It sickens me that I'm related to him!"

Ela blinked, trying to absorb Caitria's furious babble. "Ruestock? How is he involved?"

"He visits and hovers—a living blight. He told my lord-father that if I should bear Akabe a child, then I would rule as regent-queen when Akabe died. *When*. As if Akabe's death was planned! Not that I knew for sure. I was chased away after hearing this— I'm nothing but a silly girl to my family." Some of Caitria's wrath faded. "Power and money . . . my lord-father couldn't resist the temptation! I'm sure he believed he could hide until the uproar faded. I was instructed to be loyal to my lord-father and the Thaenfall name." Groping for a linen scarf, she blew her nose. "Horrid name! I'd been proud to be raised a Thaenfall. But now it means nothing! I'm nothing!"

"Lady, that's not true."

"It is! Akabe hasn't slaughtered Ateans unjustly, but it's clear that *Thaenfalls* and their sorts conspired to kill Akabe's entire family. It's all so wrong!" She swallowed. "Ela, I must protect him!"

Caitria hugged her knees again, clearly swept into wistful thoughts of Akabe. "Besides Naynee, he's the only person to ever defend me. And he's amazing—the handsomest, dearest man! For both our sakes, I've tried to keep my distance from him since our wedding, but I can't! Just to see his dimples when he smiles and hearing his voice makes me weak. I feel so safe in his arms—so protected! His kisses are—"

Ela lifted her hands. "No, no! He's my king, and I *don't* want to know about his kisses!"

A hint of a smile brightened Caitria's exquisite, tear-streaked face. "I suppose I'm glad you feel that way." Her pleasure turned desperate. "Ela, what should I do? I love Akabe more than anyone alive, but I'm so trapped and useless!"

"Are your father and brothers plotting against the king's life?"

Pressing both hands to her head, Caitria shut her eyes. "I don't know! I'm going mad with the uncertainty, particularly after my cousins tried to kill him. But yesterday—watching Akabe mourn for his family—I loathed being a Thaenfall and Atean."

Cautious, measuring her words, Ela asked, "Are you Atean in deeds, or only in name?"

The queen studied her, wary now. "Am I devout, you mean? Have I offered sacrifices or attended Atean rites?" She shook her head. "No. I was taught to offer prayers and nominal sacrifices, but I haven't been trusted enough to join the rites. I'm loyal because my family follows the goddess. We've been Ateans for generations."

"You're loyal to your heritage, then. Not to Atean ways."

"I suppose." Her tone hardened now, resistant to further questions. Defiant to her Creator.

All right. At least she was calmer. Ela stood, aware of sunlight peeking into the chamber. Her own calm faded with the brightening glow. She was unable to prevent what must happen, but at least she could prepare.

Watching the sunlight's telling angle, she said, "My loyalties are first to my beloved Creator, the Infinite. Then to my husband. And . . ." She threw a half smile at the queen, who looked ready to argue. "I'm loyal to our anointed king. Believe me, Kien and I will do everything within our power to protect Akabe, even if it means giving our lives."

Her coolness easing, Caitria nodded. "Thank you. I honor your views, though I disagree with your religion."

Ela studied the sunlight again, trying to measure it against her vision. Trying to quell her nausea. By now the king was far enough away. Safe. Infinite, let Pet sense nothing!

Speaking gently to avoid upsetting the queen again, Ela said, "Lady, please let me find a cloak for you, and pins . . . and your leggings and some boots. You'll need them today, and for the next few days."

"What are you talking about? I'm not going anywhere."

"Before midday, we will." Ela crossed to the window and checked their horses, grazing undisturbed down in the ragged central yard. "I need to warn our guards. Belaal's soldiers approach. King Bel-Tygeon intends to capture me—and his men think I don't realize it." Quietly, she said, "Majesty, you must depart with our guards."

"What are you talking about? I'm not going anywhere without my husband." Caitria stared, then sniffed, lifting her chin. "Oh. You're suffering a deluded prophet's fancy."

Ela shook her head. "If I'm wrong, I deserve to die. The Infinite's prophets must always declare the truth. And I've seen the soldiers' faces." Nausea pressed in again, making Ela grip the stone window frame. Infinite? Help me manage the queen! "Majesty, at least humor me enough to don your riding clothes and boots." Releasing the cold rocks and mortar, Ela scanned the chamber, then headed for Caitria's pile of belongings.

Caitria stood and stepped in front of her. "You needn't wait on me. Anyway, you're wrong—I'll enjoy laughing at you tonight. Besides," she darted a taunting glance at Ela, "*I* don't need my leggings and boots if the soldiers are coming for you."

"Yes you do. They've been commanded to seize everyone with me—meaning you, which is why you *must* leave with our guards."

"Oh? Well, I suppose one ought to humor the deluded. I'll dress, but I'm *not* leaving, whatever you say!" Caitria dug through her tumbled heap of gear and shook out her cloak, taunting, "Should I also don weapons, Prophet?"

Such regal mockery! Ela bit down impatience. "By all means, take weapons. But hide them inside your boots or leggings. If you fasten them to your belt, the soldiers will see and confiscate them at once."

Caitria stared over her shoulder. "Lady Aeyrievale, you're actually serious."

"Yes. And it's a blessing our husbands departed before the soldiers arrived. Otherwise they would have been captured. Possibly killed."

"Stop! You're making me nervous."

"Heed your fears, Majesty!" Ela retrieved a pin and a comb from Caitria's gear and offered them to her. "Please reconsider. You *must* leave with the guards."

"I'll not!" The queen glared, proud, furious, and resolute.

"Majesty—"

"No!"

Ela swallowed. "Very well. Please, excuse me. I must prepare."

"You're odd," Caitria complained. "Seriously. For a while, at least, I could pretend you were a normal lady."

"Your perception of normal will change as the day proceeds." Ela sped down the stairs, through the hall, and outside. Two guards spied her as she halted before the gate. Catching her breath, she called up, "Sirs, you know I'm a prophet! I've suffered a vision, so listen to me. Belaal's soldiers will attack soon, and you and your comrades are too outnumbered to fight them."

"Lady," one guard protested stoutly, rapping the butt of his spear on the ground for emphasis, "I cannot abandon my watch!"

"Listen," Ela ordered. "As prophet, I command you to leave this gate! Either hide in the woods with your comrades, or wait to be captured and killed. Those are your choices, so choose!" Oh, such rebelliousness! And she hadn't even commanded them to seize the queen. Could she? Ela frowned. Likely not. By the time they managed to drag Caitria downstairs, it would be too late. Even now, the guards were bickering amongst themselves— squandering time and possibly their lives. She gave them her most ferocious prophet-stare. "I command you! *Go!*"

Returning to the tower, Ela carefully banked the hearths' ashes in the hall and the kitchen, then rushed to her chamber, trying to think. Leggings. Boots. Cloak. Branch. She dressed and braided her hair.

She returned to Caitria and found the young queen properly

clad, her hair in a thick light-brown knot at the nape of her neck. Seeing Ela, Caitria folded her arms. "Satisfied, Lady Aeyrievale?"

"Not entirely, Majesty. But let the Infinite's will be done." A chill prickled over Ela's scalp and slid along her arms. Closing her eyes, she saw her enemies. "They arrived at the base of the hill before I came up here and realized my vision is today. Even then it was too late. But if we'd confronted them earlier, my destroyer would have sensed our danger and our husbands would have returned and been captured, so be grateful."

Reminded of her husband, Ela crossed to the window and looked out over the yard. Nothing yet. Though the birds had stopped singing. She sank to her knees and rested her forehead against the branch, praying. *Infinite? Please let our guards escape! Kien . . . dear husband, wherever you are, stay away! Protect the king!*

A sound drew her into the present. Caitria sat nearby, watching as if trying to decide whether she ought to pity Ela, or tie her up. "Lady Aeyrievale, you're ill."

"My visions always make me ill." And souls threatened by an eternity of fire only worsened her nausea. Depending heavily on the branch, Ela stood.

Caitria said, "Perhaps you should return to your chamber and rest."

Eyeing the sunlight slanting just so through the window, Ela shook her head. "There's no time. They're here. Majesty, tie your leggings, please."

Even as she spoke, Ela watched the horses stir in the yard, huffing and tugging on their ropes. Distant sounds lifted beyond the gate. Metal clinking. Men's voices. Dread weighed upon Ela's spirit. *Infinite? I am afraid!*

Are you My servant?

Always.

In her hands, the branch turned metallic. Its inner fire spiraled toward the vinewood's changing surface, sending light through Ela's fingers. Bracing herself, Ela hissed to Caitria, who now stood beside her staring openmouthed from the branch to the dark-cloaked men gathering before the gate. "Majesty! You'll need your leggings. Whatever happens, don't return to the window, please."

Caitria sat beside her gear. Hands shaking, she obediently knotted the leggings' laces. Finally! Ela turned toward the window. Beyond the courtyard, a man's cloaked form entered the gate. He looked up at the tower, obviously seeing the glowing branch. And her. Malevolence contorted his tawny face, making Ela shiver. Infinite? Why such hatred?

In answer, her Creator sent whisperings of the man's thoughts and hints of his soul. Mortal arrogance personified. Pride mingled with ambition and the longing to avenge the shame he'd suffered at Parne by ensuring her personal degradation and suffering. No! Ela shut her eyes, gasping, horrified by what would happen. Kien, love, stay away! "Infinite! Bless Your Name!"

The leader's voice called up to her. "Prophet! Our king, Bel-Tygeon—Light of the Heavens—commands you to come down!"

White fire flared from the branch, pouring through Ela, giving her courage despite her tears. Her voice echoed through the yard, bold and defiant. "If I am the Infinite's prophet, let His holy fire devour you and those renegades beneath your command!"

White flames descended from the blue sky as a curtain of lightning upon the screaming men, sweeping their bodies from life into death and their souls into eternal torment.

Weapons, buckles, and clasps fell amid a clattering of bones and sifting ashes. A terrible silence replaced the sounds of destruction. Ela gulped, staring at the scattered bones and weapons. Behind her, Caitria cried, "Ela! What's happened?"

"Caitria, stay back, please!" Closing her eyes again, Ela prayed through welling tears. Infinite? Let Your will be fulfilled—may Your enemies bow!

A commander's distant cry summoned other men to replace the vanquished ones—a single word reaching Ela with horrifying clarity. "Forward!"

Now the second commander screamed at her in a fit of killing rage, "Prophet! Come down at once, or we'll set this place afire!"

She heard his thoughts. His resolution to torture the woman who'd destroyed his comrades. In Ela's hands, the branch sent out fierce spirals of light, lending her strength. "If I am the Infinite's prophet, let His holy fire devour you and those renegades with you!"

Again a curtain of fire fell and swept over the men, cutting off their agonized cries in a haze of ashes and a tumble of weapons and bones. Behind Ela, Caitria screamed. When Ela turned, Caitria backed away, then sat as if her legs failed to support her. Eyes huge, she covered her mouth and stared, her tears matching Ela's. Silently begging for mercy. For help. Ela shook her head. "I'm sorry! Pray the survivors heed their Creator."

As Caitria wept, a renewed clatter drew Ela's attention toward the bone-cluttered gate. Living men replaced the dead. Slowly this time, their heads bowed. And when their leader approached the fortress gate, picking his way through the skeletons and weapons, he knelt and lifted his hands toward Ela in supplication. "Prophet of the Infinite, pity us! We follow the ruling of our king—we are commanded to bring you and your companions to Belaal. Have compassion on me and on my men! Be merciful and let us become servants through your kindness!"

A twist of dread unwound in Ela's soul, allowing her to breathe. "Infinite?"

Her Creator's Spirit murmured, *Go with those men. You will be safe in their care.*

Trembling, Ela called out, "The Infinite sees you! He chooses to be merciful toward you and your men—you won't die today." As the commander's men hurried toward the tower to apprehend them, Ela looked down at Caitria. The queen gasped as if seeing a lethal apparition. She snatched a pair of small sheathed daggers from Akabe's belongings and shoved one inside her right legging, the other within her right boot, then stood and straightened her long tunic.

At least she hadn't tried to use one of the daggers on a certain prophet. Ela shifted the branch and listened to their captors rushing up the stairs, their boots echoing inside the stairwell. "Don't be frightened, Majesty, but we must go with these men. The Infinite commands this, and I cannot prevent it. Now, either we walk down quietly, or they will tie us for fear of their king."

The men entered the chamber, hands on their swords' hilts, cautious but clearly determined to fulfill their orders. Ela led Caitria past them and marched down the stairs.

Caitria remained silent until they walked out of the tower. Then, eyeing the seared bones and skulls tumbled around the gate, she shook her head at Ela in disbelief. "You killed them. . . ."

Meeting the young queen's horrified gaze, Ela said, "Don't be afraid!"

Caitria's breath wheezed, and her voice squeaked. "You set them ablaze!"

"The Infinite did—to protect us."

"I cannot believe this!" Shaking her head, Caitria stepped away from Ela. "I've been talking to a-a—living fury! What will you do next?"

What next? Ela shivered at the possibilities. More than anything she wanted to run away. To Kien. Yet she longed to serve her Creator. She must. Oh, Kien, stay away! Survive and protect the king!

Silent, she crossed the yard to her small dun horse. One soldier linked his visibly trembling hands, offering Ela a step up. As Caitria followed her example, Ela rode toward the gate. Toward their enemies in Belaal.

✦ 23 ✦

The Infinite exists? He must! Nothing else could explain what had just happened. Biting her lip to stifle another dry sob, Caitria slid a glance toward her so-called companions as they rode through the hills. Thus far, not one of these armed horsemen had threatened her. But really, they'd no need of threats.

The prophet, or whatever Ela was, proved herself more frightful than their captors. Oh, those poor men—obliterated! Caitria choked down fresh tears, remembering the ashes. The screams . . .

Infinite . . . I— Caitria's courage evaporated before she could finish the tremulous thought. What a cowardly queen she'd proven herself to be! And so wrong.

A whimper escaped before she could prevent it. "Akabe!"

One of the soldiers riding alongside her turned, eyebrows raised. "Lady?"

"Nothing." Caitria swallowed. Yet her heartbeat fluttered wildly like a snared bird's. She must be calm. She must conquer her cowardice, and she must not say Akabe's name. These men mustn't suspect they'd captured Siphra's queen, useless though she was. Oh, Akabe!

Tears rimmed Caitria's eyes, blurring her vision. She blinked them away. And heard Cyril's cruel voice taunting in her thoughts: *Weakling! No wonder we can't trust you!*

Would her brother's scorn hurt forever? Yes. Even now, merely remembering his voice, she wanted to throw rocks at pretend-Cyril targets. Gritting her teeth, Caitria mentally shoved her brother aside.

She *would* return to Akabe. Even if he ultimately set her aside as queen . . . Caitria's breath snagged. Set aside! Though she'd proposed the idea, it would wound her more deeply than any of Cyril's taunts or Father's cold-eyed silences. She clenched her hands into fists around the reins. Stop. Deal with being set aside as Akabe's wife when it happened. But first, she must escape these men and return to her husband. Then, when Akabe deemed it safe to return to Munra . . . Caitria flexed her aching fingers, resolute. She'd behave as an adult and speak to her lord-father.

Might Father join some plot to overthrow and kill Akabe as she feared? Please, no! How could she endure such torment? And surely she'd be accused of joining any conspiracy—too many courtiers and members of the royal council mistrusted her.

Yet Akabe held her ultimate loyalty. He must survive. Just knowing her love was safe from his enemies would help her to endure being set aside, or worse.

She would speak to Father. And Cyril.

Now, however, she must face Ela, prophet of Parne, and the Infinite.

Lifting her chin, Caitria looked ahead at Ela, who rode with her head bowed. What *are* you? Why did you kill all those men? Caitria shuddered, remembering their screams and the ash-dusted bones.

To think she'd actually trusted Ela enough this morning to spill out all her thoughts and feelings. Fool! Caitria berated herself until the lead commander lifted one hand, halting them. He glanced from Ela to her, then nodded, somber as a schoolmaster. "Dismount for ten sayings of the Vlesi!"

The what? Caitria turned to her guard. "What is the Vlesi?"

Wary, he offered her a slight bow of his dark-curled head, then nodded toward a gray-bearded comrade, who'd begun to chant singsong, holding a knotted counting cord between his fingers. Caitria's guard explained, "In the language of our priests, the

Vlesi is our prayer for the safety of our king, Bel-Tygeon, prized of the heavens."

Prized of the heavens? Disgusting! King Bel-Tygeon certainly had a high opinion of himself. Akabe ought to teach this prized king a few lessons. At least her guard seemed humble; too nice of a man to be stealing ladies. And respectful as he helped her to dismount from the horse and guided her to the edge of the road to stand with Ela.

The instant her guard stepped away, Caitria glared at Ela and muttered beneath her breath, "Why didn't you warn us all sooner? And *why* did you have to kill those men?"

Though her eyes were red-rimmed as if she'd been crying, Ela studied Caitria with enviable calm. "I didn't warn you, lady, because I am mortal. I didn't know *this* was the day of my vision until I walked into your chamber this morning. I cannot be shown everything at once—such a vast vision would crush me. Therefore, the Infinite shares only as much as I need to know to fulfill my work as His servant. But even after seeing the most recent visions, I was scarcely prepared for . . ." Her voice caught a little. "For what happened."

"Even so, those men are dead. Charred skeletons!"

Ela stiffened, though fresh tears glittered in her eyes. "The deaths of those men saved hundreds of lives. Perhaps thousands!" She took a quick breath and whispered fiercely, "Do you really believe we could have escaped? No! I've prayed while we rode this morning. Bel-Tygeon's soldiers were oath-bound to find us! If those men had lived, you would have died by now—after you'd been assaulted. Their souls held no honor. None!"

Souls. Again. And by now . . . she would have died? All the hairs rose on Caitria's arms and scalp, making her shiver. Worse, that staff in Ela's hand took on a metallic gleam too alarming to ignore, its light drawing her gaze and her reluctant thoughts toward the Infinite.

Ela continued softly. "And I would be near-dead now, spared only to fulfill the king's edict. Because of your death, Siphra would soon be at war with Belaal, thereby threatening count-less lives, including our husbands'! Yet the souls of these men you've wished to save—their love of wickedness—would have never changed, however long they lived."

Stern now, Ela said, "At times the Infinite allows miracles of destruction for the sake of many—as a surgeon will remove putrid flesh to save a body. This was one of those times. Tell me, lady, whose wisdom do you prefer? Yours or His?"

Caitria shivered. Doubts cut away at her indignation until nothing remained but fear. Trying to conquer her fright, Caitria accepted the hard, flat rim of bread offered by her courteous guard. "What will happen to us?"

Ela stared at her own food as if seeing past it, into the future. Toneless, she whispered, "I must confront the 'prized of the heavens' Bel-Tygeon. And you—" Ela shot her a warning glance. "As for you, lady, whatever happens, please don't try to escape! If you do, you'll fail, and you'll mourn the consequences."

"Such as . . . ?"

"I'm unsure. The penalty will be decided by another. I only know that you'll mourn."

Caitria shuddered, swept by another bout of skin-prickling chills. But she scowled at Ela's warning look and took courage. What was Ela thinking? Escape must be their only goal!

Caitria broke off a chunk of the dry bread and chewed it. If the chance came, she'd take it. Alone. But was she alone?

Cautious, she formed a testing, questing, silent word.

Infinite?

✦ ✦ ✦

Astride her horse with the branch tucked into its place along the saddle, Ela tried to conceal her fears. Caitria had disappeared within a sheltered grove to tend to her needs—and had been gone for much too long. Was she already attempting an escape? Their gray-bearded timekeeper had long since finished chanting his allotted number of Vlesi and was now pacing, conspicuously agitated. The guards conferred among each other, arguing in ferocious whispers.

The leader—the commander who'd pleaded for the lives of his men—approached the thicket and called out, "Lady, if you delay us, you ensure our punishment when we arrive in Sulaanc!"

Caitria emerged from a sheltering clump of bushes, her pretty face mutinous. Particularly when the leader approached to personally escort her to the waiting horses. She sniffed. "Did you think I would run away?"

The commander inclined his head, perfectly courteous, but he gripped Caitria's upper arm and led her to her horse. "We are grateful you did not. As would be your husband. Forgive me, lady." He shifted the edge of Caitria's cloak and unclasped her wedding armband.

As Ela gasped, Caitria clutched at her golden armband in a fury. "No!"

Holding her off neatly, the commander slipped the gold from Caitria's arm. Apologetic, formal, he kept her at arm's length, saying, "Lady, this will be returned to you."

The commander looked up at Ela now, wary. "Prophet, you know I dare not lie to you and your Infinite. I, Rtial Vioc, give you my word that I am required to identify all prisoners, particularly the highborn."

Despite the sick gnawing in her stomach, Ela maintained her composure. "I am not your prisoner, sir. The Infinite directed me to accompany you as His servant. You and your men would be unable to restrain me if it were against His will."

"Nevertheless, Prophet, it is known you married a nobleman who owns destroyers. We are required to identify your rank." Still courteous, the commander extended one big hand. "Your armband, please. It will be returned to you."

Kien. His expression on their wedding day—his joy as he'd presented the elegant plume-patterned band . . . his tenderness in fastening it around her arm—made Ela long to argue. Yet the damage was done. Commander Vioc held Caitria's insignia.

Siphra's queen would soon be identified, and Ela could do nothing to help her.

Ela slid her right hand beneath her cloak and unfastened the concealed band. Obviously, the soldier who'd spied on her wedding ceremony had wasted no time in announcing her marriage among the authorities in Belaal. She forced herself to hand the exquisite armband to the commander. Vioc took the gold, inclined his head reverently, then turned, ordering his men, "To your horses. Proceed at double-pace!"

Caitria, trembling visibly, mounted her horse. She sent Ela a pleading look, as if begging her to do something—anything—to retrieve the wedding bands.

Grieving, Ela shut her eyes and prayed. *Infinite? What now?*

She wove her fingers through her horse's mane, trying to control herself as an earlier vision returned. The detestable soldier who'd spied on her wedding stared at her now, his hatred tangible. The vision lengthened, making Ela's heart thud. Unmet enemies stepped forward in her thoughts, their scarred faces pitiless, their lips uttering curses, wishing Parne's last prophet dead.

Ela opened her eyes against the vision, unable to scream. Yet the vision continued. And the dry bread roiled in her stomach as she witnessed torments she'd wish on no one.

✦ ✦ ✦

Hushed within a thicket bordering the narrow valley, Akabe drew back the bowstring, anchored his shot, then aimed at a fine eight-point stag that had paused to scent its surroundings. As the light breeze slipped past his face, Akabe released the arrow and watched it strike his quarry just behind the shoulder. The creature dropped, thrashing.

At once, his men charged from their hiding places toward the fallen beast, jubilant. Akabe wished he could share their exultation. All morning, he'd been uneasy. Instead of hunting and isolating himself from Caitria to protect his heart-wounds, he ought to be with her. *Infinite? Was I wrong to leave today?*

216

His conscience mocked. *Why not? You've been wrong about everything for most of this year.*

From the trees behind Akabe, Scythe's low, restless destroyer-rumble rippled through the air, increasing his disquiet. Decision made, Akabe left the wood and strode toward his men. "We've two. It's enough. Let's prepare this one and be finished for the day."

The leader of Akabe's guards nodded. "Yes, sir. We'll hurry."

Just as well. Evening would be fast-approaching by the time they returned to the fortress. His home. Tonight he would talk with Caitria again. And again. Until he wrested information from her lovely, stubborn soul.

Planning their conversation, Akabe marched back into the shadowed trees, where Kien waited with Riddig Tyne and Scythe, who was laden with their earlier prize, a smaller six-point stag. Akabe lifted a mock-serious eyebrow. "My friends, why do I hear destroyer-grumblings?"

"He's caught my mood," Kien admitted, shifting the quiver of arrows on his back. "I'm wondering if five guards were enough to protect the fortress."

"Trust you to raise my concerns to fear, Aeyrievale." Yet he must admit he was uneasy. During his years as a rebel, this same unease urged him to decamp in haste, often saving rebel lives—a blessing he could only attribute to the Infinite. "Well-enough. We're leaving as soon as the men tether the stag." He crossed to his horse, checked it, and mounted. Kien and Riddig followed his example and then waited. Just as Akabe turned his horse to ride past Scythe—a mouse beside the monster—his guards yelled in the meadow beyond. One of them dashed into the wood, hissing, "Sir, there's a host of men approaching from beyond, ready to fight! Leave now!"

"I will not!" Akabe drew his sword.

"Sir!" the guard pleaded. "You needn't fear! We're evenly matched—they must not capture you! *Go*—hide yourself and your lady!"

Caitria! Because she'd brought Siphra the temple's lands, she was indeed a target. Infinite— "They'd kill her!" Akabe turned his beast once more and rode through the wood, followed by Kien and Riddig, their weapons drawn.

Leaving the shouts and clamor of a warlike clash in the meadow.

◆ 24 ◆

Shifting his horse's reins, Akabe tensed, acutely aware of Riddig, Kien, and Scythe's unnatural quiet as they followed him upward through the trees, approaching the fortress.

Too quiet. Akabe gripped his sword and looked around, studying every shadow. Listening. No tree frogs croaking, no birds calling, no bugs rasping as on the night before. Not even a breeze rustled the trees' leaves. Stillness closed around Akabe like a shroud.

Unnerved, he glanced at Kien and Riddig. Both men rode amid the oppressive shadowed hush, swords readied. Akabe exhaled, praying. Infinite? Protect Caitria! Though it's my fault, she's in danger for the sake of Your Holy House. Please, to honor Your Name, save her from our enemies!

As Akabe neared the fortress, Scythe snorted, sounding prepared for battle. Akabe's steed balked before the gate. Akabe dismounted, staring at . . . skulls. Weapons. Ashes.

Sword in hand, Riddig dropped from his own skittish mount. "Sir, do you recognize anything? Any of their swords or badges?"

"No. We'll check as soon as I've found my wife." He turned as Kien swung himself off Scythe, who'd stilled. "Surely the Infinite has done this!"

Kien stared at the skulls, weapons, and ash-strewn bones, then at Akabe. "Ela!"

Akabe hurried toward the gateway, giving the two smaller horses ample room for their growing panic. More vertebrae. Ribs. Hands. Feet. More skulls. And daggers, buckles, arm guards, greaves. . . . Surely an entire regiment was strewn at his feet amid ashes. Where was Cait?

Heart thudding, Akabe picked a path through the tumbled skeletons and charged inside the yard. Caitria and Ela's horses were gone. Where were the five guards? Infinite . . .

Kien rushed after him through the sagging gate, calling out again, "Ela?"

Praying his fears would be disproved, Akabe sped across the wide, dilapidated yard and rushed up the stairs, into the tower. "Cait! Are you here?"

Riddig clattered in after them as Kien ran upstairs to the chambers above.

They searched the quiet fortress, calling everywhere for Ela and Caitria. No one answered. At dusk they returned to the main keep. Staring into his chamber, at his wife's jumbled belongings, Akabe lowered his sword and hammered a fist against the wooden door.

Infinite? Have I cost Caitria her life?

✦ ✦ ✦

In the kitchen, Kien half-knelt beside the hearth and clenched one fist to his forehead, resisting panic. *Infinite? What must we do?*

His Creator spoke into his thoughts, stunningly swift. *Wait.*

What? No! But we must search for—

Parent-stern, the Infinite cut off his argument. *Wait here!*

Reeling beneath the command's physical impact, Kien planted both hands on the tiled floor, sucking in air. Blood thumped in his head, yet his thoughts protested to his Creator.

Infinite, as You say—we'll wait. But why? What's happening to Ela?

If she never returns, will you yet trust Me?

The response gripped Kien like a giant's hand, stilling the breath in his lungs. However . . . Yes, even if Ela could never return. You are the one true God—my Creator. I trust You!

If she dies, even then, will you trust Me?

If she dies . . . if she dies . . . Kien forced himself to think beyond those words. He'd given Ela up for dead in Parne. Agony! And yet . . . In a whisper, he agreed. "Yes. Even then, I would trust You."

Gather weapons and be ready.

Weapons? Kien sat up, dizzied, prepared to obey the confusing order. Confusing because the only weapons that needed gathering lay in the ashes near the fortress's stone gate. Fine. He'd gather the dead men's gear, before the sunlight vanished completely. Senses swimming, he stood and realized Akabe and Riddig were staring at him.

Akabe approached, wary. "You were praying?"

"Yes. And swiftly answered." But Akabe wouldn't like the Infinite's command any more than Kien did. "The Infinite orders us to wait. We're not to go looking for our wives."

"You've heard from Him?" Akabe stared, clearly incredulous.

Kien pressed both hands to his aching head. "Yes. He orders us to wait."

"That's impossible!" Akabe clawed the air in a gesture of wild frustration. "You must be mistaken!"

"I'm not. And I've the headache to prove it. Furthermore—" Kien raised a hand to arrest Akabe's protest. "If we disobey the Infinite and leave to search for our wives, we'll die."

Akabe halted. "How do you know this?"

"Because if a prophet disobeys the Infinite, the sentence is death. I'm not exactly a prophet, but I am His servant. Therefore, I'll obey. Meanwhile, we're ordered to gather weapons."

Riddig nodded toward the smoldering grate. "Someone banked the fire."

Kien studied the hearth. Someone had indeed covered live coals to save them, though it couldn't have been nightfall when this fire was banked. And if Kien had to guess between Ela and Caitria . . . "Ela! She must have expected something to happen if she banked the fire so early." Kien stifled a growl. Headstrong little prophet! Why hadn't she told him?

Akabe scowled. "I'm going to check those weapons!"

Beneath the blood-red sunset, they rummaged amid the bones, gathering swords, daggers, foreign coins, exotic clasps, and buckles and carried them in bunches into the tower.

As darkness closed in, Kien noticed Scythe circling them. Not grazing. Only circling, his destroyer-nostrils flaring as he issued occasional threatening snorts toward the woods.

Realization slid over Kien as Scythe tightened his pace, closing his restless, watchful circle around Kien—and Akabe and Riddig.

They were in danger. But from whom? Local thugs? Atean assassins? Or was another contingent of soldiers approaching from Belaal? "Sirs?"

Drawing his sword, Kien motioned Akabe and Riddig toward the tower.

✦ ✦ ✦

Was this the place? Ela stared as they rode through the evening light into the military encampment. Yes. She winced, seeing those tents positioned exactly so amid this field. And the golden pennants, the moveable stands of shields and spears . . . All were as she'd seen.

Commander Vioc ordered his men to dismount. Ela followed their example, removing the branch from her saddle as well. While she shook out her robes and stretched, Caitria hurried to meet her, whispering, "If they haven't guessed my rank by now, I'm certain they will. Ela, what might they do?"

"Commander Vioc will treat you with as much or more courtesy than ever. As for Bel-Tygeon, he is less predictable." Ela felt her throat go dry. She was being watched, just as in her vision. She nodded toward a gathering pack of soldiers. "Lady, I'm about to be threatened by those men. Whatever happens, don't run! Remain still and quiet."

Caitria paled. "You're going to burn them? Ela—"

"No!" Her voice emerged a pitiable squeak, nothing like a proper prophet's voice should be. "I'm not going to burn them. Unless these men retreat, they'll suffer an ambush of scalns."

Caitria's voice rose. "Scalns? But—"

A man's harsh, low voice cut off her words. "Prophet!"

Ela looked up and met the now-familiar gaze of the soldier who'd spied on her wedding, then tracked her through Siphra. "Hyseoth." The instant she spoke this soldier's name, the branch turned metallic, silvery fire threading visibly along the vinewood's grain.

"You cursed my men in Parne!" Hyseoth accused. "By your words, they died. Then your husband cut down my comrades in Siphra!"

"I did not curse your men in Parne! You and your king refused to heed the Infinite's warnings; therefore, your men died. As for my husband—he *rescued* me. You would have done the same for any of your loved ones!"

"None of my loved ones weave spells and pronounce curses, sorceress!"

Gritting her teeth, Ela willed herself to remain calm. The branch glowed now, dazzling blue-white in the lowering sun. The angry soldier and his men squinted, their features stark within the branch's light—all wound-marked and hateful as she'd seen. Please, let them listen, for their eternal sakes! "I am the Infinite's prophet from Parne, not a spell-weaver. I warned your men before, Hyseoth, and I am begging you and the men with you now to return peaceably to your tents—at once. If you curse me or my Creator, then this has been your last day of life."

Commander Vioc spoke from Ela's left, ringing and authoritative. "Hyseoth, listen to me if you won't listen to her! Two deputations of men ignored the prophet's warnings in Siphra and divine fire turned their flesh to ashes! My men and I survived only because we did not threaten this woman—we honored her warnings."

Hyseoth tensed with fury, his deepened color outlining a scar that lay like a cord against his cheek and throat. He swore, seeming to take courage. "We honor no murderers! We kill them and denounce their false deities who blaspheme against Bel-Tygeon, lord of all!"

The men around Hyseoth spat curses at Ela. Against the Infinite. One soldier, whose face was tightened with purpled disfigurements, yelled, "Restore health to those you've wounded, and we might allow you to live!"

"Retreat, all of you—now!" Ela warned as the branch sent fiery tendrils of light through her fingers. "Or you'll die in an ambush of scalns!"

One of Hyseoth's companions flung a spear at Ela, but its straight, ferocious path veered sharply to the left the instant it reached the vinewood's dazzling glow.

Caitria muffled a shriek. Commander Vioc stepped in front of her to stand beside Ela. He snarled at the offender. "Cease! You will not threaten these ladies!" To Caitria, he said, "Majesty, lady, remain there, I beg you."

Hyseoth studied the fiery branch, then bellowed, "I'm no coward to be shaken by false magic! Vioc, you traitor, you will die for this! As for you, Prophet—" He spat at Ela, cursing her and the Infinite. Hyseoth's men took courage, adding their foul oaths to his as they lifted their curved bows and set arrows, taking aim.

Ela shuddered, longing to close her eyes against what she'd already seen and felt. Against what she saw and heard now. Hissings from her nightmares merged into lethal reality, making her scarred legs burn with searing memory. An ambush of scalns charged into the encampment and attacked, raking their poisonous red claws through mortal flesh, sinking blade-sharp teeth into the screaming men's bare legs, arms, and throats. Ela cried, reliving the torment of her shredded skin—the poison burning through her blood.

"Infinite . . . ! Majesty, don't run!"

❖ 25 ❖

Scalns!

Caitria gaped at the creatures. Even if Ela hadn't warned her, she would recognize them from childhood lore—manuscripts, sculptures, drawings, and her writing master's stories. But no secondhand account matched these beasts in the flesh.

Their guttural liquid snarls. The venom slopping from their gaping, jagged-toothed red jaws. Their powerful red-leathern bodies revoltingly graceful and pitiless, the scalns tore into the pack of soldiers who'd threatened Ela. Slashing, clawing, biting . . . spilling blood before their victims could draw swords. Caitria shut her eyes, too aghast to move.

The men's terrified shrieks and cries lifted beyond any torment she'd ever imagined. A stench permeated the air, as if the dying men's flesh had already begun to decay, and the odor's thickness filled Caitria's nostrils. Suppressing the need to vomit, she gulped, then slapped both hands over her mouth, stifling her inward screams. Quelling her impulse to run. Stay! She warned herself. Hush! Scalns chase anything that flees. Any raw, moving flesh becomes scaln-fare—her studies had taught her that much. But how had her peaceable studies come to such dreadful life? This could not be real!

Trembling, she fought her instinct to run, and her thoughts babbled in frantic cadence, be-still-be-still-be-still!

Needing support, she gripped Ela's shoulder. The men's screams lessened now, replaced by heart-wrenching groans and the throaty sounds of feasting scalns. Caitria shut her eyes tighter, sending tears down her face. As she wept, she felt Ela shudder, the movement accompanied by a telltale sob. Caitria leaned toward Ela, hearing her gasp, "Infinite, who is like You!"

Then, as Caitria opened her eyes, Ela straightened, her strength seeming restored. She looked over her shoulder at Caitria, calmer, though her eyes and face shone wet with tears. "Wait here. I'll return."

Lifting her eerily bright vinewood staff, Ela walked directly toward the tumult of scalns and dying soldiers. What was she *doing*? Madwoman! She'd die too! Caitria covered her eyes, her stomach knotting so hard she wanted to scream. "Ela, no! Infinite, save her!"

Beside her, Commander Vioc hissed in disbelief. "She's stalking death!"

Would the scalns turn against Ela? "Oh no, don't! Please! Infinite . . . ?" Caitria peeked between her fingers, ready to close her eyes the instant the scalns charged, before the inevitable happened and Ela died.

But Ela planted the glowing staff in the bloodied grass and yelled, "By the Infinite's Holy Name, He commands you to depart!"

As one, the ambush of scalns shrank back from Ela. Then, hissing and snarling, they fled from the encampment, their movements sinuous and sure, touching none of the survivors. Only the men who'd threatened Ela were dead or dying in the shorn field, their bodies stained crimson by blood and by the lowering sun.

Now Commander Vioc followed Ela, though he halted a short distance from the bodies, his frozen stance betraying shock.

For a brief time, Ela stood before the scene of slaughter, her head bowed, the branch's glow softening to the metallic sheen of moonlight. As if unable to bear the sight of such carnage,

Ela turned, her cloak and robes aswirl with the movement. She hurried to Caitria again, appearing so ill that Caitria was sure the prophet would collapse.

Just before she reached Caitria, Ela stopped and knelt, hugging her vinewood staff and trembling violently.

Caitria kneeled beside her, an unnatural hush closing about them. The surviving soldiers stared—their faces carved with fear. Closing her eyes to the men, Caitria hugged Ela tight and cried. Praying. To the Infinite.

✦ ✦ ✦

In the stone-walled, firelit hall, Akabe surveyed the cache of weapons. Forty-two swords, thirty daggers, twenty pikes, and seven battle-axes. All were serviceable soldier's armaments with keen-edged blades and sculpted ivory hafts, their silver pommels shining in the firelight. As for the coins, Akabe reached for a thin oval of silver. A stylized sun gleamed at him, its rays interspersed with the curling script of Belaal. Akabe's stomach tightened.

Cait and Ela had been taken across the border.

Kien crouched beside him, studying the weapons, then turning a coin between his fingers. "Bel-Tygeon's troops took our wives."

"I agree." Well-enough. Bel-Tygeon's soldiers must be halted. As soon as his men returned, Akabe would muster them for a sortie into Belaal. He gathered the telltale coins and dropped them into his money pouch, not bothering to look at them or count them. "There ought to be enough silver here to last us for a few days, if not a week."

"Us?" Kien tossed the oval coin to the stone floor, its thin bell-like tone drawing Akabe's glance. "Again, sir, I'm not leaving this place and neither are you." As Akabe drew breath to argue, Kien said, "You are no ordinary man trying to rescue his wife. You are Siphra's king. You must serve Siphra above yourself and the Infinite above all—and *He* commands us to stay here!"

Akabe gritted his teeth at the reminder . . . then against the force of his own rebellion. He froze, stunned. When had he turned against the Infinite? What had he become? A ruler who trusted his own power more than his Creator's sovereignty. Guilt swept at him like a spiritual torrent, threatening to bring him down. Horrified, he pleaded, "Infinite . . . forgive me!" He'd brought this upon himself and his friends with his own pride—his sin against his Creator. What could he deserve but death?

Even so, Infinite, save Caitria and my friends. I've brought them down with me. . . .

Kien approached now, his voice lowered with concern. "Majesty? What is wrong? Why are you—"

A tap at the hall's broken door halted Kien's interrogation. Riddig leaned inside, his white hair in disorderly spikes, his eyes wide with tension. "Sirs! Your weapons!"

Akabe straightened. *Infinite?* Had Bel-Tygeon's men returned? Or had the Ateans found them? Heart thumping, Akabe checked his sword and joined Kien, grabbing extra daggers, his frustration welling to a murderous fury. They rushed across the hall and sidled through the broken, leather-lashed door, Akabe's prayers quickening with their pace.

Outside, the deepening dusk revealed shapes in gray and black. Akabe stared, his eyes adjusting to the dimness. There. Two cloaked figures entered the gate, black against the grayed gloom beyond. Now lurking at the gate's left, Scythe huffed, then lunged toward the moving cloaks. A man yelled and fled. The other backed against the wall like a trapped animal, screaming, "No! Wait! Augh!" The man's cry heightened as Scythe clamped down on his arm and lifted him off the ground.

Before Scythe could fling away the unknown enemy and shatter him like a clay flask, Kien raised the Azurnite sword and bellowed, "Stop! Bring him here!"

Grumbling warnings despite his full mouth, the destroyer carried the dangling form across the yard and dropped it in a limp heap before Kien and Akabe. Kien rested the Azurnite blade over their adversary's throat, then nudged him with a booted foot. "Unconscious, sir. Unless he's dead."

Riddig Tyne unsheathed his dagger, bent and sliced open the man's sleeve. Even in the dimness, Akabe saw the unmistakable black-etched coils covering the man's bicep. An entrenched Atean.

Riddig huffed, "He's alive." He removed the assassin's belt, using it to bind his feet as Kien removed the fallen man's weapons.

Akabe retrieved a coil from his horse. Riddig wrapped the Atean's cloak cocoon-snug and bound him with fiercely cinched knots. "That should restrain him. I'll tend his wounds if need be."

Casting a wary glance at the gate, Akabe said, "Thank you, Riddig. Continue your watch with Scythe. Kien and I will call you when we've dealt with this man. Alert me when our other men return." What was taking them so long? Disquieted, Akabe crouched beside their prisoner.

Obviously guessing Akabe's intent, Kien grabbed the Atean's booted feet, ready to carry him inside the tower.

✦ ✦ ✦

In the fortress's kitchen, the bruised, cloak-swathed man glared up at Akabe, his dark eyes glittering in the firelight, revealing all the hatred of a man within arm's reach of an unattainable enemy. Aware of Kien lurking to his left, his Azurnite blade readied, Akabe smiled. "I wish we could talk under more agreeable conditions."

"Conditions will be agreeable only when you're dead!" The Atean worked his mouth as if preparing to spit. Kien swung the flat of his glistening blue weapon against the man's lips so swiftly that Fightmaster Lorteus would have gloated. Though Kien stopped short of actually striking, the startled man flinched.

Akabe leaned forward and scowled, baring his teeth at the traitor. "Attempt a phlegm shot and I'll stuff a live coal up your nostril! Trust me, I'm in a foul mood and will be only as merciful as you allow. Attack us in any way and I'll reciprocate with the most savage methods your fellow Ateans used on my men in the Snake Mountains!"

As Kien lifted his sword, Akabe nodded at their now-hushed

prisoner. "Better. Let's keep this civil, shall we? How did you know I was here?"

"It's become known that you're the son of Aythan Garric." With a smirk that made Akabe long to gut-kick him, the man added, "Most of us saw through your ploy."

Akabe muted his reaction, praying the other Ateans were defeated or lost in the DaromKhor Hills. To gather knowledge, he retorted, "But some of you were killed today!"

The prisoner's expression darkened, betraying knowledge of Atean losses. Good. This man was a wellspring of information compared to previous assassins. Not a professional killer.

Kien shot Akabe a conspirator's glance. He nudged the Atean with a booted toe. "Did you see all the skulls before the gate? They died this morning. Impressive isn't it? Forty-two swords." Kien nodded at the nearby cache of weapons. "We're looking forward to adding more."

Their prisoner paled visibly. Akabe scowled. "How many men accompanied you here?"

The Atean looked Akabe straight in the eyes, but his face tensed and his nostrils flared. "Twenty!"

"Liar!" Akabe studied the man, certain of his conclusion. "Only two of you made it this far after your confrontation with my men." For tonight at least. "Otherwise your entire horde would have attacked us outright while we were in the yard."

"So say you, fool!" the man taunted. "Yes, we suffered losses! But so did you! Others are coming. You're dead—all three of you!" He laughed and refused to elaborate.

Enough. Akabe stuffed a dirty cloth into the Atean's mouth, then nodded to Kien. "Grab him by the heels. We'll toss him into the root cellar and let him rot."

The instant the man was stashed away, writhing and howling muffled protests from beneath the cellar's door, Akabe muttered, "Let's make our plans. We can't depend upon my men returning." Were they all dead? Akabe nearly wept at the thought. Instead, he swallowed. "No doubt we've more assassins on the way and only the three of us to meet them. Four—including Scythe. The gate's left side won't take more than a few solid strikes to break it open. How are you with snares?"

"Not proficient. You'll have to teach me."

"Of course." Though his thoughts spun plans for myriad traps, Akabe almost heard his own death dirge. Three men and one destroyer against a throng of attackers who were certainly on their way. . . . Hopeless! He and Kien weren't prophets, able to call upon fire from the Infinite. They couldn't possibly overcome a horde of Ateans. Yet he must be grateful.

Infinite? Thank You for removing Caitria and Ela from the coming attack. Help us—

Kien chuckled darkly, interrupting Akabe's prayer. "Wait. If we're outnumbered, then we're going about this all wrong. Forget the snares for now. Lorteus won't approve, but . . ."

He outlined his plan and Akabe laughed. "I could almost kiss you."

"Don't."

26

The capital of Belaal, the city of Sulaanc, stunned Caitria with its opulence. Dazzling gilded domes crowned pristine white towers. Blue-tiled walls surrounded private residences, which remained unseen except for their elegant soaring spires and ornately carved stone rooftop balustrades. Broad, low-walled white bridges spanned extraordinary canals brimming with pale green water. Intensely blue flowers framed perfect gardens of lush, perfumed red blooms. And everywhere, palm trees—living images from Caitria's childhood tomes—curved gracefully against the most vivid blue sky she'd ever seen.

Fragrances wafted toward her from the crowded marketplace, making her inhale deeply as they rode by. Roasting meats, the tang of pounded spices, and enticing floral scents offered a feast of aromas. Wherever she looked, Caitria saw flowers. If only she could be an ordinary visitor to this city. With Akabe. Her breath caught in longing for her husband—his captivating gaze, the warmth of his voice, his radiant smile, and most of all, his embrace. Yet another night she'd spend away from him—the third! *Why* couldn't Akabe be a merchant? A craftsman? Even an ordinary hunter? They'd be safe. Able to live and perhaps love each other without fear.

However, she was no ordinary visitor to Sulaanc. By now, all the soldiers knew they'd captured Siphra's queen. How could she escape? Infinite? I've no right to ask, but . . . help me!

They approached an immense gatehouse patterned with deep blue tiles, depicting menacing water-dreki—spiky, sinuous amphibian-dragons that made her shudder. Did these creatures exist in Belaal? Infinite, spare me from meeting them! The scalns had been enough.

"Majesty." Commander Vioc drew his horse alongside hers. Dismounting, he assisted Caitria and Ela from their horses, then bowed. "This is where I bid you farewell. May your Infinite bless you."

Caitria nodded, her thoughts—her soul—clinging to the blessing. "Thank you, commander." Would her Creator, yet so new to her, deign to bless her with an escape? She glanced at Ela, who rested her head against the vinewood branch and closed her eyes. Ever since the scalns' ambush, Ela had been ill. Too tired to say more than a few words at a time. Unable to eat or sleep. All worrisome in the extreme.

As much as Ela intimidated her, the prophet had proven herself a friend. A maddening friend who dragged Caitria into horrifying adventures and chilled her to the heart by knowing her thoughts. But a friend nonetheless.

If Ela's illness progressed and she died . . . Caitria's throat tightened at the thought.

Commander Vioc saluted her and started to turn away his horse. With her wedding band! Caitria stopped him. "Sir, where are the armbands? Mine and Lady Aeyrievale's?"

The commander's squared face gentled, revealing a bit of sympathy. "They've been sent onward to the king. He will summon you from the Women's Palace when he has time to speak with you and the prophet."

"The Women's Palace?" She followed Commander Vioc's gaze toward the huge dreki-adorned gatehouse. "This is the Women's Palace?"

Looking surprised that Siphra's queen didn't know what

everyone in the world must know, Vioc shook his head. "No, Majesty. This is the king's residence. The Women's Palace is within his own—for the safety of all his women."

All his women? Now including her and Ela? Caitria clutched at her horse's mane, longing to fling herself onto the beast and make a wild dash for Siphra. Before she could manage another word, Commander Vioc and his men departed and were instantly replaced by a contingent of formidable armor-clad guards, who swiftly surrounded Caitria and Ela.

Two of the new guards led the horses away, while the new commander bowed to Caitria. "Majesty. Enter in peace."

Peace? No! She must resist. Caitria looked from the impassive new commander to the huge gatehouse, which resembled a flamboyant blue-tiled prison. A cold, gentle hand touched Caitria's, making her turn. Ela.

Her movements wearied, her face bloodless, Ela whispered, "Remember my warning, Majesty. If you try to escape, you will fail. And you'll mourn the consequences."

Caitria patted Ela's hand, then gripped her arm, supporting her. "I was just thinking what an exasperating friend you are, and now you've reminded me that I'm right."

Ela's mouth turned upward in a smile. "Thank you, Majesty."

"Of course." Caitria frowned at the guards who rudely herded them toward the ominous palace gate. "Boors!" Bad of her, yes, but she was in no mood to be polite.

Inside the magnificent paved entry yard, they were met by an imperious little woman swathed in flowing crimson robes and crowned with a pert crimson turban. Her dark, unsparing gaze swept Caitria and Ela from head to toe, and her full mouth went prim as if she wasn't the least pleased with what she saw.

Commander Vioc's replacement bowed to the proud woman, whispering to Caitria and Ela, "This is Lady Dasarai. She rules the Women's Palace. Wisdom itself trusts her opinion."

Oh? Who did Lady Dasarai bribe to spread that grand rumor?

Caitria tightened her grip on Ela's arm and smiled. "Lady. We will follow you." Only because they must.

The superior Dasarai inclined her head, the movement graceful as if she'd practiced all her life—and she probably had. In a snobbishly cultured accent that made Caitria feel uncouth, she intoned, "Lady. One is most grateful for your kindness."

Really? Well, this *one* wanted to swat that pert little turban off the impeccably groomed Dasarai and run for the gate. But the guards would snatch her instantly. Caitria sighed and tugged Ela along. She supposed she ought to behave until she was freed from Bel-Tygeon's control.

Would Siphra consider its queen worthy of rescue? Perhaps not. But Akabe might.

No, he mustn't place himself in danger!

Perhaps, for her husband's sake, Caitria was worth more to Siphra as a captive in Belaal.

Mourning the thought, she bit down tears.

✦ ✦ ✦

Following the Lady Dasarai, Ela forced herself to walk down a grandiose palace corridor, though her muscles burned, as if she'd tangled with another aeryon. Infinite, strengthen me. I . . .

Ela gasped, nearly halting as murky translucent flickers swayed to her left and right. Silhouetted forms writhed upward like smoke from jewel-edged golden niches framed within the walls. Deceivers! Shadow spirits! Infinite . . . Ela quickened her prayers and her pace in the corridor. The dark spirits each turned as she approached, revealing their phantom faces, all twisted by revulsion at her presence.

More accurately, by the Infinite's presence with her.

Clearly, the Adversary, the self-aggrandizing spirit foe of the Infinite, had established this palace as a deceivers' stronghold among mortals. Infinite? I know You've revealed these deceivers to me as a warning. How must I deal with them?

Those renegades are a mere symptom of this kingdom's illness. Your concern is with the disease itself.

Flashes of imagery filled her thoughts, provoking a headache that made Ela press the branch to her forehead. How could she deal with this now? All her strength seemed consumed just by the effort to walk. And, obviously, she wasn't even walking properly—Caitria clasped Ela's arm now, supporting her across an inner courtyard, leading her toward a pavilion shielded by elaborate gold-fretted screens.

Caitria's grip locked down on Ela's forearm. "Ela! Why are you lagging? Look . . . just a few more steps and you'll be carried to wherever we're going. Not that we want to go where they're taking us."

Ela blinked, noticing three chairs, each set on a pair of golden poles and each attended by two pudgy, soft-jowled men. They regarded her, Caitria, and Lady Dasarai blandly, as if studying three pieces of rather boring sculpture.

Lady Dasarai glided past the six men as if they didn't exist. She settled herself delicately in the lead chair and motioned languidly for Ela and Caitria to seat themselves in the two remaining chairs. Ela sat and anchored the branch against the chair's built-in footrest. Grateful. Until the two smooth-skinned men waiting nearest her each took hold of her chair's poles and lifted them up to their shoulders, causing Ela to sway aloft and clutch the branch and an armrest. Queasy, she took a deep breath and fixed her gaze on the long, glittering blue-and-gold corridor ahead. Better. And revealing.

Unseen by other mortals, still more deceivers fled in advance of her arrival, departing like plumes of smoke exhaled from extinguished lamps. Obviously, by the fragrance of incense around her, the deceivers—under the guise of Bel-Tygeon and dead god-kings—had been receiving devotions from the palace's inhabitants.

Symptoms of the disease, the Infinite said. Well, the current god-king, Bel-Tygeon, would soon learn the cure. Provided the

Infinite's prophet could summon enough coherence to tell the king what he needed to hear.

Praying for strength, Ela stared ahead through the endless corridor. Why had Bel-Tygeon demanded her presence? He hadn't a clue as to the chaos he'd instigated.

She gripped the armrest as her two porters threaded their way through a maze of tunnels and gates, all protected by stocky, cold-eyed armored female guards who glowered at Ela as she was carried through the gateways. Her two porters finally set her down near Caitria and Lady Dasarai within a large indoor courtyard garden, enclosed by two tiers of apartments. Ela stood, watching servants dash along the apartment walkways, tapping on doors and calling out, "Ladies! Ladies!"

Multitudes of women in gauzy jewel-bright robes and sheer mantles—which failed to conceal their embroidered foundation garments—fluttered from the lower apartments, while on the balconies above, more women peeked around the edges of ornately fashioned metal screens.

Caitria sidled up to Ela and whispered, "We're a sensation! Listen to them chattering."

"They sound like a flock of birds," Ela murmured. Seeing Lady Dasarai approach, she straightened, bringing the branch closer to herself.

The elegant woman inclined her head, allowing Ela and Caitria a stiff little smile. "Ladies, if you please, baths first, then food and rest as we await the king's decisions."

Caitria folded her slender arms, her lovely face hardening. "What sort of decisions?"

Dasarai's brown eyes widened as if shocked that Caitria had asked any sort of question. "The king's decisions concerning the two of you, Majesty. Until then, one waits."

And one slept, Ela hoped. "A bath sounds wonderful, thank you, Lady Dasarai."

"Certainly." Dasarai's smile thinned as if she didn't have much hope for making Ela presentable. "Prophet, do you use some ordinary name?"

Straightening, Caitria spoke with authority. "She is Lady Aeyrievale—one of my own ladies and my friend."

Dasarai smiled again, her voice liquid and sweet as she nodded
toward Ela. "Lady Air-ee-veil. You are a prophet and a noblewoman? Belaal has never known such a rarity. Baths. Now."
She sent away the porters, then led Ela and Caitria through the
courtyard, shooing servants ahead of her and directing the other
women. How many lived in these apartments?

Ela stopped counting at one hundred forty. No doubt she could
safely double that number, then add twice as many to account
for the maids attending these fluttering, gossiping ladies.

They entered a large room equipped with several sparkling
blue-tiled bathing pools. There, the Lady Dasarai halted and
eyed the slaves with the bored expression of one who'd repeated
her duties too often. "Be sure they are scrubbed, then checked
by the physician."

The slaves stepped forward, but Caitria glared at the girls who
prepared to take off her boots. "I will remove my own clothes,
and no one will touch them—I command it!"

Ela jumped, remembering Caitria had concealed Akabe's daggers in her boots. Would the queen be punished? She hurried to
Caitria's side. "Majesty, let me help you. I'll guard your clothes
while you bathe."

Dasarai's mouth tightened with disapproval, but she nodded at the slaves. "The task will take twice as long, Majesty, if
you and Lady Aeyrievale insist upon following Siphran bathing
etiquette."

"We insist." Ela kept her voice pleasant—and the daggers
hidden—as she unlaced Caitria's boots. Even so, she wanted to
hurry. Her body ached with fatigue, and she desperately needed
rest.

The haughty ruler of the Women's Palace sniffed and swept
away in a stylish sulk, no doubt brooding over the injustice of
being burdened with Siphra's fussy queen and its vexing prophet.

The slaves scrubbed Caitria and Ela, swathed them in light

robes and delicate sandals, then notified the physician, a wiry, efficient woman who examined them both from scalp to heels. To Caitria, she said, "You're a bit too thin, Majesty, yet otherwise healthy."

But she surveyed Ela in silence, frowning at the scaln scars on Ela's legs before she checked Ela's pulse. As the examination continued, the physician's gray-brown eyes narrowed with obvious outrage. Ela tried to maintain her composure. Why did the physician glare as if Ela had slapped her? To her relief, the woman stalked from the bathing area, though she snapped over her shoulder at one of the maids, "Send a eunuch to wait outside my door for a message. The rest of you, continue your duties!"

Eunuch? Ela winced, remembering the castrated slaves in Parne's marketplaces—trusted men who traded gems and gold for their foreign masters. Yes, undoubtedly those porters who'd carried her chair were eunuchs. Slaves. If only she could help free Belaal's slaves. . . .

The instant the physician departed, the slaves again took charge of Ela and Caitria, drying, combing and perfuming their hair. As they worked, numerous women took turns staring at Ela and Caitria from the corridor, some chattering, others giggling, all beautiful—though many darted malicious looks toward Siphra's queen and the prophet, clearly regarding them as enemies.

Infinite? Shelter us from their schemes! Let me do Your will. Let Kien . . . Feeling herself weaken, she closed her eyes. She must not think of Kien.

✦ ✦ ✦

Seated beside Ela in the enclosed courtyard, Caitria tugged her sandaled foot away from the stout female metalsmith who'd clamped a smooth gold band around her left ankle. "No! You won't tag me like an expensive pet!"

Her lips tight, the metalsmith nodded to the pudgy guards who surrounded Caitria and Ela. Visibly irritated, the guards locked their soft hands around Caitria's arms and her feet, anchoring her to the ground despite her kicks and struggling. Ugh! Akabe would have beaten those men bloody!

Biting down humiliated tears, Caitria watched the metalsmith lift a bit of heated metal from the nearby firepit, drop it onto her gold ankle band, then swiftly stamp it in place with a seal and a hammer. Each hammer blow struck Caitria to the heart.

Finished, the metalsmith nodded at the pudgy guards, who released Caitria and immediately grabbed Ela.

Though Ela looked as disgusted as Caitria felt, she didn't resist while the metalsmith fastened a similar gold band around her bare left ankle.

Marking them both, Caitria realized, as slaves.

✦ ✦ ✦

"Lady." A young woman's gentle voice roused Ela from her evening nap. "Forgive me, but you and the queen are summoned. Please hurry. Our lord-god-king waits."

The king? Ela pushed aside the light coverlet and dragged herself from the cushioned pallet. She shook out her thin tunic and headed to the corner where she'd piled her clothes and the queen's. "I require my mantle."

The girl faltered, "B-but . . . that is the traditional attire of the king's women. He might be offended if you reject our ways."

Truly? Hmm. This mantle was lovely, but inappropriate for a royal audience. "I'm cold, and I'm not one of the king's women." Best to make herself understood now, whether Bel-Tygeon liked it or not. She swept a mantle over her shoulders and then snatched Caitria's, checking for Akabe's contraband daggers. Gone. Had one of the slaves removed them?

The slave—now hovering near the queen's sleeping pallet— held no daggers, only a comb. "Majesty, I beg you, wake."

Soft-voiced, but obviously alert, Caitria asked, "What is your name?"

The slave twitched and stammered, "M-Mari, Majesty."

"Well, Mari, as far as *I'm* concerned, your lord-god-king can wait for his entire mortal life. But for your sake, we'll hurry." She flung back the coverlets and stood.

Mari smoothed the queen's hair and adjusted the thin tunic. Ela waited, pointedly dangling Caitria's mantle. Just as pointedly, Mari ignored her. "Thank you, Majesty. You're ready. Please, follow me." She crossed to the door and waited.

Caitria frowned at her fragile tunic and reached for her mantle. Ela draped Caitria's mantle around her shoulders, taking enough time to whisper, "Where are the king's daggers?"

Hushed as a breath, Caitria replied, "I buried them while you slept." Raising her voice she said, "Thank you, Lady Aeyrievale. I believe we're ready. Lead us, Mari, please."

As Ela turned, the branch took shape, gleaming pale blue-white in her clenched hands.

Mari gasped, stared, then fled their chamber.

Caitria raised an eyebrow at Ela. "I hope you have the same effect upon the king."

✦ ✦ ✦

In the depths of the kitchen's root cellar, Akabe dumped more dirt over the Atean's body. Not the way he'd expected to spend this afternoon. Beside him, Kien added another shovel-full of soil, tamped down the heap, and scowled in the dim light. "I can't believe he swallowed that cloth! If he hadn't driven himself into such a frenzy, he would have lived."

"Just long enough to betray us when his fellow killers arrive."

Kien exhaled. "It's been three nights of cold food and waiting. Everything's ready. Those traitors should have arrived by now, unless the Council learned of their plans and arrested them all. I can't help wondering . . . why haven't we heard from the Council? Or from your men? We should have by now."

Akabe hefted a final scoop of loosened soil from the cellar's broken clay floor. "Perhaps they're lost in the hills. It's happened before." That scenario was better than his alternate theory, involving the assassins finding and killing the Royal Council's

242

messengers and soldiers. Along with his royal advisors and all the workmen at the temple site—including Dan Roeh.

Infinite, save us all!

Muted footsteps overhead made them both look up, toward the cellar door. Riddig Tyne descended the ladder and closed the door with such noiseless care that Akabe stilled.

The assassins had arrived.

Staring up at the single razor-thin break of light showing through the cellar door, Akabe slid the sword off his back and waited in the near darkness. Beside him, Kien and Riddig quietly readied their weapons.

His gaze fixed on the cellar door, Akabe prayed.

27

Gripping his sword's hilt, Akabe tensed as someone clattered through the kitchen above. If the intruder was the least bit observant, they'd find the cellar door.

Infinite, please, let them fall for the ruse!

The clattering stopped as a deep, exultant voice boomed through the kitchen. "Uzleon, hurry! We have the proof—let's be gone before we're turned to dust. This place is cursed!"

From just above the root cellar door, a man answered, "Yes, yes, I'm coming. I'd hoped to find some extra food."

"Don't waste your time," the loud one bellowed. "I'd eat worms first! The food here is likely poisoned, and that cursed destroyer won't be soothed, so come on—we're leaving."

Uzleon growled audibly. "Go ahead. I'll hurry." After a short silence, then more scraping and thuds above, the root cellar door opened, silent on its freshly oiled hinges.

Sweat lifted over Akabe's skin as he waited for the man to yell to his comrades. Instead, Uzleon sniffed the air, tapped the ladder with his sword, then clambered down the rungs. Riddig was on the fool in a blink, stifling him and clubbing him with the flat of a metal axe. Even as the man fell, Akabe hurried up the rungs and quietly closed the root cellar door.

Together, they gagged the unconscious man and tied his hands and feet. While Akabe wrenched the knots tight, voices echoed through the kitchen. "Uzleon? Uzleon! Where are you?"

"Curse the man!" the now-familiar big voice boomed. "He said he'd be out directly."

Someone flung something metallic—Akabe heard it ringing across the kitchen as a second man roared, "Uzleon, we're leaving before we lose our horses! That destroyer's turned vicious! Make your own way home!"

At Akabe's feet, the hapless Uzleon stirred to consciousness. Riddig clouted him again, and the soldier stilled. Akabe pressed his fingertips to the man's throat and waited. Uzleon's pulse faded. Akabe sighed. He should have told Riddig to spare the man for questioning. His skin crawling with unease, Akabe waited for the next disaster. At last a destroyer's rumbling vibrated through the walls, accompanied by a telltale hoof-thud. Kien muttered, "Scythe's calling us. They must be gone."

Riddig Tyne grunted. "Seems they were taken by the hoax, sirs."

His voice indignant, Kien protested, "Hoax? As if my inspiration was a con's trick!"

Akabe hushed them. "It was a brilliant plan, sirs, so let's not argue. I want to see what evidence those Ateans considered to be the best proof of our deaths."

Weapons readied, Akabe abandoned Uzleon's body and led his friends through the silent kitchen and the narrow stone passage, then into the keep's great hall. Empty. Except for the evidence. Good. Akabe hurried to inspect their death scene. He and Kien had traded grim jokes while sweeping the area clean of their boot prints, then selecting the skeletons most like themselves and arranging them on the hall's tiles before garnishing the death scene with ashes sifted from the hall's central hearth.

Riddig had abandoned keeping watch just long enough to critique their work and to add his silver royal military-surgeon insignia to "his" skeleton. Now, Akabe noted, Riddig's insignia was gone. As was Kien's sacrificed dagger, a signet, and Akabe's most ornate and recognizable sword and ring—with various coins and some clasps they'd removed from their clothes.

Halting just beside Akabe, Kien rubbed a hand over his stubbly dark beard, looking rueful. "I was hoping they wouldn't steal *all* the clasps—we're now a savage trio."

Akabe ran his knuckles through his own beard. "Soon no one will recognize me if they stare me in the face." He studied the skeletons. "These ought to remain here, untouched. We'll continue to take turns keeping watch and praying our wives return soon."

Riddig heaved a sigh of mingled relief and concern. "I wonder how long it'll be before searchers come after that Uzleon fellow."

Sheathing his Azurnite sword, Kien crouched on the stones near the hall's central hearth, brooding over their death scene. "Yes. And I wonder how long it will take those Ateans to realize they didn't see our wives' skeletons near ours."

Indeed. But of course, thankfully, there'd been no women's skeletons. Akabe frowned, pondering an equally troubling possibility. If the Ateans should meet the rogue who'd escaped Scythe three nights past, they'd all no doubt exchange stories and realize they'd been duped. Sliding his sword into its scabbard, Akabe shrugged. "At least this ploy bought us some time."

A low, vibrant rumble coursed through the air, beckoning them all to the tower's entrance. Scythe loomed in the yard, chewing a mouthful of twigs and eyeing Akabe balefully.

Was the beast blaming him for the commotion? Well-enough. Akabe couldn't fault the monster. Unable to resist some destroyer-gibing, Akabe asked, "Have you cleared the yard, Master Scythe? Rest assured, I'll be inspecting your work soon."

Scythe huffed and turned his rump toward the king, almost making Akabe smile.

Kien grinned. "I'd best take him for a run."

"I'll return to watch duty," Riddig said.

Akabe nodded at his friends. "Good. I'll check to see if they stole our food." And, now that they'd survived, he might spend some time optimistically praying. Infinite? Let Caitria and Ela return! Send word from the Royal Council—and speed those reinforcement guards to us before the Atean assassins return!

✦ ✦ ✦

Fighting giddiness as two eunuchs shouldered her golden chair, Ela clutched the branch and fixed her gaze on Caitria, who sat stiff-backed as a doll in her own gilded seat. She could imagine what Caitria was thinking. Ela guessed her own thoughts were much like the young queen's. Fury. Distress. And longing for her husband.

Was Caitria appealing to the Infinite for safety? What a relief— a joy—that she now trusted Him. Eyes wide open, Ela prayed to her beloved Creator. Give me courage! With strength enough to accomplish whatever task You might command of me this evening . . . I beg You!

I am here.

"Thank You!" She relaxed in the chair, blessing Him. Loving His voice—His presence.

The corridor ended at a gilded gate, guarded by three big armor-clad female guards who glowered at Ela as if they believed her to be living poison. Yet they nodded her eunuch porters through. Beyond the sparkling gate, a short passageway opened into a magnificent room of blue and gold marble, its walls lined with gold-cushioned benches. A place where multitudes of people might sit and wait for an audience with their god-king.

Ela swallowed hard as the eunuchs lowered her chair to the floor, causing her to sway, making her queasy again. Supporting herself with the branch, she stood, still exhausted despite the nap. The instant she and Caitria stepped away, the porters lifted the chairs and departed without a word or a glance.

Still watching Ela, female guards shut the gate, locking Ela and Caitria inside the blue-and-gold room. Caitria sidled near. "What now?"

"We wait, Majesty."

"I feel nothing like a 'Majesty.'"

Another soft-faced eunuch emerged through a concealed door that opened in a far wall, his hulking form clad in gold robes and wafting dignity like a perfume. He bowed to Ela and Caitria, beckoning them in a delicate, girlish voice. "Ladies?"

As they crossed the golden receiving area, Caitria whispered to Ela, "Why do so many of the king's men sound like that? It's—"

Ela tweaked the queen's sleeve, murmuring, "They're eunuchs."

"Truly?" Caitria gasped like a shocked child. "I've read about them, but . . ." She swallowed and gazed at the eunuch with pity.

Ela understood the queen's reaction. Neither Siphra nor the Tracelands kept slaves or eunuchs.

Imperturbably calm, the big man bowed them through the doorway. As they entered a huge golden chamber, he bowed once more, then departed, closing the door softly. Leaving Ela and Caitria with Bel-Tygeon. In his bedchamber. Infinite!

Ela halted her impulse to run.

The king, who'd evidently been pacing and reading letters, flung aside a parchment and strode toward Ela and Caitria, his gold-embroidered yellow robes flaring. Bel-Tygeon seemed arrogant as ever, but younger than Ela had realized. And even more handsome than she'd remembered from Parne.

His thick black hair gleamed in the evening light, and his dark eyes burned with such ferocity that she nearly stepped back. A scowl hardened his perfectly sculpted face, and he pointed at Ela as if he wanted to doom her forever. "*You* are pregnant! Don't deny it—the physician recognized the signs. It's annoying enough as it is to heed the words of a female prophet, much less trust one who is pregnant!"

What? Ela stared at the king, too shocked to speak. Pregnant? No! But . . . pregnancy might explain the physician's odd reaction and . . . certain symptoms. . . .

Stunned, Ela appealed to her Creator. Infinite? Am I?
Yes.

Oh no! And yet . . . Aware of Bel-Tygeon's unrelenting glare and Caitria's openmouthed surprise, Ela sucked in a breath. As Kien would say, *steady*. She clenched the branch and looked the furious king in the eyes. "It's not my words you should trust, O king, but the Infinite's. Furthermore, if I am pregnant, it's my husband's concern and mine—not yours!"

"There, you are wrong!" Bel-Tygeon stood almost toe to toe with her now, smugness lessening his indignation. "As my slave, you have no husband! You and your child are mine by law. You are *my* belongings!"

"Then it's a vile law! Who are you to defy what the Infinite has ordained? You, Bel-Tygeon, are no god!"

The king's aristocratic nostrils flared and his upper lip curved in contempt. "So you say, Prophet. But where is your Infinite now, when you are powerless and under my rule?"

"He rules from His throne, but you do not! And your estimation of your own power will swiftly diminish."

Bel-Tygeon leaned so near that she could feel his breath warm against her cheek. The fragrance of rich spices surrounded her as he murmured, "Is that a threat from my prophet?"

"It's the truth. And I am not your prophet!" She shifted the branch, reminding herself not to wallop the god-king. How dare he smile so! Quietly, she warned, "You were determined to bring me here against my will—so here I am! You'll regret your decision. However, if you believe Belaal requires a true prophet, the Infinite might consent to your wish."

Infinite? Truly?

Yes.

Ela went sick inside. How long would she serve in Belaal? Yet she knew the answer: as long as the Infinite required—even to the day of her death. But what about the baby? Kien's baby . . .

Controlling herself, Ela continued. "The Infinite warns that your kingdom is diseased, and He will take *you* apart—body and spirit—until you acknowledge His Holy Name!"

"When?" The king stepped back, lifting his hands in a mockery of astonishment. "Where is your Infinite to challenge me?"

"He is here. Watching you." Fresh tendrils of light seeped from the branch. Bel-Tygeon lowered his hands and studied the glowing vinewood like a man suspecting some trick. Ela planted the precious insignia between them. "This is the truth, Majesty. You are no god. Almost one hundred of your men perished because they defied the Infinite and threatened evil against me, and you are no better than they were! Our Creator threw you into the dust at Parne, remember? Now, to bring you to understanding, for your own sake and Belaal's—to the glory of His Name—He will humble you again. This time in your own realm."

Bel-Tygeon laughed, and his smile was dazzling despite his contempt. "Let Him try! Parne was a mere windstorm!" Then the radiant grin faded, replaced by sudden severity. "I've been threatened by myriad foreign priests and prophets swearing retribution from their gods. Your Infinite is nothing to me!" He lifted his chin. "The only reason I'll endure you, Prophet, is that you predicted what would happen in Parne. You have the gift of divination that my prophets lack. Therefore, I swear now, for as long as *I* say and until you fail me, you are my prophet, *my* slave! You will prophesy my victories and proclaim the downfall of other lands—as you declared Parne's."

"I will not." Ela looked from the king's too-attractive face to the glowing branch. Why was he obsessed with her foretelling his victories? Had his resolve or his armies been weakened enough that he needed some spiritual reassurance before planning another war? Perhaps.

Infinite, let Belaal be too weakened to risk a war with Siphra!

Ela frowned at the cold-eyed king. "If you don't heed Him, then everything you know, all that you possess, will be removed for your own sake. Your Creator is *that* concerned for you!"

For one heartbeat, Bel-Tygeon seemed to reconsider. To heed her warning. But then he raised a hand and turned away from the branch. "We shall see. Until then, you are my slave. As is your child." He grinned at Caitria now, sweeping her with such an appraising look that she blushed. "You are Akabe of Siphra's wife? I see why he resisted his beliefs to marry you."

Caitria lifted her chin. "He married me to acquire sacred land for the Infinite's temple. But never mind that. Where is my armband? And Lady Aeyrievale's?"

"Your wedding trinkets?" The king crossed the room to his desk and picked up the bands. "Take them." He tossed the marriage symbols at Caitria's feet. "They mean nothing in Belaal."

The blush deepened over Caitria's face. Ela guessed by the tense line of the young queen's mouth that she was fighting to suppress her temper. As Ela retrieved the bands and cautiously stood again, Caitria said, "Perhaps they mean nothing to you or to Belaal, sir, but Lady Aeyrievale and I treasure them—as we cherish our husbands."

"I remind you both that you have no husbands. In my palaces, my slaves are not allowed marriage. However . . ." He paused, looking thoughtful. "Belaal has never captured a foreign queen. Interesting. Tell me . . . where is Siphra's king?"

As Caitria's beautiful face hardened in unspoken defiance, the Infinite's warning whisked through Ela's thoughts, making her jump. When Bel-Tygeon eyed her, she said, "Sir, Siphra's king is not your concern. What's more, your Creator declares that if you or your men enter Siphra now, you will die. And your royal dynasty will end."

For a long instant Belaal's king stared at her, clearly assessing her warning and possible intent. Quietly, he said, "I will deal with Siphra's upstart king when I please. For now . . ." He smiled at Caitria. "What should happen to you, Lady of Siphra? Imprisonment? Ransom?"

Paling, Caitria said, "I'm a divisive queen—hardly worth ransoming."

Bel-Tygeon lifted a lock of her soft brown hair, smoothing it between his fingers before allowing it to fall. "Then I'll keep you." His tone insinuated far more than mere keeping.

Ela tilted the still-glowing branch, using it like a sword to divide the air between the young king and Siphra's queen. "She is not yours."

Bel-Tygeon shot her a killing look. "Prophet, you overstep!"

Did she? Ha. Arrogant, spoiled young man! Fury forced her to speak through gritted teeth. "*You* overstep, sir, and the sooner you realize your mortal failings, the better for you and your people!"

He swept one long, powerful hand toward the branch to snatch it. Light flared and a sizzling noise cut through the air as his fingers passed through the vinewood. Caitria gasped and stumbled backward. Sparks hissed past Bel-Tygeon's shimmering black hair. For an instant he looked as shocked as a boy unexpectedly scolded by his father. Ela softened her tone. "If you test your Creator, O king, you'll fail. Please abandon your pride and listen. Your Creator calls to you."

Bel-Tygeon stalked toward the nearest wall and yanked a golden cord. Within three breaths, the big gold-clad eunuch opened the hidden door and bowed. The king snapped, "Return them to the Women's Palace and tell Lady Dasarai I'm retiring for the night."

Again the eunuch bowed. Radiating dignified displeasure at Ela and Caitria, he motioned them through the doorway into the golden room beyond. Ela nodded at Caitria. "Majesty."

Caitria edged toward the doorway, and as she passed Ela, whispered, "You should have toasted him!"

"I think not." Ela followed her, praying Bel-Tygeon was shaken enough to consider his Creator.

✦ ✦ ✦

In the tiny walled garden outside her chamber, Caitria snatched up a decorative stone and flung it at the farthest wall with all her might, raging inwardly at Bel-Tygeon. A hit to his pretend nose! A bash to his imaginary left eye—then his right! She sent a volley of rocks at each target, venting her rage and fear.

If only her self-defense could be real. If only she could knock that egotistical god-king senseless and escape! What would she do if he summoned her to his bedchamber again to fulfill his implied threat? Caitria paused to catch her breath, sickened by the thought. She would *die.*

A whimper lifted in her throat. "Akabe!" If only she could see her husband's beloved face and cherish the joy of his embrace once more.

Infinite . . . help us escape!

She could almost believe He might indeed help her. The sizzle of Bel-Tygeon's hand, the shock on his face, those blue-white sparks singeing past his hair as if to set it afire . . .

Nevertheless, why should the Infinite be concerned with her? Surely she was nothing to Him. Therefore, she must think objectively. She must escape. How could Akabe and Siphra be expected to ransom an undeserving queen who'd inspired such conflict? She wasn't worth ransoming, not even for the temple. She must escape!

A light footstep in the doorway made Caitria turn. Ela. Watching her.

As if reading her thoughts, Ela pleaded, "Majesty, don't do anything desperate."

Escape was logical, not desperate. Hoping to distract her intuitive prophet-friend, Caitria smiled, envying her. "Are you truly with child? Congratulations!"

To her shock, Ela's tensed expression crumpled, giving way to tears.

✦ ✦ ✦

Pregnant? Infinite, no! Ela leaned against the doorframe, trembling. Sobbing. Thus far she'd seen no escape from Belaal. Would Kien's baby reside in Belaal as a helpless slave? Unacceptable! How could she endure such grief?

Infinite, please . . .

Arms enfolded her. Caitria sighed. "Poor Ela, I'm sorry! I pray the Infinite protects us."

Ela blinked away more tears. "It helps just hearing you say those words."

Caitria offered a wistful smile and a nod. "You thought I wasn't listening to you or to the Infinite. Well, only a fool would not!" She rubbed the edge of her mantle over Ela's tear-streaked face. "Now, it's your turn to listen. As your queen, I command you to stop crying. I'm glad we have a reason to celebrate."

Reason indeed! Heart-torn, Ela hugged her and sniffled, blessing their Creator.

✦ ✦ ✦

Unable to sleep after his turn at watch duty, Kien removed some squares of parchment from his small travel desk, unsealed an ink vial, and settled down to write.

Dear Father, Mother, Beka, and Jon,

If you read this, know that I am gone. Remember that I have loved you all beyond measure, and I thank you for every instant of our time together. Believe me, I departed with no regrets, strengthened by every fond remembrance any man might hope for in life. I pray the Infinite blesses you all. . . .

Kien paused and studied the words. It was his duty to remain cheerful and optimistic for his comrades. For his king. But alone with himself, he must face the truth. When the assassins returned, no ploy would deter them a second time. Death waited, and he would be ready.

Resolute, he contemplated his note. This one for his family and friends in the Tracelands and one for Ela. Dear adorable Ela! Who could imagine a zealous little prophet would bring him such happiness? Certainly not the insufferably self-certain Kien Lantec he'd once been.

He'd also ink a note to Bryce and Aeyrievale.

"Infinite? Am I forgetting anyone?"

Your Creator.

Kien almost smiled. True. All things considered, he'd been blessed far more than he deserved. "What, then, should I write to You, my Creator?"

He hardly expected an answer, but it came at once, swathing him in comfort.

Write your love for Me on your heart, where My Spirit finds it always.

Kien pondered the words, then nodded, swallowing hard. Excellent advice, of course. No ink needed. He prayed, then tapped his reed pen in the ink jar again and finished the note to his family.

Preparing to die.

✦ 28 ✦

Stomach roiling, Ela sat up in her pallet when Lady Dasarai entered the chamber.

Elegant and severe in a flowing crimson gown and bejeweled headdress, the noblewoman studied Ela, then the drowsy Caitria, as if considering how to conquer their doldrums. Evidently deciding her tactics, she smiled. "One must not mope in the Women's Palace. We are the blessed in Belaal, granted the privilege of delighting our enduring sovereign, who is Prized of the Heavens. We must take joy in each day as we seek to serve him."

"Why?" Ela couldn't prevent mortal disgust from edging her words. "He's no god! And he has stolen us from our husbands and our country. We are not his!"

Smoothly, as if she hadn't heard, Dasarai said, "Each day is your gift to him and to yourself. You are encouraged to join your palace sisters in seeking to improve yourselves for your king's sake. You may offer him religious devotions, compose songs, write, play games to gladden your souls, beautify yourselves—"

On the other side of the chamber, Caitria sat up in her pallet. "Oh, this is too much! Offer him religious devotions? Beautify ourselves?" Siphra's queen glared. "I'll bathe in manure and wear the stuff if it'll keep him away!"

Dasarai's sculpted eyebrows lifted. "Respect for your rank and his, Majesty, ought to prevent you from taking such a dire step."

"Why should I respect his rank when he has none for mine?"

Ela winced. While Caitria argued and Dasarai frowned, an insight bloomed unpleasantly in Ela's thoughts. And a sudden pulsing headache compounded her nausea. Did the overseer of the Women's Palace truly expect her to worship Belaal's god-king? Well, evidently Dasarai was one of Bel-Tygeon's few faithful in this sad place. "Lady Dasarai, it seems our 'palace sisters' enjoy gambling, fighting, and gossip far more than worshiping their god-king. Why have you left those particular pastimes off your list of recommended activities?"

Still poised, the noblewoman stared, and then shook her head as if denying unpleasant news. "One hopes two ladies of such renown would devote themselves to providing examples of perfect conduct for others to admire and follow."

Ela flung aside her coverlet. "My Creator does expect me to provide a good example for others. I might not meet His expectations; however I'm always willing to try. But my good conduct involves never worshiping a false god-king, however glorious he appears!"

Dasarai stiffened, rage visible in her tensed, now flushed face. "You will not provoke a rebellion in this palace, nor in this land!"

Staring at the noblewoman's lustrous, wrathful eyes, Ela recognized a familiar glint. A family resemblance. *Infinite? Am I right?*

Flickers of new imagery and emotions whisked through Ela's mind. Betrayals, terrors, and rebellions in this glittering palace. With acts of self-sacrifice that clenched Ela's heart. She gasped and fought the spinning sensation as her Creator said, *Yes. Speak to Rethae. Warn her.*

Some of Ela's misery faded. She grabbed the branch from its resting place beside her pallet and stood. Humbled by fresh understanding, Ela gentled her approach to the irate Dasarai. "Lady, I will not provoke a rebellion. But the Infinite might, unless your king renounces his pride and ceases to oppress people beneath his rule." A chill prickled over Ela's skin, wrought by terrors from her past. "The Infinite has made Bel-Tygeon king, but that can be undone, as it was in the kingdoms of Istgard and Siphra." Softening her voice further, Ela added, "Rethae, you are the king's half sister. You raised Bel-Tygeon as your own, and you love him beyond your life. Please, persuade him to listen to the Infinite—for the sake of his people and for himself."

Rethae gasped, her sparkling headdress teetering slightly as she jerked backward. "How did you know my name? No one in the Women's Palace knows it—they're too young to remember the past."

"Nothing is hidden from the Infinite. Lady, as you love your brother, speak to him. You *know* he is mortal and—"

The noblewoman lifted her exquisite hands as if to cover her ears. "No! Every king of Belaal is consecrated to godhood! You do not know our ways, and I'll not listen to you!"

Ela's spirit sank with disappointment. How could she inspire this one living person whom Bel-Tygeon respected? "Very well, Lady. It's your decision. Even so, I promise you, the Infinite watches and waits. He loves you, as He loves your brother. I also give you my word that the queen and I will say nothing to anyone of your name or what we've discussed this morning."

"Yes," Caitria agreed, hugging the coverlet over her knees. "I agree with Lady Aeyrievale. We'll say nothing. But . . ." She flung Dasarai a pleading glance. "Won't you at least send us some decent robes? We're not used to such inadequate tunics!"

The ruler of the Women's Palace sighed. "I cannot countermand our traditions—and those tunics are appropriate to our climate and the palace. Nevertheless, I'll send you more gowns. Use them as you deem best. I'll also send in your meals today, as neither of you are well enough to visit with your palace-sisters."

A timid scraping at the doorpost made them turn. Ela hurried to the door. Mari, the young slave who'd tended them earlier, shivered visibly in the entry. Fragile and no more than fifteen, her hazel eyes wide, she clutched an ornate box and stared at Ela as if she expected to be cursed.

Ela smiled. "How may I help you?"

The slave showed Ela the box. "For the Lady Caitria. From the king."

Ela gaped at the small, elaborate box of silver-black metal, patterned with golden flowers and sprinkled with jewels of every imaginable color. Why would Bel-Tygeon send this to Caitria? "Thank you. Please come in and speak to the queen."

The girl trembled as if Ela had invited her inside to be eaten by a monster. All right. She smiled at the slave again, gently held her arm, and coaxed her inside. "We're probably more frightened than you are."

Lady Dasarai looked from the box to the girl. "Mari, whose is this?"

Stepping backward onto Ela's bare toes, Mari stammered, "Lady C-Caitria."

The noblewoman rubbed her temples, seeming hit by a sudden headache. She motioned the slave toward Caitria. As Siphra's queen accepted the exquisite token, Dasarai said, "You are invited to visit the king tomorrow night. Refusal is not permitted."

Still looking pained, Dasarai signaled to Mari, who followed her through the doorway without a word of farewell. The door thumped shut.

Ela stared at Caitria.

Siphra's queen threw the bejeweled box squarely at the closed door. The superb trinket cracked against the carved wood, spilling its glittering gemstone contents as it fell to the tiles below. A dent marred the door. "Oh! I'll give him a refusal! How dare he! I'll—"

As Caitria ranted, Ela sighed, thinking of the young slave and feeling like a failure. When would she learn to fully trust her Creator? She'd been so fixated on being enslaved herself that she'd nearly missed a vital portion of the Infinite's purpose: to reach the king, and all the souls in this palace and beyond.

✦ ✦ ✦

Refusal is not permitted. "Oh!" Hands clenched, Caitria paced through her small garden.

Only a king who imagined himself to be a god would dare to take another king's wife. How could she escape this trap? She could just imagine Bel-Tygeon gloating as eunuchs carried her kicking and screaming into the royal chamber tomorrow night. Or gagged and bound hand and foot, because that is what must happen: She would not go peaceably.

Caitria stalked to the corner of the garden and lifted the broad paving stone she'd chosen on the afternoon of her arrival. Cautious of dirtying her hands and creating suspicion, Caitria slid a flattened leather bag from beneath the stone. She opened the bag and removed one of Akabe's small, plain daggers from its scabbard, contemplating her options.

Bel-Tygeon and his palace were so heavily guarded that if she wounded or killed Belaal's god-king in self-defense, she'd probably be executed in turn.

Was she ready to die? No. She wanted to see Akabe again. Therefore, daggers were out. But she must concoct a credible escape from Bel-Tygeon's invitation. Infinite, inspire me. . . .

Ela entered the garden. "Majesty, our morning meal has arrived."

"Thank you. I think. Truly, I'd almost rather starve than eat his food." She scowled and eyed Ela. "Do you have any suggestions, Prophet?"

A sweet smile lit Ela's tired face. "Pray to the Infinite for your safe rescue."

Caitria hid the daggers again. "I have prayed."

"Then continue." Ela's smile faded and she stepped back, silently insisting upon Caitria's precedence as queen. "Meanwhile, I'm also praying for you with all my heart. Trust your Creator's plan. Not your own."

How did she *know*? Caitria crossed their comfortable room and kneeled beside a low table. Ela joined her, lifting the beautifully patterned domed ceramic lids from various dishes.

Caitria stared at the food. Soft flatbread, of course, surrounded by dishes of fragrant sauces, steamed herbed grains and vegetables, fresh berries, and tender chunks of roasted meat. She wanted none of it. Furthermore, the berries would give her a blooming, itching rash guaranteed to send Naynee into a panic if dear Naynee were here.

Berries? Even as Caitria considered the delectable, dangerous fruit, Ela spoke, her tone soft. Careful. "Majesty . . . how terrible is your reaction to berries? Is the rash spectacular?"

"Yes." She hadn't even touched the berries, but already Caitria's skin crawled wildly and invisible bands seemed to tighten around her throat and lungs.

This would work without too much trouble, wouldn't it?

Not allowing herself to fully acknowledge the prayer taking shape in her thoughts, Caitria reached for the glowing red berries. "Eat some, Ela, if you enjoy them. I need only a few."

✦ ✦ ✦

Caitria watched the Women's Palace physician, that lean, grim female swathed in gray robes matching her sparse, tightly coiled gray hair. The doctor opened a polished black box and removed a round stoneware jar. The sludge-green ointment inside the jar looked positively lethal. Caitria winced. "Will it sting?"

Worse, would it heal her?

"Not at all, Majesty." The doctor glopped some of the ointment on Caitria's splotchy forearms and rubbed it in, her touch ice-cold. "This should ease some of your misery. Alas, it will not cure you. Have you eaten anything new recently?"

Oh, lovely—a too-clever doctor with chilly hands. Aware of Ela watching and listening, Caitria told a not-quite truth. "Some of the sauces I was served this morning looked unusual, but they were delicious."

The doctor's mouth turned downward at the word *sauces*. Peevish, she scolded Lady Dasarai, who stood near the door. "Your young ladies are forever eating those rich sauces, Lady, though I have warned you against them. Such exotic fare provides hiding places for poison—with miserable results!" She gestured at Caitria's hive-covered arms and swollen face.

Dasarai sniffed. "I doubt the queen was poisoned. If so, she'd be dead by now. Furthermore, the sauces mightn't be to blame, and the ladies will riot if they're served nothing but plain steamed foods. My questions, good doctor, are first, can the queen be cured quickly? And second, is she contagious?"

"Not quickly. And possibly yes to contagious. Keep her isolated."

Triumph! Caitria hid her glee by scratching her welted arms and her scalp. The doctor slathered more ointment on her arms and in her hair. Its gooey chill slid down Caitria's neck, making her shudder. Before she could protest, the doctor snapped, "No scratching the hives, Majesty, lest you cause scars."

"I won't hold you responsible," Caitria promised. "However, I'd prefer to apply my own ointment. Will Lady Aeyrievale be safe if she remains with me?"

The doctor's narrow face seemed all the more pinched. "If you are contagious, Majesty, it is too late to protect *her*." Sounding hopeful, she asked, "Do you wish the prophet gone?"

"Not necessarily."

"Ha!" Ela gave her a pretend-angry scowl. "See if I don't remember that!"

Caitria laughed, then wheezed as her throat tightened. At once the suspicious doctor snatched a long ominous-looking gold tube. "Open your mouth, Majesty. If you can swallow, I will give you a remedy to bring you rest."

✦ ✦ ✦

Ela kneeled beside Caitria's pallet, trying to ease her growing fears. The queen was pale beneath the welts and her every breath rasped. "Is this how you always react to berries?"

"Yes. Naynee says I also become irritable with the hives—just warning you."

"Majesty, are you risking your life with those berries?"

Definitely cranky, Caitria huffed, "I'd rather risk berries than *his* attention!"

Not reassuring. Ela clasped the branch, knelt, and closed her eyes. Infinite . . . ?

"You're praying, aren't you?" Caitria sounded so petulant that Ela opened her eyes.

Hmm. Siphra's soft-eyed queen was turning quarrelsome. Bad berries. And the physician's remedies were obviously affecting her. "Yes, Majesty."

"Well, pray aloud!" But before Ela could pray, Caitria continued, rambling beneath the effects of the doctor's medicines. "I now believe He exists. Yet there's so much I don't understand. His followers are no different from any others," Caitria muttered. "Just as Ateans offer sacrifices to Atea to placate her, the Infinite's priests offer sacrifices to placate Him."

"To protect us, through obedience to Him, yes. Yet sacrifices offered by mortal priests are also imperfect. Perfection requires faultlessness and, someday, the Infinite will provide a perfect sacrifice for us all. Until then, we wait and trust Him as children trust their father."

Caitria's eyelids were closing. Her words drifted. "Except for my lady-mother . . . and Naynee . . . you and Akabe and . . . Kien have been the only people to treat me kindly. Dear Akabe . . . ." She yawned. "You say the Infinite is . . . as a father. I want *my* lord-father to be a father. . . ." Her breathing eased, and she dozed.

Satisfied that Caitria's coloring looked better, though the splotches didn't, Ela relaxed. She prayed, then set aside the branch. After washing her face and combing her hair, she donned fresh layers of fragile tunics. White, pale blue, then deep blue, covered by a sheer, flowing, embroidered white mantle. Lovely. But not her own. Wearied, Ela turned to lie down on her pallet—just as the branch flared alarmingly in her hand.

A breath of air whisked past her face, making her heart skip with fear. "Oh no!"

The air current closed about Ela like a mighty fist and swept her away.

✦ 29 ✦

As the whirlwind released her, Ela drew in a shaky breath. Mercy. One more shift like this and she would certainly retch. Where was she? Ela swept her rumpled hair away from her face, then focused her gaze on the glittering spectacle before her.

Bel-Tygeon was seated several marble steps above her on his gold throne, clad in gold from his crown to his shoes, his long fingers tensed over a crystal-and-gold scepter angled toward the polished floor. For an instant, the king stared at her, clearly perplexed. Then his dark eyes widened and his lean, handsome face tensed. "Prophet! What are you doing here?"

Good question. Infinite? What am I doing here . . . in Belaal's throne room?

Amusement permeated His voice. *Look.*

Ela pressed one hand to her head and stared into the brief vision. Absorbing her task, she hid a smile. "Majesty, what should a prophet do, but warn the king?" And shake his throne.

If a threatening stare could strike her down, Bel-Tygeon's glare would do so now. "*You* are tempting death by entering this place uninvited!"

"As any prophet expects. Sir."

A voice boomed behind Ela, gruff and hateful. "Sire, shall I remove her?"

General Siyrsun, Ela knew without turning. Belaal's general of

265

the army and leader of the first attack on Parne. She'd seen him in her vision, his face marred by rippling purpled scars earned in Parne. Ela suppressed a shiver as the Infinite allowed her some of the general's thoughts. He cursed her daily for those scars and longed to carve the same over Ela's face and down her arms—before cutting out her heart. *Not* what she'd wanted to know. Ela blinked, then focused on Bel-Tygeon instead.

The king didn't smile, but he leaned forward, clearly interested. Toying with the gold-and-crystal scepter, he said, "You would kill her, general, the instant you drag her outside."

The general's voice neared Ela. Along with his footsteps. "As we all say, sire, you are Wisdom itself. Why should I not wish to kill your enemies?"

Ela suppressed a shudder and fixed her gaze on Bel-Tygeon. He smiled a taunt at Ela as he told Siyrsun, "Yes. Remove her."

Without turning, Ela cried out, "General Siyrsun, by His Holy Name, the Infinite commands you and your men to stand where you are until He releases you!"

The general's furious growl answered. Around the gleaming throne room, exclamations of surprise punctuated the air as Ela's enemies obviously tried and failed to move and apprehend her. Ela shook her head at the king. "Bel-Tygeon, the Infinite's will is for you to live and to celebrate eternity, *if* you listen to Him. And I am His faithful servant, not your enemy."

"A nice sentiment, though inadequate." Bel-Tygeon waved his scepter toward her, its crystal glittering in the light. "But enough. Your theatrics have our attention. Tell us what your Infinite wishes to say, and then leave."

"You and your counselors have planned a ceremony for your naming day, involving sacrifices and worship. To you."

"Yes. And why not?" Bel-Tygeon stood and descended from his throne. "It is our tradition, as it has been for generations. Why shouldn't I continue in our ways?" He lifted his arms in a gesture of arrogant displeasure. "Why am *I* the first king of Belaal chosen for your Infinite's wrath? What is your true game, Prophet?"

"This is hardly a game, O king! You are the first ruler of Belaal to command exclusive worship for yourself, banning all other gods as you enslave your people!" Watching his expression chill to majestic remoteness, Ela continued. "Your arrogance stinks to the heavens and will only continue to grow unless you are corrected—which the Infinite is concerned enough to do. You've done nothing to deserve your place in this life. Your Creator has granted you *everything*, yet you cannot see beyond yourself."

"I see perfectly. You need not worry." Bel-Tygeon sauntered past Ela, toward General Siyrsun. For the first time, Ela turned to look at the proud military leader, and the sight was not appealing. Siyrsun's powerful, scarred face was livid with rage, but he remained silent as the young god-king circled him, paying particular attention to his booted feet. Bel-Tygeon's lips pursed thoughtfully, and he nudged Siyrsun's left boot with his own gold-embellished shoe. "General, are your feet dead as stone, or do you sense pain?"

"There is no pain, O king, but neither are my feet dead. They simply refuse to move."

"Interesting." Bel-Tygeon's mouth twitched as if suppressing a grin, and for one horrible instant, he reminded Ela of Kien contemplating mischief. Impossible! Pursued by the Infinite or not, this fraud-god was nothing like her charming Kien.

Bel-Tygeon swept a cool glance over the crowd of men in the huge golden chamber. Some shuffled from foot to foot, but many were clearly held in place and not the least bit happy. Then Bel-Tygeon returned to Ela, stood directly in front of her, lifted his crystal scepter, and commanded, "Free them. You've performed an interesting trick, but its fascination has ended."

Hmm. Short attention span. Seeing the branch change from a subtle metallic shade to glowing blue-white, Ela braced herself inwardly. "I cannot free those men, sir. Your Creator commanded them to remain where they are. He will release them when it pleases Him to do so."

Bel-Tygeon studied the branch and muttered, "*He* does not rule here."

"So you say." Ela paused as the Infinite whispered questions into her thoughts. Finished listening, she raised her voice, defying the proud king before her. "Bel-Tygeon, the Infinite asks, 'Who are *you*? Did you create the heavens? Were you present when the foundations of Belaal were set in place and the mountains were raised to shelter your lands? Can you cause those lands to shift beneath the feet of mortals?' No! But He does—*now*!"

Gentle, but deliberate, she rested the end of the branch against the shining floor. Ferocious light blazed from the base of the branch down through the marble and ripped along the throne room's floor, lifting the stones beneath the feet of Bel-Tygeon and all his courtiers, bringing them to their knees.

Clinging to her vinewood insignia, Ela watched huge cracks open outward through the marble from the branch like fiery blue-white roots. Lightning-brilliant spirals snapped in the air above—outlining the translucent form of a burning tree. Ela's hair swept about her in an arc and lit to molten silver beneath the Infinite's fury. As He spoke into Ela's thoughts, she called out His warning, barely recognizing her own voice, "When the Infinite created this world, mortals were mere dust! Your pretensions cannot affect Him—yet He calls to each of you. Seek Him!"

A vortex of air encircled her now, closing in, sweeping her away.

Leaning on the branch, Ela found herself in the tiny enclosed garden adjoining the chamber she shared with Caitria. Watching the garden walls spin, Ela sank to her knees and retched. Thoroughly miserable, she finally lifted her head and took a full breath. "Infinite?"

I am here.

Ugh! How humbling to know that her Creator could see her in such an inglorious state. Well, He'd seen her looking worse. But she definitely needed that nap now. Ela staggered inside the chamber, poured a goblet of water, and drank.

Finished, she crossed the chamber to her pallet. Caitria woke up and blinked at her. Sleepy-voiced and still splotchy from the berries, Caitria mumbled, "Ela? You're a mess. What happened?"

Dizzied, Ela flopped onto her pallet. "I think the Infinite just . . . destroyed Bel-Tygeon's throne room. You'll hear about it soon enough. Until then, I need to rest."

✦ ✦ ✦

Outside in the broad yard, now well trimmed thanks to Scythe and the smaller horses, Akabe checked the soil over the cooking pit. At least pit cooking conserved wood and yielded no smoke. If only it could conserve food. They had no other supplies apart from their stash of dried venison, a small clay jar of flour, and the remains of his family's now-wild kitchen garden—which was thankfully walled off from the horses in the central yard. Where were his men—along with Faine's reinforcements and Faine's report of their plan's success or failure? "Infinite, I beg You, protect my men!"

Calming his thoughts, Akabe tested the ground. Slightly warm, but not enough to deserve another layer of soil. Sweating a bit beneath his protective vest, Akabe stood and looked around. The quiet air and silence weren't reassuring. No birds were singing. Surely something was afoot. If Kien didn't reappear with Scythe soon, Akabe must presume other ominous creatures were roaming through the trees on the slopes below. Such as assassins.

Even as Akabe thought this, thuds shook the ground, reassuring him. Obviously the destroyer was returning from his daily run. No wonder the birds were silent. Akabe approached the massive pit he'd dug in front of the gatehouse with Kien's help—and with Scythe dragging away the excess dirt. The same Scythe who was now shaking the ground. Best not to walk too near the trap until the destroyer halted. "Riddig! A little help!"

"Already on my way, sir!" Riddig's footsteps echoed on the wall above as he scurried to the gatehouse stairwell. The surgeon soon emerged from the narrow stone portal, his white hair wild, his beard a mass of pale bristles. "Allow me, sir." Shifting his bow onto his back, Riddig tugged up one of the swords impaled between the slabs at the gate's base. Swords served as unconventional bars, but they worked.

To Kien, Akabe bellowed, "Keep to the side—remember the pit!"

"How could Scythe and I forget?" Kien called from beyond the wall. "We're both blistered from digging the thing!"

Akabe grinned and set down the swords. "Stop complaining, my friend! Our blisters are well-suffered! You know I'm right!" The pit—spiked with numerous half-buried swords and pikes—might slow down their attackers long enough to allow a few volleys of arrows to thin their numbers.

As they hauled open the creaking gate's intact side, Akabe muttered to Riddig, "I hope all our work is wasted—that the Ateans never appear." To Kien, he yelled, "The way's clear!"

Akabe listened for Kien to make another smart retort, but he merely urged Scythe inside, his voice low and abrupt. "Go. Hurry!"

At once, Riddig shifted his bow and quiver of arrows, his squared face tense. In silent agreement with his guardsman's apprehension, Akabe snatched a sword, ready to slam it into place as soon as the destroyer cleared the gate. Scythe grunted as he stomped inside, lowering his big monster-head to avoid scraping the gate's archway. After a nervous-seeming turn around the yard's fading grass, he bent, allowing Kien to drop solidly to the ground.

Satisfied that Kien and Scythe were unharmed, Akabe slammed the sword in place and reached for another to secure the gate. "Welcome back. You seem uneasy. What's happened?"

Kien nodded toward Scythe. "I don't know what's made him edgy today, but it's affecting me. I'm ready to attack every shadow." He grabbed a third sword and slid it in place and tamped it with his boot. Grim-faced, he looked from Akabe to Riddig. "Do you suppose the Ateans waylaid Lord Faine's reinforcements?"

Akabe slowly lowered the last sword into place. He owed Kien and Riddig honesty. Their lives were as much at risk as his. "I fear so. It's well past the time Faine and I agreed upon. I pray they're safe." Forcing a smile, he stepped back from the gate and dusted off his hands. "For now, however, I believe we've time to eat. Let's dig up our food."

Staring at the pit and the blade-guarded gate, Riddig said, "I'll take my meal up to the wall. I agree with Lord Aeyrievale—I'm nervous." He looked at Akabe now, forthright. "Majesty, if I die, I've left a note for my family in my chamber."

Kien nodded agreement. "I've done the same. My notes are inside my knapsack. I carried them with me until I realized blood-ied notes might be difficult to read—not to mention excessively upsetting to my wife and parents."

They'd written farewell notes to their loved ones? Akabe qui-eted inside. They expected to die. As did he. But . . . "I didn't consider notes. Even so, it'll be short work. I have only Caitria. And Siphra."

"Sir," Kien murmured, "with the exception of the Ateans, your people love you—as the queen surely must."

Polite of him to mention the queen. If only the sentiment were true. If she could love him after he'd endangered her life . . . Akabe shook his head. "Well-enough. I'll write the notes after we eat. But this doesn't mean I expect we'll die. I've faced worse odds than these and survived. We'll bury the Ateans and rebuild the temple. You'll see." If it pleased the Infinite.

Fighting emotion, Akabe hammered each of them with a fist before returning to work on their midday meal. They shoveled the heated soil away from the cooking pots, which they'd filled with venison, wild herbs, and old root vegetables culled from the old kitchen garden, then sat down to eat. Akabe chewed some meat and shrugged inwardly. He'd eaten worse. "Needs salt."

Kien tasted his and grinned, some of his usual good humor returning. "I have just the thing to improve our meal. Wait here, both of you."

He hurried into the tower and soon returned, unrolling a parchment-lined leather packet. "Taste this."

Akabe studied the brown cubes. Oddly dried meat chunks. Were they edible?

Kien chose one and ate it quickly, as if enjoying the taste. Riddig added two to his wooden bowl of food, then hurried up to the wall. Akabe finally selected a cube, popped it in his mouth and chewed . . . solidified salty vomit. "Augh!" He spat out the filth, then backhanded Kien, who laughed. "You're trying to kill me ahead of the Ateans! That's Bannulk cheese!"

Kien—the show-off—ate two more cubes, then wrapped the remainder and tucked the packet behind his protective vest inside his belted overtunic. "Your venison tastes better now, doesn't it?"

"By comparison, yes!" Akabe pretended a glare at Kien. "If we survive, I'll repay you, my friend—you know I will."

"I pray you will, Majesty."

Seated on the wall walk above them, Riddig suddenly coughed and spat down into the yard. Akabe laughed. "He tried the cheese."

"Both cubes at once, I'd say."

They finished their meal and scoured the pans and dishes in cold well water. As Akabe and Kien were gathering utensils, Scythe huffed and circled them. Swift. Agitated.

Flattening his ears and snorting threats toward the gatehouse.

On the wall above, Riddig flung his empty dish into the yard, offered Akabe a frantic wave, then ducked out of sight.

Beyond the gates a horse whickered. And Akabe saw Riddig scuttle into the gatehouse as they'd planned, his bow and arrows readied. Akabe's heart thudded as he and Kien ran for their curved hunting bows, arrows, and shields. Riddig's warning whistle sounded from the gatehouse, also as agreed. Akabe shifted his hunting bow. "It seems our foes have arrived."

To Akabe's right, Kien adjusted his bow and grimaced. "Of course they've arrived! Our last meal included that wretched Bannulk cheese! Infinite, be with us . . . and with our wives!"

Scythe closed his swift-moving circle around Kien, trying to herd Akabe as well.

"Easy, good monster." Setting an arrow in the bowstring, Akabe took a deep breath. So much for writing a note to Siphra. Or Caitria—his love. Infinite, please save my wife and, if You will it, Your temple!

Aloud, he added another prayer to Kien's. "Infinite, there is none like You! Bless us, protect Riddig, and speed his arrows to the Ateans!"

❖ 30 ❖

Kien concentrated on breathing steadily as he listened to men's agonized screams and horse hooves thudding just beyond the gateway. Obviously, from his vantage point at the bow loops in the gatehouse's tower, Riddig had landed arrows in more than one man. Kien set his arrow, pulled it back until the bowstring creaked, then kept his gaze fixed sternly upon the weakened side of the huge gate.

If only that gate had been left intact! Useless to wish for what could not be changed—or repaired. Yet he meant to survive. For Ela. And to protect Akabe and the temple. Already the Ateans were hammering on the gate's damaged side. Kien watched the huge metal-protected door shudder, and he prayed with all his might. Let the trap work! Let fewer than ten men pass beyond the sabotaged gate. Those odds might give them success.

Scythe moved in front of Kien then, blocking his view. And Akabe's. The king snapped, "Destroyer, back away!"

"Scythe!" Kien glared at his formidable protector, holding the beast's battle-hungry gaze. "Let us shoot down our enemies before they're within reach! Come here!" He stomped the ground to his left and snarled, "Now!"

Rumbling ominous complaints, the destroyer turned aside, standing off to Kien's left. But he aimed sullen looks and huffs toward the gate's quaking weaker side. Two more men screamed beyond the wall, prompting Kien to send up additional prayers for Riddig's aim. Riddig had about twelve arrows, Kien knew. He and Akabe each had three—they'd used the others in hunting. Each arrow must hit a target—preferably Atean.

Beside Kien, Akabe adjusted his hunting bow, praying aloud, "Infinite, protect Your servants. . . ."

The gate's weakened side groaned open. Two men charged inside and tumbled into the pit, onto the swords and pikes so laboriously spiked within. Screams shattered the air, just as a nobleman urged his steed through the gate—too swiftly to notice the trap. The horse fell inside the pit as the nobleman bellowed a futile, "Halt!"

Outside, his cohorts filled the air with harsh sibilant curses. Sweat filmed Kien's skin. His fingers twitched with the longing to shoot, but—as Akabe commanded—they must use their few arrows efficiently, only as the Ateans entered the fortress. However, the Ateans had retreated. A shriek echoed from outside as Riddig apparently hit another target.

Beside Kien, Akabe hissed, "Steady! We alternate shots, remember? Wait."

"I *am* waiting!"

At last, one Atean rebel crept inside the gate, wielding his sword and shield. Three others followed. Akabe unleashed an arrow, hitting the first man in the eye. Howling, he staggered and toppled into the pit.

Kien chose his target and caught one Atean's shoulder over the edge of the man's shield. The Atean reeled against the closed side of the gate, but didn't drop into the pit. Kien slapped another arrow into his bowstring and aimed for a third assassin. Akabe's arrow slammed into the Atean instead, felling him against the closed gate's central metal-clad edge.

Fine. Kien focused on the fourth man, who maneuvered his shield astutely, guarding his way as he edged along the pit. It would take time for him to step across the wounded men sprawled against the gate, and then he must cross the central yard before he became an immediate threat. Three more men rounded the gate—easier marks with their attentions fixated on the pit. Kien released his arrow, striking one in the side as Akabe struck his nearest comrade just below the ear with his last arrow. Both fell in the open gateway. The third stepped over them, adroitly shielding himself as he edged along the grave-like pit.

By now, the astute one had reached the broad central yard. Kien abandoned his last arrow and swiftly hefted Akabe's shield, holding it as the king slid his hands through its straps. Some distance away, the attacker shifted his own shield and looked from Kien to Akabe, his eyes narrowed. Followed by his comrade, he moved toward Akabe, who waited, sword readied.

Depending on Scythe's looming presence for protection, Kien crouched, gripped his own shield's heavy straps, then stood and unsheathed the Azurnite blade. Its glistening blue-gray sheen drew attention from both rebel swordsmen, briefly stilling them. Akabe seized this advantage and lunged, snarling at his potential killer.

Infinite! Kien advanced on the second aggressor, aware of the man tracking the Azurnite blade. Right of the Atean to be wary, but the best sword meant nothing if its owner became overconfident.

Seeming to take courage, the Atean roared and brought his sword in a downward arc, targeting Kien's head. Kien swung his shield up, received the blow, then retaliated, slashing the Azurnite blade at his foe. The man stepped back, curving his shield toward Kien. The Azurnite slammed against the shield's surface and sent a layered chunk of the inferior metal and wood flying. The Atean's eyes widened in obvious shock. Behind Kien, Scythe grunted.

Two more exchanges of metal ringing against metal and wood left the rebel's shield dangling in pieces from his now-bleeding arm.

In apparent desperation, Kien's opponent dropped the splintered shield and swung his weapon at Kien's neck. Kien countered the blow with all his strength. The Azurnite snapped the Atean's blade and sent its upper half flying.

At Akabe's attacker.

The man yelped as the blade cut into his upraised arm, giving Akabe the chance to finish him. Kien's foe stepped back again, blinked at his broken sword, then cast it aside and reached for his dagger. Fearing the man would throw it Akabe-style, Kien lunged and pierced the Atean's chest. The rebel gasped thickly and fell beside his dead comrade in the trampled yard.

Feeble moans of the wounded lifted from the pit. Beyond that, silence reigned, heavy and blood-scented.

Akabe shook his head at Kien. "Surely there are more."

They waited. Nothing moved in the big central yard except one of the wounded men stirring at the foot of the gate's unbroken door. Akabe flicked a glance at the wounded Ateans. "Do we tend the fallen and risk being attacked? Or do we leave them in the pit?"

Remembering Fightmaster Lorteus, Kien quoted, "'Even now, fatally wounded, they can kill.'"

"Well-enough. We leave them in the pit. If our reinforcements arrive in time, we'll drag up the Ateans and tend them—unless they kill themselves first."

Riddig crept onto the wall walk now, huddled over, as if hiding from someone. Kien motioned to Akabe, then pointed his sword at their guardsman. Riddig pantomimed his concern, prompting Kien to whisper, "One man remains outside beyond the gate. Do we go after him?"

"Might be a trap."

"Can we afford survivors?"

As they spoke, a bird fluttered over the gatehouse, then sped high above the yard, gray and slightly plump, its crimson talons bound with . . .

Chilled, Kien hissed, "A message! They're sending for reinforcements!"

"Infinite!" Akabe growled his frustrated plea. "Help us endure another onslaught!" To Kien, he said, "This leaves us with no choice." Shifting his shield and sword, Akabe stalked toward the gate.

Kien followed, sword readied. He should have known the Ateans would plan some sort of counterattack. At least he hadn't celebrated his survival prematurely. Seething, he helped Akabe lift the nearest wounded man—unconscious—from beneath the gate. At Akabe's nod, they dropped the Atean into the pit, provoking an outcry and meager curses from below.

The second wounded insurgent glared up at them, ashen, Kien's arrow in his side, his eyes cold with unrelenting hatred. He lurched to his knees and produced a sword. Kien thrust the Azurnite blade at him, delivering a final blow.

In silent agreement, Kien and Akabe tossed the man into the pit.

Riddig had descended from the wall and now emerged from the stairwell, his expression tightly composed. Lifting his third-to-last arrow from his quiver, he set its nock in his bowstring, then backed himself against the gate's closed door, keeping the pit in view as he crept toward the open area where the two dead Ateans lay. At the gate's edge, Riddig swung around, took aim at a target directly behind the gate, and released his arrow, just as his target's arrow missed him.

Something thudded against the door. Riddig backed away, then sighed, penitent. "He was already wounded. I blame myself that he released the courier bird, Majesty. Forgive me."

"Are any of us perfect?" Akabe demanded. "No. Riddig, you've done more than I required of you, so forgive yourself."

They lifted the swords from beneath the gate and opened it. A man slumped over at their feet, lifeless. They dragged the body away from the gate and Kien released Scythe to inspect the castle's perimeter.

Five bodies lay strewn amid the skulls outside. Two with two arrows each. Studying his comrades, Kien said, "We've three arrows remaining, the pit is filled, and there's no way to know how many more Ateans will arrive—or when."

Akabe grimaced. "You sound so cheerful."

"I ought to be. We've lived longer than I expected."

"Indeed we have. Blessed be the Infinite's Name." Akabe stared down at the bodies. "After we drop these into the pit and Scythe returns, we'll close the gate as best we can. Then I'll go write my letters."

Kien glanced around, heard Scythe's distant huff, and allowed himself to relax a bit.

Riddig nodded toward the five bodies. "What about them, Majesty? They won't all fit in the trap—not with that horse fallen inside."

"With the exception of the two in the gate, we'll leave them where they lie."

While Akabe checked the bodies, Kien sheathed his sword and helped Riddig drag the bodies from the gate toward the pit. By the fallen horse's stillness, Kien realized the poor beast was dead, like the Ateans around and beneath it.

Just as they dropped the second corpse into the near-brimming pit, fire stabbed into Kien's calf where it wasn't protected by his greave. Jolted, he looked down into the face of the Atean he'd wounded twice. Deathly pale, the man was standing on the bodies of his comrades, even now ready to kill.

The ground shook with the thunder of destroyer hooves as Kien whipped out the Azurnite blade. He landed it against the rebel's exposed neck just as the man slashed a sword upward. Kien twisted away, but not quickly enough. Riddig yelled, "My lord!"

A thin burning pain tore along Kien's lower abdomen just beneath his boiled leather vest.

Scythe's agonized groan rumbled through Kien as the Atean slumped back into the pit. Kien sat, holding his bloodied lower right side. Afraid to look. Something had given way, and it was *him*.

Looming over Kien now, Scythe exhaled into his hair and groaned again. Not good.

This, then, was how he, Kien Lantec, would die. Rotting in a broken fortress, digesting stinking Bannulk cheese while a destroyer mourned over him, breathing down his neck.

Infinite, let me die quickly!

❖ 31 ❖

Lying in the yard, trying to subdue his anxiety, Kien held his bloodied abdomen, stared up at the sky, and waited. Scythe nuzzled him again, destroyer-panic evident in his repeated vocalizations of distress. Despite his own fears, Kien smoothed the monster warhorse's big face with his free hand. "Calm yourself. Deafening me with your noise and drowning me in slobber will only defeat your hopes." And Kien's. Was this wound truly his death sentence?

Finished securing the gate as much as possible, Akabe and Riddig kneeled beside him, their faces as distressed as Scythe's. They unbuckled Kien's boiled leather vest and the padding beneath, then lifted it away. Gripping his dagger, Riddig ordered Kien, "Remove your hand from the wound, my lord."

Sickened by the wound's bulging slipperiness, Kien obeyed. "Do I want to see this?"

Riddig slit open the fabric above the wound. "No, my lord."

Akabe eyed the wound and winced. "Riddig, what do you need?"

"The pot of water I set to heat above the hearth—as soon as it steams—with a cup and some of that stinking cheese Lord Aeyrievale fed us earlier, please, Majesty."

The Bannulk cheese? Mistrustful, Kien asked, "Why?"

281

Ignoring him, Riddig called after Akabe, "Wash your hands, sir! Blood of the dead must not taint blood of the living!"

"Meaning what?" Kien demanded. "Are you giving me up for dead?"

"Not yet, my lord. Did you save any of that foul cheese?"

"Perhaps. Why do you need it?"

"To determine the extent of your injuries. *Not* for a jest." When Kien hesitated, Riddig turned a bit testy. "My lord, hand over the cheese."

Grudging every syllable, Kien said, "It's inside my tunic."

"Well," Riddig observed, "it ought to be ripened strong enough to serve its purpose." He slit Kien's tunic and snatched the contested packet. "You need to eat this, my lord. Every cube."

All? Kien eyed the warm sludge-brown cubes. He could stomach two or three without puking. More would be debatable. Torture, actually. "This is your revenge for my joke, isn't it?"

The field surgeon smirked, his silvery beard bristling. "I enjoy knowing there's a bit of retribution in your treatment. Now, eat, my lord."

"Fine." Kien chewed cube after rank brown cube. The stink set Scythe's nostrils a-twitch. Moaning, the beast backed off. Kien muttered, "Coward!" As he bit into the last cube his stomach clenched painfully, threatening revolt.

Evidently noticing Kien's squeamishness, Riddig said, "Whatever you do, my lord, you must not vomit. Remain still. I'm going to wash my hands."

Kien swallowed and willed his stomach to settle. His eyes watered with the effort. He should be written into a Siphran epic for such a feat. Infinite . . .

Akabe returned with a small kettle of steaming water, a mug, and a respectably clean white tunic. "Here's the water. I'll prepare some bandages." He knelt beside Kien, then froze. "Augh! What is that stench?"

"Lord Aeyrievale's medicine, Majesty." Hands now clean, Riddig unfurled a leather roll, revealing a gleaming array of small, vicious-looking tools. Grim-faced, he poured some of the steaming water into the cup and offered it to Kien. "Drink, my lord. If your guts are pierced and fluids are draining from your stomach, we'll smell that cheese through your wound."

"And what if you don't smell it?"

Unnervingly quiet, Riddig said, "If we don't smell it, then there's a chance you'll live."

A chance. Kien drank the steaming water, then settled down. As they waited, Riddig Tyne unfastened Kien's greave and inspected his leg wound, muttering as if reciting lessons. "Now the actions of healing are these . . . purge, anoint, stitch, and bind." Almost ceremonially, he poured some of the heated water over his clean hands, then some over Kien's leg.

Kien gasped at the liquid's sting. "How will a scalding cure me?"

Riddig ignored him, opened a vial, and drizzled a dark honey-like substance over the gash. "Remain still, my lord. I'll be stitching a tube within your wound."

Gritting his teeth against the repeated stabs, Kien held still. But Scythe paced, twitched, and groaned throughout the procedure. While the field surgeon bound his wound, the warhorse breathed moisture on Kien's face. Kien reached for the destroyer's halter. "Easy, monster."

Kien hesitated. What would become of Scythe if he died and Ela didn't return from Belaal? And if the next mob of Ateans descended on them while Kien was downed with his wounds, how could Akabe and Riddig defend themselves alone? Decision made, Kien beckoned Akabe, who tore another bandage from the clean formerly royal tunic. "Majesty, look Scythe in the eye."

One eyebrow lifted in his wearied, rough-bearded face, Akabe complied. But he asked, "Why the destroyer-staring contest, my friend? Aren't you too afflicted for pranks?"

"This is no prank, sir." Kien tightened his grip on the destroyer's halter. "Scythe. . . . *Obey!* Do you hear me? Obey the king!"

Scythe huffed, then growled and shut his eyes, clearly in a sulk.

"Good monster-horse." The best. Sighing, Kien shifted his Azurnite sword in its scabbard, pushing it toward Akabe. "Guard this. With Scythe. If I don't recover . . . turn them against your enemies."

The king's expression set into stubborn lines exaggerated by his beard. "I'll guard them *until* you recover." A rueful smile lit his face. "I'm praying your guts won't stink. That would be a miracle from the Infinite!"

Kien grimaced and shut his eyes. No doubt if he survived, he would laugh about this later. "Majesty, I ate *all* the Bannulk cheese. One way or another, my guts will stink."

✦ ✦ ✦

Ela lowered her comb. Why was she fretting so for Kien? Fears had invaded her sleep, stirring her to pray before she'd even opened her eyes. "Infinite? What is—?"

Frantic tapping sounded from the base of the chamber door, with the now-familiar voice of Mari, the young slave woman. "Prophet? You are summoned at once!"

Smoothing her hair and robes, Ela hurried to the door. She flung it open. "Yes, Mari?"

Mari quavered, "The k-king is in the Women's Palace. Come out at once!"

"I'm surprised he didn't arrive sooner. I'll hurry." Ela whisked through the chamber to snatch the branch and then to lean into the garden and warn the still-splotchy Caitria, "Majesty, the king is in the Women's Palace—I'm called for, but don't worry. I'll return soon."

"Just don't bring *him* with you!" Caitria scowled. "Ela, can't you simply roast him?"

"I think not." Outside, Ela scurried through a labyrinth of elegant corridors to keep up with the frightened slave. Mari led Ela to Lady Dasarai's rooms, knelt, and rapped on the door. Bel-Tygeon himself answered, no longer crowned, but still clad in his golden robes. Instantly he grabbed Ela's arm, dragged her inside his sister's apartments, and slammed the door in the frightened slave's face. His voice dangerously quiet, the king said, "If you expect to live, Prophet, you will repair the damage you've caused to our throne room!"

Repair the damage? She'd never considered it. And wouldn't, unless . . . Infinite?

Tomorrow. At the same hour it was shattered, and before the same witnesses, the floor will be repaired according to My plan.

All right. Ela repeated her beloved Creator's words. Bel-Tygeon slammed a fist against the door beside them, making Ela jump. "*His* plan! What is that supposed to mean?"

"I don't know, sir. The Infinite hasn't revealed it to me—I'm only His servant."

The young king's proud face tightened. "Only His servant? After that performance? You mock me!"

"I've warned you, sir!" Ela retorted. "Furthermore, my actions were no performance! Unless you change, your reign will destroy this nation and you with it, to the everlasting agony of your soul. The Infinite calls you, Bel-Tygeon! Despite your pride, He is present to you—to everyone! He *loves* you. Turn to Him and live!"

His peculiar remote expression returned, slipping over his smooth, handsome face like a mask. "I intend to live—and exactly as I please. I'll worry about everlasting agony if it arrives."

Ela's entire being stilled. "You would not speak of eternal torment so lightly if you'd experienced it, sir."

A quirk of humor broke his composed facade. "Are you about to tell me that you have experienced eternal torment?"

"Yes!" Shuddering, Ela recalled that brief fragment of time, the absolute soul-searing torment. She gazed at the darkness, forcing words past her lips. "I was trapped inside everlasting fire. I could not die, though I begged for death! The agony of being wholly separated from the Infinite was so intense—I wish it on no one! Ever!"

When Ela drew her thoughts into the present, she found Bel-Tygeon studying her. He smiled and whispered, "Excellent! I almost believed you. Now . . ." He grabbed Ela's arm and pulled her close, as if preparing to embrace her, but without tenderness. "You will do as I command. If you possess the means to ruin my palace, then you possess the means to restore it. Don't defy me, or I will *destroy* Siphra's queen. Do you understand?"

A bluff. This had to be a bluff. He wouldn't dare risk a full-blown war with Siphra by destroying the queen, she was almost certain. Almost. Surely his demand that she declare his future victories meant that this proud god-king feared another humiliating defeat such as the one he'd suffered in Parne.

Gathering her courage, Ela said, "You needn't threaten me or Siphra's queen. The Infinite has declared He will restore Belaal's throne room tomorrow. His word is always true. Fear Him, sir! Seek His heart before you suffer calamity."

"The calamity will be your own if you defy me." Bel-Tygeon released Ela and strode from the room as if he could endure her no longer. Soft rustling alerted Ela to the Lady Dasarai's presence. Ela cast the woman a pleading look. "Lady Rethae, beg your brother to consider the Infinite's warnings! I've no wish to see him or Belaal suffer for his pride."

The noblewoman lifted her chin. "With pride, he honors his birthright. One hopes you will eventually see the aptness of his ways. Now—" she waved a bejeweled hand toward the door— "you may return to your chamber."

Feeling every bit the unwelcomed guest, Ela departed. As she prayed and followed the still-agitated Mari back to her chamber, a feminine voice beckoned, "Prophet!" Ela halted.

Followed by blue-clad slaves, a lovely, bright-eyed young woman approached, her dark hair and bare arms glittering with jeweled ornaments. Breathless, she snatched at Ela's sheer mantle. "I hoped to speak with you. We've all heard what happened to the throne room—no doubt you're a true prophet. Please, may I ask you a question?"

Listen. The Infinite's words permeated Ela's thoughts so swiftly that she shut her eyes and clung to the branch to withstand the impact of His voice. As for His news . . . no. Not what this young woman wanted to hear. "The Infinite has told me your question as well as its answer. You are Zaria, the king's current favorite, and you wish to know if you are pregnant with his first child. You are not."

The young woman flinched, then blinked away tears. Ela felt the depths of her disappointment and the Infinite's compassion for her soul. Aware of the listening slaves, she said, "I'm sorry. The Infinite declares this palace is barren. Furthermore, it will always be so unless Bel-Tygeon acknowledges who he truly is— and is not. Pray to the Infinite for him."

The young woman stiffened and dashed at the tears streaking her face. "Then I'll never become his official wife? Belaal's queen? That's been my only goal while being enslaved. And now you tell me I'll fail . . . I cannot accept it!"

"*You* haven't failed. Only the king is able to change this circumstance. But until he relents, for however long he lives, Bel-Tygeon will have no child and no queen."

"I won't endure this! You're wrong!" Zaria fled, pursued by her slaves. Ela drooped, praying the young woman would ultimately accept the news with grace. If anyone was the failure here, it was the Infinite's own prophet. How had she missed such a critical detail? Infinite, this is why Bel-Tygeon and Lady Dasarai were so offended by my pregnancy—because he has no heir.

Yes. Unless he acknowledges his faults and conquers his pride, Bel-Tygeon will be the last of this royal house. He will obliterate his father's name with his self-destruction.

Yet You—his Creator—reach to him. You love him despite his rebellion. Infinite, help me to set aside my anger and see this overbearing god-king as You see him!

Heartened by His unspoken affirmation, she began to walk again, sending a soothing smile to Mari. The slave stared back, as if Ela might bite her. Ela sighed and gave her attention to other concerns. How long would it take to bring Bel-Tygeon to reason? Months? Years? Would Kien's child be born and raised a slave? Dear Kien . . . Would she see him again? A veiled fear lurked at the edge of her thoughts, making her tremble. No. No, if she expected to accomplish her work as the Infinite's servant, she must set aside her fears and trust Him for Kien's well-being.

Ela returned to her chamber and found Caitria in the garden throwing rocks at the tree, striking the trunk's center with such ferocious accuracy that Akabe and Kien would have cheered. "You're in a royal rage, Majesty. What's happened?"

Caitria nodded toward a tray set on a nearby table. "The doctor chose our evening meal."

"And . . . ?" Ela lifted the shining cover from the tray. A dish of steamed grain. "Oh. That's all they're serving us?"

"Physician's orders." Caitria stormed over to Ela, whispering, "Until my rash fades, this is our menu! My skin will be clear within two days! Ela, what can I do?"

"Remain calm." Ela's heart thudded. Bel-Tygeon had already threatened Caitria. What were his true intentions toward the queen? "Just remember the Infinite's warning. Don't try to escape. You'll fail, and you'll mourn the consequences for the rest of your life."

"Which means I'll survive!" Caitria argued. "Ela, I'm sick of this! It's been five days! *Five!* I want to return to my husband— and somehow I will, whether you help me or not!"

Her delicate jaw set with fury, she marched inside.

Ela suppressed a groan. Infinite . . . protect her, please.

✦ ✦ ✦

Crowds of richly clad courtiers lined the walls of Belaal's throne room, their condemning looks following Ela as she picked her way across the throne room's broken golden floor. In every direction, huge chunks of marble jutted upward at threatening angles. Far worse than she'd realized. Hmm. No wonder the king was so upset. Praying for composure, Ela stopped at the majestic room's divinely shattered epicenter and glanced up at Bel-Tygeon.

Seated on the throne above her in glittering blue-and-gold-patterned robes, Bel-Tygeon met her gaze with icy calm. He'd threatened to destroy Caitria. A bluff? Ela had no wish to find out. She studied the ruined floor, praying. Infinite? This appears irreparable.

Who am I?

My Creator . . . Who formed these stones. And I am Your servant—with all my heart.

He sent her a whisper and a flick of imagery. Smiling, Ela planted the branch in the gaping epicenter, then stepped back. Her soul lifting in exultation, she called to Him. "Infinite—Creator of all, including these stones! Who is like You in the heavens above, or here below? For the glory of Your Holy Name, restore this place!"

The branch took fire, spreading in dazzling treelike spirals above her head, its brilliant light permeating the soil and shattered stones below her feet. The floor rasped, grated, and then drew together, sealing to gleaming perfection—its golden marble now altered, set with a glowing starburst of iridescent crystal rays shot throughout the throne room's floor. A permanent reminder to Belaal of the Infinite's work in this palace. Within a breath, the branch inverted upon itself, vinewood again, balanced upon an exquisite crystal leveled at the very center of the starburst.

She'd felt nothing. But Bel-Tygeon and his courtiers had fallen to their knees, all of them covering their eyes as if they'd been blinded. Infinite? Thank You!

Go.

Obedient, Ela lifted the branch, turned, and strode through the silent throne room, her layered garments whispering as she moved across the floor's breathtaking gemstone rays.

✦ ✦ ✦

Seated beside the hearth in his parents' former chamber, Akabe kept watch over Kien as he slept. Infinite, bless his recovery! Spare his life. Spare all their lives. . . .

Lives that he had risked and perhaps lost. Had any other Siphran king been brought down so soon after being crowned? Not if Akabe remembered his history lessons correctly. According to future histories, he'd be an abysmal failure.

Even so, if his wife and friends could survive and escape—

Riddig charged through the open doorway, a wild man, his sword readied for a fight. In a harsh whisper, he warned, "Majesty! Horses!"

Akabe shot a worried glance at the still-slumbering Kien, then hurried outside, checking his sword.

✦ 32 ✦

In the lowering sunlight, Akabe stared down from the fortress wall walk at their approaching visitor. A solitary, stocky royal soldier rode up to the wall, leading a second horse. The man appeared bruised and exhausted, his official tunic torn and stained. Akabe winced. "Who sent you?"

Apparently recognizing his voice, the soldier bowed, then called up, "Lord Faine, Majesty." He displayed a red-corded leather tube slung over his shoulder. "I've his message!"

A true message or a trap? Akabe nodded to Riddig. "We'll allow him in, but be prepared for treachery."

While they worked open the sturdier side of the gate—with Scythe brooding nearby—Akabe listened for sounds from the pit. Nothing. Not even ragged breathing. Evidently the insurgents were dead. A pang hit Akabe. Rebels or not, these men were his subjects. Infinite? Was there no other way? Could I have done more to save them? Wasn't a king supposed to strive to protect his people—even to save them from their self-wrought disasters?

Dejected by fresh thoughts of failure, Akabe pried up the final sword and helped Riddig open the gate. Akabe gripped his own sword, prepared to fight. "Enter slowly!"

The servant led his two horses inside the yard, openmouthed, staring into the pit. Relief crossed the man's bruised face. "Majesty . . . you've killed all the survivors!"

Bracing the gate with his back so Riddig could secure it with the swords, Akabe frowned. "Survivors?"

"The Ateans who attacked us on the road. I'm sure these men are those who survived our skirmish."

A sickened realization turned Akabe's stomach. Was this one of his reinforcements? "Tell me you're not the only one of your company to survive!"

Gloom stole over the man's swollen features. "Three others also lived. But they were too badly wounded to continue with me."

"And what is your name?"

The servant straightened, suddenly appearing self-conscious. "Ilar Flint, Majesty. Subordinate Commander of the Inaren Royal Regiment."

"Thank you, Ilar Flint. You're one of four survivors. Of how many? What happened?"

As if remembering his task, Flint half knelt before Akabe and offered the sealed leather tube. "Here is Lord Faine's report. My company—twenty of us—were settling for the night when the Ateans ambushed us south of the Inaren River." Quietly, Flint said, "They killed sixteen, including our commander. We killed fifteen before I escaped with my comrades. I sent a courier bird to Munra, telling Lord Faine of the ambush. I requested that forty men replace us. May the Infinite send them swiftly!"

"May He indeed." Akabe relaxed as the commander spoke. No Atean would pronounce the Infinite's Name so reverently. "We're grateful you survived. Did you bring supplies or weapons?"

"Several days' worth of grains, bread, and dried meat, for one man."

Reasonable. Glancing at the sealed tube, which appeared intact, though scraped, Akabe said, "Tomorrow I'll give you directions and silver to go buy more food and supplies. Until then, rest. And if you can trade guard duty with Riddig and me, we'd appreciate some sleep."

Flint bowed. "Yes. Thank you, Majesty."

Akabe re-entered the tower, checked Kien—still sleeping—and opened Faine's message. Faine's usually tidy script sprawled over the parchment as if written at frantic speed.

Tilting toward the hearth's flames, Akabe read.

Majesty,

I pray this message finds you safe and well. To our consternation, only four of the suspected rebels and their men attacked the intended estate. Doubtless the remainder were somehow warned of the ruse. Furthermore, we have reason to fear that your current location has been revealed to the enemy. We beg you, sir—for mercy's sake—to send us word with all speed if your return is delayed, for we are, even now, hearing and refuting rumors of your death. For the well-being of all Siphra and the future of the Infinite's temple, your subjects' worries must be set at ease.

The men bearing this script are all tested fighters and faithful to Siphra's temple, as well as to the Infinite. You may trust them to ensure your safe return to Munra. Your Council prays to see you soon—may our Creator bless you!

> *Ever your subject and the*
> *Infinite's,*
>
> *Faine*

Akabe rerolled the message and gripped it hard in his fist. So Faine feared anarchy if Akabe didn't return to Munra immediately and prove he was alive?

No. Unless he proved the rumors true with his death, he would not leave here without Caitria and Ela. As soon as possible, he must take steps to find them and bring Caitria home—if that unlivable palace in Munra could be called home.

Infinite? Let Caitria and Ela return soon!

Kien stirred, drawing a deep breath. His pallor unnerved Akabe. Though Kien's vital organs had not been punctured—there'd been no hint of that vile Bannulk cheese—Riddig had quietly warned Akabe that Kien could die of a fever from his wounds.

Akabe sat down heavily beside his slumbering friend. If Kien died and Caitria never returned to him . . . Unbearable thoughts.

Covering his face with his hands, pouring all his strength into his plea, Akabe prayed.

❧ ❧ ❧

Caitria shivered as Mari worked a clasp into her new surprisingly heavy ceremonial robes. If only the shiver could indicate an illness. But, no. At dawn, that overbearing twig of a lady-physician had pronounced Caitria healthy. Worse, the physician was right. Already, news of Caitria's recovery was being noised throughout the Women's Palace as if her well-being carried momentous importance.

All morning slaves had tapped at the door, bringing notes and gifts from the other ladies. Flowers. Poems of blessings. Fragile gilded silver bracelets. An invitation to walk in one of the palace gardens. And, ominously, these robes from Lady Dasarai, with a cryptic message: *You are invited to honor our lord-king's naming day in the formal procession to his temple.*

Invited? No. Commanded.

Ela, still tired but lovely in her own new blue-and-gold robes, returned from the door with another scrolled note and a tiny bejeweled box. Caitria balked. "That's not from the king, is it? If he's sent me another summons, I'll—!"

"No, Majesty," Ela interrupted, warning Caitria with a sharp glance at Mari, who was fastening Caitria's sandals. "It's not from the king, I'm sure." She offered Caitria the delicate scroll. "The servant who delivered this message noticed the box sitting beside the door."

Mari straightened, alarm evident in her paling face and wide eyes. "Lady, if the box was left beside your door instead of presented to you personally, then it conceals an ill wish—or worse—from a rival."

Oh? Her gilded bracelets ringing thinly, Caitria dropped the scroll and snatched the box from Ela. Perhaps the ill wish would prompt more hives. Mari protested, "Lady, don't open it!"

"Too late." Caitria flicked open the exquisite gold-and-black lid. Inside, a long, cruelly sharp black thorn rested on a pale fold of cloth. "Oh. Do you suppose it's poisoned?"

Mari snatched the box from Caitria. "Forgive me, lady—I'm supposed to watch out for you. Usually poison is sent in sweet-meats or beverages to hide its bitter taste, or it's sewn into clothes to scar the receiver's skin, so I doubt it's more than a token threat. However, I'm taking this to Lady Dasarai at once—with your permission."

Before Caitria could deny her permission, Mari scurried out, her robes rustling. As the door closed, Caitria threw Ela a disgusted look. "Oh, delightful. I have a rival for a suitor I detest, and these 'palace-sisters' poison each other! Ela, we must find a way to escape."

Her expression turning bleak, Ela shook her head. "I cannot leave until the Infinite declares my work here is finished."

"And how long will that be?"

"I don't know."

"Ela, I've been separated from Akabe for seven days. Seven! I can't bear it any longer—I need to know that he's well! Aren't you the least bit worried about your husband?"

The prophet flinched visibly. "Yes. I'm deeply concerned for Kien. And Akabe. But I must trust the Infinite to protect them."

Ela's obvious hurt was painful to see. "Ela, forgive me—I'm desperate."

"Majesty, please, do nothing in haste. Remember . . ." Ela turned as Mari dashed inside the chamber again.

The young woman halted, breathless. "We're summoned immediately—they're forming the procession early." Hands trembling, she adjusted Caitria's robes, then stepped back. After surveying Caitria and Ela, Mari relaxed and nodded. "Why am I afraid? You're both as beautiful as Zaria. *She's* probably the one who sent the thorn."

Ela sighed. "I'm sure the thorn was meant for me."

A smile played over Mari's childlike face. "Of course! Because you told Zaria she would never become pregnant nor become Belaal's queen. I must say, we're all glad! Zaria would be a terrible queen." Beaming, she urged them both forward. "Please, we must hurry."

As they navigated the elaborately painted and screened corridor, a slash of blinding light appeared in Ela's hand, startling Caitria. The light formed the branch within a blink. Amazing. "Ela, how do you *do* that?"

"If I am forgetful or inattentive, the Infinite sends the branch to remind me of my duties." Ela stared at the branch as if dazed. "Something's about to happen."

"What now?"

Ela shrugged, and then her eyes became distant, as if remembering a catastrophe.

Caitria's heart thudded as they entered a huge main yard and followed the direction of a eunuch, who pointed them to their appropriate place with Mari amid the neatly ranked formation of women. Lady Dasarai presided over them all in a golden chair carried by four stocky eunuchs. Except for Ela's branch, they were easily overlooked, merely two among hundreds. Standing beside Ela now, Caitria leaned down and whispered, "What are you going to do?"

Siphra's prophet looked up at Caitria, calm-eyed. And her answering whisper was resolute. "I'll do the Infinite's will. Majesty, remember what I've said. Don't try to escape."

Venting her frustration, Caitria hissed, "If I see a chance, I'll take it—and you must come with me! Anything's better than being enslaved here for the rest of our lives!"

"For me, nothing is worse than disobeying my Creator! I stay until He decides I leave."

She meant it. Caitria saw nothing but determination in Ela's face. No doubt even suggesting escape for the baby's sake wouldn't change the prophet's mind. Ela would stay.

So be it. Once she'd returned to Siphra, Caitria would beg Akabe to rescue Ela somehow.

Caitria glanced beyond the crowd of women, studying the huge gate. Whatever it took, she would escape this palace and return to Akabe.

✦ ✦ ✦

In despair, Ela shut her eyes and prayed. Caitria planned to escape. But she would fail.

Infinite? Don't tell me the details, please. I know I'll mourn with her.

From prison.

Already, within her thoughts, Ela felt the weight of iron chains and fear. The weeping of fellow-prisoners wrung her heart enough that she prayed for them even now.

Whispers resounded from among the ranks of waiting women. "The king—there's the king!" Ela turned, looking with the others. Bel-Tygeon entered the huge gathering area, clad in gold from his booted heels to his robes and intricate towerlike crown. In the sunlight, he resembled a stunning living, moving statue. The image made Ela's spirit recoil.

Around her, the women were sighing their admiration for Belaal's god-king. Understandable. Add gold and god-king power to Bel-Tygeon's spectacular looks and most women would all but kill for him.

With the exception of the Infinite's prophet and Siphra's queen.

Beside Ela, Caitria sniffed and looked away from the king, her beautiful brown eyes narrowed. "Hmph!"

Seeming unaware of them all, Bel-Tygeon stepped up into a gold ceremonial chariot and accepted the reins from his handler. Four perfectly matched white horses waited until their king and the handler urged them forward into the glittering ranks of Belaal's royal guards. Ela took a deep breath as the women around her stirred, smoothing their garments and faces into order. Multitudes of slaves lifted innumerable glittering banners above them all.

Beyond them, the massive palace gates opened, and the pageant began.

They walked beneath the gate's colossal arch, into a broad square beyond. The plaza led to a wide main road clearly constructed for processions such as this. The citizens of Sulaanc knelt and bowed their heads, worshiping their god as Bel-Tygeon rode past.

Fear coiled in Ela's stomach, for Caitria, herself, and Kien's baby. Infinite? Give me strength!

I am here.

Taking a deep breath, Ela continued to walk among the palace women, their footsteps sounding in unison against the wide avenue's pristine stones. At the end of the street, she climbed a graceful stone ramp, which opened into a vast plaza crowded with row after orderly row of citizens and officials. Ela blinked, trying to absorb the sight. Multiple thousands of citizens and officials knelt, then bowed their heads to the stones in worship, creating an exquisitely timed wavelike ripple from one side of the plaza to the other.

Nerves and summertime warmth sent rivulets of sweat trickling down Ela's back. She took a deep breath and prayed. Infinite? Help me to remain calm!

From the plaza they approached stairs, where Bel-Tygeon descended from his chariot, strikingly godlike. Lady Dasarai, equally regal, left her golden chair and followed him up the steps.

The stairs led to a high terrace. The terrace gave way to a great temple with wide, stately marble columns.

Ela shivered as she walked inside and breathed the scent of burning spices. The walls gleamed, gilded and gem-laden. Surely she'd walked into a giant's jewelry box. And at the head of this glittering opulence, on a marble dais, stood a magnificent larger-than-life statue of Bel-Tygeon. The perfect depiction of a mortal naming himself a god.

Ela stiffened. She would *never* bow to this gloriously handsome monstrosity!

In her hand, the branch took fire.

As the other women halted, knelt, and bowed—with Caitria hesitating among them—Ela marched forward. Praying. She moved past the guards and ignored Bel-Tygeon's groveling priests. The instant she passed Bel-Tygeon, Ela turned and stood before him, defiant.

His complexion stark in the vinewood's burning light, Bel-Tygeon stared at Ela, his dark eyes huge.

Ela placed the blazing white branch between them.

Bel-Tygeon stepped back. Not in alarm, but in tight-lipped fury. Beneath his breath, through clenched teeth, Belaal's king muttered a three-word threat.

"Don't. You. Dare!"

⋆ 33 ⋆

Dare? Oh yes, she dared! Before anyone could stop her, Ela cried out, "Bel-Tygeon, the Infinite declares that you are no god! He reveals this place for what it is in His sight—nothing!"

On the dais above them, the brilliant statue creaked, then folded to the floor as if bowing, its forehead ringing against the marble. Within the next instant, a tempest swept through the false temple, which sifted away in a glittering sandstorm, becoming nothingness as all the worshipers screamed.

As their Creator's blessed sunlight washed over them, Ela called out, "The Infinite alone is God! There is no other ruling with Him! Belaal, turn to your eternal Father and worship Him!"

Still standing face-to-face with Ela, Bel-Tygeon shook his head as if dazed. He studied the air where gem-studded walls had stood only a few breaths before. His fear reached Ela—tangible as a touch. He stared at her again, and his lips parted. Taking a deep breath, he yelled to his guards, "Bind her! Remove her to the palace prison, *now!*"

Bel-Tygeon's women and slaves screeched and scattered as the guards swarmed through their ranks, armor clattering while they raced toward Ela.

Infinite! Within a heartbeat, she felt callused hands grasping her wrists so tight that she feared they'd break her bones. Amid the scuffle, Ela lost her grip on the branch. The soldiers wrenched

Ela's hands behind her back and tied them together before they carried her away.

Infinite! Panicked, Ela strained to see beyond the guards. Where was Caitria?

No, no, no! Infinite!

✦ ✦ ✦

Her thoughts chaotic as the glistening dust whirlwind of Bel-Tygeon's once-glorious temple, Caitria fled from the site. No one stopped her.

What had she just seen? An entire building disintegrated around her without injuring a single person inside! How? And they'd taken Ela. Oh, Infinite! But she couldn't contemplate that now. Not until she was safe again in Siphra with Akabe. He would know how to rescue Ela.

Ela! Oh mercy! She'd survive, wouldn't she?

Caitria quickened her pace. The plans she'd made this morning, which had seemed to be nothing but one of her hopeless dreams, now seemed possible. She'd trade her jewelry for supplies and a horse, or transport to Siphra's border. Surely she could reach Siphra within two days!

She ran, her delicate sandals clicking wildly against the steps and street pavings. At the base of the plaza, Caitria hesitated. The white, blue, and gold city of Sulaanc seemed to open before her—to swallow her, she prayed, into anonymity.

To the east lay Bel-Tygeon's palace. To the west, the canal and the marketplace beyond. The marketplace offered her best hope. But she must barter for a plain mantle, then blend into the crowds, if possible. She would become a lady perusing wares. A lady requiring transport to her distant home.

But the marketplace seethed with turmoil as Sulaanc's citizens scurried about, craning for a glimpse of the temple as they called to each other, "It's gone! Impossible! We're going mad!"

A plain-robed woman stopped directly before Caitria and bowed her head, lifting sturdy work-worn hands in a pleading gesture. "Lady, you must know! What's happened to the temple? To our king—may his name be praised above all!"

Caitria's thoughts skittered. "I-I . . . don't know. It's a disaster! All I can think of is that I must return home! Do you know of a conveyance with a trustworthy driver?"

The woman blinked, clearly stupefied. "Should we run?"

"Run? Yes!" Caitria snatched at the word. "Who knows what will happen now? Won't it be safer if we leave Sulaanc? Help me, and I'll repay you." Caitria removed one of the fragile silver bracelets from her wrist and offered it to the woman. "What's your name?"

"Amiyra," the woman breathed. She accepted the ornament, stared at it, then nodded to Caitria. "Lady, it must be as you say. I know who can help."

By now the marketplace was emptied of all citizens but the merchants and tradesmen who'd begun to pack their wares and herd their animals from the area. Amiyra—now wearing the bracelet—hurriedly pointed Caitria into her modest stall that sheltered baskets of dried fruits, vegetables, and netted rounds of wax-covered cheese. She motioned Caitria to a fabric-draped shelter at the back of the stall. Inside, a baby slept in a basket, chubby and oblivious to the confusion outside. Amiyra checked the baby, then whispered to Caitria, "If you please, lady, sit here. I'll speak to my man."

Hoping she'd made the right choice of rescuers, Caitria sat on a heap of coarse cushions and stared at the baby. Judging by all the work evidenced in those tiny embroidered robes, this child was adored. A fine, healthy baby. Caitria exhaled, trying to control her fears for Ela and her unborn child. Let them be safe!

Before long, Amiyra reentered the shelter and offered Caitria a clay cup brimming with water. "I wish this'd be more, but it'll refresh you. Rest a bit, lady. My man is seeing to transport. Where is your home?"

Caitria hesitated, then shifted on the cushion and accepted the cup. "North. Near the DaromKhor Hills."

"I'll tell him." Amiyra backed out, flicking the rough brown curtain in place once more.

Sipping the water, Caitria focused on the baby and tried to calm her fears.

✦ ✦ ✦

Sickened, Akabe tended the fire in the kitchen hearth and listened as Riddig talked. The burly surgeon tossed a fabric-wrapped packet of herbs into a steaming kettle and sighed. "The abdominal incision is healing well. However, the leg wound is festering inside. The tube is draining unhealthy fluids and the skin around it resembles raw meat. In addition, Lord Aeyrievale now has a fever."

A fever. Akabe shut his eyes. Not good. He'd lost friends to similar wounds. The next step would be darkening, dying flesh, with the fever growing. Beyond that, unconsciousness, Akabe hoped. But more likely, the fever would set Kien to raving. Infinite, spare Kien that much, please! Focusing on the surgeon again, Akabe asked, "Is there any way we might save him?"

"I want to reopen his wound, cut out the decay, and attempt restoratives." Riddig eyed the steaming kettle. "Heat—as much as he can can endure without blistering. Then sunlight and more of the honey ointment. If only I'd purchased maggots to consume the rotting flesh!" Bleak, the surgeon added, "Majesty, with this second surgery comes the increased chance of permanent crippling. I cannot guarantee the results. We can only pray it saves his life."

"I'm already praying." Akabe stood. "Will you need me to hold him still?"

"I'll need you and Flint, Majesty. Thank you."

"No need to thank me. I'll tell him what we're going to do. Come upstairs when you and Flint are ready."

Fortifying himself with more prayer and the resolution to save his friend, even if that friend temporarily hated him, Akabe headed for the stairwell. He found Kien propped up in the stone window seat, not resting on his pallet like a cooperative patient.

Flushed with the unapproved exertion and fever, Kien nodded at Akabe, grimly satisfied. "Scythe isn't pacing, so it seems the assassins aren't yet lurking at the gate. What are you three doing?"

"We'll finish filling in the pit this evening and plan new defenses. But first, we have another task to perform." Akabe told Kien of Riddig's diagnosis and his recommendation.

Kien listened quietly, then nodded. He reached into the window seat, picked up a scabbard-shielded dagger, and removed the weapon.

Was he going to kill himself? His heart racing, Akabe started toward Kien, prepared to disarm him. "What are you doing?"

"What do you think I'm doing?" Kien set down the dagger and waved the leather scabbard at Akabe. "This will be a perfect biting surface, don't you agree?"

"Yes." Akabe exhaled and relaxed.

Kien made a face. "Majesty, did you think I'd try to hold off the three of you with a single dagger? Not likely." Wincing, he scooted from the window seat. As Akabe hurried to help him back to the pallet, Kien said, "Don't worry. I'm all for the surgery. It's better than slowly rotting to death. Just be sure to warn Scythe that I might yell."

"I'll warn the monster. Not that it'll do any good. He's been mighty testy with me."

"Don't worry. He likes you."

"Thank you." Akabe steadied his friend.

As he limped, Kien eyed Akabe's sword belt. "You're not wearing the Azurnite blade."

"It's not mine."

"It is until we know I'll survive." Sweating now, Kien persisted. "That sword was a gift from my father, and I'll refuse the surgery until you're wearing it."

"You're a rotten patient." Plagues! Bad choice of words.

Kien almost grinned. "Yes, well, if I weren't rotten, we'd have no need of this surgery."

They halted beside Kien's pallet. Steadying his friend, Akabe said, "When the Infinite's temple is completed—if it's His will that the temple be completed—I want you there to see it."

"I hope for the same. With Ela. But as He wills." Grayed by the effort, Kien settled down and shut his eyes, clutching the scabbard. "Just warn Scythe."

✦ ✦ ✦

Finally! Caitria stood, easing onto her half-asleep legs as the shelter's rough brown curtain opened. Amiyra scooted inside and picked up the baby. "All's ready, lady. My man found a way." Cuddling her child, Amiyra nodded Caitria outside. "We need to hurry."

The instant Caitria stepped from behind the rough curtain, a man blocked her path. A weapon-bearing soldier. Clad in the blue and gold of a palace guard. "No!" She ducked away, but another guard stepped in her way. Followed by a third . . . with others waiting beyond. Trapped!

Caitria gasped, then bit her lip. She would not scream. Nor would she fight against such odds. Siphra might not have an ideal queen, but at least she could behave with dignity. She lifted her chin and studied the guards, trying to pick out their commander. A particularly stoic soldier, with an extra edging of gold along his belt, handed a small heavy leather bag to a man who now stood with Amiyra.

The bag's contents clinked—the thin metallic sound of silver coins.

"I hope you were paid enough," Caitria told Amiyra. The woman seemed a bit shamed, looking down at the baby in her arms.

The lead guard approached Caitria. "Your absence was noted, lady, and your presence is commanded." He motioned her toward a carrying chair flanked by four soldiers. Voice low, he added, "I am authorized to chain you, if need be."

"That won't be necessary." She settled herself in the chair and folded her hands in her lap, conveying serenity. Inside, her stomach knotted hard and her heart fluttered, frantic as a snared bird's. She'd failed. Just as Ela said.

Now she must mourn the consequences.

Was she about to be branded? Imprisoned for life? Thoroughly ruined and shamed by Bel-Tygeon? Please, no . . .

She refused to think of Akabe.

✦ ✦ ✦

Shivering, nauseated, Ela drew her knees up to her chest amid a clatter of chains and then leaned against the cold stone wall, praying for Caitria. What now? As if in answer, the branch appeared beside her in the straw, seeming quite ordinary, though its vine-wood gleamed at her subtly, offering strength, making her smile.

Infinite? Thank You! Her chains clinking, Ela retrieved the branch.

A rough, feminine voice snapped Ela from her silent praises. "Are you drunk? You've no reason to look so pleased!"

The speaker, a tattered, emaciated woman, crouched before Ela in the filthy straw. She appeared to be Matron Prill's age, and rather pretty, though nowhere near as clean and proper. Behind her, other women were watching and listening with interest—the ragged speaker apparently ruled them all.

Ela smiled at the women. "My name is Ela, and I'm glad because even here, I'm not alone. What is your name?"

"Jemma, and get used to it, Lady Ela! You'll be a long time visiting us, with no reason to smile."

"As the Infinite wills." Ela studied Jemma's truculent face. Did she imagine the flicker of a remembered hurt? Infinite?

Listen! See her heart—as I see. The Creator whispered into Ela's thoughts, sending her images and understanding. "Jemma, rebellion brought you here. Obedience will release you, if you abandon your pride."

The woman's eyes widened, then hardened. "I don't care if I remain in prison for ten years! I was wrongfully accused, and I'll not accept blame!"

"In part," Ela agreed. "Your accuser knows this. But her status demands an apology that you must give. You have two choices. Be stubborn and remain here, or bow and apologize, so you may live."

"Did *she* send you here?"

She. The head cook in the Women's Palace. Ela shook her head. "No. Following my Creator's will brought me here. And I am content to stay until His purpose for me is fulfilled."

One of the other women crept nearer, staring at the now-shimmering branch, then at Ela. "Who are you, really? Why were you allowed to carry a weapon into our cell?"

"It's not a weapon. And I'm the Infinite's prophet, stolen from Siphra."

She had their attention now. Recognizing the Infinite's purpose, Ela settled in to tell her story from the beginning.

To reveal their Creator's love.

✦ ✦ ✦

Caitria knelt on the throne room's gleaming floor as the palace guards commanded. Mari had described the room's transformation by the Infinite, but even Mari's enthusiastic report failed to do this place justice. Caitria stared at the floor, astonished by its crystalline beauty—even as she shivered. Infinite? Help me . . .

She felt all the courtiers' stares. And Bel-Tygeon's. Obviously he'd commanded her to be brought here so he could punish her publicly. Well. Punish away—he and his gloating subjects would not see her break, she hoped.

On his throne above the dais, Bel-Tygeon spoke, his voice cold and echoing. "By law, when my property is lost through carelessness or neglect, a penalty must be paid—and that penalty is equal to the value of my property."

Property. He made the word sound so cold, yet much too personal, for he was referring to *her*. Caitria lifted her gaze from the extraordinary floor and allowed him to see her hatred.

Bel-Tygeon continued, unaffected, though he looked at her

directly. "Caitria of Siphra, here is your price." He motioned to a pair of guards, who carried a long fabric-swathed bundle.

Noticing its shape, Caitria trembled. A body? Let it not be true . . .

The guards unrolled the bundle before her as if it were nothing.

Caitria stared at the unmoving form and covered her mouth to stifle a scream.

❖ 34 ❖

Through her tears, Caitria saw welt-like burns around Mari's swollen mouth. Had she been forced to drink poison? Whatever had happened, it was lethal. Mari's blotchy skin and staring eyes forbade Caitria any hope that the young woman might be saved. Choking on a sob, she clutched Mari's cold, lifeless hand and rubbed it. If only she could return to the instant she'd fled the temple site. Mari would still be alive.

This poor girl's death was her fault! And the king's.

Caitria blinked to clear her tear-blurred vision, then stared up at Bel-Tygeon. "Why punish an innocent girl for my decision? Why kill her?"

As if noting the weather, Bel-Tygeon said, "She failed her most basic duty, which was to attend you—my most valuable slave. The next time such an impulse seizes you, lady, you will understand the consequences of your actions."

Her actions? He'd commanded this atrocity! Caitria screamed, "When will you understand the injustice of *your* actions? You're a curse to Belaal instead of its protector!"

His expression bored, Bel-Tygeon motioned to Caitria's guards, who lifted her upright, forcing her to release Mari's hand. As the guards coerced her to turn and depart from the throne room, Caitria threw a last look at Mari's motionless form, then burst into tears.

Dead because of me!

Mari's swollen, staring face reappeared in Caitria's thoughts—an image she'd never live long enough to forget. An image she must never forget. Caitria choked down sobs and the longing to scream like a madwoman. Hadn't Ela warned her?

"Infinite!"

✦ ✦ ✦

A rush of images chased Ela from her dreams into consciousness. Her heart thudding with terror, she sat up and looked around. Prison. She was still in prison.

She still had time. Infinite, please, let them listen!

Ela scrambled to her chained feet, clattered around her slumbering cell mates, and hobbled to the woven metal door. She rattled the huge grate and yelled, "Guards—help! Warn the king! Send word to Lady Dasarai! Save the king!" Caitria, pray! *Only* pray . . .

✦ ✦ ✦

Seated on a cushion in Lady Dasarai's luxurious antechamber, Caitria stared at the floor, refusing to touch her food. If she stared at Bel-Tygeon, lounging carelessly opposite her, she would spit at him.

Thinking of Mari again, Caitria pressed her hands to her aching head. Help me not to attack this man! "Infinite . . ."

The king's hatefully amused voice cut into her faltering prayer. "You've truly turned pagan. What will the Ateans do if I restore you to Siphra?"

Did Bel-Tygeon have spies everywhere in Siphra? He seemed entirely too familiar with Siphra's politics. "The Ateans will kill me as they've been trying to kill my husband. And that would please you, wouldn't it?" Digging her fingers into the cushions, Caitria finally looked at the king. If she had Akabe's daggers, she would throw them now. To her own ruin. Be calm. Self-controlled.

Clearly enjoying his late-night meal—and considering her

as entertainment—Bel-Tygeon's handsome face twisted with a sardonic smile. "If you've turned pagan, they would indeed kill you."

"I'm already a target for the sake of the Infinite's temple! Anyway, how can I be pagan if I worship the one true God who created all? You're the pagans, you and the Ateans!"

"My philosophers would love to crush you in a debate. As for myself, I think you've turned delusional." The king straightened and raised his dark eyebrows at Dasarai, who'd just reentered the room from answering a tap at her door, for they'd sent out all the servants.

Dasarai knelt, arranging herself decorously on a cushion. "The prophet is clamoring in her cell, causing unrest among the prisoners. Should she be ignored?"

The king dipped a crisp wafer into a spiced meat sauce, ate it, then shook his head. "No. I intended to tell her in the morning that she will restore my temple as she restored the throne room. It's just as well that I speak to her tonight. Bring her here."

A delicate crease fretted Dasarai's forehead. "She will need a bath and clean clothes after being in the prison—not to mention delousing."

Taking another bite of the bread and meat concoction, the king shrugged. "Order her here. We'll speak with her in the corridor. I've endured enough today—I'm tired."

He'd endured enough today? Caitria sniffed.

While Dasarai glided away to do her god-king's bidding, the false idol frowned at Caitria. "Eat. That is a command. Otherwise, I'll feed you myself." Bel-Tygeon studied her now, interested. "Actually, I might enjoy carrying out that threat."

Caitria took one wafer, crushed it to bits on the empty gold dish, then ate one crumb.

The king lifted an eyebrow. By the time Dasarai returned, Caitria had eaten three crumbs. Bel-Tygeon shoved a gold dish at her, its gelatinous dark red contents quivering with his sudden motion. "Enough! Eat, or I will do as I've said, and more."

She ate. Disgusting substance—too highly spiced. Eyes watering, Caitria reached for more wafers to settle her stomach and the fire in her mouth. When she finished, the king smiled. "You look better already." He tossed a fine linen cloth onto the table and stretched. "If I sell you to Siphra, I will demand the Darom-Khor Hills and two hundred thousand Siphran coins. The ones you call gold nobles."

Caitria gripped her hands tight in her lap, hoping she hadn't revealed the depths of her shock. He wanted the DaromKhor Hills? But . . . according to her history lessons, those hills were Siphra's natural border against Belaal. Remove all the border lords, then give Bel-Tygeon control of the DaromKhor region— with time to gather his forces—and he could overrun Siphra! Could? No, he would.

As for the payment in gold nobles . . . She swallowed, calculating.

Her father's household, large as it was, required six hundred nobles to sustain itself comfortably for one year. The average highborn household required four hundred. Bel-Tygeon was demanding enough gold to sustain one highborn Siphran family for five hundred years!

Did Siphra's treasury contain so much gold? Likely not, considering Siphra's years of strife. Queen since spring, and she'd cost her country a fortune. "I'm not worth such a price."

"Then I must keep you." He smiled again, beautiful and horrible. "Belaal needs a queen. You might bear me a son."

Akabe. Oh, Akabe . . . For an awful instant, her eyesight dimmed and a humming welled inside her head, threatening to blot out consciousness. Caitria huddled down, hiding her face in her hands. Trying to breathe. The best thing to do . . . the best thing for Siphra and Akabe . . . was her own death. How? Think!

Would Bel-Tygeon kill another innocent slave if Siphra's queen took her own life? Poor Mari! Caitria swallowed a sob.

Furtive rapping at the door summoned their attention. Followed by Dasarai, Bel-Tygeon stood and sauntered from the room—a god-king who was mightily pleased with himself.

"Infinite? Help me."

✦ ✦ ✦

Unchained, but surrounded by eunuchs and four big, stolid female guards, Ela waited in the opulent corridor outside the Lady Dasarai's apartments.

Infinite, may Your will be done. Please let them listen!

The door opened, and the guards straightened as Bel-Tygeon and Lady Dasarai stepped into the corridor. Dasarai, ever the head of the Women's Palace, frowned at Ela's rough braid and the plain linen robes provided by the jailors. Ela offered the great lady a placating nod, then snapped her attention to Bel-Tygeon.

The king crossed his arms and glared at her. "Do not think you are forgiven for today's events! You will restore my temple, on *my* terms this time, not your Infinite's!"

"But who will restore you, O king?" Before Bel-Tygeon could interrupt, Ela rushed to explain. "I was prepared to remain in Belaal, in prison for as long as necessary—for years if need be— but that is not His plan. As soon as I fell asleep, the Infinite woke me again with a dream. A blood plague has overtaken this palace. I've been sent to warn you, sir, because *you* are the plague's instigator."

His upper lip curved with obvious disdain. "I am the instigator?"

"Yes." Ela braced herself. "Because you took what didn't belong to you, the Infinite will allow the plague to take you. Unless you forget your pride and—"

"I should have known you'd return to this!" Bel-Tygeon interrupted, his icy disdain becoming contempt. Careless of the branch, he leaned toward her, furious, his chin lifted in regal defiance. "It's clear you're referring to yourself and Siphra's queen! But I'll take whatever I please. You're both my property and that will *never* change! As for your Infinite, what if I admit that He exists? Why does He hate me? I've done nothing that my ancestors would not have done to consolidate their reigns!"

"But there's the point! You've done what none of your ancestors dared to do. You've declared yourself the only god, sweeping all others from your lands. Ultimately, you'll threaten your people with their lives if they disagree." The branch now shone metallic and severe, throwing harsh light over the king's pale face and burning eyes.

Ela continued. "Your Creator loves you, sir! Never doubt it. But you'll destroy others who love Him—and you are destroying yourself with your pride. What should any loving Creator do to gain your attention?"

Bel-Tygeon turned from her in obvious disgust. Watching him, Ela also glimpsed doors closing all along the corridor. Every woman roomed along this corridor had been watching and listening to their dispute. The king yelled to the would-be onlookers, "Do not open your doors until you're commanded to do so!"

He spun around to face Ela again, pointing at her. "Let your Creator do as He pleases—*you* will obey me!"

Lady Dasarai's terrified gasp cut through the air. "Ty!" She snatched at his gold-embroidered sleeve, lifting it from his forearm. Ela knew what she would see on the king's arm, but she looked again at what she'd been shown in her dream.

Huge dark blisters lifted over Bel-Tygeon's arm. As they all stared, a blister broke, dripping blood at the king's feet. Sickened, Ela tottered, then knelt. "Sir, these blisters will move inward—even to your heart. Please, please listen. You can halt this! The Infinite commands you to return me at once to Siphra, with the queen, for I am *not* your prophet, and she cannot be your wife! The instant we cross the border, you'll recover. Obey Him. Send us away, or you'll slowly bleed to death!"

"Go!" Dasarai ordered. To a eunuch, she cried, "Give the prophet and Siphra's queen everything they need and be sure they're safely returned to their husbands!"

"Majesty!" Another eunuch's thin cry echoed down the corridor. Gasping, the man halted some distance from Bel-Tygeon. "Blessed One, a plague has struck two slaves. . . ." He stared at the king's dripping arm, then knelt shakily, weeping. "Oh, save us! The plague's found you."

Remarkably composed, Bel-Tygeon adjusted his sleeve to cover the blood, and he spoke to Ela. "I will give the order now. You and the queen will leave at once, with full honors." Quietly, he added, "Pray to your Infinite that I recover."

Her Infinite. Not his. All right. At least Bel-Tygeon admitted the Infinite's existence. Obedience and a partial admission were enough for now. "I will, Majesty. Thank you."

✦ ✦ ✦

Akabe helped Kien to his feet, glad to listen as his friend complained. "The muscles in my leg seem permanently tightened, and I'm so weak, I'm useless!"

"You're walking," Akabe argued. "And your fever is down. That's what we've prayed for, isn't it? Let's move you into the sunlight and—"

Scythe's threatening huffs and stomps from outside made them both turn. A long trumpet call resounded from the gatehouse where Flint kept watch. Akabe waited, fearing another warning blast. It rose high and piercing through the evening air, accompanied by distant battle cries.

Kien grasped Akabe's arm. "More Ateans have found us. Help me to that wall, give me your old sword, then do whatever you must to survive, sir! Forget I exist—I'll manage."

"Not for long with your wounds!" Akabe half dragged Kien to the nearest wall. "Lean here—I'm running for more weapons!"

✦ ✦ ✦

"Lady." His armor clattering and glinting in the afternoon sunlight, Commander Rtial Vioc bowed his head as he drew his horse up beside Ela's. "Are you well?"

She couldn't help smiling at his earnest tone and the sincerity behind his question. He knew she was pregnant, and he'd been hovering near for the past two days as if fearing she'd be too fragile for such a rushed journey through these tortuous hills. "Yes, commander. The queen and I are both well—only tired and eager to reach our husbands."

"We're in Siphra," Vioc told her. "My men and I will accompany you to the fortress."

"Thank you, commander."

"My duty and honor, Prophet." He nodded, then rode ahead to speak to Caitria.

Contemplating his words, Ela's heartbeat quickened. They'd crossed the border. She'd see Kien soon! Another thought halted her exultation. Infinite? Has Bel-Tygeon recovered?

Can I forget My word? Belaal's king is spared the plague.

Within her thoughts, Ela saw Dasarai and Bel-Tygeon checking his arms, legs, and face for blisters that no longer existed. Ela sighed. Thank You! But what will happen to him now? What about those who have turned to You in Sulaanc? They've no prophets, no holy books, no—

Aren't they My concern?

Yes. I know You are always right—and that You love them. Forgive me, please.

She allowed herself to relax slightly, though Commander Vioc was increasing their pace once more. Why had she been fretting? Of course the Infinite would bring another prophet and His Sacred Books to the new faithful ones in Belaal.

And surely other souls in Belaal would be called by His Spirit. Perhaps even those who'd hated her. Please, *please* let it be so! She'd seen too much death as the Infinite's prophet.

Too many souls endangered by their own rebellious natures.

Soon their procession turned onto a narrow winding road, and Ela nearly dropped with relief, recognizing its contours. This road led to Akabe's fortress home. To Kien!

Ela leaned forward, urging the small horse ahead.

✦ ✦ ✦

Caitria blinked back tears, seeing the fortress on the hillcrest above. Everything within her wanted to abandon all dignity and run through those woods and up the hill into that battered castle while screaming for Akabe. He'd think she was a wild woman. And if he was wise, he'd run. The thought almost made her smile.

Scanning the walls more closely now, Caitria bit her lip. Where were Akabe's watchmen? Why couldn't she see plumes of smoke from at least one or two cooking fires?

Ela drew her horse up beside Caitria's and stared up at the fortress above. "No banners, no guards on the wall walk, no smoke . . . where are they?"

Distant horn blasts and battle cries cut toward them from the hillside above. Was the fortress under attack? Ela urged her mount forward and called to Caitria, "Majesty, stay here!"

"Not for my life!" Caitria goaded her horse after Ela's.

They abandoned the procession and urged their horses ahead into the trees as Commander Vioc yelled, "Stop—Majesty, no!"

✦ 35 ✦

Caitria heard Commander Vioc's men chasing after her, their horses' hooves thundering, armor and weapons clattering. Would they try to stop her? Panicked at the thought, Caitria leaned forward, urging her horse onward. "Go!"

She rode after Ela up through the trees, toward the bare hill-crest. As they rounded the final turn, Caitria glimpsed a body falling from the far side of the gatehouse wall to the ground, and her breath caught in horror. The fallen one wore Akabe's colors. "Oh, Infinite, no!"

An arrow whisked past Caitria, provoking yells from Commander Vioc's men. Vioc bellowed, "Majesty, lean down!"

Unnerved, Caitria bent, hugging her horse's neck and scanning the area. Two leather-clad horsemen waited near the gatehouse, guarding a number of horses—none of them belonging to Akabe. One of the men wielded a bow, and he stared straight at her, as a hunter with the prey in sight. Just as he reached over his shoulder to lift an arrow from the quiver on his back, Caitria's would-be killer was struck with two of Belaal's arrows to his throat and chest. His companion turned his horse to flee, but was hit by an arrow to his side.

To Caitria's right, Ela cried, "The gate is open!" She dismounted, branch in hand. "Others have entered the yard!"

Caitria slid off her horse and knelt, removing one of Akabe's

321

daggers from her boot. Could she use it if she must? Infinite, grant me strength! She started toward the gate.

Vioc roared, "Wait until we've secured your path!"

She halted. "Hurry, please! My husband is in danger!" Accompanied by Vioc and his men, she stepped around the horrid skulls and sped after Ela through the gate. They slipped into the yard, briefly startled by a massive mound of soil, piled and piked—a bristling barricade inside the entrance.

Ela rounded the side of the mound, halted and gasped. "Pet—Scythe!"

Lathered and disheveled, the monster warhorse stood amid multiple trampled bodies before the tower's entry, his powerful jaws clamped tight on the luckless remaining soldier's arm. Scythe flung the screaming man away, then rushed him again, clearly too overcome by battle rage to pay the least attention to Ela or Caitria.

Recovering, Ela charged toward the tower, her bright robes and blue mantle fluttering as she ran. Behind Caitria, Vioc sucked in a breath. "Has the monster vanquished all your enemies?"

"I hope so!" Praying in frantic silence, Caitria dashed after Ela. Infinite? Where was Akabe? Inside they hesitated.

Vioc hissed, "Majesty, allow us to help you! Identify your husband and his men, that we may strike only your enemies and fulfill our task!"

"My husband's men wear crimson and gold—usually. . . ." Distant voices echoed from the stairwell, making Caitria turn. Akabe's shout and a man's cry. Dagger in hand, Caitria rushed past Ela and scurried into the stairwell. Clambering up the winding stone stairs, she followed the voices toward Kien and Ela's chamber and froze in the open doorway.

Rough-bearded and wielding the blood-streaked blue Azurnite sword, Akabe stood at the far wall, guarding Lord Aeyrievale, who held a sword, but was obviously weakened and supporting himself against the wall's stones. Another man's body—a stranger to her—sprawled at their feet in a pool of spreading blood, evidently just cut down by Akabe. Caitria gasped.

Akabe saw her and his eyes widened, clearly horrified. She backed toward Commander Vioc in the stairwell, but a man reached from inside the chamber doorway and snatched Caitria's hand. He crushed her fingers around the dagger's hilt, then wrenched her against his chest. Stumbling, shocked by the pain in her hand, she looked up and recognized the man at once. Lord Siymont, father of Barth, her favorite little palace page. "My lord, what are you doing?"

His grip cruel, he twisted Caitria's hand, pointing Akabe's dagger upward beneath her chin, while blocking her further with his sword. In throaty, roughened tones, Siymont muttered, "I'm setting Siphra aright, lady, and you're the very instrument I require for the task." To Akabe he said, "I'll skewer her like meat on a spit if you take a single step!"

Caitria grimaced. He would surely break her hand, then kill her. Infinite! Save the king!

Ela edged into the room now, her dark eyes wary and huge. "My lord, I beg you—it's not too late! Release her or you will die instead."

"Not before I rid Siphra of you, Prophet! You, your puppet-king, and his temple!"

"He's the Infinite's king, and you'll fail," Ela pleaded, her tone making Caitria shiver. "The Infinite offers you—"

Lord Siymont snarled, "Hang your Infinite and yourself!"

Caitria could smell Siymont now, reeking of horse and his own traitor's sweat. Speaking carefully through her pain-clenched teeth, she added her plea to Ela's. "My lord, think of your son!"

"I'm saving my son from a future of being controlled by your Infinite and those superstitious temple priests! How did you think I'd react, Majesty, upon hearing that you'd sent my son and heir to the Prophet for lessons? You *all* should have died then!"

Akabe's voice cut through the chamber, low and furious. "Siymont, release my wife and—"

"And *what*?" Siymont wrenched Caitria hard, making her yelp.

"Shall we bargain, Akabe Garric, lord of nothing? I'll spare her in exchange for your life. Turn your sword on yourself. Now."

"No!" Caitria struggled. Feeling the blade's edge stinging beneath her chin, she tilted her head just enough to speak. "Akabe, don't! They'll kill me anyway! Don't—"

A jolt interrupted Caitria. Siymont grunted. "Ungh!" His grip went slack, and he released the dagger. As Caitria staggered, shocked, Siymont dropped his sword, then fell, taken down by Commander Vioc. Without looking up, Vioc asked, "Lady, are you well?"

Caitria wobbled. "Yes. Rather."

Akabe lowered the Azurnite sword, stepped over the man he'd slain, then gathered Caitria in an embrace. "You're alive! Cait . . ." He kissed her fiercely, his whiskers scraping her face. "Oh, Cait—my dear, brave wife—bless the Infinite! I feared I'd led you here to die!"

"Bless Him indeed! I'm well." She hugged him with all her might. "And you're safe!"

Across the room, Ela—in tears—hurried to kneel beside Kien, who'd eased himself to the floor, his face waxen and drawn in pain. Unnerved, Caitria looked up at her husband. "Was Lord Aeyrievale wounded?"

"And stitched, yes. I'll tell you everything later." He kissed Caitria's lips so gently that she melted. But then he shook her, becoming stern. "Never charge into a clash! I was about to attack Siymont when you appeared."

"Sorry, I didn't know." She hugged him, fighting fresh tears. "I *had* to find you! But you're safe and nothing else matters. Except . . . he was Barth's father! How will we tell him?"

Akabe didn't answer. Instead, he looked at Commander Vioc. "Thank you, sir. Should I ask who you are?"

"I am a servant of my king, who decreed I must be sure your wife reaches you safely." Vioc slid his dagger into its scabbard and bowed his head. "To be certain of that—with your forgiveness, Majesty—I ordered my men to search this place and subdue your foes, if any have survived. When we are certain Siphra's queen is protected, we will depart in peace."

Akabe sighed. Caitria felt the tension fade from his body as he spoke. "Thank you, sir. I'll ask no other questions. However, you and your men may shelter here for the night."

"Our thanks, with gladness, Majesty." Commander Vioc bowed again and retreated.

Now Akabe answered Caitria's question about Siymont. "How can I possibly tell that little boy his father is a traitor?" He shook his head. "I'll pray over that as I take care of these men—after I find Riddig and Flint. Infinite—have they survived the attack?"

Dismayed, Caitria remembered the first death she'd seen as she and Ela approached the fortress—one of Akabe's men falling from the gatehouse. Had her husband lost all his men? Bracing herself, she tucked her unbruised hand in his. "I'll go with you to find them."

✦ ✦ ✦

Followed by the battered and miserable Riddig Tyne, Akabe knelt with Caitria beside Flint's body and stared, heartsick. "A good man. Dead, because of me."

Her touch featherlight, Caitria smoothed his beard. "My lord, you cannot blame yourself for Siymont's rebellion. Flint died serving Siphra."

"Even so, I'm responsible." Akabe embraced his wife and kissed her soft cheek, marveling again at her presence and praising the Infinite for the transformation he saw in her. Later, he would ask Cait for details and rejoice in their newfound intimacy. But not now. Not while gazing upon the stilled faces of dead Siphrans. Caressing the graceful line of her throat—and checking the small bloodied nick left by Siymont's attack—he murmured, "Beloved, go inside. Riddig and I must bury our dead."

She kissed him, smoothing his beard again. "I'll have bathing water warmed for you."

Akabe watched her reenter the fortress, then sighed and nodded at Riddig. "We bury Flint first. Then Siymont." He prayed aloud, sickened. "Infinite! How will I tell young Barth?"

They'd just finished wrapping and tying Flint's body when the sounds of horses alerted them to visitors. No . . . Akabe listened hard, hearing orders and responses given by the unseen men's respectful, well-trained voices. Accompanied by the customary trump-call of his personal guards, alerting all to their approach.

"Majesty!" Riddig breathed, some of his misery vanishing, "Your men are here!"

Akabe stood and lifted his dirtied hands in praise. "Bless You, Infinite!"

As he watched, five of his personal guards emerged from the woods, emaciated and obviously worried. When they knelt before him, Akabe recognized the five as the guards he'd left with Caitria the morning she was stolen. One of the five moistened his cracked lips and said, "Majesty. Forgive us, but we were ordered to flee. But . . . we became lost in the hills. Until our reinforcements appeared . . ."

"Stand," Akabe commanded. "There's nothing to forgive. Bless the Infinite that we've survived!"

✦ ✦ ✦

Kien opened his eyes, blinked hard, and saw Ela enter the now-clean chamber, carrying a tray set with a bowl, a towel, and a spoon. Definitely not a dream, though she was more than beautiful enough to be a dream. Infinite, thank You!

He smiled, loving the curve of her mouth, the line of her cheek, and the way she raised those dark eyebrows at him, looking— Kien was sure—for any sign that he required some vile herbal remedy. Ugh! Inspiration for a swift recovery.

Caitria followed Ela, bearing a pitcher and clearly continuing a conversation, which sounded more like a debate. " . . . then, just like that—upon an instant—the Infinite would forgive the worst reprobate? Or a Siymont-sort who has hated Him for a lifetime?"

"Or an Ela, a Kien, or an Akabe," Ela agreed, placing her tray beside Kien's pallet. "Not to mention a Caitria. We're all guilty. But He loves us as the best of fathers and seeks a way to bring us home. Think of it as a spiritual adoption."

A spiritual adoption. Kien almost grinned at the comparison, then paused. Adoption?

While Ela and Caitria talked, Kien turned over the idea in his thoughts, picking at it. Trying to find any flaw while viewing adoption according to the Tracelands' legal codes. And . . .

Infinite? Of course! You're brilliant!

At last Caitria departed, and Ela fussed over Kien and coerced him to eat. Finished with his meal but too tired to ask for parchment and ink, Kien closed his eyes and mentally composed his letter. *Dear Father and Mother, I pray this letter finds you well. I am recovering from a skirmish. . . .* No. Don't mention the skirmish or the wounds. Not until he'd healed.

Kien frowned, feeling exhaustion take hold, blanketing his thoughts in a haze. Sleep threatened. Best to keep the letter short. *Dear parents, if you love me still, and if you persist in the notion of permanently and irrevocably restoring my legal status as your son, then adopt me!*

Softly, Ela kissed him awake. "You cannot sleep yet, sir. I must tell you our news."

For her sake, Kien opened his eyes and tried to look interested. "More good news, I hope." There'd been too much evil news lately.

"Yes, we pray you think so."

"We?"

✦ ✦ ✦

Grateful for the promise of a solid night's sleep, Akabe donned a comparatively fresh robe, then ran a hand over his now-shaven jaw. Being clean for the first time in weeks eased his gloom. As did the beguiling sight of his wife, who sat on her pallet, combing her hair to gleaming smoothness. She smiled up at him. "You look much better, sir."

He returned her smile. "But you need no improvement, lady.

Indeed, you look remarkably well for everything you've been through."

She shrugged, seeming rueful. "I'd have been far better off if I'd listened to Ela. She was right about everything!" Caitria shivered visibly. "The way Bel-Tygeon's temple disintegrated around us . . . and what happened afterward . . ."

Suspecting she was close to tears again, Akabe sat beside Caitria and pulled her into his arms. "You didn't know Bel-Tygeon would order that girl's death."

"Yet she'd still be alive if I'd listened to Ela—to the Infinite." Caitria sniffled moistly and leaned against Akabe's shoulder. "I'll never forgive myself, nor will I forget Mari."

Rocking her slightly, he murmured, "Believe me, I understand."

Caitria straightened. Not looking at him, she said, "I still say you should set me aside."

Her words jabbed him like verbal darts. After everything they'd been through, *why* was she bringing up this matter again? Frustrated, he held her shoulders. "Cait, look at me." She looked him steadily in the eyes, but he felt her tremble. "As you live, tell me the truth. Do you want to be rid of me?"

"No." Her words firm and controlled, she continued. "I love you. But setting me aside might be best for you, and for Siphra. I'm too—"

"You're my wife! Our marriage was blessed by the Infinite, and I won't release you from our vows. I refuse!" Her eyes brimmed in the lamplight, and her composed expression crumpled. Sensing victory, Akabe swept her into his embrace, kissing her. "Never bring up this notion again—I don't want to hear it. Ever. If it's the Infinite's will, when Siphra's temple is dedicated, I want you there standing beside me. Do I make myself clear?"

"Perfectly!" She returned his kiss fervently and snuggled against him.

Akabe glimpsed a flash of gold on her slender ankle. "Where did you acquire that? I'm certain I would have remembered it." Though he admired her feet more than the ornament.

She grimaced. "It's from the Women's Palace in Sulaanc. Ela and I were forced to wear these. All of Bel-Tygeon's women wear these anklets."

"What!"

By the time Caitria finished answering all his questions and showing him her gold anklet—which he intended to break at once—Akabe's heart was thudding as if prepared for battle. Though he'd seen enough death for a lifetime, he wanted to kill a certain god-king.

❖ ❖ ❖

In the kitchen's morning light, Akabe faced Siphra's most fearsome prophet as she lifted a flat round of bread from a griddle. "What of the temple? Is it against the Infinite's will for Siphra to rebuild?"

Ela slid the hot, brown-flecked round onto a dish. "I've been praying, asking that very question." She paused and looked up at him. "No house built by mortals can contain the Infinite. Yet He will bless Siphra's work." Tears filled her eyes, though she smiled. "Parne's sacred Books of the Infinite will be sheltered there."

Akabe listened, her words rending his spirit, even as they offered joy. "What your Creator truly requires of you, Majesty, is that those sacred verses be found engraved in your heart and soul, as you ever seek Him in love. As you restore peace to Siphra."

Incapable of speech, his soul crying praises to his Creator, he nodded agreement.

Forgiven.

❖ ❖ ❖

Determined to set his Royal Council aright, Akabe flung the document onto the Munra palace's meeting table. "What do you mean you've confiscated Siymont's properties?"

"Sir," Faine began soothingly, "Siymont was the ringleader. Barth was his informant."

"He is six years old! *Six!*" Akabe stood, glaring at each of his lords. "I thank you for everything you've done, my lords, and I'll reward you for your loyalty, but this is wrong! Evil may walk this world, sirs, through the actions and inspirations of mortals, but I'll never follow it or commit it willingly. Instead . . ." He caught his breath, remembering his parents, his brothers, and Deeaynna's innocent little face. "I prefer to forgive and show grace, as our Creator wishes."

Certain they were all listening, Akabe said, "I command that document destroyed and Barth's inheritance restored. When you've done so, then order Master Croleut to bring the boy to court again—I want to speak with Barth. Find Thaenfall as well, and Ruestock. I intend to settle matters now, so we can rebuild our temple in peace."

Trillcliff, Piton, and the others shifted. Faine coughed. "Yes, Majesty."

36

Though all his stitches burned and pulled enough to make him grit his teeth, Kien managed to keep his seat on Scythe while he rode into Aeyrievale with Ela and their guards. It helped that the black monster-horse moved cautiously, as if realizing Kien might truly unravel.

Riding before them in the cushioned chariot Kien had just abandoned, Ela called over her shoulder, "Will riding beneath the gates be too much for you?"

"No." Kien hoped it was the truth. It wouldn't do to enter his fief yelling in pain. Controlling himself, he looked around. Aeyrievale in summer's glory proved a good distraction. As did the celebratory greetings from his tenants. Doubtless they were grateful he'd lived—the mining operations would continue uninterrupted, providing sapphires to adorn the Infinite's temple. The realization made Kien grin.

Waving at Naor, who bellowed a pledge to visit, Kien turned Scythe onto the broad stone track cut into the gray cliff. Inwardly, he cringed each time he ducked to allow Scythe through this series of gated arches. By the time they reached the manor that crowned the cliff above, he was sweating. Inside the main courtyard, Kien ordered Scythe to kneel, then edged gingerly off his back. "Home!"

Kien exhaled his relief. Until he saw the welcoming committee.

Bryce and Prill rushed toward Ela and Kien, exultant. Followed by Lorteus, the royal fightmaster. An unpleasant grin widened in Lorteus' battered face, and his voice grated harsh in Kien's ears. "Welcome, sir! I've been sent ahead by order of our king to direct your recovery—seeing's how you nearly died by failing to heed my lessons. Good of his majesty, isn't it?"

Oh yes. Killing good. Kien rested a hand on the Azurnite sword—just in case—and he managed to look stern. "Fine. But not now, Lorteus!"

"Of course not, sir," Lorteus agreed flatly. "Tonight, I clean the weapons. At dawn, I'll fetch you for work—to overcome your failure. Be ready."

As Ela linked her arm in his, Kien hissed, "He's going to kill me!"

"Hmm." Ela smiled and hugged him while they crossed the courtyard. "*We* think he's already done some good, sir. You're walking faster now."

Kien bit down a smile—which Ela undoubtedly saw—and he grumbled, "It's a sad thing when my own family sides with my tormentor!" Before he'd limped into the manor's doorway, Kien had fully composed a letter of protest to Akabe, with mock-promises of revenge.

✦ ✦ ✦

"Majesty." Master Croleut's mannerly tone permeated Akabe's private study. "Lord Siymont has arrived, with his mother."

Akabe nodded at the portly tutor. "Thank you, Master Croleut. Show them in." Akabe exhaled quietly, covered his ink jar and returned his pen to its gilded tray. His formal complaint to Bel-Tygeon could wait. Akabe turned his chair but remained seated, determined not to intimidate Siphra's youngest lord, or his mother.

Barth sidled into the study, neatly clothed and combed, but sadly downcast as if he'd been asked to carry the entire world on his small shoulders. A sensation Akabe remembered all too well after his family's deaths. A dark-clad noblewoman followed Barth, her face haggard with obvious melancholy and muted resentment. Had Lady Siymont known of her husband's plans? No proof had been found, yet Akabe wouldn't be surprised. He cleared his throat. "Sir. Come here."

After a wary glance at his mother, Barth crossed the study slowly, staring at Akabe as if doubting what he saw. A few paces off from Akabe, the boy halted and bowed. His tone fearful, he whispered, "Majesty." He straightened and swallowed hard.

Akabe held out a hand. "I've been worried about you, Barth— I'm glad to see you."

"Sir." Barth accepted the handshake. "I'm glad to see you too." As if hesitant to mention the subject, the boy looked down at the tiled floor. "I was afraid you were dead."

"I'm not."

"They said my lord-father tried to kill you, but he died instead."

Akabe could just imagine who *they* were. Wretched gossiping courtiers! "And how did you feel about that, sir?"

The boy's face puckered. He looked down again, shaking his head. And he sniffled.

Beyond enduring, that sniffle. Akabe looped an arm around the little lord's shoulders in a fierce hug, but the consolation failed. Barth sobbed into Akabe's shoulder. Loudly—all his heartbreak mingled with those sobs. Near the door, his mother stared, then burst into tears. Akabe mourned with them. If nothing else, he prayed for Barth to regain his spirit and, hopefully, learn to trust the Infinite.

At last, Akabe shook the boy kindly. "Barth, whatever anyone's said, you're not to be blamed—believe me! And if you ever wish to speak of your lord-father, I'll listen. As long as you don't neglect your lessons with Master Croleut."

"But they said I couldn't stay here."

"I say you can. And whenever *they* say something that concerns you, my lord, you come talk to me—I command it."

Barth sniffled again and wiped his nose on his sleeve. "Yes, sir."

Later, Akabe resolved, they'd discuss wiping noses on sleeves while ladies were present.

To Lady Siymont, Akabe said, "The Infinite requires that I forgive you as He forgives—completely and with perfect mercy. For your son's sake and for Siphra's, lady, I request peace."

Lady Siymont straightened, wiping her tears. "It may not be a perfect peace, Majesty. Yet we'll attempt it."

"Thank you." Akabe mussed Barth's hair, provoking a gap-toothed smile from the little boy. Reassuring.

And Lady Siymont's hostility had faded somewhat. Perhaps work on the Infinite's Holy House could proceed undisturbed.

Infinite, I beg You, let it be so!

✦ ✦ ✦

Wearing crimson robes and a gem-studded tiara—and protected by her guards—Caitria eyed Ruestock as he entered the reception room. The elegant lord approached, clad in rich green robes and gold rings, his dark hair sleeked back beneath a gold circlet, his arrogant face showing a mocking half-smile. Obviously the meddlesome nobleman was gloating at the sight of her as queen and congratulating himself on the success of his own schemes.

Caitria winced inwardly, wishing for the thousandth time that he couldn't claim kinship with her.

Ruestock bowed, his glance caressing and admiring her inappropriately, even now. "Majesty, you surpass every ideal as our queen."

Remembering Akabe's counsel following his visit with Lady Siymont and Barth, Caitria forced herself to remain pleasant. "Lord Ruestock, if you seek a place in my husband's court, we must be honest. I loathe flattery, so please restrain yourself."

He smiled. "I will try, Majesty. But it is no flattery to tell you how delighted I was to receive your summons. In whatever you command, I am your most humble servant."

Oh, no doubt—until she interfered with his ambition. To honor the Infinite and her husband, Caitria bit down her sarcastic impulses. "Thank you. My request is simple. We know you have ties to the Ateans. Persuade them, for the sake of Siphra and for the many lives already lost, that we must have peace."

His smile vanished. Eyes cooling, he asked, "Do you expect me to neutralize their presence entirely?"

"We don't believe that all will be persuaded, no. But isn't the Atean leadership now greatly diminished and in turmoil?"

A bit of admiration crept into his face and tone. "Majesty, you surprise me. Queen for only a few months and you have recruited spies."

"Yes." Through Barth and Lady Siymont, whom she intended to protect. "Which is how I also know you didn't take part in the plot against my lord-husband." Curious, she asked, "Why didn't you? I thought you loathed the king."

She saw the conflict play out over his face. Wariness, discomfort, even a trace of amusement. Now, as serious as she'd ever seen him, Ruestock said, "Let us say that I have had dealings with the Infinite, and given the prophet's warning, I've no wish to provoke Him. It seems He protects the king and I bow to His Divine might, though I prefer to continue our family's traditional worship without . . ." Ruestock chose his next words carefully, " . . . priestly restrictions."

Our family's traditional worship? Ha. He'd experienced the Infinite's might firsthand and still wished to flirt with the mortal-created Atea? "That choice is yours. He waits for you, sir, if you ever change your mind, and He is concerned for you. I speak from my own experience."

"Yes, well . . . Suffice it to say, Majesty, if it pleases you to do so, then who am I to argue?" He bowed again, then threw her a smirk. "Above all, consider me your servant. I will speak to those you have mentioned and sway them to the best of my meager powers."

For some reward to be collected at a later date? Caitria sighed and dismissed him. "Thank you, my lord. I'll trouble you no further."

Ruestock departed, and Caitria's father sent in word that he'd arrived. Heart pounding, unable to believe they'd found him alive, she nodded to the servant, who immediately escorted Cyan Thaenfall inside.

Caitria lifted her chin, trying to remain calm. Her father paused, looked her up and down, eyed the guards, then approached, his gold-edged green robes lifting with his swift pace. Did she imagine these past few months had aged him? He looked thinner, with more silver hair at his temples. Yet nothing could touch his ever-present Thaenfall arrogance and that chilly composure. An arm's length away, he halted, hesitated, then bowed with fluid elegance.

For an instant, she considered removing her tiara, then squelched the notion. "Sir."

"Majesty." And he smiled, with pride, not warmth. "You look a proper queen."

"I'm glad you're pleased, sir. And I'm glad you're safe." Her throat dried. She swallowed and forced herself to continue. "You have no clue what your ambition has done."

Father's eyes narrowed. "Is he setting you aside?"

"No, sir. We love each other."

"Then why have you summoned me—guarded as if I'm some felon?"

Infinite . . . why couldn't Father behave as a father and be glad to see *her*? His coldness would tear her to pieces if she allowed it. Caitria straightened. "The king has ordered guards to attend me and, given recent events, I won't argue with him." Even so, she led him to the other side of the room, allowing the guards to protect her, without overhearing. Her question must not be gossip-fodder for courtiers. "Sir, in confidence, have you ever plotted against my husband?"

A corner of his mouth lifted. After a pause, he said, "Before you became queen, yes. Afterward, no. I am not such a fool." He looked her up and down again. "Are you with child?"

She prayed so. It had been four weeks since her return to Akabe in the DaromKhor Hills, and she had reason to hope. But she wasn't about to enlighten her father. Not before she told Akabe. "Time will tell, sir."

"I say you are." His eyes shone. "To think that one of my daughters will give me such a legacy—I will be the grandfather of a king!"

"What about being the father of a queen? Or of a daughter who has always loved you?"

The question surprised him. "What are you talking about?"

Caitria shook her head, giving up. "Never mind, sir. I pray the Infinite blesses you and Cyril."

"The Infinite?" His stunned look would have been comical if she weren't so upset.

Well, what had he expected when he threw her into the arms of the Infinite's anointed and faithful king? Really! It was enough to make her indulge in a royal tantrum and send him away for such . . . such . . .

Wait.

Now that she thought of it, Father couldn't leave her presence until she dismissed him. Ha! Oh, she would be sure he understood protocol! She was the queen, and she had a captive audience! Elated by the realization, Caitria tucked her hand into the crook of her father's arm. "Walk with me, sir, I command you. I have so much to tell you—this could take days."

✦ ✦ ✦

Ela settled back against her pillows, as her mother, her former chaperones, Tamri Het and Matron Prill, and Ara Lantec chattered around her. Ignoring them, Ela smiled, lost in adoration of her wide-eyed infant son. Caed. Had any baby boy ever been so handsome? Not likely. With the exception of Kien.

Ara Lantec's cooing voice broke through Ela's doting reverie. "Oh, Ela dear, isn't he perfect?"

"Yes, he looks so much like his father." Mesmerized, Ela

shifted against her pillows and studied Caed. He stared at her in turn—his tiny face quizzical, as if preparing to question her about *everything*. Dear, beautiful baby boy! She could never tire of gazing at his dark blue eyes—surely they'd turn gray like Kien's. Would she live long enough to hear Caed talk? To see him play and laugh and learn about the Infinite?

Grief tightened Ela's throat and tears threatened.

Her mother leaned over them now, smiling. "He looks like you too, Ela. And Jess—look at his curls!" Kalme fluffed Caed's dark hair, making him blink. Ela blinked as well, fighting back tears.

Finished placing a kettle of soup at the chamber's hearth, Matron Prill straightened and frowned. "Ela, for mercy's sake, why are you crying?"

Ela swiped at her tear-streaked face. "I'm remembering Parne's prophets—'*A silver-haired prophet has failed.*' Do you suppose my little boy will remember me?"

"Of course he will! Goodness, Ela, you're a long way from finishing your work in Aeyrievale and Siphra, let me tell you!"

"Prill, you don't know for certain."

Sitting tentatively on the edge of the bed, Kalme soothed, "Ela, stop! Hasn't my fear taught you anything? You'll make yourself sick with worry!" She hugged Ela now. "Listen to your mother who loves you. What if the Infinite intends that you never become silver-haired?"

Infinite? Wait . . . don't answer!

She couldn't bear to know. Mother was right—she mustn't make herself sick with worry. Sniffing back the rest of her tears, she kissed Caed's baby-soft curls and snuggled him close.

Voices and laughter from outside made her look toward the terrace doorway. Kien's sister, Beka Thel, marched in, holding her nine-month-old daughter, Aliys. Rosy from her walk in the chilly late-winter air, Beka beamed. "Ela, Aeyrievale's so charming that I could live here forever!"

Kien's voice taunted from beyond the doorway, "I doubt it— you'd be bored and missing East Guard's political affairs within a week." He strode inside with only a hint of a limp, carrying Ela's baby brother, Jess, on his shoulders.

Delighted, Jess whooped and tugged at Kien's hair, making Ela smile. Kalme laughed and hurried to take charge of her son.

Beka scowled at her brother. "You have such an opinion of me! That's the thanks I receive for championing your adoption petition through the uproar in the Grand Assembly."

"Children," Ara stood, scolding tenderly, "Don't fight—you're spoiling my visit."

Beka settled herself primly at the foot of Ela's bed. "*I* was happy until he said something."

Kien landed a kiss on his sister's perfectly arranged hair. "Oh, fine! I apologize if I upset you. Enough pretend sulking."

"Who's pretending?"

As Beka unwrapped the pink-cheeked Aliys, Kien took possession of his mother's vacated spot on the bed. His expression softening, he ran a knuckle lightly along Caed's round cheek, then leaned over and kissed Ela's lips—so tenderly that if she'd been standing she would have swooned, she was sure.

Nose to nose with her, his gray eyes shining, Kien whispered, "Thank you, love!"

"You're welcome," Ela murmured. "But you should thank the Infinite instead."

As should she.

"Yes, Prophet, I do—and I always will." He straightened and grinned, reaching for his son. "Are you finished with him for now? May I take him outside?"

Ara complained, "Kien, darling, it's cold enough to snow—Caed is not a toy."

"Yes he is! Besides, Father and Dan sent me to retrieve him. They've decided you've had Caed long enough, and everyone in the village wants to see him. I'll bundle him up snugly . . . if someone will show me how."

While Ara, Tamri, and Prill wrapped Caed in extra robes, a warm little cap, and an Aeyrievale fleece, Kien leaned toward

Ela again. "Next time, I want a Tzana with big brown eyes and a bad temper like her mother's. She'll be perfect."

Tzana. The mention of her departed little sister's name wrung Ela's heart. Thankfully, Mother was chasing Jess through the chamber and hadn't heard. Just hearing Tzana's name made Kalme sigh and grieve. Before Ela could respond to her husband's plan for "next time," Kien was crooning warmly to the unsuspecting Caed, "Come with me, son! The destroyers are waiting to meet you, and we must discuss swords and lessons with Lorteus—you'll enjoy hating him."

"Ela." Prill's words dripped with disapproval as Kien swept out of the room with Caed. "You have no choice but to live and keep those two out of trouble!"

"I pray you're right." Exhausted, Ela closed her eyes. Infinite? Forgive me, but I must ask . . . what will happen?

He answered, not with words, but with an image that took her breath away and made her smile. She entered the vision with joy, approaching His Holy House.

Infinite? Bless You!

EPILOGUE

Akabe's soul lifted in exultation as he guided his chariot along Munra's crowded, banner-draped main thoroughfare, his people cheering him onward. Five years of unrelenting work had led to this day—this dream come to life.

Trumpets blared, calling worshipers toward the temple for its dedication. All along the way, he prayed under his breath, "Infinite, though nothing built by mortals can contain You, let Your Spirit be present here! Let Siphra's heart be turned toward You whenever they see this Holy House! Let those who have rebelled against Your way and Your love be moved to repent and call upon You!"

He stepped from his chariot and looked up at the magnificent gold-crowned white marble temple, amazed by the fragrance of incense that swept down to enfold him before he'd even approached the steps. There he paused to greet Siphra's new high priest, Ishvah Nesac, and the temple's servants and workers.

The temple's chief stone mason, Dan Roeh, father of Siphra's most eminent prophet, beamed at him—the smile of a man who has realized a lifetime dream. Akabe grinned and nodded at Dan in perfect understanding.

Ela Lantec, holding the lively little Tzana in her arms, waited

341

nearby with Kien—now Siphra's ambassador to the Tracelands. Before them, Barth stood at attention with remarkable eleven-year-old patience, guarding young Caed Lantec, who wielded his blunted miniature sword, clearly ready to charge at the temple. Adventure-prone as his illustrious parents.

After today's dedication, Barth would depart with Ela and Kien to train in courtly service to Aeyrievale and Siphra. Akabe saluted the boy, proud of him as any parent.

Barth grinned and bowed, prompting Caed to bow as well—the perfect future royal page.

A gentle, beckoning hand rested on Akabe's arm, and he turned at once, recognizing that beloved touch. Caitria. She and the children had followed him here in their own chariot. Exquisite in her crown and robes, Caitria smiled up at him, her soft brown eyes sparkling, clearly celebrating this day they'd anticipated for so long. Akabe kissed her, provoking cheers and applause from the crowd.

Caitria offered him a graceful bow, copied by their delicately pretty four-year-old daughter, Deeaynna. Beyond them, Dee-aynna's toddler brother, Aythan—held firmly in the faithful Naynee's embrace—caught sight of Akabe and yelled, lunging toward him, small arms outstretched.

Unable to resist, Akabe reached for his heir. Aythan hugged Akabe's neck, then straightened, plugged his thumb into his mouth, and looked around at the crowds. A ripple of excitement and heightened shouts from the opposite side of the plaza announced the appearance of another king. Bel-Tygeon's glittering entourage now approached, headed by the erstwhile god himself—on foot.

Following Bel-Tygeon, his beautiful queen glowed as she gazed up at the temple—her delight revealed in her smile, which surely dazzled the crowd as much as her gold-and-blue robes.

She is my gift from the Infinite, Bel-Tygeon had written to Akabe amid their lengthy, increasingly friendly correspondence. *My sign that the curse upon my kingdom has been lifted.*

On either side of Belaal's queen, attendants held her eighteen-month-old twins, a boy and a girl, both with their royal father's dark eyes and gleaming black hair. It would be a joy to visit with Belaal's royal family this evening.

First, however, they would approach the Holy House and worship the Infinite together.

Infinite . . . by Your will.

By the noise ringing in his ears, Akabe judged that almost every citizen in Munra was now cheering. Overwhelmed by their fervor, he waved. Then, led by Siphra's high priest and the Infinite's preeminent lady-prophet, and accompanied by his family, Akabe of Siphra climbed the steps toward the Infinite's Holy House, his soul singing for joy, praising his Creator-King.

✦ ✦ ✦

Smiling in the lamp-lit, nighttime hush, Akabe settled at his desk, smoothed a clean piece of parchment, tapped a plain reed pen in ink, then wrote,

In the first year of his reign, King Akabe of Siphra proclaimed to his people the rebuilding of the Infinite's temple in Munra. . . .

DISCUSSION QUESTIONS

1. What is your first impression of Akabe in chapter one? Does he seem to be a potentially successful king?

2. In the first few chapters, does Akabe reveal any traits that might cause difficulties, either spiritually or in his role as Siphra's king?

3. Does Akabe make sacrifices for his people? What are some issues that frustrate him in his new role? Would you feel the same if you were forced into a similar position of leadership?

4. What do Akabe's friends and advisors think of him? Do they reveal concern over his decisions? Are those concerns justified?

5. Does Akabe's situation parallel events in the lives of any Old Testament kings? If so, do those parallels illuminate favorable or unfavorable aspects of Akabe's relationship with his Creator?

6. What are your thoughts and impressions of Akabe's queen? What situations in the Scriptures portray similar political

or spiritual concerns for a queen, or is she truly powerless in her role as a king's wife?

7. Do you believe that Akabe faces and resolves his personal, political, and spiritual issues by the final chapter? Would you have reached a similar conclusion if you were in Akabe's situation?

8. What do you think of the Infinite's role in this story? Do you believe He is actively working for each character's well-being? Do you believe there is a reason for His prolonged silence?

9. Who is your favorite supporting character in this book, or in this series? Why?

10. How did you feel after finishing the final page of *King*? If you read the entire series, which book's spiritual or "life-lesson" theme affected you the most?

ACKNOWLEDGMENTS

My love and thanks to everyone who has supported me throughout the past three years while I was absorbed in writing this series—you are my blessings! To Jerry, my dear husband, and our kids, Larson, Robert, and Katharin, thank you for all your help, and for cooking, cleaning, running errands, doing dishes, and drawing maps and other artistic contributions (Katharin!). I truly appreciate you! (Readers, check out Katharin's fun art at www.facebook.com/pages/Fish-Spaghetti-Art and on www.rjlarsonbooks.com/Art.html.)

Tamela Hancock Murray, David Long, and Sarah Long and the whole Baker/Bethany House team, I have truly appreciated your input and encouragement throughout this process. The BOOKS OF THE INFINITE series has been a joy to work on, and you've added to the fun.

Thanks again to my fightmaster-brother, Joe Barnett, for offering crucial advice during a late-night bout of writing, when I was too tired to see the scene clearly. Did I say you're brilliant? ☺

Special thanks to you, dear reader, for sharing the adventures! I'd love to hear from you at www.rjlarsonbooks.com, where you can also link to my blog. You can also connect with me on Facebook! (facebook.com/RJLarson.Writes)

Above all, thanks to our loving Creator, for His grace and blessings in all things as we journey together through this world and onward!

Ever yours,
R. J. Larson

ABOUT THE AUTHOR

R. J. Larson is the author of numerous devotionals featured in publications such as *Women's Devotional Bible* and *Seasons of a Woman's Heart*. She lives in Colorado Springs, Colorado, with her husband and their two sons. The BOOKS OF THE INFINITE series marks her debut in the fantasy genre.